MW01152702

THE TAINTED KHAN

Also by Taran Matharu

The Soulbound Saga
Dragon Rider

TARAN MATHARU

THE TAINTED KHAN

HARPER Voyager
An Imprint of HarperCollins*Publishers*

HarperCollins books may be purchased for educational, business, or sales promotional use. For information, please email the Special Markets Department at SPsales@harpercollins.com.

Originally published in the United Kingdom in 2025 by HarperCollins Publishers Ltd.

FIRST US EDITION

Library of Congress Cataloging-in-Publication Data has been applied for.

ISBN 978-0-06-322762-0

25 26 27 28 29 LBC 5 4 3 2 1

For my mother, Liege.
Your love and wisdom have guided
every word on these pages.

Northern Tundra
Dansk Kingdom
Samarion Lands
Latium
The Eyrie
Plague Pits
The Manticor
Silver Seas
Sabine
Damantine
West

FROSTWEALD
YALTAI MOUNTAINS
PETRUS MOUNTAINS
PORTICUS
GREAT STEPPE
HUDDITE LANDS
KIDARAN LANDS
PETRUS MOUNTAINS
RUFUS'S HIDEAWAY
KENNA'S GALLIPOT
MPIRE
NAMBIAN DESERT
SHAMBALAI
LANDS

Chapter 1

Jai's head throbbed with every jarring bounce as the khiro's massive hooves pounded the ground beneath them. The rough sack over his head chafed against his skin, but the discomfort barely registered; he was too preoccupied with clinging to the rhino's coarse fur, desperate not to fall upon the rushing green long grass below.

He could sense Winter beside him, straining against the same ropes that trussed her to the lurching beast's side. Jai comforted his dragon with a thought, but it did little to quell her terror. It didn't help that she could sense the same in him.

The khiro's pace began to slow, the great muscles beneath him shuddering as the thunder of hooves slowed to silence. The creature's breath was heavy, punctuating the quiet that had settled.

Then the air around Jai and Winter grew tense, as if filled by some signal with the yammering of men, Steppespeak so heavily accented even Jai's childish understanding could not discern a single word.

Rough hands grabbed Jai, pulling him down from the khiro's back. He stumbled, disorientated, as he was dragged across the ground, the sighing of the breeze suddenly muffled as his feet found flat ground. The sack was yanked from his head, and a sudden rush of light and air left him gasping. Blinking against the glare of a fire, Jai struggled to bring the tent's interior into focus, even as he was shoved to his knees.

The tent was made of animal furs, and lashed bamboo, large as a three-horse stable. The smell of smoke and leather hung in the air, mingling with a faint scent of herbs. At the centre of the space, a firepit smouldered, casting shadows that danced upon the tent walls.

As his eyes adjusted, a woman stooped into a crouch at his front, hawkish eyes boring into Jai's. She was a Steppewoman, and undoubtedly one of status. The finely braided plaits in her hair, adorned with bones, teeth and precious stones, spoke of her standing among her people, if what little Jai had glimpsed before his blindfolding held true. Even without the symbols, the woman's posture exuded a confidence that came from leadership, her gaze sharp and calculating.

Summoning his courage, Jai opened his mouth to speak, but a swift slap to his cheek silenced him. The Steppewoman tugged Jai's head down, examining his scalp, appraising him like a piece of livestock. Jai's head reeled from the blow, but he held the woman's gaze, refusing to let fear rule him.

She grinned at Jai's defiance, then squinted as if spotting something, clucking her tongue as if in disapproval, checking Jai's fingernails and tugging Jai's lips apart to view his teeth, even sniffing a lock of his hair as if trying to glean some hidden information. The indignity of it all burned in Jai's chest, but he knew better than to resist, not wanting to be slapped again. Instead, he reached inward, drawing on the bond he shared with Winter, finding comfort in their connection.

The woman sat back, sighing and clapping her hands. She bit her lip, looking pityingly at Jai, as if on the verge of speaking. Then she shook her head, turning and striding out of the tent's curtained entrance.

Jai took a breath. Then another, and another, attempting to quell the hammering of his heart. He knew not where he was. Nor even who had taken him. But he was alive . . . and far from Magnus and his ilk, if the journey's bruising of his ribs was anything to go by.

Yet he had no way of knowing if Erica and the Huddites had been so lucky.

By all accounts, he had succeeded in his mission. These were his people, after all. But not *his* people. Not the Kidara.

For as Jai examined his surroundings, he knew this was no great tribe of the steppe. In his childhood, Balbir had spoken of their tribe and the world they had left behind. He knew, in his childhood pride, that the picture he had built in his head was far grander than it likely was. But these dirt floors and ragged pelts were not the rich tapestries, rugs, and embroidered cushions Balbir had once described.

He sniffed, his stomach groaning at the smell of cooking nearby. Jai could hear the stirring of pots, laughter of women and children. He had been taken into the heart of their camp. No . . . their village. One that moved with their herds, as all Steppefolk did.

A wheezing from the corner spun Jai's head, such that he almost fell, turning with his bound feet. In the corner, an old man stared at him with beetle eyes, trembling beneath a hairy khiro pelt. Beside him, an old woman spooned a thin milk into his mouth, using a wooden spoon and a burnt clay bowl.

This was a small tribe, and a poor one at that. And they were keeping him alive for a reason.

The two elders ignored him, as if the sight of a battered, bleeding captive was nothing new to them. But then, he supposed it would not be, if Balbir's tales were to be believed. No people warred more than the Steppefolk. Nor did any take more captives. Half the fettered in the Phoenix Empire were made up of the defeated captives of the steppe.

Footsteps approached, and Jai was swift to cast down his gaze, returning to the position he had once been in. If escape was an option . . . he would do well to appear compliant.

A diminutive man stumbled into the tent, shoved by a hand unseen. Then another entered, shouting in jest over his shoulder.

It was a Steppeman this time, though he shared the woman's features. Those same hawkish eyes, compounded by a hooked nose that could only be familial.

A brother of the Steppewoman perhaps, or a cousin. Certainly he seemed of similar standing based on his fine furs and adornments, though there was a cruelty in the man's smile as he turned his eyes upon Jai, one that had not existed in the woman's gaze.

He clapped a hand upon the smaller man's shoulder, forcing him to kneel in front of Jai. He was trembling, and flinched as his superior stabbed a finger at Jai.

'I am Feng,' the man muttered, his gaze fixed firmly upon the ground. 'They say you speak High Imperial. Is it true?'

Jai said nothing, if only in shock at the fluency of the man's speech. The other bristled at Jai's silence.

'Speak, lest Zayn angers,' Feng hissed.

'I do,' Jai blurted.

Zayn clapped Feng's back in a sudden movement, laughing in delight. Then, as suddenly as he had laughed, his face turned into a scowl, and he gripped the back of Feng's neck.

Zayn spoke, spitting his words in guttural bursts. His eyes never left Jai's face.

Feng translated, his querulous voice a poor imitation of the venom in Zayn's own.

'Where did you steal this from, half . . . breed?'

Zayn tugged something silver from the furs that adorned him, letting it fall into the dirt. Jai's breastplate. Even as Jai's gaze turned to it, Zayn seized Jai's face in a vice-like grip, lifting it back up at him.

'Speak, worm.'

Jai curled a lip, then spat off to the side, though in truth his mouth was so dry it was little more than a gesture. The man grinned . . . then slapped Jai so hard his head spun.

It was the blow of a soulbound, and a powerful one at that. Dizzied, Jai's vision swam, even as a curved blade flicked in front of his eyes, Zayn dangling it like a toy over a cooing babe.

'You're not listening,' Feng translated, as Zayn snarled out the words. 'It seems you've no need for your ears.'

Jai groaned and felt the cool of the blade against his cheek, slipping down towards the side of his head.

A shadow darkened the tent entrance, and a voice rang out. Muttering as if disappointed, Zayn lifted the knife, before striding out of the tent. Outside, voices were raised, followed by the slap of blows.

Only when there was a curse, and a final, hard thud, did the tent entrance darken once more. The first woman entered, blood staining her lips and teeth as she offered Jai a smile.

Feng translated, as the woman spoke:

'I am Sindri, khan of the Valor tribe, and I apologise for the behaviour of my brother, Zayn. He can be . . . impulsive.'

Sindri's tone, even in the harsh speech of Steppespeak, was almost gentle, a stark contrast to the violence that had just unfolded. 'How came you to our lands?'

Jai hesitated, weighing his options. He decided to speak the truth – up to a point.

'My mother was not of the steppe, and my father was Rohan, khan of the Kidara. I was raised as a hostage in the imperial court. My two older brothers were framed for treason and executed at the hands of Emperor Titus, but I escaped. I have travelled across the empire in search of my tribe.'

Sindri listened intently, her expression thoughtful.

'I know little of the . . . politicking of the larger tribes,' she said after a moment, Feng stammering as he searched for the correct words. 'But we well know this Rohan of whom you speak.'

Sindri drew a blade from a sheath at her side, and Jai flinched back. She raised her free palm in peace, and cut Jai's bonds with two deft slashes of the dagger. She straightened, half-turning to the tent's exit.

She spoke, and Jai listened intently to Feng's words.

'You are free to walk among us, but your beast will remain captive until I decide what to do with you. But know this, so-called Jai of the Kidara:

'Try anything, and it will be more than an ear you'll lose.'

Chapter 2

It was not long after Sindri had left that Jai realised he had been holding his breath. He let it out, releasing the fear he had hardly been able to stifle.

Beside him Feng shuffled his knees, his head bowed.

'It's okay,' Jai whispered. 'She's gone now.'

Feng's eyes flicked to the elders behind them, and gave a shake of his head, pressing a thin finger across the crease of his lips.

Only now, as he slightly raised his face, could Jai get a good look at him.

Feng looked a little older than Jai, perhaps in his late teens or early twenties, with dark, intelligent eyes that seemed to hold an unspoken sadness. His face was thin, with a hint of moustache dusting his upper lip. His hair, unlike the braids and adornments of Zayn and Sindri, was simply pulled back in a short ponytail, and his facial features seemed different than that of the other plainsmen, telling of mixed heritage. Something in his features that reminded him of the Phoenix emperor's diplomats and traders that had rarely made the long journey to Leonid's palace from the far east.

Jai studied Feng for a moment, wondering what thoughts lay behind that guarded gaze. He needed to tread carefully if he was to gain Feng's trust, or perhaps even his help. Clearly, the man was as unwelcome a guest as he was.

'Thank you for translating,' Jai said, his voice soft. 'Your High Imperial is very good. How did you learn to speak it so well?'

Again, Feng said nothing, instead standing and heading towards the light of the entrance. Jai followed, rubbing his wrists and aching ribs. He had long run out of mana, and had not had a chance yet to soulbreathe so he could heal – Jai had figured out pretty quickly that being strapped upside down to the back of a khiro was not conducive to soulbreathing.

Outside the tent, the vibrant pulse of the nomadic tribe's everyday life thrummed around them. Men and women busied themselves at cooking fires, preparing meals with knives and pots, while children darted playfully among the tents, their laughter rising with the last of the day's heat. Beyond this centre of activity, older men lingered at the edges of the camp, their presence an uneasy contrast to the familial atmosphere. Some gathered in circles, playing and laying bets on games of knucklebones, while others sat and stared into the distance, sipping from their horn flasks. All were clearly armed.

Most captivating of all were the khiroi, which grazed contentedly nearby. Their massive, shaggy forms moved with surprising grace, the curved horns atop their heads like masts in a fleet of ships. Jai was relieved to see Navi among them, her scarred, smaller frame and grey fur easily discernible amid the hulking beasts. The older youths of the village were gathered there, keeping watch, their eyes never ceasing to search the horizon.

This tapestry stood in stark contrast to the sterile halls of the imperial palace, and despite the fear coiling in his belly, Jai found the scene strangely comforting.

Feng led Jai to a quiet spot near the edge of the camp, where they could talk without being overheard. Beyond the circle of tents, Jai had to stop and take in the view.

It was a sea of green, stretching out from horizon to horizon. A moving sea, stirred by the eddies of the wind, blushed by the first hint of sunset.

Feng pulled at his sleeve, tugging him to sit amid the grass. Glancing back the way he came, he finally answered Jai's earlier question.

'Like yours, my father too was a plainsman,' he said, his voice soft and distant, like a memory that had begun to fade. 'But my mother was a trader from the far east. It was she who taught my sister and me your language, as well as her own tongue. I guess that's why I was chosen to be your . . . minder.'

Jai could hear the bitterness in Feng's voice, even if the young man tried to hide the pain in his eyes. It seemed that, like Jai, Feng was caught between two worlds, never truly belonging to either.

'We ventured into the steppe to trade with my father's people, and to avoid the Sabine tax collectors. He and my mother paid for it with their lives. My sister and I were traded back and forth, until we ended up with Sindri three years ago. I made myself useful enough to not be traded away once more, as they so often do.'

Jai recoiled, the story sullying the peaceful scene before him. It was all starting to make sense. Jai had gone from being a Sabine hostage . . . to that of his own people.

'And your sister?' Jai hardly dared ask.

'Still here . . . for now.'

Feng did not meet his gaze, instead tugging at a strand of grass with his fingers.

'I'm sorry,' Jai said, finding no need to force sincerity. 'I know what it's like to not belong.'

Feng's gaze met Jai's, and for a moment, it seemed as if the walls between them were softening. But just as quickly, Feng's expression closed off once more, and he looked away.

'We should get you some food,' Feng said abruptly, standing up and brushing the dirt from his clothes. 'Come on, I'll show you around the camp.'

Jai found it hard to focus, for he could sense Winter, still struggling against her bonds. She knew his own had been cut, but far from calming her, she was panicking that he would be taken away. Jai knew she would not rest until she laid eyes upon him, but also knew to not push his luck just yet in seeking her out.

He had but a moment to close his eyes, entering the half-trance that let him hear Winter more clearly.

Jai! Jai!

His name, his scent, his very soul. She was crying out for it. Yet he could offer her no lies to calm the hammering of her heart, let alone his own. Instead, he sought out the glimmer of hope buried deep within him, and offered it up to her like a salve, before the clamouring in his mind quelled to a gentler dread.

'Hurry, before the light fades,' Feng's voice called from his retreating back.

As they walked through the camp, Jai took in every detail, trying to memorise the layout and the routines of the tribe.

The camp was alive with a harmonious blend of function, chaos and beauty, with plant-dyed tents of lilac and woad arranged in an orderly fashion around a central open area. This space seemed to serve as a gathering place for the tribe, for Jai could see people congregating to share meals, stories and laughter.

Most interesting of all was the symbol painted on each tent, and even stitched into the clothing of the villagers: a crossed pair of flowering lupins. That explained the purple everywhere.

The air was filled with the rich aroma of spices and herbs that he had only experienced before at the imperial palace's most lavish feasts. The scent was enticing, a heady mixture of fragrances. There were aromas he couldn't quite place, but knew were foreign to the Sabine cuisine he was accustomed to.

Curious, Jai was careful not to stare too long at those around him, even if they did not share the same qualms. Children pointed, giggling, at his hair, for it was far shorter than the long braids of every man and woman there, children included. He smiled at them, only for them to squeal and to run behind their mothers' skirts.

Feng settled by the central campfire, and Jai was curious that the captive was handed a bowl of simmering stew without hesitation. Feng gave it to Jai, and then took one for himself. It seemed the prisoners here were treated well, at least. Sindri had been true to her word so far.

Jai took a tentative spoonful, and was surprised by the complex flavour. It was unlike anything he had tasted before, rich in spices, herbs and more. But even as he moaned with pleasure, his mouth began to burn.

Within moments, he was gasping like a beached fish – much to the amusement of those watching.

Jai lifted his chin defiantly, and spooned more into his mouth . . . only for him to splutter, as a fresh wave of heat hit home. Another bout of mirth followed, one man finding it so funny, he was bent over double.

'Here,' Feng said, passing Jai a drinking horn. 'You caught one of the chillies. You should leave those in the pot.'

'You . . . gave it . . . to me,' he gasped.

Feng shrugged and nodded at the jug.

Jai took a deep swig . . . and gagged. For it was not water, but rather milk. Sweet, fat and acrid milk, with claggy lumps that coated his tongue and mouth.

'Interesting taste, no?' Feng asked, grinning as Jai handed it back with a foul face. 'But worth it, right?'

And Jai wanted to disagree, but the heat in his mouth was soothed, and Jai found himself reaching back for it but a few seconds later. Feng nodded his approval as Jai took another sip.

'Fermented khiroi milk,' Feng said. 'Sithian fuel, some call it. Most call it *khymis*. Not too much now, it's strong.'

Jai raised a brow, and took another swig. Then spooned some more stew into his mouth, careful of what came with it. Surprisingly . . . it worked.

He survived the meal with the alternating heat and cool,

until he was sated with a full belly and left with a pleasant buzz. That feeling was fleeting, though, his soulbound body processing the booze faster than he might have wished it.

He could have used a little numbness right now.

Despite Jai's full belly, he felt uneasy. His eyes caught Zayn, the man watching him darkly with an entourage of beetle-browed men. Their gazes locked for a brief moment, and Zayn shook his head, his expression a mixture of contempt and disdain.

Sindri might have welcomed him, but her brother clearly did not like the fact that he was sitting among them.

And that he still had his ears.

Chapter 3

Zayn and his men were gathered around a strange depression in the ground, not far from the central campfire, where the grass had been flattened. Along the edges of the rough circle, tufts of grass were tied together in tussocks by scraps of red-dyed cloth, forming a makeshift border.

Jai watched as Zayn shoulder-barged a nearby Steppewoman, a strange mix of aggression and playfulness. The woman looked resigned, but allowed herself to be cajoled into the circle, after a brief exchange Jai could not hear.

Through it all, Zayn's eyes seldom strayed from Jai. It was evident that Jai was meant to witness whatever was about to happen. His curiosity piqued, he watched the impending confrontation with trepidation.

Zayn and his opponent faced each other, their eyes locked in a fierce stare. No sooner had the pair entered the arena than the circle became crowded, men and women calling bets, others simply watching with eager eyes.

It started without preamble, for it seemed to Jai they lunged for each other, arms outstretched, searching for a hold. Zayn's movements were fluid and precise, judging each move with careful coordination as he slipped under the shorter woman's grasp. With a sudden, savage jerk, Zayn hurled his foe to the ground, her body landing with a crushing thud.

As the fallen woman gasped for breath, Zayn stood over her, triumphant. He looked to the crowd, his eyes seeking out Jai's. There was a dark promise in their depths.

'Zayn is one of the few soulbound warriors here,' Feng whispered, as Jai dragged his eyes away from the still-staring Steppeman. 'That was the other.'

'What was that?' Jai asked. 'Do they wrestle, as the Sabines do in their Ludi?'

Feng stared at Jai for a moment.

'You really don't know? Perhaps you *are* who you say.'

Jai shrugged, hating the fact that he was so ignorant of his own people.

'It's the fighting technique of the Steppefolk,' Feng said. 'Talvir. It is an ancient art, forgotten by many, more so since the peace treaty. But some still practise it.'

Jai nodded silently, replaying the fight in his mind. It had a brutal, fluid efficiency to it. It fascinated him.

'Mostly it's fought with a falx,' Feng said, seemingly awkward at Jai's reticence. 'Rarely on khiro-back, strangely enough, though it lends itself well. Tradition supersedes practicality in that regard.'

Jai could see now why Zayn was so feared and respected among the tribe, his prowess in Talvir was analogous to his place in their hierarchy.

'The falx is a curved longsword,' Feng continued, his voice a soft murmur. 'In the hands of a skilled Talvir practitioner, it is a terrifying weapon. And in the hands of someone like Zayn . . . well, I wouldn't want to be his enemy.'

'I know what a falx is,' Jai snapped, perhaps a little harshly.

He had not known the depths of his shame, at the little he knew about his own people, until that moment. Jai watched, as another pair of men entered the fighting ring, this time armed with bamboo poles. Their movements were elegant, ducking and weaving amid a clatter of wood. Jai's desire to learn the art of Talvir himself, a pull as natural as wanting to know the plainspeople's language or comfort Winter.

'I wonder if my father trained in this,' Jai wondered aloud.

Now it was Feng's turn to shrug.

'Nobody even knows if he was soulbound. The legends say he was.'

Jai bit his lip, thinking on it.

The idea of his father being soulbound was familiar to Jai, though Balbir had never confirmed nor denied it when asked – and now Jai realised it had been because she had secretly been soulbound herself.

In truth, Balbir had always said few knew his father well, her included. It was his mythical status that had allowed him to unite the tribes, and it was a mystique his father had cultivated. Why, many Sabines still believed he had been a seven-foot-tall giant, who ate babies for breakfast.

Once more, Jai cursed his own capture, wishing he could seek out his own tribe. At least there, he could get the answers he sought. Let alone claim his birthright.

Jai's focus shifted when he noticed Sindri's imposing form pushing her way through the onlookers. A long khiro horn was held in her hands like a club, and Jai felt a surge of fear, until he saw Sindri lift it to her lips.

A rich note reverberated, so deep and loud Jai could hear it in his chest – silencing the Steppefolk. The sudden quiet was eerie, and only the soft susurration of the wind-stirred grass disturbed the air.

Folk shuffled closer to the fire, and not a word was spoken. Even Zayn greeted Sindri's arrival with no more than a scowl. Feng clutched Jai's wrist, tugging him away, as men and women crouched down, resting upon the balls of their feet. Soon, they hovered at the far back, too low in the pecking order, Jai realised, to be allowed any closer.

Sindri strode towards the central campfire, her footsteps heavy and deliberate. As she did so, she lifted the horn like a trophy, waiting for everyone to take their places.

Feng leaned in, waiting to hear Sindri's words and speak them in Jai's ear.

'Brethren,' Sindri called out. 'I call a Great Council, so that we may decide what to do with this stranger, this so-called son of Rohan.'

Still, silence.

'The Kidara tribe have grown fat,' Sindri growled. 'They have spent these years as traders, buying Tainted captives from the Phoenixians and selling fettered to the Sabines.'

The word 'fettered' was spat, as if it were a dirty word. Jai didn't understand. Was he not their captive too, to be sold on to the highest bidder? And what did 'Tainted' mean? It sounded familiar, an insult his brothers had used long ago. But the memory was faded to nothing, and Feng was too busy translating to get clarification.

'They reject us from their High Councils. Refuse us trade, keep the best bloodstock for themselves. But now . . . we have something they want. Now, we have them by the nethers.'

A murmur of agreement swept through the gathered tribe.

Zayn stood, his head bowed, arms outstretched. Sindri hesitated, almost imperceptibly, then placed the horn in his hands.

'I have seen this boy,' Zayn said, his voice low and dangerous. 'Made my measure of him.'

He turned, and stabbed a finger in Jai's direction.

'He is a thief and a liar!'

Jai wanted to protest, but he found himself unable to speak, his voice caught in his throat. It was just as well.

'He may be a half-breed runt from the palace,' Zayn growled, striding into the circle's centre, 'but he is no son of Rohan. Hands as soft as a milkmaid's. Not a braid to speak of, nor a word of his father's tongue. Why, I would not be surprised if he is yet to pass the Rite. He has stolen this artefact . . . he has . . . he . . .'

Zayn ran out of steam, his finger trembling in the air, giving Feng time to catch up with his muttered translation.

Sindri held out a hand, and Zayn grunted, letting the horn fall into his sister's palm.

'And yet,' Sindri said, just a hint of impatience in her voice, 'is this not what we would expect, from a captive prince raised in the gilded embrace of our enemies? Is he not soul-bound to a *dragon*? What servant could steal Rohan's armour from Leonid's private chambers? And what servant would have *this*.'

Jai felt the blood rise to his face as Sindri brandished a tattered notebook, clearly stolen from the rucksack that had yet to be returned to him.

'Penned in Leonid's own hand,' Sindri announced. 'Bloodied by his own blood. A chronicle of his wars against our peoples.'

Zayn snatched the horn from her, his face dark with rage.

'He knows nothing of our traditions, nor our struggles.' Zayn's voice was filled with contempt, and worst of all, Jai could hardly defend against it. 'He's worse than a Sabine. He's a traitor to his own blood. He does not deserve to live.'

Feng's voice shook as he translated, and Jai shrank beneath the accusations. On the one hand, how could Zayn possibly discern that in just their few moments together? On the other . . .

Maybe he was right. Maybe he'd been with the Sabines too long to claim his heritage.

The tribe murmured in agreement – seemingly in agreement with that latter thought – casting suspicious gazes upon him. He could feel the weight of their judgement, and lowered his eyes.

Sindri raised a hand for silence once more, taking back the horn.

'We must be cautious, my brethren,' she said. 'Deception is a fickle thing. Let us say, for a moment, that my brother is right.'

Zayn almost looked surprised, his brow furrowing.

'Imposter or not, traitor or not, it matters little if *we* believe him to be the son of Rohan. What matters is that the *Kidara* believe it.'

She tossed her hair and then motioned for Jai to stand.

He didn't want to, but Feng nudged him urgently even as Zayn made an almost imperceptible step towards Jai, making it clear that he was going to stand one way or another.

He stood.

Sindri said, 'A lost prince is worth far more than a servant thief. It is up to us to make him a prince. He must be taught our ways. And in the meantime . . . we ride east. In search of the Kidara.'

And though Jai had just wished for that very thing, he felt nothing but dread, his heart heavy as the fast-approaching night.

Chapter 4

Jai woke to the resonance of a horn. He lay still for a moment, his eyes closed. Listening to the movements of his surroundings, until a hand jostled him awake.

Men and women stretched around him, paying him almost no heed, talking among themselves. Only the one who had woken him, a young woman, offered him a fleeting, soft smile before ducking out of the tent. Jai recognised her as the other soulbound here, who Zayn had faced in the fighting circle.

It had been an uncomfortable night, spent in the same tent he had found himself in that morning. As it turned out, it was a place for the elderly and infirm – a poor prison, had Jai wished to escape. But the truth was, Jai had been exhausted – one moment, he had calmed his mind to soulbreathe, the next he woke to the morning reveille rumbling in his ears.

Still, even if he had soulbreathed through the night, and an opportunity to run had presented itself, he wouldn't have made it far. And he couldn't leave without breaking Winter free.

His dragon was held in another tent, chained to a stake. She had communicated as much to him. Since his ascension, he could understand her better. She could shape intention – not words exactly, but . . . meaning. He hadn't had much chance to explore their renewed bond since escaping the Sabines.

Now he sought her out in his mind, and found her sleeping. He let her rest, opting instead to join the elders as they emerged from the tent.

Jai rubbed his eyes, adjusting to the dim light of daybreak. The camp was a hive of activity; warriors sharpened their weapons, khiroi being saddled, and the tent behind him was collapsing even as he stepped out of it.

It was fascinating to see the village disappearing before his eyes, and the great beasts of burden loaded up like humpbacked oxen. Within minutes, all that remained of the village was trampled grass. Indeed, Jai could see the green shoots already growing in the exposed dark soil. Soon enough, it would be as if they had never been there at all.

If Jai had imagined that they would be riding east on the backs of the khiroi, he was mistaken. The majority of the khiroi bore the weight of furs, nets, baskets and assorted belongings. Others were harnessed to bamboo sleds, mostly the oldest, or youngest of the khiroi.

A few, though, did ride. At their head, Zayn sat astride the largest of them, its horn standing proud and tall above the others. To Jai's dismay, he saw Winter chained to Zayn's saddle, her mind still bleary from sleep.

Her sapphire eyes turned on him, widening as she let out a yawp of recognition. He worried for her, but soon a flash of her love through their bond told him she was happy enough to be out in the open air, and within sight of him. He promised himself he would hold her in his arms soon, but dared not approach as Sindri barked orders and men and women hurried to ready themselves.

Those on foot had gathered at a series of central fires, where children handed out steaming dumplings wrapped in waxy leaves. Jai took one, savouring the rich filling, a tangy, meaty centre, mixed with more spices that set his tongue tingling, and warmed him from the inside out.

'Come,' Feng said.

Jai turned to find the young man hunched behind him, a heavy pack upon his shoulders. Beyond, the khiroi were already on the move, with the Steppefolk trailing the path of flattened grass that otherwise would have reached their waists.

Together, they ploughed a furrow through the green expanse, following the vanguard of warriors who led the way.

Jai and Feng walked in silence for a while, and Jai was amazed at the deep quietude that had settled over the steppe. The dawn air was still, but for the shuffling of feet, and the plodding of the khiroi. Not a bird to be heard, nor the soft chirr of an insect. It was as if the very world was holding its breath, waiting for the sun to crest the horizon.

Still, before long the Valor began to speak, a murmuring begun by the play of bored children. Jai walked on in comfortable silence, only stopping to relieve an old lady of her burden as she shuffled behind them, a large basket that he slotted under his arm.

But then he remembered something that had disturbed him last night.

'Feng, I never got a chance to ask at the . . . gathering . . . who are the Tainted?' he asked. 'I didn't know what Sindri meant last night.'

Feng glanced at Jai, his eyes reflecting the weight of the question. He responded in a low voice, though the rest of the tribe had already given them a wide berth as they trudged through the long grass.

'The Tainted,' Feng said, 'are a caste among Steppefolk, relegated to the fringes of their society. Though in truth, almost a third of those that call this land home are so-called. They were born into a cursed lineage, or so it is believed. They are not welcome to join with other tribes, nor marry with others outside their caste. They are denied breeding rights for the khiroi, forced to tame wild ones and start fresh bloodlines anew.'

Jai was beginning to understand. It was no wonder he held such value to this tribe, if they could force a trade with the

Kidara. Especially if it meant bringing new khiroi, bred for generations by the Great Tribes of old.

'So all the Valor are Tainted?' Jai asked.

Feng nodded.

'Why are they cursed?' Jai asked.

'Some will say they know the truth of it, but none that I've heard are worth repeating. The original transgression was long forgotten, yet the punishment remains. Fear and superstition force the burden of a sin they never knew.'

Jai shook his head, disillusioned. He had always pictured the Steppefolk as beyond the prejudice of the Sabines. Yet it seemed they were not so different after all.

'If they are so reviled, how can they treat you the way they do? How can they hold others captive?'

Feng halted, his brow furrowing. 'Treat me how?' he asked. 'I have as many rights as any among the tribe. I am simply forbidden to leave . . . unless I can purchase my own freedom.'

Now it was Jai's turn to be confused.

'But Zayn . . .'

'Zayn is a bully to everyone,' Feng sniffed. 'But me especially. To the others, I am just another tribe member. Even if they don't see the value of my labours, the way Sindri does.'

'You're . . . a captive, and an equal?'

Feng walked on, shaking his head.

'I am no fettered man, nor a hostage as you once were. The tribes of the steppe war so often, it is common for men to be captured, if not entire villages. Do you see a prison here?'

Feng spun slowly, his arms outstretched.

'It is the way of the steppe. In defeat, you become your enemy. So says their mother goddess, and so it has always been. The merging and breaking of the tribes are as ever-changing as the eddies of the wind. Why, some misguided souls within the Valor fear Zayn will leave and form his own tribe, taking all that would follow him, as is the right of any royal. But the tribe is far too small for such a schism.'

'And if one of these captives were to wish to leave?' Jai asked.

Feng shrugged.

'Then they must earn or buy their freedom. Just as any Steppefolk wishing to leave their tribe must.'

'Oh?' Jai raised a brow.

'Upon their Rite, every Steppeman and Steppewoman must swear allegiance to their tribe leader, one that can only be broken by blood, khiroi or gold. And it's the tribe leader who sets the price.'

Jai was fascinated at this. Did this mean he might buy his own freedom?

'Rite?' Jai asked. 'Sindri mentioned this as well.'

It sounded familiar, but he could not remember what Balbir told him about it. He'd been so young when she was taken from him.

Feng looked at him, almost with pity, and again the shame from the day before punched Jai in the gut. *I know so little about who I actually am*. But the other man didn't speak with disdain when he said, 'It is the rite of passage, before a tribesman or woman must settle upon a tribe. It is why so many of the young will leave their tribes and travel the steppe before their adulthood. They must return with a gift for the khan of the tribe they wish to join, and swear the blood oath there and then. They must do so alone, or with other riteless, and the gift must come through conquest. Some may never come back, riting themselves to another tribe. The Tainted stick with the Tainted, however, and the untainted with their own. It is the way it has always been.'

Jai wanted to ask him more, but a yell from ahead had Feng scurrying. The same girl who had woken him was calling to them, for they had drifted far behind the rest.

'I think I understood that,' Jai said, as he jogged to catch up with Feng. 'I'm getting used to the accent. Something about limping?'

Feng grinned and nodded.

'Well done! It comes back to you. I was the same when I first came here. Come on, we can practise as we walk.'

Jai grinned, even as Feng cast a dark look over his shoulder. It seemed his soulbound mind was finding it easier to learn the language than in his childhood.

'She's right you know,' Feng said. 'We shouldn't drift behind.'

'Oh?'

'Wouldn't be the first straggler picked off by a sabretooth.'

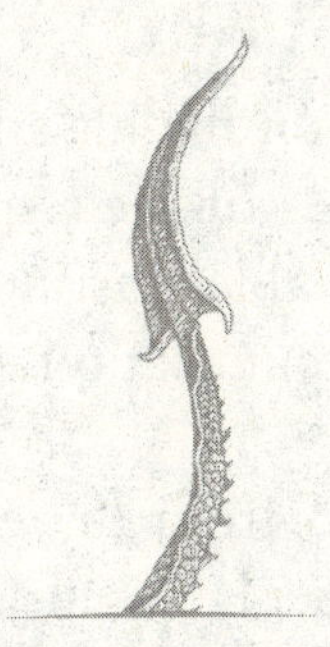

Chapter 5

As morning turned to noon, Jai's heart hurt with a bittersweet memory as he listened to the giggling of the Valor youth when they stared at him and Feng. He recalled how little laughter his own childhood contained.

Only one, a girl paler than the others, kept her distance. Feng's sister, Sum.

The siblings were not allowed to talk, or so Feng said. By Zayn's decree. As much as Feng claimed he wasn't a prisoner, like Jai he *was* a hostage, his sister tying him to this place and tribe. It dawned on him then that if Sum was Feng's shackle, Winter was Jai's.

Jai waved at Sum, but Feng pulled his hand down, shaking his head. Jai bit back a question about her, but was glad to see her smiling, playing in the grasses with what looked like friends.

A fresh gale of laughter brought memories of him and his brothers chattering in their father's native tongue, while Balbir walked them around the palace gardens. It had been one of the few happy memories he had – yet all too brief, the Sabine putting an end to such activity swiftly.

As such, he had never been as adept at speaking it as his brothers, especially after they had been separated. After all, he'd had nobody to practise it with. But now, in the company of Feng and the Steppefolk, he felt the lost words stirring within.

Even now, he focused on the lilt and cadence of their voices, learning the subtle rhymes of their speech. He practised softly under his breath, the syllables tasting like memory. Feng, ever patient, corrected his pronunciation and encouraged him with quiet joshing.

It was strange to learn from the chatter of infants, for few others would converse openly yet in Jai's presence. Jai tried not to be offended. He was an oddity, at the very least.

Even as the great furrow of trampled stalks stretched behind them, the Steppefolk dipped on and off the beaten path, their hands deftly collecting the small tubers, herbs, seed pods and grains that grew there. He marvelled at their keen eyes, able to discern the subtle differences in the swaying blanket of green. How connected they were to this land.

Jai remembered the deep love Erica held for her people, when he'd experienced some of her memories after consuming her dragon's soulgem. He was beginning to understand it.

The thought of Erica was like a twisted knife in Jai's heart, and he was forced to push the thoughts of her away. Right now, there was nothing he could do for her but hope.

Feng tried his best to teach Jai new words, once Jai had worked his way through the puerile insults he was mostly overhearing. Jai's new companion gladly shared his knowledge, even stooping to snatch herbs from the grass, explaining the uses of each find, interjecting with Steppespeak wherever he could. Jai listened with rapt attention, amazed by the depth of their understanding of the land and its offerings. But then, Feng too was half Steppeman, like he. And he had known his parents, while Jai . . . had not.

One of the Steppefolk began to hum a soft, melodic tune. Gradually, the others joined in, their voices weaving together to create a haunting harmony. He strained his ears to pick up familiar words, catching a few phrases here and there. They sang of the vast steppe, of the love for their land and the mother goddess who watched over them.

Jai found himself entranced by the rhythmic cadence of the voices around him, a marching song by all accounts. At times, the song would dwindle to a whisper, a single voice carrying the melody, only to rise again as others joined in, filling the air with a chorus that seemed to resonate with the very soul of the land.

Spring had sprung, if the buds emerging from the grass were any indication, and the afternoon sun was warm enough that Jai was tempted to remove his top. Certainly, several of the men and women of the tribe had done so, with little more than beads and fallen hair to cover their modesty. But his Sabine upbringing held him back, even as his fingers nudged the hem of his tunic.

As the pair ducked to examine a tuber amid the trampled grass, the shadow of a large khiro passed over Jai and Feng, casting a momentary relief from the sun's heat.

But the relief was fleeting, as Jai saw Zayn glowering down at him. The man snorted, and turned away, but not before his steed kicked a pile of khiro dung in Jai's direction.

This didn't bother Jai in the slightest, though, for Winter was rushing towards him, chain clinking, finally within sight of her master.

Catching her in his arms, Jai felt the warmth of her iridescent scales against his skin. He held her close. For a fleeting moment, the world around them seemed to fall away, leaving only the two of them, bound by a love that transcended language.

Then the moment was shattered. Zayn's fist suddenly jerked the chain attached to Winter's neck, pulling her away from Jai's embrace with a sudden sidestep. Winter choked and gasped for air, her eyes filled with fear and confusion. Her claws scrabbled at the ground, tearing clods, until she fell back, dragged across the grass like a carcass.

Jai felt his face contort with rage.

'Bastard!' he bellowed at Zayn.

Zayn turned, his hand resting upon the hilt of his sword, his eyes dark with challenge. Though he did not speak, the air between them became charged with the unspoken threat of violence.

Jai's anger threatened to boil over, but the sight of Sindri observing the scene forced him to bite back further words. Jai turned his back instead, spitting into the grass.

Now it was Zayn who spoke, cursing him with a snarled word. Jai already knew its meaning.

'Half-breed!'

Jai ignored him, but the rest of Valor watched until a snapped order from Sindri set the others moving once more. Jai tried to think of Winter as he took a few breaths. For who knew if Zayn would not take out on her what he was forbidden to do to Jai?

Feng avoided Jai's gaze as Jai caught up to him, but muttered beneath his breath.

'You would do well to avoid Zayn's ire. Should the Kidara refuse you, the Valor will find another buyer if they have no use for you. One that might not be so welcoming.

'Or he might simply get his wish and get to kill you.'

Jai shrugged at the threat, still simmering with rage as he stared at the man's retreating back. Only then did he notice something peculiar.

Zayn held no reins. Yet the khiro seemed to be moving with a mind of its own, weaving between the mounted warrior vanguard as Zayn conversed with his comrades.

Of course. Zayn was soulbound to it – what need could he have for reins? Jai looked closer.

He wondered if there was a reason it was so much larger than the others, draped in dark, shaggy fur that cascaded over its hulking form. Its feet, like massive dinner plates, effortlessly supported the behemoth's weight, while its conch-like ears twisted back and forth. The sheer presence of the beast seemed to command respect, as if acknowledging a force of nature brought to life.

'Why is it so big?' Jai asked, trying to distract himself from plotting Zayn's comeuppance.

Feng glanced at Zayn's mount before answering. 'That is an Alkhara – the largest among khiroi, akin to the head of a lion's pride or an alpha direwolf. They are bigger, darker and bear a silver streak in their tails. Alkhara are the strongest and most dominant of their kind. Every wild herd has one. Many tribes do not.'

Jai looked at the impressive beast. It was no wonder his father had chosen an Alkhara as a sigil for his tribe. He remembered now, Balbir speaking the word Feng just used. But he had long forgotten when, or how.

'And how did Zayn come to possess such a beast?'

'Most Alkhara among our tribes are born and raised tame, nurtured by our people before soulbonding with a chosen warrior – those who are respected for their strength and wisdom. But sometimes, a young warrior like Zayn will seek to tame a wild Alkhara during their riting, to soulbond with it.'

'Is that what a riting is?' Jai asked.

'Not always, but for some it is the taming of a beast and gifting it to the tribe – it is usually returned to them. For most who choose this path, they seek a khiro doe, for they are far smaller and more docile. A warrior wishing to make a name for themselves might take on a khiro bull. Zayn . . . he was bravest of all. He took on an Alkhara, and brought it to the Valor.'

'He was not of the Valor before?' Jai asked.

Feng shook his head. 'Zayn and Sindri were orphans both. They formed a tribe years ago, before they were conquered by the Valor. Sindri married the former leader, and upon his passing, she inherited his position. Thus, she rules.'

Something struck him then. 'How can they keep you and your sister apart?' Jai asked. 'Surely they of all people understand.'

Feng looked down. 'They treat her well enough. But I am

too valuable to them, so they keep my leash tight. Without me, they could never trade with as many tribes as they have. Nor sell their wares to the traders of the Phoenix Empire.'

Jai stared at Zayn's retreating back, feeling the rage building within him once more. Feng prodded him.

'Don't even think about it,' he hissed. 'An Alkhara-bound warrior is a rare power. Even for a dragon-bound prince such as yourself.'

Jai didn't doubt it. But it told him one thing: unless Winter learned to fly, and grow to three times her size . . . there was no way he'd escape here. Otherwise, Feng might have done it first.

His best and last hope was to be traded back to the Kidara tribe. And he had to do everything possible to make that happen.

'From now on, we must only speak in my father tongue,' Jai said. 'I have to learn, Feng.'

'Then I will teach you,' Feng replied in the language of the Steppefolk.

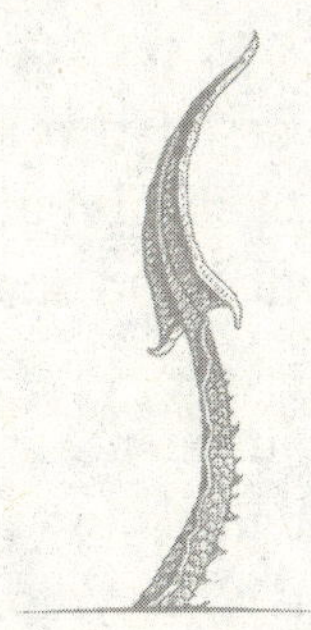

Chapter 6

As the journey continued, the song accompanied them like a living, breathing presence. It seemed to energise the Steppefolk, spurring them on through the long hours of the day. Even when the music faded into silence, it lingered in the air.

Jai longed to lend his voice to the chorus. Instead, he committed the words to memory, breathing them in a quiet chanting that Feng corrected as they walked.

Jai spent the last daylight hours talking with Feng, attempting to improve his pidgin understanding of Steppespeak, or sithosi, as the Steppefolk called it.

It was not so simple as stringing half-remembered words together. Jai had to unlearn so much of what he had taken as gospel. Indeed, even the word, Steppefolk, was what he used when thinking of his own people. This was wrong.

For they were the Sithia. Children of the mother goddess.

Jai came to realise sithosi was a rich and poetic tongue, full of nuance and subtlety that challenged him. He came to appreciate the depth of his people's connection with the land, and the many words they had for grass, of all heights, in all states.

Feng spoke too of the mother goddess, the divine being who nurtured and protected the Sithia. She was the life-giving force that sustained the vast steppe and the people who called it home. The ancient tale, passed through the generations, told that the Sithia were born of her breath and moulded from the soil she tended. This ancient bond shaped their deep reverence for the land.

It was almost a disappointment, as the sun began to crease the horizon, that Sindri called for a halt. To Jai's surprise, despite the long day's journey, the Valor moved with unwavering energy. The village seemed to rise from the earth itself as tents were expertly erected with practised hands. Strangest of all was the eerie feeling of familiarity.

Jai found himself standing in the midst of the village centre. Each tent occupied the same position it had held at daybreak, as if the village had been transported intact across the vast steppe. The only evidence of their journey lay in the long furrow trailing behind them through the grassland, and the scent of fresh-trampled grass. But he was far more interested in another smell, a promise of a hearty meal hanging in the air, drawing Jai's feet into the heart of the village.

The warm hues of twilight bathed the landscape in a gentle glow, casting a soothing warmth over the encampment.

Feng prodded Jai towards the fire, where a large cauldron bubbled and steamed, its contents emanating a mouthwatering aroma. Men and women both stooped, slicing, trimming and peeling the fruits of their forage, tossing them into the stew under the watchful eye of a wizened matron, her helpers following every twitch of her gnarled hands.

The riders, however, had not yet reached the end of their day. As those on foot attended to the camp, Zayn's warriors rode in a wide arc around the perimeter, skilfully herding the now unburdened khiroi ahead of them. The grass surrounding the camp was purposefully trampled low, Jai guessed, to deter predators, thieves and raiders from approaching beneath its cover.

Undeterred, the riders continued to patrol the camp's edges, using the fading sunlight to scan for any hint of silhouettes along the distant horizon.

The vast steppe was both sanctuary and concealment to those who knew its secrets. Yet without a khiro to navigate the endless sea of grass, even a man who grew up here would be as helpless as a raft caught on a windless sea, struggling to make any progress.

It made him worry for the fate of Erica and the Huddites. For they had no mounts to speak of, and they would have to battle through the grass with what few axes they had kept.

The khiroi were truly the Sithians' most prized possessions, serving as the vessels that voyaged this verdant expanse. Even now, while granted respite to graze, the animals were tended to by the Valor's youths. They tightened the braids in their tails and brushed the creatures' thick fur with bone combs, always checking, rubbing, touching. The khiroi rumbled with deep contentment, nuzzling their caretakers with affection.

Jai stood at the outskirts of the gathering, unsure if he would be welcomed by the Sithian youths. Navi cropped the grass nearby, hungry as he it seemed.

Feng, noticing Jai's hesitation, gave him an encouraging nod. So Jai went to Navi's side, his presence sending the youth attending to her scurrying away. He ran his hand along her grizzled fur, tracing the scars of her cruel past. Her muscles shuddered beneath his touch, yet as her wrinkled eye turned to him, she let out a deep sigh, as if acknowledging his return, and leaned against him.

He pressed himself close, hugging her, breathing in her damp animal scent. He wished Winter could join them in their embrace, but he could sense she had already been chained up in Zayn's tent again. She lingered on the edge of his consciousness, sending him encouragement. Trying to hide the fear she felt for herself. But there were no secrets between them, try as she might keep them.

For she shared the same worries as he. She too wondered what had become of Erica, and the Huddites. Had they escaped Magnus and the invading legion? Were they lost in the sea of grass? Or were they captives like he, to be sold to the highest bidder?

'Jai,' an accented voice said.

He turned to find Sindri, looking down at him from her mount.

'The moon is full,' she said. 'A good evening for a ride. Mount up, son of Rohan. Let us see if the chick falls far from the roost.'

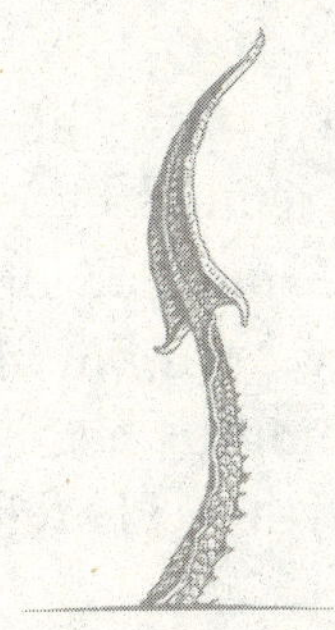

Chapter 7

Jai stared at Navi as the groom patted the saddle, but the khiro seemed more interested in cropping the grass than the fresh leathers upon her back. Despite the lack of torches, the full moon gave Jai enough light to see that the youths of the Valor were gathering to watch. Certainly, his soulbound ears could hear the jingle of coins being exchanged.

The groom, sensing Jai's hesitation, winked and knelt down, offering his cupped hands as a makeshift stirrup. Jai hesitated, then stepped up, vaulting himself onto Navi's back with a hurried thanks.

Beneath him, Navi shuddered, her legs splaying in surprise at the sudden weight. Jai held his breath. But Navi's trembling turned to shudders, her snorts betraying her agitation as her gaze flicked between the onlookers and Jai.

In one swift motion, Navi reared up, kicking her powerful forelegs. Jai flailed, falling backwards as his hands snatched at the air.

His landing was surprisingly soft. It was only when the laughter swirled around him for longer and louder than warranted that he realised he was lying in a pile of fresh dung. Jai gritted his teeth, and wiped the muck from his trousers. His pride stung far worse than the fall.

He approached Navi once more, and ran his hand along her

side, feeling the scars of her past. She trusted him, he knew she did; he simply needed to remind her.

He remembered how Arjun had once calmed a lame horse, years ago, when they were both but children. Jai pressed close, forehead to snout, breathing in her breath, and she breathing his, mingling in shared rhythm. He felt the rushing pulse in her neck. Felt it slow.

Jai lifted a leg, twisting onto her as swiftly as he dared. She bucked again, but Jai was ready for her, shifting his weight back and seizing the thick fur of her neck. She whickered in protest, but Jai soothed her, leaning down to murmur into her ear.

Gradually, the trembling of her body eased, and she took a tentative step forward. Then another, and another, as if testing their new-found accord.

The rumble of another khiro's feet made Jai turn, only to see Sindri slap Navi's rump. Navi surged into the long grass, the world around them becoming a blur of motion. Jai's heart swelled with exhilaration as they ploughed on, the wind tearing through his hair, and the scent of earth and greenery filling his nostrils.

Sindri rode beside Jai, her laughter resounding through the air, her long black hair streaming behind her like a dark banner.

It felt like an age had passed before they slowed, yet when Jai turned, he could still discern the flickering fires of the camp and see the tendrils of smoke fading into the moonlit sky.

Despite his enhanced strength, Jai found himself panting – more from exhilaration than exhaustion. Sindri chuckled, her eyes glinting with mischief.

'Ease up,' she advised, pointing at Jai's white-knuckled grip on Navi's nape. 'Lest you rip it out.'

Jai released his hold with a sigh, patting Navi's neck as the khiro snorted, her head already buried in the grass, snuffling contentedly. Sindri watched for a moment, her expression softening. 'She missed it here,' she said. 'Khiroi belong amid the endless expanse of the steppe. It's a wonder an old matron like her is still going. She has heart. You're fortunate to have her.'

She sniffed, leaning over to trace the scars that marred Navi's back.

'I had to be certain,' Sindri said. 'No khiro treated this way would let their abuser ride them. Or even a stranger. You must have a way with her.'

'You could have just asked me,' Jai said.

'Yes,' Sindri said, giving him a searching stare. 'I am beginning to see that.'

Jai met her gaze, attempting to maintain a steady expression. At last, Sindri nodded, seemingly satisfied with what she saw. She reached behind her saddle and tossed Jai a familiar bundle – his satchel.

Grinning, Jai unbuckled the top, relieved to find his sabretooth still there. However, his father's gorget, Leonid's diary and his sword were all missing. He looked up at Sindri, who raised her hands defensively.

'As Queen of the Valor, it is my right to divide the spoils of any conquests we make,' she said. 'If you are traded, I will return them to you – or, at least, to those I trade you to. But not before.'

Jai clenched his teeth, frustrated that he had been stripped of nearly all his worldly possessions. Still, he nodded in acceptance. What other choice did he have?

'Feng has taught me many things,' she said as she drew the thin volume that was Leonid's diary from beneath her furs. 'Even the letters of our enemies. Poor boy was up half the night helping me read what I could of this.' She stared at it, as if half in wonder.

'This thing,' she mused. 'It is either the work of a master forger, or an artefact of the greatest worth. It is . . .'

She stopped herself, and tucked it away.

'I believe you, Jai,' Sindri said softly, her voice carrying the weight of her conviction. 'But I am one of the few who do. My brother . . . he is a hard man, shaped by the harshness of our life before I took power here. We were nothing more than Tainted orphans, shunned even by those who might have shown us charity. I remember the days we chewed on grass just to fill the emptiness of our bellies. We scavenged carrion, following the circling buzzards in search of sustenance. He kept me alive. Beneath the scars he bears, there lies a loyal heart. Much like Navi's.'

Jai must have failed to conceal the scepticism on his face, for she smiled at him knowingly.

'Mark me, Jai. Zayn makes a formidable enemy, but a better friend. With his power, his warriors' devotion, he could wrest this tribe from me in a second. Instead, he rides night and day, keeping the direwolves from our door. Do not judge a man by his worst qualities alone.'

Jai had little to say to that. All he'd seen in Zayn was a bully.

Instead, he stared out, into the distance. Raised his brows, as he saw flickering lights far on the horizon.

'You see them too?' Sindri said. 'Zayn's been following their scent for days.'

'Is it the Kidara?' Jai asked.

Sindri shrugged.

'Whoever it is, we'll catch up to them in a few days. Send Feng to parlay, learn their identity and if the Kidara have ventured this way. They won't speak to us otherwise.'

Jai stared at her. Were the Tainted truly so reviled that they would refuse to trade for even their own heir? Sindri, ever perceptive, caught his expression once more. Jai reminded himself to be more careful of that.

'None trade with the Tainted. They only raid us, and sell us as fettered. It is our strength.'

'Oh?' Jai asked.

Sindri motioned back towards the Valor's camp.

'The Great Tribes of the steppe have grown fat in peace, Jai. They no longer follow the old ways. They sell fettered to the west, and buy fine silks, baubles and trifles from the east. If you are to learn the ways of the Sithia, Jai, you will find no better teachers. Heed our lessons, for the Kidara are not the tribe they once were.'

She turned away, clucking her khiro into a trot.

'You can ride Navi tomorrow,' Sindri called over her shoulder. 'So you're not too weary by sunset.'

'Too tired for what?' Jai shouted after her.

Her reply drifted back to him on the wind.

'Your training.'

Chapter 8

Sindri did not linger to see if Jai could turn Navi around, leaving him alone under the vast expanse of the moonlit sky. Jai sat on Navi's back for a while, allowing the old khiro to graze on the tender grass, as he breathed in the cool night air. This was the Great Steppe in all its glory: the grasses, bathed in silver, swaying in a shimmering, burnished meadow.

His thoughts drifted once again to Erica. He wondered if she had made it to her homeland. If Hanebal and his Huddite brethren had continued east, or gone with her, to the Dansk and their Northern Tundra.

He missed her presence. Even missed her silence, in the early morning, when the world was still asleep, and Rufus was loading up their wagon.

Rufus too weighed heavy in his thoughts. Had the big man won his battle with Magnus? Or did the Gryphon Guard sect leader still fly the steppe, relentlessly pursuing the royal bloodlines of the Sabines' adversaries.

Jai realised he might never discover the answers to these questions. He could only hope for their success . . . and focus on his own.

Only one of his loved ones was within his reach. Winter, trapped in a life she did not choose. He knew he had to earn

Zayn's trust, not just for his own sake, but for Winter's as well. Sindri had said as much.

Taking a deep breath, he filled his lungs with the crisp night air and steeled himself to face the challenges that awaited him. He urged Navi forward, steering her back towards the camp using his heels, as his brothers had taught him long ago.

Upon his return, Jai saw only Feng had waited for him, standing forlornly at the edge of the village. Jai dismounted, awkward as he slid backwards off her rump, and was suddenly glad for the lack of audience.

'You're back,' Feng said, half to himself. 'I had almost believed you wouldn't be.'

Jai felt a surge of gratitude for Feng. He had fast become a steadfast ally, looking out for him when he could have easily turned his back. In a world where trust was a rare commodity, Jai knew the value of such friendship.

'Thank you, Feng,' Jai said, embracing the lad. 'I wouldn't leave without you.'

Feng's eyes lit up at that.

'Truly?'

But Jai hardly registered his response, for beyond them, the encampment bustled with activity.

Men and women toiled with wooden trowels, excavating two pits in the village centre. Others drove bamboo stakes into the earth, fashioning a makeshift curtain to separate the two holes.

Still more stoked bonfires, tossing bales of dried grass into the flames. They were cooking something. But what?

'Come,' Feng said. 'We must help, or we won't be allowed to partake.'

Jai grinned, and rubbed his belly, following Feng as the lad hurried back into the village.

'Good idea,' Jai said, 'I'm starving.'

Feng grinned back, but more in amusement than camaraderie.

'You misunderstand me.'

By now, Jai could feel the heat of the bonfires, the crackling of flames drowning out the chatter of conversation as the Valor went about their labours. What food could possibly need such fires?

Only now, did Jai see men scrabbling around in the bottom of the pits, lifting out stones from the soil beneath. Children grabbed them, and tossed them into the bonfires under the watchful eyes of the elders, who stoked and prodded the flames.

'What . . . ?' Jai asked.

Feng hushed him, instead leaping into the pit. Jai followed, landing in its muddy bottom with a squelch. He followed Feng and the others' example, raking his hands through the soil, clawing rocks from its sucking embrace and passing them to the grasping hands of the children above. Others hammered bamboo stakes into the retaining walls, holding back the earth.

Feng strained to dislodge a small boulder lodged at the pit's centre, eliciting knowing grins from the others as the stone slid back into the mud.

Jai sucked in a breath, and summoned the dregs of mana within his core. Things had been moving so fast, he'd hardly any mana: only what Winter had trickled through to him through the night, and some hints of the hummingbird technique, when there was a lull in his and Feng's conversation.

Nonetheless, it was enough for Jai to thrust his hands beneath the boulder, lift it with a grunt and heave it over the edge of the pit.

He ignored the astonished looks from the others, and went about his work.

'Watch out!' a voice called from above.

Jai understood enough sithosi to leap back just in time. A young girl grinned down at him as a bowlful of embers and coals tumbled into the mud behind him, sizzling and steaming.

'Come on,' Feng said, clapping Jai on the shoulder. 'Before the pit fills completely.'

By now, more embers were being tipped into the pit, and the stone diggers were swift to scoop mud over the steaming embers, burying them in a thin layer of silt, spreading them more evenly along the pit bottom.

Jai had hardly time to see how it was done before the embers stopped, and the workers were scrabbling out of the hole. A hand reached down to Jai, and he took it, surprised.

A shocking strength pulled him over the edge, and he hauled himself, a muddy, charcoal-dusted mess, onto the grass above. His helper chuckled, and gave him a poke with her toe.

It was the girl who had woken him that morning, the same one who had fought Zayn. She was a rare beauty, even among the many winsome girls in the camp, with long lashes, a heart-shaped face and wide eyes whose intense gaze Jai found difficult to meet without averting his own.

She flashed him an enticing smile before hurrying away. Jai watched her retreating back, noting the long braid that swung down to her buttocks. Unmarried, then, if what Balbir had once told him held true.

He felt a flash of guilt, for the feeling that stirred within was one he'd only reserved for Erica. She could be within Magnus's clutches that very moment.

'Little help?' Feng called out. 'Before I drown down here?'

Jai hurried to help Feng, who by now was waist-deep in water that was rapidly seeping into the pit. With a firm grip, he pulled Feng out, and the two collapsed beside the pit, catching their breath amid the laughter and chaos.

'Why the embers?' Jai asked, trying and failing to rub the dust from his hands.

'Charcoal cleans the water,' Feng panted. 'See?'

Jai stared into the slow-rising placid pool. Feng was right. The water was tinged with mud, true, but he could see far deeper than he had any right to.

Then, a red-hot stone plummeted into its centre, sending out a splash of hissing, steaming water. Another followed, and then another.

Soon it was not just stones that followed, but men. Whooping and yelling, they dove and bellyflopped into the fast-warming waters, splashing the onlookers in a near-puerile display. And bare as the days they were born, utterly unembarrassed by their nakedness, the boundaries between age and status momentarily erased in the face of shared revelry.

Jai stood awkwardly at the pool's edge, suddenly understanding what the screen of bamboo was for – for he could hear splashing and the laughter of women on the other side. He turned to Feng, only to see he'd stripped down himself, and was sliding down the banks of the pit.

Jai groaned, but knew he needed to bathe more than any here. He could not remember the last time he'd had a chance.

Throwing caution to the wind, Jai tugged off his clothing, letting it fall into the mud. Then he leaped into the water with as much grace as he could muster.

Within, the water was warm as a baby's bath, and he let out a stream of bubbles as he groaned with relief. Jai emerged with a whoop, smoothing the hair from his eyes.

He and Feng waded to the edge of the crowded pool, surrounded by the strong, battle-scarred men of the village. Jai couldn't help but count the warriors, taking note that there were perhaps thirty men of fighting age, all of them gravitating around Zayn.

Now the young boys and elders slid down into the pool, but not before they tossed baskets of rough-chopped herbs into the water.

There was a scent that rose with the steam, minty and refreshing. Jai observed as the men scooped up handfuls of the fragrant leaves, crushing them between their palms and allowing the rich, foamy suds to cascade over their heads. Strangely, a foam was gathering on the surface of the water.

'Yucca,' Feng said, gathering up a handful. 'It makes the water soapy. Then there's wild mint, lemon balm, who knows what else.'

Jai followed Feng's example, squeezing it into his hair and delighting in the silky tingling as he rubbed it into his scalp.

As he rinsed the suds from his eyes, Jai noticed the men arranging themselves in a line around the edge of the bathing pit. He and Feng joined the queue, taking their places in the chain of men. A toothless elder grinned at Jai, guiding him into position with a gentle nudge.

Each man took his place, reaching out to work through the hair and beards of their comrades, using combs they had apparently brought with them. Their fingers worked deftly, untangling knots and smoothing out the roughness that marked their lives. The scene was surprisingly intimate, and Jai was beginning to see the deep trust that bound these men together.

Jai did his best, even as his own scalp was tugged and teased, the old man tutting loudly. Feng chuckled a little at Jai's inexpert touch, and handed him the bone comb he had been using on his own charge, a young lad who seemed content to escape Feng's ministrations.

It was peaceful. Here, words were unnecessary. All that could be heard was the gentle splash of water and the crackling of flames, as the steam drifted into the star-speckled sky above.

He settled into the rhythm of it. Letting the fresh, herby scent clear his mind, and his nostrils. And all the while, finally . . . Jai soulbreathed.

Letting the mana fill his lungs, it flowed through his channels and reached the emptiness of his core. Even as the first motes entered his crystalline centre and ran down its walls to fill its bottom, Jai felt it rush to his extremities, to heal the cuts and scrapes of the last few days. Had it really only been a few days? It felt like his escape from Porticus had been a lifetime ago.

It was amazing. It was the first time he'd felt like himself in forever. Except he knew he wasn't truly complete, and once more he wished Winter could be with him. The poor dragon remained chained within a nearby tent, though he could sense she had been well-fed at least.

The little dragon was listening through their connection

intently, vicariously enjoying the scents and sensations of Jai's mind. Apart as they were, their meld was far stronger than before he had ascended.

And then, as if by some unspoken signal, the chain broke apart, the men dispersing like ripples in a pond. Jai watched, intrigued, as the warriors began scooping up silt and charcoal from the pit's bottom, gathering the dark, rich mixture and lathering themselves with it, then scraping it off with the backs of their combs.

Some slapped fine mud playfully into each other's faces and shoulders. Brotherly in their love for each other. No one did it to Jai, though.

'Go on,' Feng said. 'It's heavenly.'

Jai took a handful of it himself, only to catch Zayn's brooding eyes. The firelight danced across his face, crisscrossing faded scars. With a subtle tilt of his head, he beckoned for Jai and Feng to approach. Jai's heart seized, and he hesitated, knowing to ignore the invitation would be a grave offence.

Feng's hand pressing the small of his back made the choice for him, and he waded closer to the gathered warriors.

Zayn's eyes never wavered from Jai's, his expression shrouded. The other men's movements slowed, the air thick with anticipation as they drew near. What had been a jovial, raucous atmosphere was suddenly heavy.

Jai felt like he was walking to his own execution. He swallowed hard, feeling the scrutiny of the battle-scarred men surrounding him. Amid these bare-chested warriors, his and Feng's paler skin tones were all the more obvious.

Zayn's hand extended, offering Jai a generous scoop of the silt and charcoal mixture. The gesture was both invitation and challenge. Jai's gaze met Zayn's and accepted the offering, his hands trembling slightly as he began to lather the mixture onto his skin.

Now Zayn turned to Feng. But as the boy extended his hand, Zayn allowed the mixture to slip from his grasp, dropping it with a mocking splash. Chuckles rippled through the gathering of onlookers.

Jai's nostrils flared, and he took a defiant step back, receiving a disdainful sneer from Zayn in return. He remained unfazed. Any semblance of an olive branch held out to him was undoubtedly broken if it didn't extend to Feng as well.

The man was toying with them, only seeking to divide the pair. Jai stooped, gathering a scoop for Feng instead. He turned his back upon Zayn as he did so, catching the sudden scowls from the onlookers.

A wad of mud slapped into the back of his head, and Jai turned to see Zayn grinning at him. What was this? The politics of this place were so physical. In the world Jai was raised in, loyalties were earned in the stroke of a pen, in proclamations and debated antechambers. Politics on a grand scale. Yet here, in the mud, it was a tangible thing. A gift of earth, of knotting the hair of the one beside you. A punch in the shoulder, or an ignored jibe.

And now, Jai realised why Zayn hated Feng. It was because the boy did not fight back. Did not show defiance. Avoided the gaze of those who would challenge him.

Zayn was a man who would only respect strength – courage, in the face of a bully. So Jai would show him strength.

'When I say,' Jai muttered, 'splash at Zayn.'

'Are you mad?' Feng hissed back.

'Do it,' Jai said. 'If I get in trouble, Navi is yours.'

Feng thought for a moment. Then nodded.

Jai lowered his hands, scooping mud with one and contorting the other beneath the water. Zayn tensed, still grinning, seeing Jai crouching.

Jai knew few spells, and had practised but two of them. A gout of fire would hardly do, but Balbir's shade spell might allow him to get within Zayn's guard.

He channelled the mana through his body, feeling it circulate.

Green light flashed beneath the water, and Jai felt his body numb. Fade.

Zayn's eyes widened.

'Now!' Jai growled.

Water splashed, distracting Zayn for but a moment. Enough time for Jai to dive forward, splatting the big man directly in the face.

Jai stood there as Zayn wiped the mud from his eyes, the numbness leaving Jai's body, for he had used the last dregs of his mana.

Silence hung in the air, and Jai gave Zayn a hesitant grin. The man looked enraged. Then he broke into a roar of laughter, grabbing Jai by the arm and knuckling his hair.

The watching men, at first hesitant, joined in the laughter, one even punching Feng on the shoulder.

'Good!' Zayn announced, in broken High Imperial. 'Very good!'

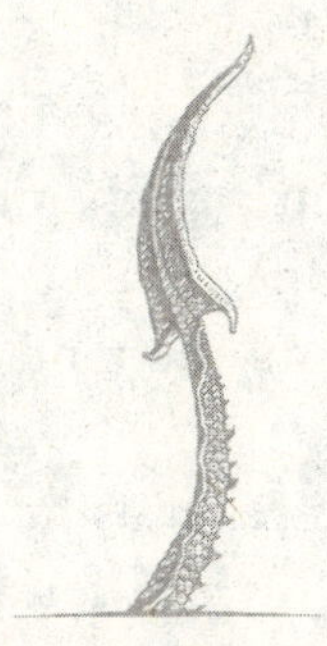

Chapter 9

Morning came all too quickly, and Jai groaned as he roused, the khiro horn announcing the morning. His night had been a tapestry of dreams, woven by threads so vivid, he had thought them real.

Jai had tasted the gamy flavour of squirrel upon his tongue as Winter dreamed of the dense forest she had been born in. The memory had been so strong, it was as though Jai himself had been scampering through the leaf-laden ground, feeling the wind on his scales, his heart racing with the thrill of the chase.

Jai sat up before the beautiful Valor girl could rouse him, for she was already there to wake any deaf elders who had not heard the horn. This time, she left him something, placing it beside him with a quiet smile. A pile of clothing to replace the rags he had been wearing since he'd arrived.

Jai felt a twinge of guilt as he smiled back at her, Erica's own smile on the edge of his thoughts.

He shook the thoughts from his head and took the opportunity to hold the clothes up to the light. He was grateful to her and couldn't help but smile as he noted the tanned leather and handspun wool, crafted to withstand the elements.

It felt like an age since he had worn clean clothes.

'What is your name?' Jai blurted, attempting to speak in a language he had hardly spoken to anyone but Feng.

She smiled at him, and shook her head, still coaxing an elderly woman from her fur rug, then motioning for Jai to leave.

'Kiran,' she called, as he blinked in the new daylight. He grinned, and hurried behind the tent, dressing as quickly as he could.

His body warmed with relief as he tugged on the new attire, almost sighing in its comfort. He felt almost human again. The leather trousers were supple, allowing him to move freely, while the woollen tunic was soft and warm against his skin.

Jai saw the Valor were wasting no time, for the village was dissolving before his eyes. He hurried to where the khiroi were being prepared for the day's journey. Amid the flurry of hurrying men and women, he found Feng, holding Navi by the reins. The khiro was already saddled, adorned with a vibrant, patterned linen beneath the leather seat.

Instead of a bit between her teeth, the reins were attached to a snug harness that wrapped around her snout. Jai knew enough about horses from his brothers to know it was an unusual arrangement. Jai reached out and fingered it, seeing where the harness ended just behind her mouth.

'No bit?' Jai asked, curious.

'You try to keep a khiro from feeding,' Feng said, 'and they'll chew any bit to nothing.'

Jai eyed the saddle with remembered trepidation, aware of the side glances from the other riders nearby. Perhaps they were hoping for a repeat of the previous day's performance. Jai surreptitiously eyed the ground for khiroi manure before gingerly climbing into the saddle.

Navi trembled beneath him, until Jai leaned forwards, patting the old beast's thick neck. She gave one last tremble, almost a shrug, before leaning down and cropping at the grass once more.

'She remembers,' Sindri observed, her voice coming from behind.

Jai clicked his tongue, nudging with the reins, attempting to turn Navi in Sindri's direction. It took a forceful yank to lift her head from her meal, but she spread her feet, obstinately refusing to move.

Sindri clucked her tongue disapprovingly, guiding her own khiro around to come alongside Jai.

'You should be more gentle,' she advised. 'A khiro doe is no Alkhara to be manhandled into submission. She must be respected, and she must, in turn, respect you. Let her eat if she is not ready to go. Until she respects you enough to go when you wish.'

Jai felt a twinge of guilt, letting the reins fall limp. Navi snorted, tugging on the reins a little harder than she had to as she lowered her head to crop the ground.

'I thought I had a way with her,' he admitted, a touch petulant.

Sindri laughed at that.

'Pah,' she exclaimed. 'If you seek to be put in your place, then I will do the honours. You are but a stripling on an old doe, one who has been ridden before. She will never charge into battle, nor trample your enemies. You try mounting an unbroken bull, let alone a wild Alkhara. That is a different beast altogether.'

Jai detected the disdain in her voice, despite the kindness with which it was intended. He crossed his arms, even as the first riders began plodding into the grassland.

'Now, you go ride with the others,' Sindri said. 'The warriors will be riding ahead, in case of ambush. Best to be careful when another tribe is near. You take Feng with you. It's about time he learned too.'

Hearing that, Feng clambered into the saddle behind Jai, and the pair sat there, with Jai now so bewildered that he didn't know whether to pull the reins or not. Instead, he stared at the twin pits in the ground, which were far more conspicuous than the last camp they had been to. Strangely, several of the village elders were scattering seed along the pit's edges, others kneeling and praying to the open sky above.

'Why are they planting?' Jai asked. 'It's unlikely we will pass this way again, no?'

'In hopes it will become an oasis,' Feng said. 'For the beasts of the steppe, and for any other tribe, if not the Valor's own descendants. A place to collect water, where the bamboo and trees can compete with the voracious grasses of this land. Some say, without the Sithia, there would be naught but khiroi and grass. The elders plant that which they shall never see. It is their way.'

It is *my* way, Jai thought as he stared, fascinated. And suddenly wished he could someday see this place, a month, or years from now. Perhaps he might see one of these oases someday, mature and fruitful, rich with the life of the land.

Ultimately, it was the absence of other khiroi that coaxed Navi from her grazing, and Jai couldn't help but feel a surge of exhilaration as she thundered over the plains, closing the gap with the warriors ahead.

The cavalry of the Valor comprised some fifty men and women on khiroi, their ages spanning from youths only slightly younger than Jai to grizzled elders who may have shared his tent that very morning. Few were in their prime, khiroi included, save for the small, tight-knit group that gravitated around Zayn, their leader, as they rode at the forefront of the herd.

They were armed as if for battle, but only a few bore the famed falxes of the Sithia. Most others were armed with an assortment of weapons – axes, spears and shorter blades. As for their clothing, it was not dissimilar to his own, but with an added layer of leather breastplates, greaves and other armour, likely scavenged from battles past.

Kiran, the soulbound woman Zayn had wrestled, was among the best equipped. Her armour, like Zayn's, seemed to denote her status, setting her apart as a warrior to be reckoned with.

Winter, to Jai's annoyance, was not with them – instead being led like a dog by the children at the back. Jai might have even complained, if he had not sensed the little dragon's pleasure as she frolicked in the grass, diving for treats. Instead, he resigned himself to the day's ride, trying to figure out what sort of training Sindri might mean.

For a while, they travelled in silence, the quiet of the sunrise blushing the world in its ochres. Only when the birds began to chirrup, and the first marching songs began behind them, did their voices stir.

Though his understanding was limited, he found himself able to grasp the essence of what was being said. He was becoming used to their accent too. Each fragment of conversation he pieced together was a small triumph.

Hours slipped by, and Jai took the opportunity to soulbreathe. He had assumed it would be difficult, for he was still mastering the art of riding Navi, his spine jostling with each step. The tight embrace of Feng's arms around him only added to the challenge. However, it was as if Jai's body craved mana, and his soulbreathing instinctively found a rhythm. He even took the chance to connect with Winter, who sorely missed him, yet aided his cultivation of mana by sending her own meagre reserves.

Jai always felt guilty when he awoke to find his core partly filled by his loyal companion – knowing that without mana of her own, she would be all the weaker for it.

But the golden motes were like a balm as they filtered out of his core, wiping away the aches and pains of his broken sleep, and exhilarating him with new energy.

He was forever grateful to Winter, and resolved to himself that he would ask Zayn for an audience with her. Surely after the last night's camaraderie, the man might see reason?

As if reading his mind, Zayn galloped up to him, guiding his imposing Alkhara to Jai's side. The pair's combined presence was imposing, for the sheer size of the beast matched Zayn's own. In comparison, Navi appeared almost a babe, for she was smaller than the rest – the years of malnourishment having taken their toll.

The powerful beast's dark fur shone in the spring sun, and as Zayn slowed beside Jai, it snorted, dancing away from the strange khiro it did not know. Meanwhile, Navi remained unbothered, grazing contentedly beside the great beast without acknowledging its presence.

'Follow me,' Zayn ordered, his voice harsh.

Feng's translation was lost in the spray of soil as the Alkhara pulled ahead; though in truth, Jai had not needed it. Understanding the Valor was becoming easier and easier. Finding words of his own was the hard part.

Barked commands divided the Valor vanguard, leaving most of the warriors behind, Zayn and his entourage carving a gap in the grasses ahead. Jai did not have long to consider whether to obey, for Navi lurched after them, her competitive spirit refusing to be left behind.

Even now, Feng's tales lurked at the back of his mind – the rumours of Zayn coveting his sister's rule, of his ruthless ambition. As they rode on, Jai found himself observing the riders around him, trying to read their faces. But he saw nothing.

It almost made him miss the cerebral undercurrents of the Sabine court, where a glance could be as heavy as a thousand words.

Soon enough, the Valor tribe were but small figures far away, the vast plains having swallowed Jai and Navi whole. His fears only grew with the distance, and he almost jumped when Zayn signalled for a halt, slowing his Alkhara without even a twitch of his reins. Jai followed suit, Navi's breathing coming in heavy snorts.

The other men seemed disinterested, instead scanning the horizon, as the Valor were wont to do. If Zayn had a plan, Jai guessed they were not in on it. Not yet.

Zayn dismounted, motioning for Jai to follow suit.

'Come,' Zayn said, again in a heavily accented High Imperial, clicking his fingers, pointing at the ground. 'Come, come.'

Jai dropped to the ground, his hand straying and then

retreating from his empty belt, bereft of the blade he instinctively reached for.

Only when they were a little distance from the others, did Zayn speak again.

'You,' Zayn said. 'Me. Teach.'

Jai nodded, smiling. He thought for a moment, then tried in sithosi.

'You teach me Talvir?' Jai asked, nodding. 'Yes. I will work hard.'

Zayn's face twisted into surprise, then darkened with a shake of his head.

'No,' he grunted, now in sithosi. '*You* teach me . . . spell.'

With new understanding, Jai felt the blood drain from his face. This wasn't a lesson . . .

This was a shakedown.

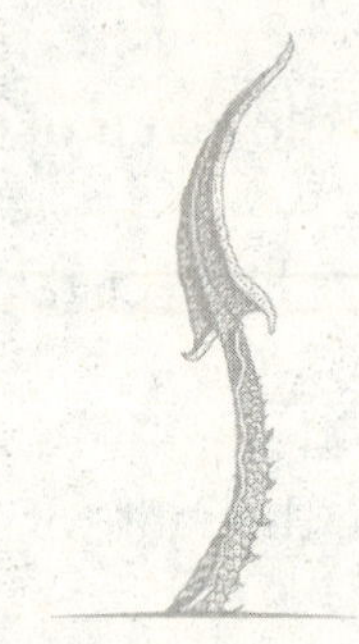

Chapter 10

If Zayn had noticed Jai's expression, he did not show it, only pointing at Jai's hands, expecting him to contort them into the shape required for the shade spell.

Jai had always hoped to pass on the spell to any and all Sithians, as had been Balbir's last wish. But now he saw the opportunity in this: for the first time, Jai possessed something that Zayn desired. What he needed to gauge, then, was how far could he push this formidable man without humiliating him in front of his followers.

'Feng,' Jai said. 'Translate for me, please.'

Feng dismounted, and Jai noticed his friend's hands trembling. The sight grounded him, reminding him of the precarious situation. They had been separated from the baggage train for a reason.

Jai took a deep breath, composing himself, before speaking in a measured tone. 'I will gladly teach you the spell, Zayn,' he said, enunciating each word with as much deference as he could summon. 'But in exchange, I request something from you.'

Feng hesitated, but then dutifully translated, and Jai watched as Zayn's eyes narrowed, weighing the proposition.

'What do . . . you want?' Zayn asked, his voice a low rumble, a hint of impatience seeping through.

'Winter,' Jai said. 'My dragon.'

When Zayn immediately stiffened, as if to reject the request, he pushed on.

'How would you feel, if your Alkhara was kept chained like a dog, away from you?'

He had noted how the big man doted on his own totem, for none among the Valor's khiroi had fur so shiny and kempt. Indeed, he had seen the man show kindness to young children in the baths. He wasn't a monster. So maybe he could see how much this hurt both Jai and Winter.

'Yes,' Zayn growled. 'You can sleep in her tent. Chain stay. Now show me.'

'And Talvir,' Jai said, pushing his luck. 'You must teach me.'

Zayn's face darkened, and he raised a trembling finger.

He barked a string of what Jai knew to be expletives, the force of his feeling apparent in the spittle that sprayed Jai's face.

'He's angry,' Feng whispered, stating the obvious.

Jai held up his hands, a show of peace.

'I am in awe of you,' Jai said, this time in sithosi, attempting the common phrase of respect Feng had taught him.

Zayn seemed to perk up at that, and his anger abated slightly. Jai kept his gaze steady, but lowered his head in deference.

'You are a formidable warrior,' Jai continued, Feng translating for him again. 'Why, the Kidara would more believe *you* were Rohan's son than I.'

Jai steadied his breathing as Zayn nodded broadly, accepting Jai's compliment as his due. Whatever Jai's status among the tribe, such adulation from an outsider only served to confirm Zayn's own. In turn, the flattery cost Jai nothing.

'I heard what you said,' Jai pressed on. 'You call me a bastard fool. A stripling not worthy to learn the sacred arts. If you do not teach me . . . the Kidara will think the same. What worth will I have then?'

Now, Zayn leaned forward, pressing Jai's forehead with his own. Jai could feel the wet heat of the man's breaths, the pressure forcing him back a step. He braced, and felt his feet skid in the dirt. And then, just like that, Zayn straightened, pointing to Kiran.

'She will teach,' he said, showing off his High Imperial once more. 'Now *show*.'

Jai knew he needed back his father's gorget, and Leonid's diary to boot. Without them, he might never convince the Kidara of his origins, if he might escape this place.

But now he wasn't so sure escape was the right option. At least, not until they found his father's tribe. A castaway does not abandon the pirate vessel that rescued him, only to be swallowed by the merciless sea. He waits for sight of shore.

He was also sure he had already pressed his luck as far as it would go today.

'Show!' Zayn barked.

Jai lifted a hand, contorting it as best he could. Zayn gripped his wrist, his eyes hungry. Behind him, Kiran leaned from her khiro, also curious.

After a few moments, Zayn crooked his own fingers, cursing as a green glow sputtered and sparked from the tips of his fingers.

Jai tried to correct the placement of the fingers, manually moving them, when a shout pierced the air: one of the men had spotted something approaching.

Zayn pulled his hand back and vaulted onto his Alkhara, standing tall upon his saddle and peering into the horizon, shielding his eyes from the sun's harsh glare.

He barked a command. One of the riders peeled off, thundering back towards their baggage train at breakneck speed. The others unsheathed their weapons, the sound of steel singing, accompanied by the creak of leather as armour straps were fastened tight.

'Jai,' Feng hissed, holding out a hand. Jai hoisted himself back onto Navi and stared in the same direction as the Valor.

Zayn barked another order, and the khiroi jostled together,

shoulder to shoulder, leaving Kiran to pull on Jai's reins and guiding him to join the line. Together, the khiroi snorted and pawed at the ground, while Navi quivered beneath him.

And within him, Jai felt Winter running. Ripping her chain from the child that held it, tearing over the grassland. She had sensed the danger before Jai had truly grasped it himself. For upon the horizon . . . they came.

At first glance, Jai thought it a herd of wild khiroi. But they were too closely packed, too purposeful in their travel. And there were riders, their shapes melding with the shuddering, humped forms of their mounts.

'What is this?' Jai demanded of Feng.

'Another clan,' Feng whispered, his voice breathless with fear. 'Come to face us. Test our mettle. Or shatter it completely.'

'We should retreat,' Jai growled. 'There are too few of us. Even if Sindri gets here in time, they look like almost twice our number.'

'The Sithia always ride out to face their enemy,' Feng said. 'The enemy should never be allowed near the village.'

Time trickled on as the sun bore down, rivulets of sweat trailing down Jai's spine. Zayn's warriors waited in tense silence.

The enemy drew closer, such that Jai could now see them in more detail over the shortened distance. Men and women both, far better armed than they, with falxes near to a man, and war banners fluttering in the breeze above.

The reassuring rumble of approaching allies reached Jai's ears, but so did the disconcerting sound of the enemy's advance. A loud chirr drew Jai's attention, and there was Winter, crouched at Navi's feet. She gave Jai but a single glance, her blue eyes expressing all that he could already feel through the meld. Her love . . . and determination to fight. Even with a rusted chain clinking behind her.

A rider lumbered to his side, then another further down the line. Jai thanked any god that might be listening. Their reinforcements had arrived from camp, such as they were.

Now some fifty warriors stood in a single row, eyes locked on the horizon. Jai could only do the same, where a far more formidable line faced them.

'See the crossed falxes upon their banners,' Feng breathed. 'The Keldar. Another Tainted tribe. One of the larger ones.'

'Allies?' Jai asked.

Feng grunted before declaring, 'No such thing. They will swallow us up. Make us their own.

'Or slaughter those who try to fight back.'

Jai held his breath as Zayn raised his blade, awaiting the command to charge. He wondered what he would do without a weapon of his own, but there seemed there were none to spare.

Channelling the meagre mana within him, Jai prepared the flame spell with his fingers, cursing his scant reserves after last night's shade spell, which were barely sufficient for a single burst of fire.

Jai felt the sudden urge to attempt escape. Winter was with him, and he rode Navi. But indecision seized him. It was too risky. There were too many variables.

Before Zayn could give the order, Sindri's cry interrupted him. Breaking ranks, she brandished a white banner on a tall pole above her head.

'Surrender?' Jai asked, incredulous.

'No,' Feng breathed, both in relief and confusion. 'Parlay.'

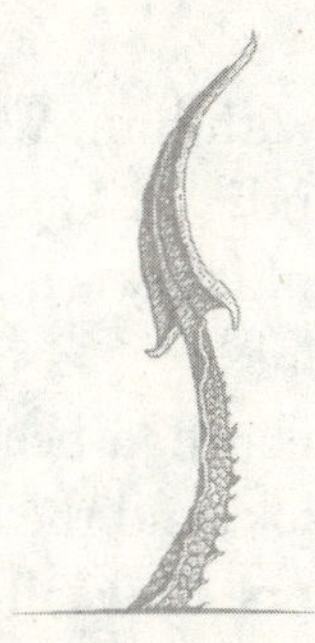

Chapter 11

A trio of Keldar riders broke ranks, advancing towards the Valor line. In a mere thirty seconds, they reached the middle ground at a measured trot.

A single held breath's space stood between the two lines clashing, and the world plunging into a chaos of blood, blades and violence.

The Valor remained silent, but Jai could already hear the taunts and jeers from their adversaries, their confidence evident.

Zayn and Sindri, though grim faced, appeared anything but disheartened. They sat tall in their saddles as they rode out to meet the riders, Zayn's Alkhara towering above the rest, for their enemy had none.

Out of earshot, the leaders spoke among themselves, while the khiroi jostled nervously. Navi, inexplicably, had resumed grazing, much to Winter's irritation.

'Knock it off,' Jai hissed.

Navi kept on, oblivious. Jai was at least thankful that his dragon was hidden in the long grass, but when he ordered her to move behind him, she stubbornly refused. They tussled mentally, but she was resolute – she would remain by his side, come what may.

He stared at the other tribe, and for a moment, the mad thought of breaking ranks and running to the other tribe entered his mind. He had Winter with him. Would it be so bad to leave the diary and gorget behind?

But of course, that would leave him with little proof of his claim to the Kidaran throne.

And then, as abruptly as it had begun, the parlay concluded. Sindri and Zayn turned back, and the Keldar did the same. This close, Jai could see the hints of wealth upon these Keldar.

Their armour was not merely crafted from boiled and layered leathers, but reinforced with chain-mail and lamellar plates. The jewellery that decorated them far surpassed the beads and polished bones of the Valor tribe, for the Keldar's braids and the fur of their khiroi were interwoven with hairpins, combs and barrettes of precious metals and gemstone, along with ribbons of scarlet silk.

'Prepare to charge,' Sindri announced. 'On Zayn! On Zayn!'

Jai half-understood, but Feng's whispered translation confirmed his worst fears. The line of Valor warriors edged closer, until Jai knocked knees with the warriors beside him. Zayn hoisted his immense blade once more, his Alkhara pawing the ground.

In the distance, the taunting of the Keldar intensified. Their voices rose in a cacophony of challenges, their blades clashing in a menacing rhythm. Some of the khiroi lunged forward, their eagerness barely contained by the firm hands of their riders, who pulled them back to maintain the line. The tension in the air was palpable, a storm of anticipation brewing before the inevitable.

In stark contrast, the Valor stood steadfast and silent. Gradually, the enemy's clamour subsided, as if disconcerted by the lack of reaction. Jai realised what this was – discipline in the face of overwhelming odds. The Valor were proving they were unfazed and would hold firm against the Keldar's intimidation.

Too calm. As if they knew something he didn't.

'Now, show them!' Sindri bellowed.

The Valor roared in unison. Once.

'Again!' she demanded.

This time, Jai lent his voice to the wordless battle cry.

To no avail. A horn sounded, and the enemy began to trot towards them.

'Hold,' Zayn roared. 'Hold!'

Jai didn't need Feng to understand. The enemy advanced.

'Hold!' Sindri screamed.

This time . . . a bone-shuddering roar. Winter, adding her voice to the throng. Enough to turn heads.

And then, just like that, the enemy stopped. Let out a last series of jeers, spitting and cussing from their mounts. Then they wheeled around, riding back the way they had come.

'WHAT WAS THAT?'

'A bluff,' Feng explained. 'To see if our warriors would break. Had we faltered, they might have charged in earnest.'

Jai rode on, contemplating Feng's words, and what he had just witnessed. They were returning to camp now, riding at a sedate pace. He longed to spur Navi on, to hasten their arrival, but he understood that Sindri likely wanted to demonstrate to her tribe that there was no need to rush. Even so, Jai could sense the barely contained fury in her voice as she admonished Zayn in hushed tones, a few dozen yards ahead of them.

'Foolish of Zayn,' Feng said. 'To divide our forces, just to intimidate you. Had the Keldar come upon us without a united front, we'd probably be dead.'

Jai didn't understand.

'Why *didn't* they attack?' Jai asked. 'Surely they would have beaten us.'

'Yes,' Feng said. 'But if we fought back, they'd lose half their warriors in the process. And we showed we *would*. Where would that leave them? Half their men dead? A poor trade, even if most of the khiroi survived the battle. A leader who throws away the lives of his warriors so pointlessly is not leader for long.'

'So they hoped we'd surrender, and when Sindri refused, they tried to scare us into retreat so they could chase us down and force our capitulation?'

'Yes,' Feng said. 'That's the heart of it. I am sure Zayn and his Alkhara were part of their calculus too – a soulbound warrior might be worth ten riders on his own. Perhaps it was Winter's roar that turned the tide, but I doubt they ever intended to fight. These sorts of confrontations are common in the Great Steppe, especially among the smaller tribes, like the Tainted. It is how tribes grow. They absorb one another, with as little bloodshed as possible.'

Jai looked down, where Winter was happily ambling alongside him. Nobody had yet come to relieve him of her, and he took a moment to awkwardly hop out of the saddle, to gather her chain in his hand.

It felt wrong to lead her this way, but she hardly seemed to mind. Jai longed to stop and cradle her in his arms, but now wasn't the time to reveal to the others what he held most dear. He gritted his teeth as they approached the baggage train.

It made for a forlorn sight. Elderly and children sat among hastily discarded piles of belongings, remnants of their homes. Isolated in the vast expanse, they appeared utterly helpless.

This was why the Sithia rode out to meet the enemy. The village was far too exposed to defend, even with the tents set up, and the ground cleared.

Jai understood well why the Sithia prized their khiroi. Only now, seeing what was left of them without the beasts in tow, did he realise just how much khiroi mattered. And had not each and every khiro, Navi included, counted in that confrontation? For there were still men and women left behind who might have carried a blade, or shored up their numbers.

As they drew close, warriors leaped from their mounts,

hurrying back to their loved ones. Families reunited, right there in the trampled grass, hugging and crying.

Jai felt numb, and alone. Winter was the only family he had left.

Or was she? For Jai knew, he had an uncle, somewhere out there. A leader of a great tribe. Holding the Kidara for Arjun's return. He wondered if word had yet reached them that their heir was dead. That Jai, a bastard son to a half-Sabine concubine, was all they had left.

It was when Feng slid down from Navi, and wandered wordlessly to the edge of the trampled grass to stare out over the steppe, that Jai realised Feng was far more alone than he.

Jai dismounted, and allowed Navi to wander back to the rest of the khiroi. He gave Winter a quick hug, watching to make sure nobody saw, and joined Feng. They stood in silence, until Jai could no longer hold his tongue.

For he could see Feng, watching his little sister, his eyes full of hurt. To be kept so close, yet be unable to speak. It was unnecessary cruelty.

'Why does Zayn hate you so?' Jai asked.

Feng sighed.

'He and Sindri were once fettered in the Phoenix Empire. It is not uncommon, when a Tainted tribe consumes another, to dispose of the riteless children. He and his sister were such children, seen as too sickly or small to be worth waiting till they would become contributors to the tribe. He and Sindri escaped their masters, long after they were fettered – it is the only life they remember. But when he sees my face, my eyes. It reminds him.'

'Fettering is a plague on this world,' Jai said. 'I did not know it was so prevalent in the Phoenix Empire.'

Feng shrugged.

'It wasn't, until the Sabines codified it into law. The Phoenix emperor did the same, if only not to fall behind. The Kashmere Road must flow.'

'So it's about money,' Jai said.

'Isn't it always?'

'I've seen no money trade hands here,' Jai said.

Feng chuckled at that.

'You might, if they had any. Or if any other tribes would trade with them. Look, there he goes.'

Feng pointed to show Zayn riding off into the wilderness, some dozen warriors in tow.

'He'll patrol through the night. Say what you want about the bastard – he keeps this place safe.'

Jai grimaced, and thought on the events of the day.

'He sees you as a weakling,' Jai said. 'He respects strength.'

'What strength could I bring?' Feng spat out bitterly. 'He could crush me like a grape. Most everyone here could.'

'And so could the Keldar to the Valor,' Jai said. 'Yet who retreated from the other? Courage is just a scared man's bluff, oft to himself. Show Zayn you can stand up for yourself. That you can be trusted to hold the line, and not retreat in the face of the odds.'

Feng remained silent, and Jai could see tears shining on his face.

'We'll camp here tonight,' Feng muttered, turning away.

He walked off, leaving Jai to his thoughts.

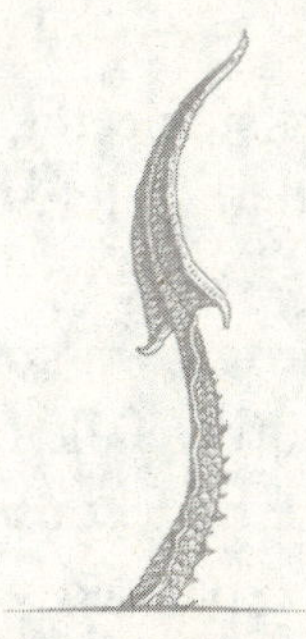

Chapter 12

The village was thrown up quickly, and the grass surrounding them cut back even further than before. There was no fire, even as the sun began to set, so their meal was a bowl of raw greens, seeds and crunchy roots – much to Winter's dismay.

When this paltry succour was finished, Jai was led by the hand by a child to a small tent of his own, just on the edge of the village.

Situated on the outskirts, where the village was most susceptible to attack, the tent neighboured the most dilapidated dwellings. Jai secured the flaps tightly, wary of sabertoothed cats, direwolves or the terror birds said to roam the eastern Great Steppe – enormous flightless avians taller than a man sitting atop another's shoulders.

The tent itself was a paltry thing made of a pair of khiroi furs, stitched together around a simple bamboo frame. The skins were old and frayed, with holes letting through the last hours of the spring sun. Another ragged fur laid on the flattened grass made for a makeshift rug, and Jai imagined he could fit the entire ensemble quite easily, folded upon Navi's rump.

Jai didn't mind. At last, he was alone with Winter.

The dragon chirred, resting her head in Jai's lap before he had even settled. It felt like ages since they had enjoyed solitude together.

Indeed, he'd had but a single night with her following his escape from Porticus, and that had been spent soulbreathing before battle.

He took her in. She had grown so much, since she had first slithered from her egg into the fallen snow. In just one season, she had gone from the size of a house cat to that of an adolescent lion. Her scales had expanded with her, smooth and hard as porcelain teeth, and the wings, once folded so tight against her back that one might guess she had no wings at all, had loosened from their purchase.

Jai dared not dream of riding her just yet, for she was still growing. And from the hunger coiling in her belly, he knew that Winter, runtish already, needed more food.

Tomorrow, then. He'd find her some meat, even if he had to hunt it himself.

Now he let his body settle, closing his eyes and letting the meld overcome him. Now that they touched, he could feel her. Feel the warmth of his forehead against hers, the hunger roiling in her belly.

The fear, and the love, all directed at him. It was overwhelming in its intensity, yet Jai could only return the same emotion. He only wished he could strike the chain from her neck.

For a while, they remained that way, revelling in each other's feelings. He ran his hand along Winter's scales, feeling the scars where Beverlai's direwolf had hurt her.

She had given so much. Travelled the length and breadth of the empire as little more than an infant, and freed him from his prison. He owed her his life, and more.

He felt tears spring to his eyes as he clutched her close, and she nuzzled into the crook of his shoulder. Now it was she who was in chains. And he who had to save her.

Someone is coming.

Again. That message, not in words, but meaning. Pulsing down their connection like a voice in his mind.

As if on cue, there was a tap on the outside of his tent, and a hand slipped through, tugging free the knot he had secured there.

Sindri ducked into the tent, and closed the flaps surreptitiously behind her. She looked at Jai and Winter, and sniffed.

'Feng tells me you speak sithosi well,' she said, enunciating clearly and slowly for Jai's benefit.

Jai nodded, surprised at how much he understood. But he supposed he had once spoken it near fluently, as a young child. It was all coming back to him.

'Zayn gave what is not his,' she said. 'Your dragon.'

Jai motioned at the grasslands outside, struggling to form the words. It was so much easier to listen to sithosi than speak it.

'You think we can escape?'

Sindri smiled.

'No,' she allowed.

For a moment, she stared at him, searching his face. Then she pulled forth the diary from her furs.

'You did good today,' she said. 'You showed . . . loyalty.'

She slapped the diary into his lap, and stood.

'Keep the dragon. And the tent.'

With those parting words . . . she was gone.

Jai stared at the diary, amazed she would trust him with it. Though the gorget she still kept from him was the real proof of his heritage, the diary might well be enough on its own.

She was showing him trust. If he kept this up, he might just get Winter's chain struck from her neck. For now, it was enough to have his dear totem back in his arms, purring contentedly.

He turned the diary over in his hands. It was in a terrible state, stuffed with loose papers, waybills, scouting reports and the like. It had suffered much in his travels, such that he could hardly read the words on the first page. Jai flipped to the second.

Today, I begin my campaign. Three legions, marching into the depths of the Great Steppe, turning off the well-trodden path of the Kashmere Road. This place is like no other I have travelled.

It is like a great, green desert, stretching as far as the eye can see.

There are no cities to march on and lay siege to. No rivers to dam, nor roads to block. There are no trees for our camp walls, nor wood to burn. Water, at least, is plentiful, for it lives but a few feet below the surface.

The grass rises high as my chest in places, and our horses can only push through it for but a few hours before they tire. The grass is unpalatable to them, and they cannot stomach it. My men bring grain for them by the wagonful.

We travel but a few miles each day, and my soldiers' arms weigh heavy from hacking it. I can only thank the heavens for Rufinus, and his Gryphon Guard. They fly above, and guide us towards the enemy. They protect our supply route, for the steppe raiders circle like vultures. Without them, we would be lost.

And there it was. On the very second page. Rufus, or rather, Rufinus, as he had once been known. It had taken so long for Jai to read more than the cover page, and then he had traded it away, like hack silver. He had been ashamed to read about Leonid's defeat of his own people. Of his own father.

No longer.

Still, Jai was left in near darkness within the tent, for the sun had at last set. Even with the slivers of moonlight cutting through the moth-eaten hides, he could hardly see the faded letters, soulbound eyes or no.

Jai closed them, and allowed the trance to take him once more, clutching the dragon to his chest. If Sindri had allowed him to keep Winter, it meant his trade with Zayn was being honoured. He would need all the mana he could get.

Chapter 13

'Jai,' a voice said.

Startled awake in the darkness, Jai saw a figure crouching at the entrance of his tent, hand outstretched. He instinctively recoiled, until Winter let out a low rumble of greeting, the calmness of her heart stilling his own.

Kiran grinned, placing a finger to her lips.

'Come,' she whispered in sithosi.

Without hesitation, Jai took her hand and followed her out of the tent. Winter followed, her chain clinking in the hushed air.

Night still shrouded the village, though the first hints of dawn brushed the horizon. To Jai's surprise, he and Kiran weren't the only ones awake. A youth was perched upon a strange, laddered bamboo structure, almost two storeys tall. A crow's nest of sorts to scan the horizon for approaching enemies.

Kiran hailed the youth with a soft greeting, but this was not what she had brought Jai to see. Instead, she led Jai on, towards the village edge. Zayn and the best of his men, some fifteen of them, lay alongside their mounts, nested into the fur of the great beasts' bellies. It was obvious they had only just returned from their patrolling, for the lower halves of the khiroi, and indeed the moccasin boots of the riders, were still coated with the morning dew from the grasslands.

'We eat,' she said. 'Then we train.'

Jai grimaced, thinking of the leafy meal from yesterday. He looked to see if there were campfires for cooking yet, but there were none. Only now did Jai notice too that most of the tents were pitched lower than usual. Such that they were barely a few feet higher than the grass itself.

It was obvious the tribe were hiding. No fire to glow, no smoke to billow, not even the scent of spiced, cooking food to drift on the wind. Nor the silhouettes of their tents to be spotted by passing marauders.

'Here,' Kiran said, nudging the back of Jai's knee with her foot, dropping him into a kneeling position. 'Learn.'

Jai bit his tongue in indignation as Kiran crouched beside him, reaching out to the dugs of the animal, her flask in one hand, clasping fingers in the other.

She milked the teat, the milk splashing rich, foamy white liquid into the bowl. It was the work of a minute to fill it halfway, and she withdrew the bowl, handing it to Jai.

Jai went to put it to his lips, and earned a stinging flick to the ear for his trouble.

Instead, Kiran steadied his hand, pulling it into position beneath the great beast's head. The khiro's small, wrinkled eyes looked at him dully, as Kiran lay her head upon her khiro's neck.

She rubbed along its throat, feeling for something. As she did so, she chewed on something, the edges of her lips stained green.

With a subtle move, she fetched a thin reed from her saddle bag, green and fresh cut at an angle. The narrow tube was raised to the neck of her khiro, and she knocked it into the beast's jugular with the flat of her palm.

The khiro twitched, once. Blood, thick and caustic, jetted from the reed into the bowl, staining the milk pink, splotched with clots of red. It was over in seconds, the reed withdrawn, and Kiran spat into her palm, the chewed-up green leaves making a poultice as she pressed it to the wound.

She stepped away, wiping her hands on the dewed grass.

'See,' she said, speaking loudly and simply to help him understand. 'Alkharas are good only for war. Doe, better. Doe feeds you.'

The horror on Jai's face must have been evident, as she rubbed her belly and waggled her brows, giving Jai a playful grin.

Kiran stirred the mixture with her reed, before popping the tip into her mouth and sucking out the juices within.

She smiled again, her lips red stained, and motioned for Jai to have the first sip.

Jai groaned . . . but knew, like everything, this was just another test. He lifted the bowl . . . and swallowed.

It was a drink you could chew, for the clotted mixture clagged upon his teeth, and the back of his throat. It was fat, and rich, and tangy, and sweet, in all the wrong ways. But Jai forced it down, offering it back to Kiran.

She grinned, and withdrew a dumpling from her saddle instead, biting into it with great gusto.

'Finish,' she said. 'It will make you strong.'

Jai took another gulp, looking with trepidation at the remainder, slopping in the bottom of the bowl.

A claw dug into his back, and a mewl from Winter made Jai pause. She pawed at him, panting with excitement. Jai didn't need the meld to know her jaws were already dripping with saliva.

Jai looked beseechingly at Kiran, who nodded with a roll of her eyes, and the hint of a smile. In seconds, Winter was snorting and slavering into the bowl, nearly knocking it from Jai's hands so she could lick every inch of what remained.

'Good,' Kiran said, taking another bite from her dumpling. 'Very good. Now . . . come. We will fight, before the others wake.'

* * *

JAI STOOD AT THE fighting circle's centre, rubbing his hands together in the crisp spring air. It was more a force of habit than anything else; his soulbound body could endure it well enough, and it did not cause him much discomfort. More than anything, it helped hide the nerves that trembled his hands.

Kiran had just finished knotting the grass edges, and now stood opposite him, contemplating Jai. Winter watched eagerly from the sidelines, hopeful with the bowl still in her mouth.

Kiran grinned and assumed a low, bow-legged stance.

'You are with dragon,' she said. 'Me, with khiro. You are stronger, yes?'

Jai nodded, though in truth he was not sure. He knew, though, that those bonded to a khiro were not the most powerful of soulbound, their progress along the so-called path stymied by the qualities of their chosen totem.

Though for one bonded with the powerful Alkhara, like Zayn's, he was not so sure. But certainly, Jai had ascended already, and he doubted Kiran had succeeded in the same yet.

'Push me out,' Kiran said, motioning at the grass with her chin. 'Easy. Quick.'

Jai hesitated, leaving himself open to a swift slap from Kiran that landed squarely on his cheek. It stung, and he could feel his face redden with the rush of blood.

Flushed with embarrassment, Jai lunged at Kiran, attempting to push her out of the ring.

She fluidly sidestepped his advance, a blow to the back of his neck sending him sprawling to the ground. Flashing a playful smile, she extended her hand to help him up.

'You rush,' she said. 'Slow, slow. A fight is like a first fuck.'

Jai groaned, even as her words stirred his loins. That strike . . . it felt like it had taken all the strength from his body, the shock of it running down his spine to turn his legs to jelly.

'I'm waiting.' Kiran prodded him with a toe.

Jai slid his feet into a crouch, rubbing the back of his neck, planning to catch Kiran off guard with an unexpected attack. He launched himself at her, yet Kiran remained poised, effortlessly dodging his move and guiding him into a stumble before pulling back.

'I see your eyes,' she remonstrated, motioning with two fingers. 'I watch your body. It betrays you.'

Cursing, Jai squared up, circling her slowly. He glanced at the surrounding tents, but all was quiet. He was glad of that. It was an embarrassing display of ineptitude.

Jai edged closer, and closer, jabbing punches as she bobbed her head back. He chased her around the circle, cautious, yet keeping up the pressure.

'Better.' Kiran grinned.

She stepped into his guard, seizing Jai's wrists. For a second, they grappled, Jai pushing her back. Her eyes widened at the sudden show of strength . . . and then Jai's soles flew up, as a hooked leg took out his knees, his feet flopping into the grass outside the circle.

He stared into the brightening sky, until her face filled his vision.

'You are strong,' she said, peering down at him with bemusement.

She tapped his chest.

'Strong is good.'

Then tapped her own chest.

'Balance is better.'

Jai lurched to his feet, slapping ineffectually at the fresh grass stains on his trousers.

'I am better . . . with a *sword*,' Jai grumbled. 'Why can't we . . . ?'

He couldn't find the words, so mimed chopping in the air.

Kiran shrugged.

'Fight with a falx, all you think is falx. Fight with your body . . . all you think is body. Learn body first. Falx . . . later.'

She tapped her head, then patted Jai on the shoulder, chuckling as he flinched back.

'Good,' she said. 'Enough.'

She spun on her heel, and stalked away, just as the morning reveille, a quieter one this time, brought the village back to life. Winter dropped the bowl at Jai's feet with a clatter, and nudged it in his direction.

Jai sighed, rubbing the back of his neck. So much for showing off the swordplay he had learned from Rufus, such as it was. It had been a short session, done in private, which told Jai that Kiran was reluctant to teach him, or be seen to do so.

He needed this training, though – he was fully aware of that. So how could he ensure he got it, and got it faster than whatever pace Kiran thought she could afford?

It's a matter of leverage, he thought. Or, as she put it, balance. After all, she was hardly powerful enough to use the shade spell. But there might be more he had to offer.

THE NOON SUN WAS warm as Navi stomped through the grasslands, alternately cropping and trotting to catch up with the rest of the herd. Jai didn't mind. After all those years of starvation, she deserved to gorge all day.

'Tonight, we can cook again,' Feng muttered over Jai's shoulder. 'No sign of the Keldar. They must have moved on.'

'Moved on where?' Jai asked, scanning the horizon for any signs of the elusive tribe.

'Who can say? The others think most tribes are headed east. Can't trade with the Sabines anymore, so they'll go to the Phoenix Empire. And everyone knows the legions are on the march.'

Jai chewed his lips, thinking on it.

'Will the tribes fight together?' Jai asked.

Feng sniffed.

'It may have been peacetime with the Sabines, but the tribes have been fighting since long before the War of the Steppe, and since. After the fettered trade began, they have all the more reason for it. If there's an alliance brewing, we Tainted will be the last to hear of it.'

'So what, they'll let the legions take their land?' Jai asked, incredulous.

'Let them plant their flags, and draw their maps. The land belongs to the Mother, Jai. No man can own it, no matter how loud they shout it.'

'What happens when they start building their cities,' Jai said. 'When they burn the grass, and plant their crops.'

Feng was silent.

'I'll be long dead by the time it matters,' he finally said.

'Tell that to the elders that plant their trees,' Jai said.

Feng had nothing to say to that.

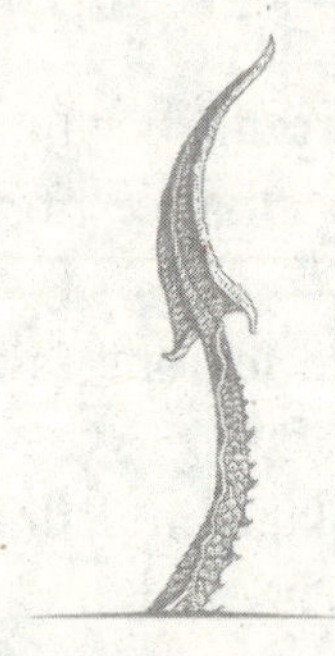

Chapter 14

Another week has passed in this endless sea of grass, and the steppe continues to test our resolve. Our progress remains slow, the days monotonous and exhausting. The nights are no respite, for the temperature plummets once the sun dips below the horizon. My men huddle together for warmth, their spirits dampened by the harsh conditions. We cannot spare the wood to burn.

Rufinus and his Gryphon Guard have proven essential, their aerial advantage providing us with information we could not otherwise obtain. They scout the land and report back on the movements of the Sithians, who, like shadows, are elusive and ever-changing.

Yesterday, my cavalry encountered a small band of Sithian warriors. The battle left us weary and battered, but we emerged victorious. My heart swells with pride for my men, for they have shown their mettle in the face of an unfamiliar enemy.

However, I must address the brutality of the Gryphon Guard. Their wrath upon the Sithians was merciless, their actions striking fear in both *the enemy and my own soldiers. I have spoken with Rufinus, urging him to temper the fury of his warriors, lest we lose our own humanity in this vast, untamed land.*

As the days bled into weeks, Jai found himself growing accustomed to the rhythm of life among the Sithians. The spring sun would rise over the seemingly endless grasslands, setting the world ablaze with gold and crimson – a far cry from the pale blue dawns of the Sabine winter he had so recently endured.

Each morning Jai would practise his sithosi with Feng, stumbling over unfamiliar words, grappling with the nuances of the language. He even began speaking to the children, whose fear of him had been replaced by fascination as Winter gambolled among them each morning. She'd taken a liking to them, though Jai could not tell if it was their innocent joy, or the jerky they fed her that drew her the most.

His progress with sithosi was slower than he'd have liked, but with Feng's patient guidance, his people's songs began to form more fluidly upon his tongue. Now he joined in the marching chorus with gusto, such that they lingered in his mind as he slept each night.

He'd been so busy with his lessons, and so tired from each day's march, that the diary had lain forgotten at the bottom of his bag since he'd read the last entry. And though he knew he should read further, he made excuses to himself, for with each page, he learned more about the cruel man Rufus had once been.

It was easy to find the excuses, for during the day, the wildlife of the Great Steppe could be glimpsed from Navi's back. Ground sloths, enormous, bear-sized herbivores, could be spotted on the horizon, before disappearing into their giant burrows as they neared.

Impala dove like dolphins nearby them, springing high above

the grass to watch for predators, before angling away to leave them in the dust. Their ten-foot leaps allowed them to move unimpeded by the thick brush. These, Feng told him, were rarely hunted, as they could outrun even a rider upon khiro-back.

While the khiroi relied on the protection of their herd, the impala avoided the sabretooths and direwolves that hunted the steppe, speeding away in great curving leaps at the new signs of danger. The Sithia watched the impala to see where predators lurked, more than anything.

Surprisingly, Jai was yet to see more than a sling for hunting among the Valor, and these were more intended for the larks and grouse that sometimes burst up from the grass as they roamed. Truly, did the Sithians rely on their khiroi above all other animals, their milk and occasional meat replacing their need to hunt.

With new understanding came new discoveries, and Jai learned the intricacies of the Valor society, noting the significance of the braids they wore in their hair. Each braid bore a different meaning, some marking the wearer as married, others signifying a warrior's first kill in battle, or his rank among the warriors. Even the smallest details held meaning, the placement of the beads threaded through the braids revealing almost as much as the braids themselves.

So too did he begin to take a liking to their cuisine. The tribe ground gathered grains into hearty flatbreads and dumplings, and the aroma of tubers cooked in a rich medley of spices and khiroi creams and cheeses would often set his mouth watering each evening. Even Winter didn't turn her nose up from it, as she typically did without meat on the menu.

Jai could feel his body filling out as he indulged in these hearty meals, his once scrawny frame slowly giving way to a layer of healthy fat and the promise of new muscle. He caught a glimpse of himself in the reflection of a burnished plate, a wave of relief washing over him as he took in the changes. No longer was he the emaciated wanderer who had arrived at Porticus, but a stronger, more robust version of himself, a consequence of the sithosi fare and the rigours of his training. Not to mention the beginnings of a scruffy beard.

As for making friends, well, it was still only the children who spoke to him, outside of Kiran and Feng. Sindri had not even glanced his way for days, and Zayn maintained his distance almost to a fault. He and Jai shared little more than cursory glances, a silent acknowledgement of the gulf that lay between them. In the dim hours of the night, Jai would often see Zayn ride off with Kiran, their silhouettes swallowed by the vast expanse of the steppe. He could only guess they were practising the spell he had taught them, for Kiran had been sure to get a proper accounting of the spell from Jai, on Zayn's behalf. He realised that Zayn's pride prevented him from seeking Jai's guidance in front of his entourage, unwilling to admit that Jai's skills surpassed his own.

It mattered little to Jai, for he had his own work to do. With Winter by his side, Jai was finally able to soulbreathe to his fullest, and it was some relief when he finally filled his core with mana. There was safety in that. How many days had he passed in Porticus, with little more than a few dregs to keep him alive? He would never let that happen again.

It was a shame, then, that he knew little of how to advance along the soulbound path once he had ascended, so instead he practised his spells alone within the relative privacy of his ragged tent.

Each night, he would summon a flame, holding the ball of oscillating fire, letting it hang in the air like a miniature sun. It was far harder to control its direction, and its shape, than simply blast a gout of flame as he had done before. So he practised in the hope that, in battle, he might have the chance to throw a fireball, as he had seen Beverlai do during their fight to the death.

Jai's training in Talvir continued under Kiran's watchful eye, and with each passing day, he grew better at balancing his new-found strength with the grace of a martial warrior. Their sparring sessions were punctuated by Kiran's laughter, her eyes alight with amusement as Jai fumbled through the intricate dance of hand-to-hand combat. Despite his initial reluctance, Jai found himself enjoying these lessons, the thrill of feeling himself get better, and Kiran's grudging praise was more than enough to keep him motivated.

During this morning's training, Jai had let out a whoop as he finally managed to heave Kiran out of the circle. While his triumph owed more to his superior ascended strength than outclassing her, it was a triumph nonetheless.

Now, some hours later, Kiran trotted beside him during the morning march, and took his reins, leading him wordlessly ahead of the tribe, as Zayn had done before.

'Where are we going?' Jai asked, smiling as Winter raced alongside, then fell back to trail just behind them, treading the easier path in the khiroi's wake.

Kiran put a finger to her lips, sitting tall in her saddle as she scanned for threats.

Today, Feng had chosen to walk, for the saddle they shared was not designed for two, and he was beginning to chafe. So it was just Jai and Kiran, riding out into the wilderness.

Kiran only stopped when they were out of sight of the others, and now she dismounted, after standing on her khiro's back, and giving one last look to the horizon. She motioned for Jai to do the same, and he did.

Only then did Kiran reach into her saddlebags, and pull forth two bamboo practice swords strapped to their side. They were as long as falxes, and had been hardened and curved over a fire.

'Come,' Kiran said finally. 'Let us begin.'

'What, no fighting circle?' Jai asked, flattening the grass around him with his foot.

'Is there a circle when you fall from your khiro?' Kiran asked. 'Or anywhere else in the Great Steppe?'

Jai grimaced at the rebuke, but took the blade, raising his eyebrows at the weight of it.

'Soil inside,' Kiran said, catching Jai's expression.

Of course. It was pointless practising with something so much lighter than a true falx. He raised the sword, glad of the rough hilt of wrapped cord at the bottom, giving him a strong grip.

He didn't have a lot of time to admire the weapon because Kiran didn't hesitate, her bamboo sword whipping towards Jai's shoulder. He deflected the blow at the last moment, the crack loud in his ears.

She pressed forward, slashing and stabbing, pushing Jai back. He stumbled through the swaying grass, tripping on the tussocks and strands that tangled his legs. Kiran's feet remained firmly planted, while Jai constantly struggled to find his footing on the shifting earth.

As they traded blows, Jai remembered the technique Rufus had taught him. Keen to impress, Jai met her next blow, their swords locking together. Jai heaved his head back, and then lunged, slamming his forehead into her nose. The impact sent blood spraying, and Jai felt instant regret.

'I'm sorry, I didn't mean to—' he stammered, dropping his sword.

Kiran's response was swift, tackling him to the ground. They grappled among the tall grass, Jai's apologies forgotten as they wrestled, Kiran's eyes burning with defiance, even when blood stained her lips and chin, turning her smile feral.

Laughter bubbled up between their gasping breaths, the thrill of the struggle turning to comedy. Finally, they stilled, breathing deep, neither willing to surrender. It was only when Winter nosed between them to join the fun that Kiran finally released him, falling back with a moan of relief.

For a moment, they lay there, staring into the expanse above, catching their breaths.

'You have some training,' Kiran said, breaking the silence. 'To force a battle of strength. We call it the Locked Horns.'

'Yeah,' Jai allowed. 'Had to do something. I'm not used to such a long blade.'

Kiran smirked, a mischievous glint in her eye as she turned to look at him.

'You know what they say – it's not the length that matters, but how you wield it,' she chuckled. 'Or perhaps you're just not used to handling something so impressive.'

Jai burst into laughter, grateful for the flush of exertion that he hoped hid the sudden warmth in his cheeks.

Here, away from the village, it was as if she were a different person. Lighter somehow. Freer. She groaned and got back to her feet, but not before wiping her nose with a torn handful of grass.

'Again,' she said.

Jai nodded and rose to his feet, grasping the bamboo sword with trepidation. Kiran took a moment to size him up, then crouched back into her fighting stance.

'Your grip is too tight,' she said, rapping his knuckles with her sword.

Jai adjusted his grip accordingly, and Kiran circled around him, studying his posture.

'Keep your feet shoulder width apart, and your knees bent,' she snapped.

As Jai shifted his stance, Kiran tutted and knocked the blade at his feet, until he had the correct position.

'Hold the sword up and out, like this. It is the best starting position.'

Jai mimicked her posture, feeling the difference as he adjusted the angle of his weapon. They began to spar again, though more slowly, Kiran narrating his progress.

'Good, but relax your arm. A tense arm is stiff, slow, easy to predict,' she said, slapping down his swing with ease, leaving the tip of his blade in the dirt.

'Now, defend.'

She demonstrated a swift, fluid sweep, aimed at Jai's legs. The move forced him to dance away, and he cursed as he stumbled for what felt like the hundredth time that day, receiving a grazed knee for his troubles.

Jai observed her movements as the minutes passed, trying to memorise the pattern of her swings. Soon enough, he attempted the technique himself in return, his first try a bit clumsy and slow. Kiran easily avoided it, and seemed none the worse. She shook her head, stepping closer to guide him through the motion.

'In Talvir, we call this the Serpent's Dance. Seize the moment that your opponent's weight shifts – strike high, then sweep low when their focus is above. That's when they're most vulnerable.'

She demonstrated a series of quick, fluid motions, her sword seeming to slither as the eponymous serpent as she weaved a figure S in the air.

'You will learn, the secret to a good defence is in the footwork,' she said, her eyes meeting Jai's. 'You are flat-footed. Try again, keep the balance on the balls of your feet.'

Jai let out a frustrated breath, slashing low and fast. It was like stabbing at smoke, her legs swift as a dancer's, her balance poised. After a few more tries, she whipped up her blade, catching Jai under the chin.

'Now, you try.'

Jai dragged himself back from the dirt, rubbing his face. This time, he managed a good ten seconds of avoiding her attacks before he was flat on his back, nursing a bruised scalp for his trouble.

He cursed, but Kiran did not press her advantage, instead looking at him with what might have been approval.

'Better than most,' she sniffed.

Jai groaned. There was something hard in the small of his back. He rolled over and picked it up. It was a rusted bowl, buried so deep in the grass, he had not seen it.

Kiran snatched it from his hand, examining it. Her face darkened.

'You're in luck, Jai,' she said, sniffing the bowl where a slim crust of food remained. 'No more than a few weeks old.'

She turned the bowl over to show the stamp embossed upon the bottom. A male khiro, perhaps even an Alkhara, complete with its enormous horn. The symbol of his people. The Kidara.

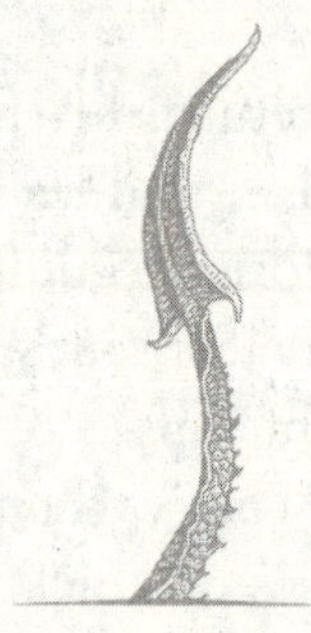

Chapter 15

In the days that followed, Kiran and Jai rode out each morning, practising amid the long grass. It was a painful training, but no worse than Rufus's had been, and one that Jai relished, even as he tried to find a comfortable position for his bruised body to sleep.

By now his sithosi was returning far faster, and he even found himself thinking in sithosi on occasion. It was just as well, for the camp was now moving with greater urgency at the bowl's discovery, and Jai struggled to keep up with the demands of the day.

Nobody knew how long the bowl had been there exactly, but the crusted food within told them it could have been recent. Either way, it was a good sign, for it was common for the largest of tribes to follow the same paths year after year.

As it turned out, the khiroi were the ones who decided where to go, following some unknown instinct, whether it was scent, the stars or memory, to guide the tribe on. Zayn led the way, but was actually letting his Alkhara go where it willed. It was proof of the trust between Jai's people and these great beasts, and Jai was once again reminded of how important the khiroi were to his people. They followed the ancient migrations of the beasts, walking paths across the Great Steppe that none but the khiroi could see, like great currents in an ocean, carrying them ever deeper into its depths. If they followed their course, Feng was sure they would catch up with the Kidara eventually, for both tribes were on the same path.

As the days passed, they found further artefacts. Tribes as large as the Kidara left a trail in their wake. Lately, the Valor had even spotted fires on the horizon. But with each glimpse of the small flames, no sooner were they seen, did they disappear. He soon learned that these fires could not belong to the Kidara, for a tribe of that size had no need to hide. Only the smaller ones, such as the Valor or Keldar, would quench their fires upon seeing those of another.

What this told them was that they were not the only ones migrating east. Clearly, word of the legions was spreading. And Jai knew, from Leonid's diary, that this would be a problem for Titus's legion. Alone, and far from supply lines, they would struggle to catch up to any tribes they wished to fight, whatever their size. It seemed like hubris to send a single legion to invade the Great Steppe, diminished though the tribes of old now were. They would commit evils untold, but one legion could never truly conquer its vast lands.

Though, with the now more numerous Gryphon Guard in tow, he doubted they were as troubled as Leonid had first been.

The Sithia marked no territory, nor upheld any borders. To them, Titus's encroachment into their lands was no more a danger than the arrival of a new tribe – if left well enough alone, they hoped the legion would return the favour. But to Jai, this was capitulation.

More, he knew that when Titus didn't get his fight, he'd send Magnus and his goons out to provoke one. And it would be the smaller tribes that would suffer most.

Yet what could he do? Even if the Kidara welcomed him with open arms, would they follow him into a war they could not win alone? Would the other Great Tribes even grant him an audience, let alone join him as allies?

He was getting ahead of himself, yet he felt responsible. He could have ended this. All those days ago, standing there with that blunted sword, the doorknob rattling as Titus made his return.

Yet he'd run, like a coward. And now his people would suffer the consequences. Unless he stopped it.

An outcry came from ahead, and Jai's hand drifted to his empty scabbard. Yet, as he spurred Navi to the head of the column, he realised they were shouts of joy.

At first, he had thought another tribe was headed for them, as he made out the humped forms of khiroi, spread across the plains before them. But as Jai and the Valor drew closer, spurring ahead of their baggage train, he recognised the sight before them was not an approaching tribe, but a wild herd of khiroi.

There must have been two score of the massive, woolly creatures, ranging from small, frolicking calves to great bulls and even a towering Alkhara at its head.

The wild khiroi were far from oblivious to the approaching Valor riders. As the distance between them diminished, the creatures grew visibly agitated; their ears flicking back and forth, and their nostrils flaring as they caught the scent of the humans and their mounts. The Alkhara issued a deep, resonant call, urging the herd to turn in unison.

Meanwhile, the Valor riders were tossed bundles of bamboo and rope by the children, tying them hastily onto their saddles and peeling away.

They spread out, whooping and spurring their khiroi, excitement palpable from the thrill of the chase and what a success could mean for them. Jai did not wait to find out what the bundles were for, instead urging Navi faster as the riders drew away.

The massive creatures ahead moved with a lumbering gait, their thick, pillar-like legs carrying them with that strangely even stride that made them almost glide over the grassland. Hindered by the slower pace of the young ones, whose short legs laboured to keep up, the Alkhara soon turned back, joining the doe mothers in urging the little ones onward with gentle nudges of their lips.

At last, though, the Alkhara's mournful call brought the herd to a halt. The adult khiroi formed a barrier around their young, their horns lowered like a row of pikes.

As the Valor riders closed in, their ranks fanned wide, encircling the herd with seemingly rehearsed ease.

Jai's heart raced as he watched the scene unfold before him. Unsure of what to do but eager to help, he urged Navi on, joining the charge with the last of the stragglers, those that had been slowed as they threw off their baggage.

Jai whooped, feeling the thundering hooves of Navi beneath him, the wind whipping through his hair. He knew in his blood that this was what it was to be a Sithian. To ride the steppe, and lay claim to whatever riches he could take.

As Jai drew closer to the encircled herd, he could see the Valor riders come to a halt, the herd contained, for now.

The adult khiroi bellowed and snorted, mock-charging at the riders in a desperate attempt to protect their offspring. Jai could almost smell their fear, seeing the foam upon the beasts' lips, their wrinkled eyes swivelling wildly.

Sindri barked a command, and the riders raised their sharpened bamboo stakes, notched like the teeth of a saw. For a heart-stopping moment, Jai feared they would hurl the stakes like javelins at the living wall of flesh and horn. Instead, they drove the stakes deep into the grass, anchoring them with boot and fist until they barely peeked out above the green expanse.

It was hardly much of a barrier, and twice Zayn had to race his Alkhara and ward off the herd moving from their place. The Valor began to gather the ropes, looping them about their arms and chests, swinging them in lazy circles. Soon, the air was filled with a menacing thrum nearly setting the herd into a panicked stampede. Only the skilled movements of the hunters headed it off before it could breach their makeshift pen.

And now the riders began to circle, at first at a slow trot, and then faster and faster, until the very air began to yellow with dust. Jai could do little but watch, devouring the scene with his eyes. He had never imagined a hunt like this.

One rider, a lean and agile woman with sun-weathered skin, expertly twirled a lasso above her head. With a flick of her wrist, she let the loop fly, and it sailed through the air, landing around the neck of a young khiro. The calf bleated in surprise, eyes wide with fear. It bolted, nearly yanking the rider from her perch as she let the rope unspool like a fisherman's reel, twisting her body to let the line loose.

Moments later, though, she'd whipped the rope around a stake, and not a moment too soon, for it snapped taut with a whip crack. Jai knew had her arm been caught, she'd have ridden off without it. As it was, the stake nearly tore from the ground, and only the calf's trembling, splay-footed halt stopped it from coming free before Kiran reinforced the anchor. She rode by, twisting a stake through the rope in another loop, and stabbing the earth deep in one deft motion.

The success spurred on the Valor, and more lassos sailed into the herd. Few made their mark. The horns, so easy to catch, slipped the ropes easily enough, and the shrill shrieks of the calf were setting the herd mad.

And then it happened: the wild Alkhara reared, a rope tangled in its horn. Jai caught a glimpse of a brown body tumbling, and the beast's great feet thundering the earth in a furious dance.

With a cry from Sindri the Valor circle split, creating an opening for the wild herd to escape. The beasts moved as one, even as the Valor erupted into screams, their voices cracking.

Jai lent his voice to the chorus, Navi heaving beneath him at her own volition, joining the tribe in a final pursuit. But it did not last long.

For once the herd broke the circle, and had gone some ways into the grassland, the Valor wheeled back, and Navi with them.

Jai coughed from the dust that still hazed the air. He raised his fist in triumph, only to falter as Navi slowed, returning to the scene of the hunt. It was no less than a battlefield, a wreckage of tangled ropes and broken spars of bamboo. The ground was torn up, a cratered, muddied no man's land.

Men and women wailed, clutching broken limbs and nursing rope-burned palms. Two calves, each hardly larger than a pot-bellied pig, were all they had to show for it. Small, pitiful things, bleating for their mothers.

The smile on Jai's lips faded, as he made out Sindri, crouched alongside a group of men. Zayn knelt in the mud, a limp body hanging in his arms.

It was an old man, almost as old as Leonid, though Jai only knew this from memory. He had hardly a face to speak of . . . for it had been caved into a single, gaping hole.

Jai felt his gorge rise, even as Sindri covered the man's head with her saddlecloth. She straightened, and wiped blood from her hands.

'Mount up!' she called. 'We go again!'

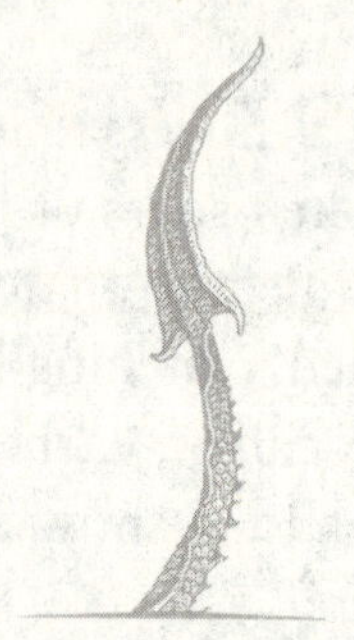

Chapter 16

The riders followed on, leaving the wounded in the dirt, preferring to secure the fruits of their labour. Jai held Navi back, for he knew he would be of no help, and more likely to hurt himself or another.

Instead, he stayed and helped the wounded, such as he could. By now, the baggage train had caught up. The children, the elders and the injured dragging the belongings on their sledges to the wreckage of the hunt, using the few khiroi still too young to be ridden.

The elders, far from being a hindrance, took immediate charge. Bones were set and splinted without ceremony, such that those first minutes were stippled with shrieks of pain under their rough ministrations.

Toothless old men and women stuffed handfuls of herbs into the mouths of the children, such that they could chew it into a poultice. When the young ones spit it out, they used it liberally upon rope burn, broken limbs and cuts alike, and capped it with clay dug from deep within the soil.

Winter, usually a scampering, playful puppy, looked cowed. She nuzzled her snout beneath Jai's arm, tucking herself into his armpit as Jai crouched in the mud. She'd become accustomed to sleeping there, somehow enjoying Jai's scent.

'Strange little thing,' he whispered to the dragon, scratching beneath her chin.

Jai scanned the camp, looking for where he could help. But the elders had moved swiftly. Already, the tents were being thrown up, and Jai hurried to do the same. The sky was dark, darker than he'd yet seen it, and he feared it would rain.

The two calves continued to call for their mothers, their calls mournful, legs trembling. They hooted at whoever approached, and the children giggled, tempting the small creatures with outstretched vegetables and clumps of grass.

'Newborns,' Feng said, trudging up to him and casting an envious glance at Jai's tent. 'Hardly a few weeks old. We'll let them loose when they start taking food. Otherwise, they'll run off.'

'Why so young?' Jai asked.

'If we weren't on the move, we'd try for some does too, maybe a runtish bull. Those take days to settle, though, and they're hard to hold. The calves are pretty tame; Sindri will get more of them. But we can't be taking wild khiroi with us, not when we're chasing down the Kidara.'

Feng tasted his finger and held it to the air.

'They'll settle when winds change. Young 'uns take years to learn how to follow the scents of the steppe, and are quick to forget their herd. They'll bond with our own herd before long. Most of our khiroi were taken young.'

'All this,' Jai whispered, gesturing at their surroundings. 'For two little calves?'

Feng sniffed, and nodded.

'In a few years, those calves will be worth far more to the tribe than the pain and suffering of today. Two more riders for battle. Milk and blood in the winter. Meat, bone, horn, sinew and fur when they're culled.'

Jai motioned at the limp body with his chin.

'Worth more than a life?'

'A long life, well lived. A fair trade, well made.'

He almost chanted it, and Jai imagined it was a Sithian proverb of sorts. That didn't mean he had to like it.

'You sound like Zayn, talking like that. There's no trading when it comes to people's lives.'

'I only meant that he's run his course. If another tribe took over this one, he'd be left behind.'

'So is he only worth what he can contribute to the tribe? Now you really sound like Zayn. Better hope they don't see you the same way.'

Feng turned away.

'I contribute plenty,' he said. 'Where would you be, without me?'

'Feng, I didn't mean . . .'

But Feng was already walking away. Jai went to follow, but he couldn't find the words. What more was there to say?

'Give him time,' Kiran said.

Jai turned to see her looking down at him from her mount.

'Feng hides his hurt, when he should hide his fear instead,' she said. 'He thinks it weakness. Let him mourn in his own way.'

Winter pawed at Jai, wanting to be lifted into his arms, but she was far too large. The little dragon was going through a growth spurt, and Jai had seen children riding ponies smaller than she.

Instead, he scratched her chin, and looked out from whence they had come.

'Not helping with the hunt?' Jai asked.

'Sindri sent me back,' she said, avoiding his eyes.

Jai understood.

'To keep an eye on me?' he asked.

'We are on your tribe's trail now,' she said, almost apologetic in her words. 'If you rode into the night, with our warriors in the midst of a hunt, only Zayn or I might have a chance of bringing you back.'

Jai let out a bitter laugh.

'I had thought you'd trust me by now.'

'Why?' Kiran asked.

Jai stared at her, at a loss.

As they stood there, a sudden commotion erupted from the edge of the camp. Jai and Kiran turned to see a group of riders approaching, their mounts lathered with sweat, their faces grim.

It was Zayn and Sindri returning. Behind them, three more calves were in tow, their ropes secured to the riders' saddles . . . tugging and jerking as they dragged a furrow through the grass. The Valor looked triumphant, but the atmosphere was heavy. Among them, a rider carried a lifeless body slung across their mount – a young girl, her face pale and bloodied. Jai seemed to be the only one who had noticed her because Kiran was crying out, 'Five!' Clapping her hands, she shouted again, 'Five!'

It was only when Zayn dismounted, carrying the young girl into the firelight, that the celebrations began to fade.

The camp was silent for a moment, and then the murmurs of mourning began. Kiran shook her head, tears welling up in her eyes.

'She was so young,' she said softly, more to herself than to anyone else.

Jai could only watch, as the girl was laid out beside the old man. To hunt the khiroi was a battle between man and beast. And if he was to be accepted by the Valor, or indeed the Kidara . . . Jai knew he might someday have to hunt them alone.

Chapter 17

As the sun dipped towards the horizon, long shadows stretched across the steppe. Jai stood among the gathered tribe members, his head bowed in respect. In the centre of the camp, a pyre had been stacked from the bamboo stakes used during the hunt, their splintered ends pointing like so many accusing fingers.

Upon the pyre, laid out on a soft bed of dried grasses, the bodies were wrapped side by side in simple linens, with the belongings most precious to them there beside. Beads, a wooden doll, even an old flute laid out beside their respective owners.

The funeral had been thrown in haste, for the tribe raced against the setting of the sun. In the Great Steppe, a fire of that size often meant only one thing – the burning of the dead. At night, it would be a beacon of weakness to any tribe that hunted others.

A Steppewoman knelt nearby, her face marred by tear streaks and self-inflicted scratches, her eyes red-rimmed as she clutched a pot of embers. In a sudden, anguished jerk, she cast them into the pyre, releasing a heart-rending wail.

One of many in the circle around the pyre, Jai watched his neighbour, Kiran, keen to follow tradition. Catching his gaze, Kiran silently handed him a corded bundle of wet herbs. One by one, the watchers threw the bundles onto the fire, tendrils of fragrant smoke coiling before they were hidden by the rising flames. Jai could feel the heat from the fire, sweat beading on his brow, but he did not step back.

The air was heavy with the scent, a smoky, herbaceous aroma that tickled Jai's nostrils and seemed to cling to the inside of his mouth. He felt himself growing lightheaded. The world's edges seemed to shudder, the flames hypnotic as they stretched ever higher, bright cinders like fireflies fading into the sky.

The mournful tones of a flute drifted through the encampment, echoing the sorrow that weighed down Valor hearts. And then . . . singing.

It started by the broken voice of the grieving mother, her voice faltering, cracked, until it was joined by the clear tones of the men and women around her, lifting her words higher and louder.

It was a song of heartbreak, of loss, of hope, willing the departed into the embrace of the Mother. Jai tried to join in, to lend his voice to the chorus, but his throat was tight, and the words were slow to come. How could they not, when he did not know if he believed?

And then the solos. Men and women, breaking through the chorus. Friends of the fallen, telling of the lives of those they had lost. Of the joys they had shared, and of kindnesses shown.

The flames rose higher and higher, engulfing the pyre in a fiery embrace. Jai found himself lost in the light and the melodies, joining where he could, careless of their meaning.

It was only when the heat subsided and the sun had travelled well below the horizon that the voices fell silent.

A hush descended upon the gathered mourners as a large, elderly khiro was led by halter into the circle, stopping beside the fire's remains. Its eyes were clouded with age, and it moved ponderously, as if burdened by a lifetime of memories. With gentle ministrations, the man who led the beast lay it down, scratching and tickling the khiro's belly. When it collapsed upon its side with a groan, he tied its legs together, earning a hoot of complaint.

Jai saw a tear on the man's face, and only now did he recognise it as the khiro Navi spent the most time with, one used to pull the smallest of the sledges. Now he felt his heart rise to his throat. For Sindri had stepped forward, clutching a curved ceremonial dagger.

'We call upon the spirits of ancestors past, begging your guidance and protection. Watch over us, and guide us, as your lineage did before you. Commend us to the Mother, and grant us her favour. Take this gift of blood, to sustain you into the ever after.'

With a swift, decisive movement, she slit the khiro's throat, allowing its lifeblood to spill into the embers, sizzling and spitting.

Even as she did so, tribe members held out their hands, and still more outstretched bowls, catching the blood as it spilled and spilled, the beast twitching as its owner clutched its head, whispering.

As the khiro's life drained away, the bowls were passed among the tribe members. Each person took a sip of the still-warm blood, paying their respects to the dead. When a bowl was handed to Jai, he hesitated, his stomach churning, though he had drunk it mixed with milk before. Kiran placed a reassuring hand on his arm, and with a deep breath, he tipped the bowl to his lips, the metallic taste of the blood filling his mouth.

Jai could not believe how much blood there was. It came in great, spouting gushes, until the bowls were overflowing, and the Valor's bellies were stretched. Still more was captured in cauldrons, saved for cooking later into the black, tangy balls that Jai had gotten a taste for. Now . . . he felt a little sick.

Once the blood-drinking ritual was over, the tribe members turned their sights to the fallen khiro. Men and women forced the beast onto its back, even as the move spurted the last remnants of its blood still sizzling in the embers.

Now they swarmed it, like whalers upon a humpback. Men, women and children alike, slicing it open to spill its yellow entrails into the flattened grass. These the children dragged away upon a skin-covered sled, running clenched fists along the entrails to push out fermented green paste. They ate it gleefully and by the handful, even as they hung the long guts out to dry, and began butchering the great, shaking slabs of organ meat.

Sindri motioned for Jai to join her, and he approached hesitantly, unsure of what was expected of him.

She, along with several other skilled tribe members, had already begun the process of skinning the khiro. They worked methodically, their movements precise, ensuring that each cut was clean and efficient. As they worked, they murmured prayers of gratitude to the khiro for its sacrifice, thanking it for the life it had given for the sake of the tribe.

Jai watched, fascinated by the skill and reverence with which the tribe members performed their task. Noticing his interest, Sindri beckoned him closer and handed him a smaller knife.

'Here, Jai,' she said softly, 'try. Split the skin from the meat.'

One slip, and the entire pelt could be ruined. Sindri had trusted him, and now he dared not betray it with failure. His hands trembled, and he took a deep breath, steadying himself.

Sindri pulled back the fur, and Jai slipped in the blade. It was like peeling the rind from the fruit of a mango, but far more delicate and bloody. The fat, just beneath the thick, white skin, was a gelatinous yellow, which the Valor elders were already trimming away and rendering down in their large terracotta cauldrons.

They continued their work, Sindri guiding Jai's hand as they made further cuts along the animal's body. The other tribe members worked alongside them, each focused on a different part of the khiro, their hands moving with confidence as they deftly separated muscle from bone, tendon from ligament.

The children began gathering the largest hunks of meat, first hanging them from a wooden frame, letting the blood drain from them fully, before carefully placing each on sheets of clean waxed cloth laid out on the ground, and wrapping them tight.

These were buried in the cool ground, and travelled by day in an insulated box. In time, it would be dried into the jerky Winter loved so much.

Torches were lit, for by now the sun was set. Jai looked down at the ground where the khiro had once lain. All that remained was a bloodied depression. Nothing had been left to waste – even the bones broken open for their marrow, and their remains pounded to dust for eating.

Sindri smiled at him as she took in his bloodied arms and the satisfied expression on his face. 'You did well, Jai,' she said.

Jai turned, only to see Winter the centre of attention among the children behind her, their work finished. Her red-tinged snout told him what her distended belly had already, as she scarfed up another offcut, dangled from the hand of a cooing child.

'Come here, you greedy thing,' Jai chuckled.

He could feel her discomfort, for she had eaten more food than ever in her entire life. Jai scratched her belly as she flopped onto her back, letting out a mewl of discomfort.

'A fine beast,' Sindri said.

'Thank you,' Jai said. 'For letting her stay with me.'

For a moment, he wanted to raise the issue of Kiran, sent home from the hunt to watch over him. Perhaps, if Kiran had stayed with the others, the young girl might have lived.

But the diplomatic side of Feng was rubbing off on him. He held his tongue, and bowed his head as Sindri patted Jai's shoulder.

'We'll make a Valor of you yet, my boy.'

Chapter 18

In the face of our slow progress, we bring scythes from the west, and fettered to wield them. Broad-shouldered Huddites, farmers turned soldiers, now become my workers. Older now, but well-broken. They cut our path without complaint, and we have no need to chain them in the day. Out here, in this vast green place, there is nowhere to run.

It is days like these, I doubt my truce with the Huddite Kingdom. Their lands feed the east and the west – far riper pickings than this green wasteland. But now is not the time, for their spies infest our ranks, and without them, I could not prosecute this war. So Huddite wagons feed Sabine legionaries, as we bounce from oasis to oasis. There, at least the bamboo is plentiful, and fires warm our hearths once more.

Once again, Rufinus is invaluable to my cause, guiding us to these places that were once known only to the Steppefolk. Every day, his demands for gold and power grow, for there is a sly fox beneath that great red bear. But we are old friends – I know it is not greed that *compels him. It is the dream of his sect's great tower that is at the heart of it. We have struck an accord, such that all the fettered soulbound will be sent to the prison mine of Porticus. Their secrets shall be pried from them, their knowledge given to the sect.*

The granite they bring forth will make the foundations of his so-called Eyrie. And when this war is won, he will have the rest of it. It is a dangerous thing to place a man with such power at the heart of my empire. But it is distance that turns a heart cold. I will keep him close, and stoke the embers.

It started slowly. A yellow stain, just on the horizon, so subtle Jai had first thought it just a trick of the light.

He was training with Kiran, a few weeks after their hunt, having ridden ahead as they did each morning to spar without being observed. By now, he was holding his own against her, though in truth this was more due to his superior strength and speed – the advantages of having ascended while she had not.

Still, he *was* improving. Kiran, for all her strict discipline, had managed to impart to Jai a great deal of knowledge and skill in a relatively short time. Each day, their sparring sessions became more intense, their movements more fluid and precise.

By now, Jai had realised why they only trained in the mornings, and so briefly. At first he had thought she was embarrassed to be helping him. But while that might have initially been a part of it, the truth was that Kiran was using all her mana just to keep up with him. She had not yet ascended, and could contain but a fraction of the mana Jai could. Yet even now, as sweat dripped from her brow, she held her own.

While they practised, Jai couldn't help but steal glances at the strange yellow hue in the distance. It seemed to be growing, spreading closer. Minutes passed, and it became clear that this was no mere trick of the light.

Kiran noticed Jai's distraction and followed his gaze to the yellow stain. Her brow furrowed in concern as she observed it. Even Winter seemed to notice now, letting out a low mewl from where she was sunning herself beside Navi, for she was too large to ride the old khiro anymore.

Even with the mystery of the horizon tugging at him, Jai could not help but admire the fine figure of the little dragon. Or rather, not so little anymore. Whether it was the glut of meat the tribe had been consuming these past weeks, or the additional morsels the children of the Valor gave her, she was growing at a pace. But it was more than size.

Her scales were more lustrous, her eyes brighter. Her body had filled out; her legs muscled, her tail thicker and longer. Though she had lived but a season, there was little left of the puppy-like features, that overlarge head and wide eyes.

She was now the size of a runtish donkey, and a child had attempted straddling her that very morning, kicking his little heels against her belly. Jai had enjoyed watching her confusion, legs akimbo and trembling, as the child slapped at her rump. She had dumped him, rather unceremoniously, in a pile of old khiro dung. Navi had clearly been rubbing off on her.

'We should return to the camp,' Kiran said, interrupting Jai's thoughts.

'What is it?' Jai asked.

She shook her head, already leaping into her saddle.

They rode back quickly, and Jai could not help but note the worry evident on her face. As they approached the camp, they saw that the rest of the tribe had noticed the peculiar sight as well, for they had come to a complete halt. The warriors of the Kidara were fully armed and armoured, their khiroi stripped of the belongings they carried.

'What is it?' Jai asked again, as Kiran slipped into the formation of warriors gathered at the front. Sindri and Zayn were among them, sitting high on their saddles, staring out at the spreading stain.

'Did they see us?' Kiran demanded. 'Is this why they turned?'

'No,' Zayn grunted. 'They know we'd outpace them. This is something else.'

He clucked his tongue at his sister, and the pair rode some way towards the crowd, until they were out of earshot of even Jai. Whatever they were to discuss, they did not want the others, or indeed Jai to hear it.

'What's happening?' Jai asked, trotting up to Feng. The young man's face was pale and drawn, and he stood among the elders and children, staring as they did beyond.

'It's a big tribe, on the move,' Feng said. 'We think it's the Kidara.'

Jai let out a breath he had not realised he'd been holding. He had thought as much, but had not yet dared to let the thought solidify in his mind. But it made so much sense: this was the dust thrown up by khiroi on the move. Hundreds, perhaps thousands of them.

'What's wrong with that?' Jai asked.

Feng chewed his lip.

'We know they were headed east, as we are. Now they head west, where we came from. Back towards the Sabines.'

Jai felt a surge of pride at that.

'Maybe they plan to make war with them?' Jai asked.

Feng looked at him, incredulous, shaking his head.

'The Kidara might have a few hundred strong warriors,' Feng said. 'And another few hundred youths and elders that could mount a khiro and hold a blade, if you had enough of either to spare. Not enough for a legion, even an untested one.'

Jai had always pictured the Kidaran army as one of several thousand. Certainly, Balbir had described it as such, though in truth she had never spoken a number. It was with sinking heart that Jai realised perhaps this single legion was not hubris after all.

'Why then?' Jai asked.

'I will have to ask that, when the time comes,' Feng said.

Jai hissed an anxious breath, letting the air escape between his teeth. He knew he should be overjoyed that they were nearing his people, but instead, he felt a growing sense of dread. There was much that could go wrong, and there was nothing he could do about it.

'Wait . . . why would you be doing the asking?' Jai demanded, Feng's words catching up to him.

Feng looked away, and for a moment, Jai thought he could see fear in the young man's eyes.

'Feng, what did you mean?'

'Do you know why they keep me, Jai?' Feng asked. 'I'm not a true member of the Valor. I am not Tainted. So I act as the Valor's ambassador to the untainted tribes. Their merchant, their messenger. When we meet another tribe, they send me, and me alone.'

'Because if they kill you . . .'

'Then no one here but my sister will mourn.'

'YOU CAN'T DO THIS,' Jai muttered to Feng beneath his breath, shifting his weight on the rug within Sindri's tent.

It was the largest and most luxurious of the Valor's dwellings – a marvel of craftsmanship, the fabric woven from khiro hair and what looked like plant fibres. The exterior was dyed in vibrant shades of purple, and the tent supported by a series of wooden poles, each carved with ornate designs, rather than the traditional bamboo Jai had seen before.

Inside, the space was divided into several sections by lupin embroidered fabric partitions; bleached hemp stitched with dyed thread. The centre of the tent was an open area, where Jai was seated with the others, though this was Jai's first invitation inside. Skin rugs and cushions, crafted from khiroi pelts, covered the ground, providing warmth and comfort beneath the feet. A small brazier in the middle of the room served to heat the space, its glow casting flickering shadows on the walls.

'So it is agreed. Feng shall approach under the auspices of the Pact,' Sindri said. 'It has always worked before. If all goes well, they will allow us an audience. We will use Feng as an intermediary, so there will be no direct trade between us.'

They were so calm about this. As if Feng had no choice in the matter. The young man was going to walk into the Kidara, alone, and blackmail Jai's Uncle Teji in front of his entire court, in his own home. How could they expect Feng to walk out alive?

Jai cursed quietly, earning himself a warning glare from Kiran.

Sindri had gathered her small council, and they sat around a fire. There was Zayn, seated beside her, and a circle of a half-dozen elders and warriors, Kiran included. Feng sat with Jai, a little apart from the others.

Clearly, he was here to see proof the trade was still intended, and there was no plot afoot. It would keep him from getting any ideas, with the Kidara so close and his safe transfer assured. Though Kiran never let him stray out of eyesight for a moment, either way.

'Take it,' Feng hissed, pushing something into his hands.

Bowls of fermented khiroi milk were poured and passed around, the sweet, acrid scent mingling with that of the dried-dung fire. To Jai's enhanced senses, the scent was overwhelming. The waiting cupbearer, holding his large wineskin, must have caught his expression, for he leaned in, dashing a handful of wet herbs into the fire. The minty smell only added to the malaise of scents, but Jai nodded his thanks.

'Not all tribes honour the Pact,' Zayn growled, his face dark and brooding.

'The Kidara will,' Sindri said. 'All the Great Tribes do.'

Zayn spat into the fire through his front teeth.

'What is the Pact?' Jai whispered. Feng shook his head.

'Why do we allow this riteless child to speak at our council,' an elder hissed. 'Be silent!'

Jai bit his tongue, if only for the moment. Sindri, it seemed, took pity on him.

'It grants all traders, lone travellers, and the unrited the right to move freely between tribes, and be heard by their khans. The rest of the Sithia do not grant this right to the Tainted, nor we they. Nonetheless, it will allow Feng an audience with their ruler, and the freedom to leave without being taken captive.'

Feng's face became cold and drawn. Had Feng's family not been traders? Surely they would have been safe if this so-called Pact held true? Obviously, the Valor did not live by it.

A wizened man held up a finger. He was the oldest among the tribe, and had been carried into the tent earlier. Jai struggled to understand him, for the man lacked any teeth, but even Zayn fell silent as the man mumbled wetly.

'What is to stop Feng from betraying us?'

Zayn cleared his throat.

'We have his sister.'

Jai started. His respect for the Valor had grown these past days. Now it was shattered. He knew he was their hostage, not a member of their tribe. Yet he had not begrudged them it.

The Tainted were in perpetual war with the rest of the Sithia. Preyed upon by their brothers and sisters of the steppe. Sold to the highest bidder, to be fettered in the east and the west, whichever was nearer. Jai was a prince of their enemy, a combatant by default.

But with Feng . . . it was different. He'd had no choice in this. A trader from a good family ripped from his life and held there. Endless servitude, shackled by a debt he'd never asked for, and a blade to his sister's throat.

Feng looked down, avoiding Jai's gaze. It seemed the answer was enough for the old man, who closed his eyes and nestled his chin into the thatch of white hair upon his chest.

'We send him ahead,' Sindri said. 'Hide our people, so if we are betrayed, we can outrun any outriders. Take only our best for the meeting.'

'And how do we meet them,' the old man muttered, eyes still closed. He lifted an ear trumpet to his ear, one made from half a hollowed dried gourd.

'Our warriors will wait with Jai a *kiri* east of their path,' Zayn said, before Sindri could answer. Jai knew this to be the measurement of half a day's khiro ride, a distance that varied with the seasons.

'If they wish to meet us, they will send an emissary,' Sindri said. 'We burn wet grass, summon them with smoke. If they do not meet us by nightfall, we leave, meet with our tribe. Find another buyer.'

'And what do we ask for?' Zayn demanded.

'As much as we can get.'

She clapped her hands, signalling the meeting was over. Zayn reached out as she went to stand, holding her in place. For a moment, the air was heavy, almost awkward.

'I want falxes,' Zayn growled. 'One for every man here.'

Sindri jerked her sleeve, giving Zayn a glare, until he lowered his gaze.

'Falxes are for war,' she said. 'The Valor have enough. We need khiroi does. Milk for our children. Transport for the elders.'

'Give me falxes,' he hissed. 'And a few more bulls. We'll take the rest from the next tribe.'

'Your men can ride the does we can spare,' Sindri said. 'And falxes for your ten best.'

Zayn spat, and Sindri struck him clean across the face. He grinned up at her, touching a finger to his teeth and finding the blood there. As an ascended soulbound, it could not have hurt him much.

She held his gaze, until he leaped to his feet, startling her back. He let out a curt laugh, then stalked out of the tent. His men followed, half the council leaving with him.

Sindri stood still, all eyes within the tent upon her. She

stooped, and helped the elder to his feet. The old man patted her shoulder, and she leaned close.

'Before you, all the Valor knew was war,' he said hoarsely. 'And look at where it left us. Our best warriors dead. Half those that remained hated us, for they had been another tribe before we defeated them. Only the blood oath kept their blades from our throats in the night. It took years before we embraced as brothers. No way to grow a tribe.'

He held up a crooked finger.

'Now, marriage,' he chuckled. 'That's the way.'

Sindri, uncharacteristically, rolled her eyes. Yet, as the rest of the tribe got to their feet, and made their farewells, her face looked drawn, and her eyes veiled.

Feng was quick to leave, and Jai followed.

'Feng, you don't have to do this,' Jai said, forced to grab Feng's arm. 'We can find another way.'

Feng laughed bitterly, pulling Jai's hand from his wrist.

'Don't you get it, Jai?' he said. 'This is what I do for them.'

'My uncle might kill you,' Jai said. 'This isn't some merchant caravan selling pots and pans. It's not a go-between for two tribes that can't talk but want to. You're there to blackmail them.'

Feng sighed, and patted Jai's shoulder.

'Come,' he said. 'Walk with me.'

It was strange, but in the face of this danger, Feng seemed all the more confident. As if . . . he welcomed it.

'If I die, my sister will be freed,' Feng said, as they neared the edge of the camp. 'Payment in blood, remember?'

'So that's your plan?' Jai said. 'To die?'

Feng sniffed.

'You think just because your sithosi has come back to you that you know our ways,' Feng said. 'I've been here three years. I've traded hostages with a dozen tribes – some weren't even Tainted. Smaller tribes, true, and for a paltry ransom, but I'm sure it's no different. I may survive this yet.'

Jai stared at him.

'It is a common thing, in the Great Steppe, especially after a skirmish. Warriors fall. Khiroi die beneath them or are wounded in battle. That is how most of these exchanges happen. But the Valor . . . they do not keep to the Pact. They'll ride down a lone traveller, a trader or the unrited making their way.'

He motioned around him, as if it should be obvious to Jai.

'The Valor could hardly call themselves a tribe, before Sindri took over. The few warriors would run, if another tribe caught up to them. The rest were the worthless elders and babies that were leftover, hardly worth the journey to be sold, or swearing their oaths to the tribes that hunted them. They'd take what they wanted and leave the rest.'

'But the khan?' Jai said.

'Just a man who called himself khan and a few fools that followed him, with a handful of sickly khiroi, overburdened and dry of milk. But it was *she* that changed all that.'

Jai listened, fascinated. It was like hearing the old war stories of Leonid. Of that scrappy kingdom that had become an empire, but on a smaller scale.

'How?' he breathed.

'Instead of war, she hunted the steppe for the smaller prey. Broke the Pact. Captured the riteless, the traders, the lone warriors. Ransomed them for what her people needed. Rited in those that would strengthen us. But Zayn . . .'

Feng scratched his chin, where a fledgling few hairs had sprouted.

'He's responsible for it too. He led the hunts, made the prisoner exchanges. Which is far more dangerous than what I'm about to do.'

'How so?' Jai asked.

'We broke the Pact,' Feng said. 'Means they've no reason to keep to the rules of parlay. Break one rule, break them all, right? Sometimes the buyers arrive looking to betray us, but they don't expect Zayn on an Alkhara, with Kiran in tow. Keeps things from getting . . . emotional, at the exchange.'

Feng rubbed his eyes, staring out into the depths of the steppe. With the sun gone, Jai could see the flickering lights of the Kidara's fires, just below the horizon. As if there, the steppe were transformed into a placid lake, reflecting the celestial dance of the stars above.

Behind them, Jai heard the rustle of the grass, and turned to see Kiran. Her steps were heavy, and she pulled Navi on a lead behind her.

'Zayn says we send him on Navi,' Kiran said. 'She's the oldest.'

Kiran held up her hands before Jai could protest.

'Just be thankful she was not chosen for the funeral offering,' she said.

Jai's heart fell, looking over the loyal old khiro. He supposed she'd have a better chance, away from the hardships of an impoverished tribe like the Valor.

'He leaves now?' Jai asked.

Kiran nodded.

'They are two *kiris* by my reckoning – he'll be there by morning, before they break for camp. Best to pass on the message before they set their course.'

He turned, only to have Feng embrace him. Jai returned it, hugging the boy close. They had shared their differences, but in the weeks past, Jai had grown fond of the solemn, soulful young man.

'Go with grace,' he whispered the sithosi farewell. 'And may the Mother keep you.'

Chapter 19

Jai crouched in the long grass, Zayn's fingers tight upon the nape of his neck. He listened to the chirr of insects around him, the grind of the khiroi chewing and the crackle of their signal fire. The air was tinged with smoke, billowing above them in a dark cloud, as a Valor squire tossed on fresh handfuls of dewed grass.

Dawn had hardly broken, but already the majority of the tribe had departed, leaving only the warriors and their bull khiroi behind.

But for their saddles, the remaining Valor had only their weapons and armour, in case they had to flee. Jai guessed for the same reason, the khiroi were fed grain-meal dumplings and watered-down milk before they too had made their way to the rendezvous.

Now they waited, with only Kiran standing, gazing out at the yellow haze that was passing them by. Their khiroi lay down, coaxed onto their bellies by their riders, a bucket of tubers laid beside their snouts.

'They're not coming,' Zayn growled. 'That coward has abandoned us.'

Sindri hushed him with a barbed curse. Alongside her, Winter mewled pitifully, from where she had been chained to Sindri's khiro's horn. Today, they were taking no chances. Even Feng's sister had been brought, a small, wide-eyed girl, watched over by Kiran.

Jai gritted his teeth, his eyes swivelling to see the falx clutched in Zayn's hand. He had no doubt for whom it was intended. This exchange was with a khan. Not a small tribe with a self-proclaimed ruler, like Sindri. If things went south, only a blade to Jai's throat would give them a chance at escape.

For a tribe of the Kidara's size would have enough riders to run them down. And more likely than not, at least a handful of soulbound warriors – more than a match for Zayn and Kiran if things went wrong.

Kiran let out a high, keening note, trilling between her fingers. Zayn spat, then mumbled.

'The little runt made it.'

Jai lifted his head, just a fraction, and Zayn relented, easing the pressure on Jai's neck as he craned to see for himself. Jai caught sight of the blot on the horizon. Riders. Coming straight for them.

'There are twenty of them,' Zayn called. 'Twice what we told Feng to agree to.'

'Do we hold?' Sindri called out.

Zayn sniffed deep, standing and cracking his back.

'He'd be a fool to send less.'

'That's not an answer, Zayn.'

Zayn lifted Jai to his feet, then clucked. His Alkhara grunted and rolled onto its feet, casting Jai in shadow as it shook its dark fur free of dust.

'Mount up!' Zayn called, taking control. 'Be ready to flee on my command.'

It was clear that in these exchanges, it was Zayn they deferred to, Sindri included. Jai felt sweat trickle down his back as the other khiroi stood, Zayn lifting him in front by the back of his shirt.

Sindri clomped a few steps ahead of them, the white flag clasped in her grip.

'Remember, Jai,' she said, her voice firm but low, 'you are a bargaining chip, nothing more. Keep your head down and your mouth shut.'

Jai nodded, swallowing hard as he settled onto the Alkhara's back. The other warriors mounted their khiroi, tension hanging thick in the air.

The approaching riders grew larger on the horizon, their figures becoming distinct as they closed the distance. They were heavily armed and armoured, the blues and silvers of the Kidara visible on their banners. The foremost banner, held high upon a bamboo frame, was unmistakable. The great horned form of an Alkhara. His father's sigil.

As they neared, Jai could see the concern etched on the faces of the Valor warriors. It was clear they were outmatched, yet they held their ground, waiting for Zayn's command.

The Kidara riders finally halted, forming a solid line ahead, so close Jai could see the armour that adorned their khiroi, and the dark, humped outlines of at least two Alkharas. In the centre, a figure on horseback held up a white scrap of cloth, signalling for a parlay.

'Wait for my signal,' Sindri hissed, her eyes never leaving the Kidara leader.

Zayn and the other warriors tensed, hands gripping their weapons tightly. The air felt charged, a dark storm cloud waiting to break.

Jai's heart pounded in his chest as the seconds ticked by, the stand-off between the two tribes hanging in the balance. Finally, Sindri raised her white flag high, jerking it, once.

Ahead, a white flag bobbed back, twice.

'Together, then,' Sindri said. 'Slowly!'

Jai felt the flat of Zayn's blade slap against his throat as the Alkhara surged forward, and the two lines approached. Equal numbers, but far from equals.

The Kidara were of another class entirely. Dressed for war . . . yet they would not go amiss in the halls of the imperial palace.

Their eyes were darkened with kohl, men and women both, with the regalia of their status on full display. Personal sigils were emblazoned upon pennants, from animals of the steppe, even birds and insects, to the tools, weapons and favoured plants of the Sithia.

They wore lamellar armour, composed of small, overlapping leather plates meticulously laced together, dyed in blues so deep, it was as if they wore the very sky itself. Even from a stone's throw away, Jai could hear the leather creaking, and the scrape of blades being loosened in their scabbards.

The hilts of their falxes, for they all bore them, were engraved and studded with garnets – more than just tools of war, but symbols of status and heritage.

Their khiroi were no less impressive, each animal groomed beyond even the primped puppies Jai had seen at the palace, coveted by Latium's dandies. Their manes and tails were braided, clipped and shaved into intricate patterns that stirred Jai's heart – flowing rivers, leafy branches and curling vines.

Though Jai had no grasp of the meaning behind these symbols and adornments, he could imagine their significance. The Kidara were a tribe steeped in tradition and hierarchy, and it was clear that every aspect of their appearance had been carefully chosen to reflect that.

The Valor were being told, in no uncertain terms, where in this hierarchy they lay.

Jai saw Feng, among them. Riding upon Navi, almost hidden by the hulking bull khiroi that all the Kidara rode.

A barked order from one of the Kidara stopped the approach. It required no order from Sindri or Zayn for the Valor to do the same.

Every one of the Kidara were fixated on Jai, and the score of eyes scrutinising him made his face burn. Still, he lifted his chin, trying to convey a courage he did not feel.

From the opposing line, a man emerged, riding out alongside two bodyguards. Jai noted the wealth of the man, for he had golden jewellery that seemed to weigh down his fingers, ears and neck. Thick golden bangles encircled his wrists, and a heavy gold pendant hung from a chain around his throat, emblazoned with a jackal. The man seemed less of a warrior, short and portly, with a little potbelly and beady eyes that darted between the Valor warriors, sizing them up.

'Bring out their negotiator,' he demanded, a smirk playing on his lips.

Feng trotted out, Navi's reins yanked to encourage her, and Jai could see a dark bruise on his face, and shadows beneath his friend's eyes. Despite the injury, Feng flashed Jai an encouraging smile, seemingly to reassure him. It decidedly did not.

The man looked Jai up and down, his eyes narrowing with doubt. For a moment, Jai wondered if this was his uncle. But he saw no resemblance. Indeed, the man had a round, almost babyish face, and yellow-tinged, baleful eyes whose gaze Jai found hard to maintain.

'I have my reservations about this boy's authenticity,' the man said, his voice dripping with disdain. 'Only on this eastern boy's insistence, even in the face of our . . . encouragement, have we come here today. That, and rumours from the west.' He cast a suspicious glance towards Sindri and the other Valor. 'But perhaps you've heard these same rumours.'

He spat, off to the side, his eyes never leaving Sindri's face. Finally, he looked down, reaching for something, setting hands to hilts up and down the Valor lines.

He tutted at the response, and slowly pulled out a small sack, which jingled with the sound of coins.

'This is all you'll get for the boy,' he said, tossing the sack at Sindri. 'There's no way of proving who he is, after all. And my king won't stoop so low as to trade directly with you. The coins are for Feng. You are just holding them.'

Zayn ripped open Jai's shirt with a swift, savage jerk, leaving him shivering in the cold morning air. The gorget Sindri had placed around his neck that morning was there for all to see.

Sindri brandished the diary in one hand and yanked Winter's chain forward with the other. The sight of Jai's dragon made the man's eyes bulge in shock, for until now Winter had been hidden by the grass. Undoubtedly, Feng would have already told them about her – it was clear they had not believed him.

'You dare doubt us?' Sindri snarled, her voice barely controlled. 'I have your proof, here in the diary of the conqueror himself. Rohan's heir sits before you in his father's armour, soulbound to a stolen dragon from the royal court he was raised in. Here he sits, with a Tainted's blade to his throat. Yet you dare insult us. You will pay more than this pittance, or you will leave empty-handed.'

The man's eyes were bulging, and it was clear that he was not used to being spoken to that way. *Particularly by a woman*, Jai thought.

The man turned, looking at the nobles that had accompanied him. Gauging their reactions.

He went to his pocket once more, but Sindri held up a finger.

'Your coins are no good to the Tainted. We've no need to buy trinkets from the east. We need khiroi does. That's all we will accept.'

The man glanced back at the Kidaran nobles once more. Clearly, he cared about what they thought. Their faces, however, were inscrutable, their eyes flicking from Jai, to Winter, to Sindri.

Finally, the man sighed, and snapped his fingers.

One of the squires lifted a khiro horn to his mouth and let out a short series of notes.

'We wait, then,' the man said.

Chapter 20

They waited in awkward silence, neither party speaking, even among themselves. Just the clinking of metal, the creak of leather and the soughing of the breeze. The uneasy quiet stretched like a spider's thread, threatening to snap at any moment.

It was not long before there was a blot along the horizon, and later, a procession of young does led by a single scout.

Jai realised now, his tribe had held these back. Even among the Kidara, khiroi were favoured above all other commodities.

'Fifteen by my count,' Sindri scoffed, sitting upright in her saddle. 'Not nearly enough.'

Yet Jai discerned the bluster behind her words. The Valor possessed no more than fifty adult khiroi, plenty of which had long since seen their prime. These does held the promise of calves of their own someday too. This was their entire tribe's future, and she knew it.

The Kidaran's lip twitched, and a muscle in his jaw tightened. There was rage there. Controlled. Calculated.

'Greed will cost you,' he said. 'The more we give, the more worth hunting you down in the days to come. At the moment, we are not insulted, and fifteen is not worth the hunt. Do not push it.'

Still, Sindri held firm. She sensed a weakness, Jai could tell, though he saw none.

'Blades,' she said.

'No,' the man snapped back.

'Nazeem,' one of the Kidaran women whispered. 'Do you—?'

'No blades,' Nazeem said firmly, nodding to the bag of coins. 'You could keep that. Trade for them elsewhere. But—'

'With who?' Zayn muttered under his breath, earning himself a look from Sindri. 'It's hard enough to trade with you.'

Jai yearned for her to accept. But was it enough? Their plan was going perfectly, but greed could scupper it all.

Nazeem held up a finger, silencing the murmurs.

'Jai,' he addressed him, his voice changed. Kinder. Slower. 'Have they anything of yours?'

Jai's eyes found Navi and Feng. Feng met his gaze, his face inscrutable. Yet Jai pointed, his voice strained as Zayn pressed the blade against his throat.

'I want Feng and his sister.'

Sindri cursed.

'We need him,' she stated, crossing her arms.

'He's served his purpose – let them have the runt,' Zayn snarled. 'And the brat. Doing us a favour.'

Nazeem hesitated, surprised at the request.

'If he is willing?' Nazeem asked.

'I am,' Feng called.

Sindri's shoulders slumped, imperceptibly. Zayn had sealed it. She made a show of pouring the coins into her palm, a mix of gold and silver, many in currencies Jai did not recognise. She hissed through her teeth, then nodded, once.

'I agree to your terms,' Feng said swiftly, keeping up the charade of acting as intermediary. 'Both of yours.'

'Release them,' Sindri ordered.

Finally, the blade retreated from Jai's throat, and Zayn shoved him from the saddle into the dirt. Sindri's gaze met Jai's for a fleeting moment before she stuffed the diary into Jai's satchel, tossing it to him. Sum ran to Feng's side as the khiroi does were led by the Kidaran squire, their horns bound by ropes. At the same time, Kiran attached the lead doe to her saddle.

'We ride!' Sindri commanded.

The Valor surged forward, the earth trembling beneath their hooves. None spared Jai a second glance.

Only Zayn remained, his blade outstretched, baring his teeth at the Kidara. Giving his people a head start, in case of pursuit – his Alkhara would soon catch up. Jai dared not step out of the blade's reach.

Minutes ticked by. Finally, Zayn leaned out, and unlocked the shackles around Winter's neck. She raced over to Jai, standing between the Alkhara and him.

Zayn spat, giving Jai a scornful look.

'Good luck,' he said. 'You'll need it.'

And with that . . . he too was gone.

JAI STOOD THERE, IN the dirt, massaging his neck. It was strangely silent.

'Vizier, do we follow? We could have them by dusk,' asked one of the Kidaran knights.

Nazeem flapped a hand, giving Jai a wild smile.

'No need,' he said. 'We got the better of that deal. Let us not sully this joyous occasion.'

Jai returned the smile, even as Winter nuzzled up to him. He scratched her under her chin.

'Come, my boy,' Nazeem said, not unkindly. 'Sit behind me.'

Jai's heart thundered in his chest, the words of the tense exchange still ringing in his ears. He sought solace in the eyes of Feng, who was clutching his sister in front of him in the saddle as if she might suddenly fly into the sky.

Jai strode towards Nazeem, who extended a hand and stirruped foot to help him onto the khiro.

As Jai found his seat behind the portly man, the Kidaran

nobles burst into jubilant cheers, blades rattling from scabbards as they held them high in the air, whooping and hollering.

Winter, her shackles a memory, bellowed a triumphant roar, joining the cacophony of celebration. The primal sound quelled the noise, leaving an uneasy silence in its wake. The Kidaran warriors traded uncertain glances, some breaking into a nervous laughter, staring at the creature they had just welcomed into their ranks.

Nazeem clucked, nudging his Alkhara's sides with his feet and wheeling it about. Jai felt tall, up there on the enormous beast.

Sum clung to her brother upon Navi's back, her eyes wide with wonder as she took in the vast expanse of the world beyond the Valor camp. The sight of her joy and curiosity warmed Jai's heart, a small flame against the chill of his recent ordeal.

He gave one glance back, seeing the fading shapes of the Valor khiroi in the distance. He would miss the Valor, in his own way.

And then . . . they were flying. Hurtling across the steppe, Jai's world scored by the hiss of grass and clomping of khiroi. Winter leaped and bounded beside them, uttering yelps of joy. She sensed Jai's relief. Felt it too.

It flooded him. Like a great weight had lifted from his shoulders, even as he rode into the unknown. For he was with his people. People who *wanted* him. Who would sacrifice great treasures, just to get him back.

He was back with his people. His family.

Jai was home.

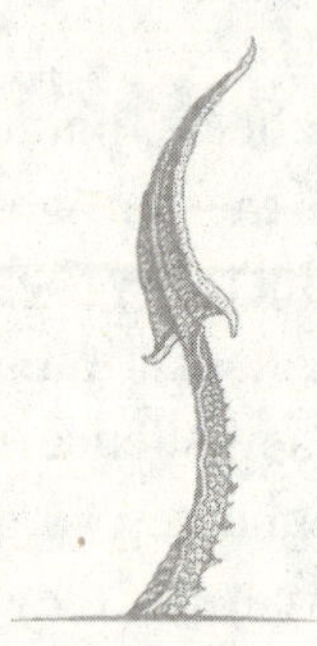

Chapter 21

The wind snatched away any words that Jai attempted, so he could do little but grip Nazeem, and hold back the tears that pricked his eyes.

The soldiers were riding roughshod, and Jai could understand why. Had a war band as large as the Keldar's come across them, they'd be wiped out. It had been a risk indeed, carrying so much wealth with such a small party. No wonder they'd kept their offerings some distance away.

Soon enough, he could see the outline of the Kidaran camp, blue blots upon a green canvas, crested by a hundred trails of smoke.

But before the camp had come into view, they were joined by another group, riding towards them. Two squires, boys barely older than himself, standing beside another dozen or so does. Baskets hung from the khiroi's sides, neatly stacked with an assortment of blades and armour, gleaming in the sunlight. It was clear that the Kidara had been willing to pay a high price for Jai's ransom, more than he or the Valor could have imagined.

Jai didn't know what to make of the sight. Was it a compliment that they had been prepared to offer so much for his safe return? Or was it an insult that Nazeem had haggled so fiercely, and put Jai's freedom at risk. It mattered, in the end, little. Jai was here now. Back with the Kidara.

Had he truly walked among them, all those years ago? His memories were fleeting, fantastical things, distorted by the passage of time and the whims of his imagination. He was left to wonder if those few memories he had treasured were nothing more than figments, conjured by his mind to fill the void.

Ahead of the camp, Jai was astounded to see another forty riders, gathered in a milling mass at the edge of camp, blocking his view. The nobles around Jai raised their swords high, whooping, riding into their midst alongside him.

This was clearly the war band, ready to be summoned if the exchange had been an ambush. Jai had never seen so many khiroi in one place.

And it was not just the riders. Beside the camp, there must have been more than a hundred more, cropping the grass under the supervision of a dozen squires.

This was no village. It was a city.

There were paths, lined with embrasures for the night. The tents, if the grand pavilions could be called that, were in stark contrast to those Jai had seen among the Valor. Some were adorned with vibrant banners, while still more boasted intricate embroidery of flowers and wild beasts, denoting the clans of those who owned them.

The camp was alive with activity; the air filled with the sounds of everyday life: craftsmen plying their trades, tailors sewing garments in the open. There were even merchants offering an array of goods, from spices and fabrics to pottery and metalwork.

Children played among the tents, chasing each other and fencing with thin bamboo for swords. Some paused in their games to stare at Jai and the entourage, wide-eyed and curious. Jai couldn't help but feel apprehension at the sight of this thriving Kidaran community, so different from the harsh world of the Valor he had come to know. This was especially true because he had fallen in love with the simplicity of the Valor. There, the rules were clear, each knowing what was expected of them. But this place . . .

It was another world entirely.

In the heart of the camp, a pair of blacksmiths were hard at work, sweat glistening on their brows as they hammered molten metal into shape. The glow of their forges cast flickering light across their sooty faces, yet none turned to watch as Jai went by. The same went for the leatherworkers as they shaped saddles and harnesses for the khiroi, or the others he observed stirring great vats of blue dye as fermented leaves frothed indigo at the surface. And still another artisan nearby was diligently preparing tendons, stretching and scraping them to remove any excess flesh or fat before allowing them to dry under the sun.

There was an urgency in their movements. Something he recognised before, from his time among the Sabines. It was as if . . . they were preparing for war.

Jai's heart surged at the thought, though he had no way of knowing for sure. But in his heart of hearts, he *knew* his estranged uncle, Teji, would not let the Sabines walk over them. It was no wonder the Kidara were headed west.

Because the Kidara had fought the Sabines before, and had handed Leonid the greatest of their defeats. Surely now they would rise in the Sithia's defence again.

They reached the centre of the camp as he thought this, coming to an enormous plaza, as large as the market squares in Latium.

At its heart stood a massive tent, more akin to a palace than a temporary dwelling. Rich blue fabric adorned with golden embroidery flapped in the breeze, with a half-dozen guards standing sentry along its edges.

Nazeem swung down from his ride, handing the reins to a waiting squire.

Jai's heart pounded in his chest as he dismounted too. He had been dreaming of this moment for so long, but now that it was here, he felt almost afraid.

He took a deep breath and walked up to the tent, his eyes

fixed on the guards. They stood aside, bowing their heads, as he and Nazeem approached.

'The creature stays here,' one said. 'Same rule for everyone, soulbound included.'

Jai nodded even as he bristled at the word 'creature'. Still, he requested Winter wait with a thought. She did not like it, sensing Jai's apprehension, but she did as he asked, sitting upon her rump and glaring at the curious onlookers, as if it were their fault she was being separated from her master.

Nazeem pulled back the curtain, a smile on his face.

'Come, Jai, son of Rohan. Your uncle is waiting.'

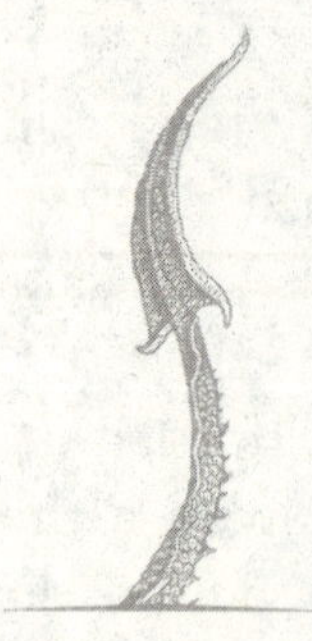

Chapter 22

Stepping over the threshold of the grand tent was akin to crossing the boundary of worlds. From the sunlit openness of the steppe, he found himself cocooned within a realm of cool shadows and soft whispers.

The tent was bathed in a dim light that filtered through the blue fabric overhead, tinging the vibrant tapestries that adorned the walls, rendered in rich dyes. Each one was a mythic tale, a piece of pageantry, or a recounting of history, of Rohan's victories, woven with threads of dyed wool and silk.

In the centre of the tent, atop a raised platform of polished wood, stood a throne. It was a grand, imposing sight. The chair was crafted from the massive bones of the great khiroi, shaped and polished until they shone like ivory in the cool light. The seat was upholstered with a thick fur, the shaggy hairs knotted into a plaited, soft matt. The back rest was fashioned from a fan of imposing, curving horns, each larger than any Jai had ever seen, their sharp points aimed skyward.

Yet it sat empty. Instead, a dozen men and women sat cross-legged on an enormous rug in front of it, murmuring among themselves in hushed tones. Waiting for something. *For someone*, Jai thought.

Jai went to join the waiting Kidara, only for Nazeem to tut and pull him back. The tent was not just one big space, but had a heavy curtain dividing it in two, just behind the throne. Nazeem and Jai walked down the length of it, the whispers of the waiting subjects fading behind them as they made their way to the other side of the grand tent.

Pulling back the curtain, Jai was met with a much more intimate setting. This half of the tent was quieter, warmer, the air thick with the sweet aroma of spiced fruits and wine.

There, reclined on an ornate bed draped in fur, was a man Jai immediately knew to be his uncle, Teji. He was the spitting image of Samar, though he did not look like the warrior Jai had envisioned. Instead of the hardened, fearsome man of his imaginings, Teji was a vision of regal leisure, dressed in a robe of silk, a fine pelt of curls erupting from his chest. His features were softened by years of easy living, his body fuller than the wiry fighters Jai was accustomed to among the Valor.

Around him, three women worked diligently, each from a different part of the world judging by their looks. One was pouring wine into a finely crafted goblet held in Teji's hand, tasting it diligently, then wincing and turning aside, before handing it to her king.

Another was massaging his feet in her lap, while the third wafted at him with a peacock feather fan.

Courtesans, by Jai's guess. Just like his own mother had been. The realisation stung, but he pushed it aside as Teji turned his heavy-lidded gaze towards them, a slow, lazy smile spreading across his lips as he recognised his nephew. His voice was a low rumble, slurred by the wine.

'Arjun,' he drawled, smacking his purple-stained lips. 'Come closer, boy. Let's have a look at you.'

'It is Jai, uncle,' Jai said, hurrying forward. 'Rohan's third son.'

His uncle, far from giving the embrace Jai had hoped for, instead flopped a bejewelled hand from the bed. Jai stared at it for a moment, and his uncle twitched it impatiently. One of the courtesans, a dark-skinned woman with a tight cap of curls upon her head, mimed kissing her own hand. Bemused, he heard

Nazeem cough gently behind him, and despite his revulsion, Jai lowered his head, kissing the largest of the rings there.

'Good,' Teji said, closing his eyes and readjusting himself upon the tasselled cushions that propped him upright. 'Very good.'

Nazeem approached then, and bowed his head.

'My lord, your nephew has travelled across the breadth of the empire to find us. Shall I organise a welcome feast?'

'His visit has cost us enough already,' Teji said, not even looking at Jai, instead prodding the masseuse at his feet. She giggled, but Jai saw her laughter did not reach her eyes.

'But surely—'

'I'm not in the mood,' Teji grunted. 'My belly pains me again. Leave us.'

He shooed at Jai and Nazeem with a limp wrist, reaching out a hand and pulling the masseuse closer. Jai felt the sting of disappointment and embarrassment, but knew better than to argue. He let Nazeem take his hand and drag him outside, his heart in his stomach. It was a bitter welcome. He turned to Nazeem, his only anchor in the sudden maelstrom of the unknown.

'He is better in the mornings,' Nazeem said, giving Jai an apologetic smile. 'Your arrival was a surprise to us all.'

'He mistook me for Arjun,' Jai murmured, only just concealing his contempt. 'Does he know . . . that Arjun was murdered?'

Nazeem looked around, and Jai saw the eyes of the waiting Kidara dart away.

'That is a delicate matter,' Nazeem said in a low voice.

He guided Jai out of the tent with a hand on the small of Jai's back, until Jai was blinking in the bright afternoon sun. Winter ambled up to him, nudging his hand with her snout. He scratched her absently between the small nubs of her horns, just where she liked it, and at least one of them was content.

'Our conversation will continue,' Nazeem stated, keeping a

wary eye on the dragon. 'But first, refresh yourself. Rest. I'll have a manservant arranged for—'

'Feng,' Jai interjected. 'I want him, and his sister. He's probably feeling as out of place as I.'

A furrow creased Nazeem's brow.

'But, Jai, he's not one of us, not Kidaran. Can he be trusted? He failed to mention your dragon, or your father's armour when he first arrived. We almost didn't come.'

Jai was taken aback, puzzled. Why would Feng withhold such information? Nazeem, reading his expression, nodded.

'We'll ensure he's sent off with the next band of merchants, back to his people in the east. He made the journey to us alone, and argued your case. There's a certain bravery in that.'

Jai started to protest, but Nazeem propelled him down the path with a soft hand.

'So it's settled,' he said. 'I have a great boy, eager to please. He'll draw you a bath.'

'Send Feng,' Jai ordered, with as much confidence as he could muster. 'If he lied, he can explain himself to me.'

Nazeem faltered in his steps, then bowed his head.

'As you wish, my prince.'

My prince, Jai thought. *Damned right.*

But then he remembered the curt scene in the tent. The dismissal from his uncle.

Then why don't I feel like one?

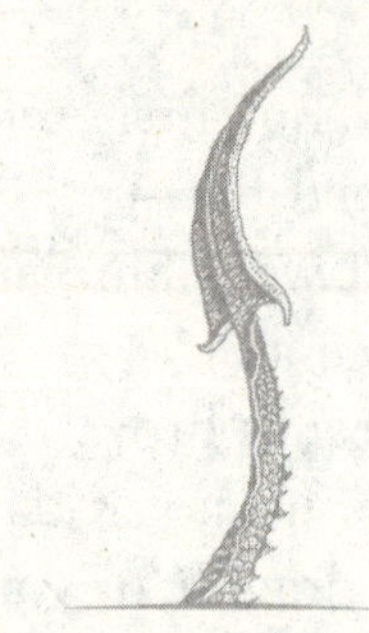

Chapter 23

Jai lay on the furs of his tent, staring up at the ceiling. It was enormous. Larger, even, than Sindri's had been. Too large for Jai to pack away on his own.

He found himself grappling with the realisation that servants would now do that for him. Yet, as he lay within the empty tent, an unexpected pang of yearning gripped him.

He found himself longing for the modest tent the Valor gave him, where the wind would rustle the khiroi furs, and the scent of dew-kissed grass was always lingering. He yearned for the hum of life just beyond the fur walls, where laughter ebbed and flowed like a merry stream, the chatter of voices weaving tales yet to be heard.

Now he was engulfed in a silence that seemed to swallow all sound. It was just him and Winter, nestled in his lap, her rhythmic breathing all that disturbed the air. He pulled off his satchel, and then the ripped shirt.

It was time to take stock, for the tent contained nothing in the way of furniture – only the furs that kept him from sitting on bare grass. It was hollow luxury.

Which reflected his feelings precisely.

More than inside, though, he possessed little. The worn shoes that had journeyed with him from Latium itself, the simplistic Valor attire now torn and fraying at the edges. The gorget that graced his throat, and Leonid's diary. His other possessions were but the detritus of his travels – a shrivelled carrot top, a single Sabine coin, and a sabretooth fang. His sword, however, was gone. It seemed Zayn had not been joking when he said they needed swords.

He had nothing, and yet he had everything. Everything that mattered. Winter.

A surge of emotion welled within him, too powerful to contain. His vision blurred as tears began to fall, each a remembrance to his brothers who would never see this day.

He was home. A dream he had never truly allowed himself to believe in. And yet here he was. Alone amid the grandeur, save for Winter's unwavering presence.

He ran his fingers along Winter's pearlescent scales, his heart swelling with the love he held for his faithful dragon. Winter, with her bottomless eyes and her warmth that seemed to seep into his very bones. She was his constant, her love the beacon that guided him in the darkest of hours. It was her love that gave him the strength to bear the unbearable, to find hope in the hopeless.

He reached for the diary. In this place, now, more than ever, he wished to read about his father. Even from the mouthpiece of the man's nemesis, the scribbled writings were near all he had of him now. He would learn the truth soon enough, from his father's people.

Our first major defeat today. Thirty cavalrymen, ranging our trail. Gone in an instant. Our men hardly dared collect the bodies, so quickly did these Steppefolk seem to come and go. Our horsemen are no match in open battle – they, who are more used to the cleaving of a retreating man's back than the rigours of battle on beast-back. I was told by a survivor that they numbered only ten, and were not even seeking a fight. A band of shepherds, it seems, slaughtered my men.

On further investigation, these so-called skirmishes we had won in days past were little more than ambushes of small bands, traders and heathen families. No true victories, only the boastful tales of cowardly soldiers, embellished beyond recognition.

This war will not be won if it is one between horse and khiro, those great stinking beasts that are these heathens' chattel of choice. I have sent every cavalryman back, but for a handful. And these too shall not range far beyond our camp.

Still, my spies have been busy at work, crossing the palms of Phoenixian traders with silver. Rumours, and whispers abound, but these shadows begin to take shape. I hear of a warlord who does not take kindly to my invasion, or any incursions into their lands. A man who is feared, even among his people. Only when silver turned to gold did they dare even speak his name.

Rohan.

There was a tapping on the entrance to the tent, and Jai swiftly wiped his eyes with his sleeves. Feng ducked his head into the tent before Jai was finished, and cast his eyes downward as he and his sister, Sum, shuffled into the tent.

In this moment, Jai's stomach twisted. For Sum was so young. And now she was to be cast out, with Feng. Left penniless, with whatever merchants that rode the plains.

And it was his fault.

She smiled at him, shuffling forward. Her eyes were fixed on Winter, and she twisted her little hands. She couldn't have been much older than eight or nine.

'She likes scratches around her horns.' Jai winked, gently moving Winter's dozing head and standing.

Sum clapped her hands with glee, and Jai felt his spirits lift as she descended upon Winter with grabbing hands. The dragon didn't seem to mind, rolling onto her belly and letting out a panting yap of pleasure.

He'd neglected her these past days. No longer. She was all he had in this world. That much was clear.

'Feng,' Jai said. 'I thank you, for your part in what happened this morn—'

'No thanks needed,' Feng said hastily, holding up his hands. 'You have done far more than any have for me before.'

Jai rubbed his eyes, trying to consider how to broach what Nazeem had told him.

'We need to secure the entrance,' Feng said. 'Did Sindri leave you a weapon in that bag?'

Jai shook his head, bemused by his friend's antics.

'Why would I need one?' Jai asked. 'I'm in the safest place I could be.'

Feng stared at him, and Jai stared back. It was strange; Feng was looking at him as if *he* were the mad one.

Feng ran his hands over his face, shaking his head.

'You have no idea, do you? Mother help us.'

'What aren't you telling me, Feng?' Jai asked.

But in his heart, he knew what it was. The cold reception, the empty room, the hard negotiation. There was more to this.

'The obvious!' Feng snapped, wincing as Sum and Winter went quiet at the sudden noise. Feng smiled to them, though Jai saw it didn't touch his eyes.

'We're just playing a game,' he said to his sister. 'Don't worry about us.'

He took Jai by the shoulder, and pulled him a little further away.

'Jai. You may have lived among royals, but you know nothing of the politics of our people. You're in more danger here than you *ever* were with the Valor.'

Jai felt his worst fears confirmed. He didn't want to believe it. He was home now. He was safe. This was all a trick, a manipulation. He *needed* it to be.

'Why should I trust a word you say now? You didn't tell Nazeem about Winter,' Jai said, careless of the anger in his voice. 'Nor the diary, nor the armour. Everything that would prove that I am who I say. Why?'

Feng shook his head.

'I was trying to help you,' he muttered. 'Now you treat me li—'

'Just tell me,' Jai said, forcing out a breath to calm himself.

Feng stepped away, and Jai could see tears in his eyes.

'I didn't have to help you, you know,' he said. 'I could have told them the truth – made them think you really were the heir. You'd already be dead.'

'I'm sorry, Feng,' Jai said. 'Truly. I just . . . I've dreamed of coming home my whole life. Now, you're telling me I'm in danger? Help me understand.'

Feng chewed his lips, and wiped his face with his sleeve.

'Sindri valued me for more than a middleman for the untainted,' Feng explained, his eyes holding Jai's firmly. 'To survive as a trader in the Great Steppe is to master a treacherous dance, playing one tribe or clan, or even sect against another. My father danced it well. But he was too trusting of the Pact. And we paid the price.'

Feng motioned at the fur-lined floor, and Jai sat with him, the chortling of Sum discordant in the heavy atmosphere.

'Trust, Jai,' Feng said. 'That is the heart of it.'

Jai leaned close, feeling his joy evaporating like rain in a hot skillet.

'I learned at my father's feet,' Feng continued, his voice steady. 'Then by his side. I sat through every negotiation, every parlay. Believe me, Jai, when I say this – I know of what I speak.'

Jai nodded silently, his mouth dry.

'Tell me,' he whispered.

'Jai, you are the rightful heir,' Feng asserted. 'Your uncle may act as regent, but that's all he is – a placeholder. The nobles loyal to your father never let him forget that fact, or at least, they did when we traded with them last. He is king only in name.'

'What does that matter?' Jai asked.

'In Sithian succession, even a courtesan's child can hold greater claim than a sibling,' Feng explained. 'With Arjun lost, you are not just a prince, Jai, but a king in waiting.'

Jai nodded slowly, understanding beginning to dawn. He had thought he would rule alongside his uncle. Or inherit it when he was passed, for his brothers had told him the man had no children of his own. He didn't want to believe it.

'I've no intention to oust my uncle. He paid for me. Kept my father's tribe for my brothers and I. He'll be right by my side.'

Feng shook his head, as if Jai were speaking in a foreign tongue. Jai's confusion mounted.

'What does any of this have to do with concealing my identity?'

'Because had they suspected you were the *true* heir, we all would be dead by now. Sindri was reckless to even attempt the exchange.'

Jai's stomach churned.

'Why . . . why would they . . . ?' he stammered.

'Because you are going to take his crown. If he had suspected, he would have orchestrated an "accident". Claimed you were an imposter, that the Valor staged an ambush. None would be the wiser.'

Jai felt the ground shift beneath him. He was in the eye of a storm.

'Why even agree to the ransom?' Jai muttered aloud.

'Because many Kidara are loyal to your father's memory. Men and women who fought for him, whose families died for him. Many more remember your father fondly. So Teji had to show them he was taking the ransom seriously. All those weapons and khiroi you saw on your way in? It was a show, nothing more. Politics.'

'How?' Jai pressed.

'When I delivered the Valor's ransom terms, I ensured there was an audience. I spent the whole morning in that damned tent waiting for enough nobles to be within earshot before Nazeem's men hauled me off.'

'So Teji and Nazeem thought I was a fraud?' Jai asked.

'I did everything short of proclaiming it outright. I dropped enough hints under duress for that parasite Nazeem to conclude he'd extracted the truth from me. They thought they'd buy a tarted-up street rat for a handful of gold, and parade you around as the imposter they thought you were, to convince everyone that Rohan's line was extinct.'

'And instead, they got . . . me,' Jai said. 'The thing they feared most – the true heir.'

Feng glanced at the tent entrance, and scratched his head nervously.

'They won't attack us in broad daylight. But from now on, only eat food from the communal pots, and do not accept any drinks you are offered.'

Jai laid his head in his hands, taking deep breaths to calm himself.

'That Nazeem is not what he seems,' Feng murmured, his gaze intent on Jai, making sure he was heard. 'He has his tentacles wrapped around Teji, guiding his moves. He is the puppeteer behind the scenes.'

'If that's true, why didn't he kill me at the exchange the moment he realised I was the true heir?' Jai asked.

'His arrogance was our saving grace,' Feng said with a wry smile. 'So convinced was he you were an imposter, he invited your father's loyalists to witness it. Thank the Mother he did.'

Winter nosed close, sensing Jai's distress. He clutched her tight, drawing comfort from her warm embrace, and Sum toddled over, wrapping her arms around her elder brother. For a moment, they sat there, revelling in the reprieve they had bought, and fearing what was to come.

'These loyalists, then,' Jai said. 'It's time I met them.'

Chapter 24

Jai stood at the tent's centre, resisting the urge to pace. Winter remained at his side, sitting straight backed, sensing the gravity of what was to come. Her keen eyes were fixed on the tent entrance, as though her very gaze could summon the anticipated visitors.

Feng had vanished discreetly from the rear of the tent, orchestrating an exit by uprooting one of the anchoring pegs that kept the canvas taut. He had been accompanied by his sister. Jai had extended an invitation for her to stay, but Feng had responded with a resolve that brooked no argument – she would never again leave his side.

By now, it was obvious why Nazeem had wanted Feng gone. To prevent the very conversation they'd just had. He'd declare Feng his bannerman no sooner he had the next chance. So long as Feng would have him.

So now he waited, as Feng sought out the woman who had seemed sympathetic to Jai's cause – based on nothing but an interruption when Nazeem had refused them the blades. It was a risky thing to do, especially with Nazeem knowing Feng had tricked him. Jai did not know what he had done to earn such loyalty.

He replayed the encounter he'd had with the nobles, that fleeting interaction that had hinted at a desire to rescue him.

He tried to recall their faces, their expressions, as they looked upon him: the supposed prodigal son returned.

Many would be men and women who had served his father, bled for the crown, for the tribe, but would they extend the same loyalty to him?

His thoughts were interrupted by a soft rustling outside the tent. His heart hammered like a call to war. It was time to step out from the shadows of his father and brothers and assert his own name.

He was no longer just a son, a brother, a survivor. He was Khan Jai of the Kidara, first of his name. A legacy reborn, a destiny claimed. Rohan had lived by his own legend. It was time for him to blaze his own.

The tent entrance darkened as figures began to crowd its threshold. Jai's heart lifted in his chest as Feng, Sum and a half-dozen men and women stepped inside, their presence filling the expansive interior. These were the individuals whose allegiance could very well be crucial, the ones whose loyalty could tip the scales of his tenuous claim to rule.

Seeing their numbers, there were more than he'd dared to hope for, a sign that perhaps his cause wasn't as impossible as it had seemed. At the same time . . . he could not trust any of them. One of Nazeem's spies could well be in their midst.

The assembly knelt in fealty, save one – the woman who had been the catalyst of this meeting. She met his gaze with a subtle bow of her head before speaking, her voice quiet in the tent.

'We must be swift. Nazeem surely has men watching this tent.'

Jai nodded, stepping closer.

'You are truly Jai, son of Rohan, brother of Samar and Arjun?' she asked.

Jai nodded, for his throat was as dry as a desert. But she simply kneeled in response, averting her eyes as the rest had done.

Feng cleared his throat, and Jai knew he had to say *something*. This was all happening so fast.

'Who are you?' Jai asked.

'I am Harleen,' the woman responded. 'I fought with your father in the War of the Steppe. With me are the sons and daughters of those that died with him in the last battle.'

He was not schooled in the etiquette of his father's court, so he lowered himself to their level. The Valor had far simpler rules – and he preferred them.

'Your grief echoes my own,' Jai said. 'And your loyalty to my father will not be forgotten.'

Harleen's face was etched with the stern lines of a seasoned warrior, her bushy eyebrows and the burn mark on her cheek a reminder of the battles fought in years past. Her question, though respectful, carried an undercurrent of bitterness.

'Your presence here raises questions. Tales of the palace massacre, the Black Rehearsal as it is now known, reach far and wide. Rumours of your brothers' plotting with the Dansk have spilled into every corner of our world.'

'I watched them die,' Jai stated. 'Saw Titus slit their throats. This plot was not of their doing. It was Titus. All of it. He killed his own father to seize power. We were but the scapegoats.'

An unsettling silence fell upon the tent, every eye a weight upon him, his words hanging like spectres in the air. He saw the shadow of pity flicker across a young man's face. Pity he did not need.

'I didn't come back to mourn,' Jai said, with as firm a voice as he could muster. 'I came back to fight. For the Kidara, for my father's memory and for the legacy of our people.'

His voice strengthened, his resolve hardening with every word.

Harleen motioned at the others to sit, and they did so, some groaning with relief. Clearly, he had passed their first test. His every phrase was a labyrinth to navigate, as they sought truth in his tale, his countenance and his conviction.

'And the dragon?' she asked. 'The armour? What of Leonid, and his death? Did Titus kill him too?'

Jai hesitated.

'Leonid I killed,' he lied. 'In the name of my father. The armour, I took from his room. And the dragon, a gift, from a Dansk princess. We came here, together, before the Valor captured me.'

'Lies,' one of the boys muttered.

'Oh?' Jai said.

The boy glanced at him, then lowered his eyes. Still, he wasn't so cowed as to fall silent. 'No Dansk would part with a dragon.'

'Somewhere out there,' Jai said, 'far to the west, there will be some thirty Huddites, escaped from the prison of Porticus. The princess is with them. We travel west, do we not, to meet with the invaders? Until then, I will ask my uncle to send search parties, to find them.'

Harleen shared a weighted glance with the others before speaking, her sigh just as heavy. 'We ride west, yes. But not to engage in war.'

'Then why?'

'To pursue peace.'

Jai stared at her, incredulous.

'They *killed* my brothers.'

'So *you* say. And while I believe you,' she said, holding up her hand to stave off his protests, 'your uncle has laid the blame upon their bodies.' Harleen said, 'Greedy fools, he calls them. You, he never mentioned. In truth, few of us knew you even existed. You were with us for such a short time.'

'I share the blood of Rohan.' Jai's voice was steadfast. 'My mother may have been a courtesan, but my lineage remains unbroken.'

'So you say,' the same boy blurted out.

'Quiet, Gurveer!' Harleen snapped. 'Show some respect.'

The boy silenced, but Jai saw the tension in the young man's shoulders.

'Who else could I be?' Jai asked.

Gurveer's lips twitched, as if trying to contain himself, only to fail as words burst forth.

'Some think you are a Sabine puppet. That your life was spared for your treachery, your betrayal rewarded by a dragon. Then you were sent into our lands to locate us. To gain power, and then turn against us.'

There were a few murmurs of agreement, and Jai felt his heart quicken.

'It is Teji who betrays us!' Jai called out. 'And it will not work. Titus dreams of war. Of finishing what his grandfather started. There will be no peace between the Sithia and Sabines.'

Gurveer scoffed.

'Believe me, or don't,' Jai shot back, his voice echoing around the room. 'But I am here to reclaim what is rightfully mine. I will not stand idle while the legacy of my father is tarnished.'

'You claim a lot,' Harleen said, getting to her feet. 'But words are wind. Actions are the currency of trust.'

'I am prepared to act,' Jai retorted, speaking loud to keep their attention as the men and women stood. 'I did not come all this way to stand here and be doubted.'

'Then sit,' Gurveer snapped. 'Or prove yourself.'

Still more nods, pursed lips, and then Gurveer made his exit from the tent, a train of supporters trailing behind him. Jai grimaced in the sudden silence – it was evident Gurveer's word carried considerable weight among the younger generation. Harleen exhaled, her head sinking slightly.

'We will speak more,' she said. 'But you can see, our blood runs hot. Gurveer's father was executed alongside your father. Most of their parents were, if they did not fall in battle. That is why I brought them. But over the years, Teji and Nazeem have spun such tales that you are practically a Sabine to them. Please, forgive their anger.'

'Do they blame my father?' Jai asked.

Harleen allowed him a smile, now that they were alone.

'Your father was the best of us. To blame him would be to blame their own parents. They believed in his cause, just as much as he did.'

She turned to leave, and Jai blurted a question.

'Say you believe me,' Jai said. 'What would you have me do?'

Harleen paused at the tent's entrance, glancing back at him. Her face held a thoughtful expression, as though carefully weighing her next words.

'Prove them wrong, Jai. Show them you're not the enemy they imagine. Stand with them, fight with them.'

And with those words . . . she was gone.

Chapter 25

Another battle lost. My son, Constantine, hides from me in his disgrace, for it was his own actions that led us to this folly. Three ingredients, poorly mixed, made for this fine sauce:

Rumour of a nearby tribe, whispered from a passing trader at the camp brothel; liberal libations indiscriminately imbibed; and sprigs of bravado from men fresh off a strumpet, now sent back home where she belongs. A too heady mix, for this untested son of mine.

So they rode out. All hundred of his bodyguard, the cream of my legions, making for this so-called camp in the dead of night. A hundred horses, each one fed their own weight in grain for every league we travel.

Gone.

Wasted.

Seven returned. Were I not so relieved Constantine was among them, he would have received a hiding not felt since his youth. Pride is the little poison, but it is what pulls a man from the gutters. But like all things, it is needed in moderation. Too much, unearned, is the culprit in this.

He has learned his lesson well enough. And I too have learned. It seems, this Rohan is no fool. He too has his spies and agents. He too tracks our movements. It is no coincidence it was my son's ears that heard tell of this so-called tribe. He has made this personal.

So too will I.

Jai startled awake, a hand on his shoulder drawing him from the depths of sleep. The dim figure of Feng loomed above him, the pre-dawn light casting long shadows across his face. Winter nuzzled her snout against Jai's cheek, her tongue a cool salve against his sleep-warmed skin.

With a good-natured grumble, Jai indulged the beast, scratching her belly until she gave a sigh of contentment and rolled away.

'What happened?' Jai asked, his voice hoarse with sleep.

Feng's eyes were dark rimmed, but a small, crooked smile played at the corners of his mouth. 'You succumbed to sleep,' he said, 'right after Harleen left. We were talking, and next thing I knew you were snoring. A needed respite, I imagine.'

'And you've been up all night, keeping guard,' Jai said.

'On and off,' Feng confirmed, casting a fond glance at the dragon. 'Though Winter here proved a worthy sentinel. Nothing to report. There were a couple of men hanging around near the tent; I think they were eavesdropping, nothing more. They got an earful of your snores instead.'

A sigh escaped Jai as he pushed himself up to a sitting position, his eyes searching the emptiness of the tent. Only Sum remained, deep in slumber, and of course, Winter and Feng. He watched as Winter yawned, her jaws snapping shut with an audible clack. His playful days of letting her gnaw at his fingers seemed far behind him; the dragon was growing fast.

He held a fleeting vision of himself, mounted atop Winter,

soaring through the sky. But such a future required living long enough to see it.

'What do we do now?' Jai asked.

Feng considered this, his brow furrowing as he chewed on his lower lip.

'A messenger arrived while you slept, bearing news of a Great Council to be held, ostensibly to formally welcome you into the tribe, but I suspect their intentions are less than sincere. If you aim to lay claim to the Kidaran throne, today will be our only opportunity to gather support.'

Jai felt the blood drain from his face.

'It's *tonight*?'

Feng nodded, his face grim. 'They don't want to give you a chance to make your case. They want everyone to decide while you're still a stranger.'

'Then they were stupid to leave my quarters so empty,' Jai said. 'I have no cause to linger here in the shadows. Let's step into the light.'

Jai did not wait for Feng's protest, for he was sick of being cooped up within this empty tent, waiting for an assassin to finish him. These were *his* kin, *his* tribe, and he refused to be painted an outcast among them.

Outside, Jai was bracing for a scene of chaos, of the Kidara bustling in preparation for travel. Instead, he was met with a picture of calm. His people moved unhurriedly, each one engrossed in their own tasks or simply strolling and murmuring in relaxed conversation.

'Why aren't we on the move?' Jai asked.

'Because this place is home to upwards of five thousand souls, perhaps more. The Kidara only move every two days, sometimes three. This is true of all the Great Tribes. That is how the Valor were able to catch up to them. It's the rhythm of life on the plains – one that keeps smaller tribes from being swallowed by larger ones. The bigger the tribe, the slower they are.'

'I guess you know this from your merchanting days, huh?' Jai asked.

Feng chose silence over an answer, his eyes fixed on the sprawling camp around them. Jai followed his gaze.

Yesterday had been a whirlwind, but he had only caught a glimpse of the beating heart of the Kidara. Barely a stone's throw away lay the bustling plaza at the core of the moving city.

'Should we bring Winter?' Jai asked.

'I would suggest otherwise,' replied Feng, his voice conciliatory. 'Yes, they all know about your dragon totem. But today, they need to perceive you as one of their own, a true Kidaran. You can't be seen as a pampered princeling flaunting his foreign beast. That's exactly what Nazeem wants you to do. Why do you think he left you with so few comforts? He *wants* everyone to see Winter on the streets.'

Feng's words stung, but it was a harsh truth that Jai had to grudgingly accept. Today, he was a Sithian prince, not Jai the Sabine. He relayed his thoughts to Winter, who had been observing them keenly from the tent's entrance. With a reluctant mewl, the dragon retreated back into the safety of the canvas shelter.

Nazeem wouldn't expect him to go out without her to protect him. But Jai doubted a rushed murder attempt in broad daylight. No, this would have to be done quietly, with a well-placed assassin and a ready scapegoat. That would take time.

'Come,' Jai growled, his gaze steady. 'Nazeem be damned. Let's meet my kin.'

Side by side, they navigated the labyrinthine arrangement of tents, the bustling plaza gradually unrolling before them like a Phoenixian rug.

This was the true heart of the camp. There were baths at its edge, for Jai could see plumes of steam ascending into the sky, their privacy maintained by veils of fine netting, fresh-planted saplings and bamboo. Here, the structures also had a woven roof, as if to trap the steam. And, as was everything here, they were far larger than that of the Valor.

So too were there further differences, for there were great reed mats that covered much of the ground, where clusters of seasoned men and women sat hunched in circles, gnarled fingers working their way through mounds of fresh harvest: onions, garlic and various tubers were methodically peeled and chopped, while stalks of fresh leaves were stripped and prepped.

In another part of the plaza, the mature shoots of spring grass were piled in sacks, their seed-laden heads ground into a fine powder by scores of children with mortar and pestle. The soft, rhythmic whisper of stone against stone was almost calming. Others mixed them with milk and water, before slapping them on steaming-hot stones, making great piles of flatbreads.

Still more churned milk in buckets, or sieved milky barrels for white nuggets of curds, pressing them into squares between tightened boards.

The foods' scents were so strong that it made Jai almost sick with hunger, his empty stomach twisting and churning.

Not a morsel of food had been sent to him the previous night, in stark contrast to Nazeem's earlier show of friendship and guidance. It seemed the pretence had evaporated just as quickly as it had been established, particularly after Feng and Harleen had visited his tent.

Nazeem was nothing if not a shrewd operator; Jai was beginning to appreciate the depth of his cunning.

But Jai was determined to surprise him.

His gaze was drawn to the heart of the plaza, where a large ring was rapidly becoming the focus of attention. Encircled by woven grasses, the space was easily twice the size of the Valor's fighting circle. Already, the ring was starting to throng with men and women, their hands clutching the tell-tale bamboo poles of Talvir.

For all his savvy, Nazeem would have no idea that Jai had not idly spent his time among the Valor. That he had immersed himself in their culture, their language, their ways. Despite the differences of the Tainted, Jai knew Talvir was a shared bond across the Great Steppe. And that meant he could show he was as much a Sithian as a son of Rohan should be.

So let Nazeem believe he was orchestrating a moment of humiliation. Jai was about to turn the tables. With determination tugging his lips tight, he made his way towards the growing crowd, ready to show them not only the Kidaran prince returned from exile, but the seasoned fighter who had survived far worse than a pampered upbringing.

This was his chance to prove his worth to them, in a language they all understood – the dance of Talvir.

Chapter 26

Jai waited on the fringes of the Talvir arena, eyeing the combatants within. Without Winter by his side, he could blend into the crowd with relative ease. The clothing he and Feng wore, a product of their time with the Valor, didn't stand out among the less affluent Kidara congregating in the plaza, and it seemed in a place this large, there were more than a few members of mixed heritage, traders included. He was yet another face in the crowd, and he found it refreshing.

Gone was the foreign savage that he had been in Latium. No longer was he a hostage among the Valor, where each tribesman knew the others as they knew their own reflection.

These were his people. He was *home*.

Jai's gaze was drawn to the circle's centre, as one contender after another vaulted into the arena. They entered a series of duels, some simultaneous, some taken in turns, the result of unheard challenges between opponents meeting within the ring. Every display, every bout, was an act of prowess.

Instead of being awed, however, as he was the first time he had witnessed the Valor compete, Jai was calculating. His eyes, trained by relentless practice and Kiran's supervision, could still easily pick out the wasted movements, the overly wide swings, the failed feints. He found himself mentally stepping into their shoes, analysing their strategies, imagining what he would have done differently.

All around him, onlookers leaned forward, their voices loud with both cheers and jeers, bets being won with swift exchanges of promised wares and swift-palmed coin. It was strange to see money here, once more being reminded of the stark difference between a Great Tribe and that of the Tainted.

He didn't ruminate on it too long, however, as the crowd's timbre shifted. A hush fell over the throng as a woman entered the ring. Her tall, wiry figure cut a sharp contrast against the stocky strength of the previous contenders. She was clothed in simple garb that accentuated the hardened, sinewy lines of her body. Hair, dark as raven's wings, was pulled back from her stern face, revealing a pair of sharp eyes.

A collective groan rippled through the crowd.

'Not her,' a voice muttered close by.

Jai turned to see a well-dressed noble shaking his head, his face a picture of sad resignation.

'What's wrong?' Jai asked of him.

The man barely gave him a look.

'That is Priya,' he muttered, turning away with a shake of his head. 'She's the best here, soulbound to an Alkhara. Not worth betting on. Not worth fighting. She always wins.'

Around the circle, the fevered energy had fizzled like wet wood on a fire. It had been replaced by a restless anticipation. Men shuffled their feet, women murmured among themselves, all keeping their distance. Even Feng had paused his mingling, catching Jai's eye and returning hurriedly through the crowd.

There was an elegance in her solitude. Like a lone wolf daring its pack for a rival, a challenge that was both invitation and a warning. The circle was her territory, and she the undisputed sovereign.

Priya smirked, and put her hands on her hips. Jai knew it would be foolish to face her. He'd hardly bested Kiran more than a handful of times, and she wasn't even the best fighter among the Valor. But something told him Kiran and Zayn were special cases.

Perhaps . . . perhaps he'd hold his own.

Compelled by this lingering thought, Jai made to step forward, only to find his path impeded by Feng's firm grip on his tunic.

'Jai!' Feng's whisper held a tinge of panic. 'What are you doing?'

'I'm going to fight,' Jai answered.

'You'll lose,' Feng said. 'Nobody is even taking bets against her.'

'If I beat on one of these others, I'll look like a bully,' Jai said. 'None of them are soulbound. But if I beat *her* . . .'

'And when you lose?' Feng asked. 'You've had but a few weeks of training.'

'And I was training for months before then. And at least I'll have tried. There's respect in that.'

Jai caught Gurveer in the crowd, his eyes wide, fist pumping the air. Feng's words drifted through.

'Jai, you don't understand . . .'

But Jai's feet were already moving. Because what Feng seemed to not understand was that he had no choice. *This* was the opportunity the Great Steppe was providing him, and to not take it was to lose everything anyway.

He shrugged off his tunic, the garment falling to the ground in a discarded heap. His chest was bare now, vulnerable under the gaze of a hundred eyes. It revealed the steel blue of the Damantine gorget around his neck, marking him as the son of their greatest khan.

A collective gasp swept through the crowd, the whispers among them becoming a dull roar.

Fresh bets echoed around the arena, a frenzy punctuated by the clink of coins changing hands. Jai felt the lingering doubts evaporate, as he heard calls for bets on him to win. People were willing to take a chance on him. Even now.

Jai saw Feng among them, and tried to put it from his mind.

This was his moment. His one opportunity to prove himself a Sithian.

Jai stalked to the stack of bamboo swords at the edge of the circle, trampled grass crunching softly under his feet. Selecting one, he tested its weight in his hand, the familiar grip steadying his nerves.

He approached Priya, bamboo sword at the ready. Her eyes, dark and unreadable, flickered over him, taking in his armour, and the confidence in his stride. He could almost see her appraising him anew, her earlier smirk replaced with wary interest.

Jai bowed, as was the custom, and she returned it.

'I will not go easy on you,' Priya said.

'I'm counting on it,' Jai retorted.

He adjusted his stance, welcoming her to make the first move. He would not reveal his skill. Let her come to him.

Priya did exactly that, her sword sweeping in a wide arc. He countered, once, twice, thrice, their bamboo weapons clashing in a staccato rhythm that echoed through the open air.

The crowd roared their approval, even as Priya danced back, her sword lancing forward in a contradiction Jai did not expect. He arched his back, the blow missing its mark, only for the sword to sweep up and graze his lips.

He tasted copper in his mouth, and spat a glob of blood into the grass. It was a reminder – a message written in pain – that Priya was no ordinary opponent. Jai bared his teeth, even as she lunged again. Her attacks grew fiercer, the winds that drove her becoming a storm, her sword a lightning bolt.

He blocked and parried as best as he could, but she was relentless, her feet dancing her out of range with every rushed counter he could manage. The fight was no longer in his control.

And yet . . . yes, an opening; an overconfident lunge bringing her close. He barrelled forward, locking blades with her. Forcing a battle of strength, in the Locked Horns of Talvir. Priya's eyes widened as he pulsed mana into his body, just as Rufus had shown him.

The roar of the crowd blended with the roaring beat of his pulse in his ears, his world reduced to the twin staves edging ever closer to Priya.

Seizing the moment, he launched his forehead into her face, a brutish trick from Rufus's repertoire. Priya staggered back, but even as Jai heaved to press the advantage, her leg wrapped around his, and a surge of power was pushing back, flipping him onto the grass.

He scrambled to rise, only to find the tip of the bamboo blade pressed into his throat. Priya, her nose dripping with claret, offered him a bloodstained smile.

'Do you yield?' She extended her hand, and for a moment he thought he needed to fight on. His mind a whirl, a decision was formed, and Jai reluctantly took her hand.

There were cheers from the onlookers, but he knew not who it was for. He bowed to his opponent, who returned it with grace, and made his way back to the ring's edge. Only then did the hands clapping his back confirm the applause . . . and his decision to both fight *and* yield when he did.

He might have lost, but he had also won. Not the fight, but the respect of his people. At least some of them, it seemed.

The well-dressed noble shook his head at Jai in amazement, before handing something to Feng, his fingers reluctant to part with it before Feng yanked it free.

Jai expelled a breath he didn't know he was holding and let Feng lead him away.

'We should return to the tent,' Jai muttered, touching his lips to see his fingers stained red.

Feng chuckled drily. 'Oh, but we've got much more to do. There's always a trade caravan following in the Kidara's wake. We have wares to peruse, haggles to win.'

'With what money?' Jai asked.

Feng opened his purse, showing Jai the glint of gold inside. 'I bet your tent, and everything inside.'

Jai looked at him, confused.

'But I lost . . .' Jai said. 'Don't tell me you bet against me.'

'Hardly any money in that,' Feng chuckled. 'I bet you'd last more than thirty heartbeats. Truth be told, it was a narrow call. But it seems this morning was a time of gambles for both of us.'

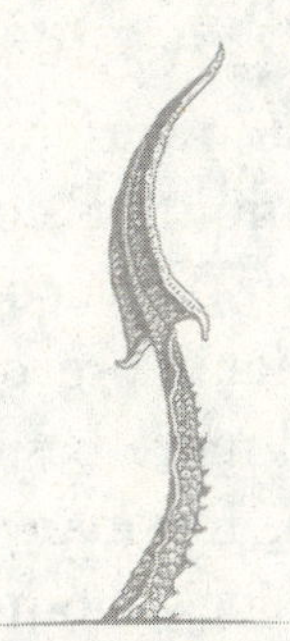

Chapter 27

'What are we buying?' Jai whispered.

They stood at the back of the camp, where the wake of the Kidara's passage through the Great Steppe was evident.

A great furrow had been torn through the grasslands, one that stretched as far as the eye could see. And yet, already, Jai could see the new shoots sprouting, staking their claim to reconquer the land.

But it was the caravans within it that drew Jai's gaze, for there was a chaotic tableau of trade happening in the midst of the great trail, like a bustling satellite town springing up in the trampled grass and mud. Caravans with stretched awnings and tables of wares were scattered in haphazard fashion, the air punctuated with the calls of sellers, the chime of coin and the aromas of exotic wares from distant lands.

Nearby, Jai could see horses, grazing on cut piles of grass, mixed in with grain. He knew from Leonid's diary, they were difficult to keep fed, or to even move them through the grasslands. It was no wonder they followed the Great Tribes, taking advantage of the flattened ground and protection from those that did not honour the Pact.

As a Sabine hostage, he had seen myriad exotic items paraded in front of Latium's royalty, the Sabines' peculiar tastes ranging from the intriguing to the downright grotesque. Yet those items were often the culmination of countless trades along the Kashmere Road, and almost never from the original seller.

Here, the folks were far more diverse, hailing from every corner of the empire, and more besides. There was a distinctly eastern influence, though, for many seemed to hearken from the Phoenix Empire, as Feng's mother had.

Jai could see Feng tense at the sight. It must have reminded him of home. The boy sniffed, and shook himself, as if willing away ill thoughts that clung to him.

'We need to find you more suitable clothing,' Feng said. 'In this place, you must display your bloodline, and wear garments according to your status. No one will follow you dressed as you are.'

He walked into the midst of the strange settlement, without waiting for a reply. Jai followed, trying to resist his mild annoyance at Feng's domineering. He was only trying to help and, if he was being truthful with himself, it was help he desperately needed.

The sheer vibrancy of it all was a stark contrast to the tranquillity of the surrounding grasslands, and it felt as if they had stepped into a different world. Amid the hustle and bustle, the common language was commerce, a tongue that Feng seemed to think he spoke fluently.

Jai was entirely in his hands. He had hardly ever handled coin in his service of Leonid. The royals hardly had need for petty change. Now thrust into this world of haggling, he found himself completely at Feng's mercy.

'How much do we have?' Jai asked, pulling Feng away from the awning of a vendor. His was one of silks, dyed in a dozen colours that drew Jai's eye.

'Perhaps not enough for a full outfit,' Feng said. 'But maybe a shirt to go beneath your gorget. It'll be dark enough in his tent; they won't notice your trousers.'

Feng returned to the table, one draped with an assortment

of cloth in vibrant hues that would have looked more at home on a peacock's tail than in the midst of the Great Steppe. Their vendor, a woman of middle age, wore a dress that showed off all its colours, the rainbow hues clashing with the black of her hair. She glanced up, her eyes bright with a shrewd yet friendly gaze.

'I am Lai,' she said, gesturing to her goods with a flourish that bespoke of a performer. Her hands moved quickly, touching the fabrics with an affectionate familiarity. 'Here to be of service. But remember, if you muddy something with those dirty paws, you're buying it.'

Feng returned her comment with a cheeky smile, holding his hands up to the morning light.

'Don't worry, I've been thoroughly house-trained.'

'And that one?' she asked, motioning at Jai with her chin. 'He looks like trouble.'

Feng grinned once more. 'That there is a Kidaran royal,' he said flippantly. 'So mind your manners.'

'Oh,' she chuckled drily. 'Sure. Next, you'll tell me you're the Phoenix emperor's prized eunuch.'

Jai wiped his nose with his sleeve, glad to see the bleeding had stopped. He looked over the silks. His attention was caught by a bolt of deep blue fabric, the colour as fathomless as the midnight sea.

'Popular here,' Lai said, catching Jai's gaze. 'The royal Kidaran colours, dyed by my own hand. And the finest silk.'

'But it seems the nobles aren't buying,' Feng said, tapping his nose. 'You've brought more of it than old Teji and his nobles wanted.'

Lai waved away Feng's claims, as if they meant little. 'What need have *you* of it then?' she muttered.

'Never you mind,' Feng said, lifting the bolt and holding it to the sunlight. 'Thirty *denarius* for a shirt made from this, by sundown.'

Lai spluttered in exaggerated shock.

'Fifty, surely.'

'Take it or leave it,' Feng said, dropping the bolt as if it were a sack of cold vomit. 'See if any other tribes will wear the royal blue of their rivals.'

Lai grimaced, then took a rough grip of Jai, lifting his arms and laying marked string along their lengths.

'Come now,' she said, kicking his legs akimbo.

'Wha—'

Lai brooked no nonsense, measuring him up in brusque fashion. She eyed his crotch.

'Hangs to the left . . .'

Jai reddened and she winked.

'Finest silk in all the land, sold to a ruffian,' she muttered good-naturedly under her breath. 'You know what this silk can do?'

'Tell me,' Jai said.

'You think it's merely made for style and comfort? Silk, dear boy, is a warrior's wear. It resists a light blow, for it challenges even a tailor's shears. Should a javelin strike you, it won't tear or shred like other fabrics. It'll wrap around the barbs, making it easier to pull out.'

'Really?' Jai murmured, unable to keep a touch of intrigue from his voice. He looked down at the fabric with new-found respect, his fingers grazing its surface.

'And on top of that,' she continued, eyes back on her work, hands navigating his dimensions, 'it's a blessing on a hot day, and a comfort in a cold night. It breathes and warms.'

'The perfect material for the steppe,' Jai concluded, earning himself a nod of approval from Lai.

'Indeed,' she agreed. 'But such virtue comes at a price. Forty-five *denarius*.'

'Thirty-five,' Feng countered.

'Fine,' she said. 'But only because this one here looks like he could do with a bit of luck. That's a bad cut lip if I've ever seen one. Mind you don't bleed on it.'

Jai swore he would not, even as she gave him a light nudge, letting him know she was done. She did leave them with one final bit of advice, though.

'I'm told a man wearing a shirt of my silk always finds luck. Whether in battle, or in the boudoir.'

Feng burst into a hearty laugh while Jai's cheeks flushed a light shade of pink.

'If it doesn't work, at least you'll look great while doing it,' he chuckled.

Jai sighed, and watched as Feng counted out the gold, and the pair argued over the values of the various coinage, weighing them on a set of small scales.

He felt lost. If it had been the Sabines' plan to keep him unprepared for the rigours of this world, they had succeeded in at least this part.

Perhaps he *was* what he knew Teji would make him out to be. A pampered princeling, who knew not even the value of a coin.

'Come on,' Feng said, interrupting his thoughts. 'We've still some coin left over. Let's make a prince out of you.'

Chapter 28

Stepping into his tent, Jai felt the day's excitement tugging at the corners of his mouth, forming a smile. There was an unfamiliar thrill coursing through him, a thrill he soon realised was the joy of *shopping* – owning things that were truly his own. All his life, he'd been clothed in Leonid's castoffs, wearing another man's life on his back.

Now he had a new shirt, and even fresh trousers, unpretentious in their design, but crafted from fine, supple leather that seemed to mould to his form.

The once-familiar feel of his ragged shoes, so loose and worn that he could feel the breeze with every step, had been replaced by sturdy boots. These fresh keks were held tight by sturdy hobnails and were capped with steel, all bound together with thick leather laces.

And while his shirt was yet to arrive, Jai was glad he would finally own something made for his size. Something *he* had chosen.

But upon entering, Jai's eyes were drawn to an unusual sight. A massive barrel, open at the top, took centre stage, with a soap bar, a comb and a jar of oil resting on its rim in a silent invitation. A young boy, no more than twelve winters old, was attending to it.

At the sight of Jai, the boy straightened up, his eyes wide

with a mix of fear and awe. Behind him, Winter sat with a watchful eye, suspicion stamped across her reptilian features.

The boy executed a hasty bow before promptly returning to his task. He was transferring red-hot stones from a wheelbarrow into the water-filled vat, using leather gloves. A soft hiss erupted each time a stone hit the water, sending ripples that shimmered under dimming sunlight that filtered through the canvas above.

The water, already simmering, gave off a pleasant steam that unfurled before vanishing in the dark tent's recesses. The only light came from a beeswax candle, hung on a lantern on the central pillar.

'At your pleasure, my prince,' the boy said, dropping the last of the stones.

Feng held up a hand, before Jai could speak. He hurried to the barrel, tasting the water from a dipped finger. He sniffed at the oil, then picked up the soap, crumbling it in his hands. Testing for poison. Winter, not wishing to be left out, sniffed the same.

Satisfied, Feng shooed the boy away, but not before dropping a small coin into his hands for his troubles.

'I have no way of knowing,' Feng chuckled, as the boy left. 'Just watched his face. He's no assassin.'

'Should I not bathe with the others?' Jai asked. 'Show I am a man of the people?'

Feng shook his head, embracing Sum as she ran up to him.

'No, Jai,' he said. 'Your fight in the ring showed the people you're no spoiled princeling, but the nobility of this place need more than that to change their loyalties. They need to know you are a king in waiting. A man who can guide them safely through the coming war. Even profit from it.'

'Profit?' Jai asked. 'What man could profit in such a time?'

At this, Feng sighed. 'This world, Jai, is one of greed. It was not always this way. Before the War of the Steppe, the Great Tribes followed the old ways. Their wealth was in their khiroi, in the people that served them and they, in turn, protected. But now they seek the luxuries of the east and west. They measure their worth in gold, not in bannermen, or khiroi flesh. And they expect their king to provide that.'

He shook his head.

'We will talk more. But first, you must bathe – the hour grows late. Sum and I will leave you for now – we will go check on Navi, make sure she's being looked after.'

The pair left. Jai undressed, and was surprised to find a burnished bronze looking glass left propped against the barrel. He lifted it, examining himself, even as Winter dipped her snout in the water, churring contentedly at the steaming heat.

Jai examined himself. Touched the beginnings of a beard grown along his chin. Saw the circles beneath his eyes, but also the fullness of his features. He had spent months on the run, and though his diet had left a lot to be desired, he knew the mana had sustained him too. His body, once scrawny, was now corded with tight muscle, his belly taut and creased, his chest proud, and covered in a soft down of black curls.

The man staring back at him from the mirror seemed like a stranger. He had still thought of himself as a mere boy at times, if he thought of himself at all, yet the reflection offered undeniable proof: he was a boy no longer.

Winter chirred impatiently, and Jai set the mirror aside, easing himself into the water with a sigh. It was heavenly.

The heat seeped into his skin, dissolving the aches and pains like a healing spell wiping away a wound. He took the green soap in hand, enjoying its pleasant, minty scent, and the slippery luxury of the rendered khiroi fat. He worked it into a lather, then scrubbed at the grime and sweat of the last few days, and rinsing his tangled hair for good merit.

Then he began the long process of combing out his hair, the horn comb left for him a marvel. The oil he poured and rubbed into his scalp was heavenly, and it was not long till he could pull the comb through without a snag.

Alone at last, he reached for the diary, careful to keep it free from the sudsy water.

If Rohan had hoped to starve us out, he has failed. It keeps Rufinus from my side, but his Gryphon Guard keep the grain shipments coming, and by now we have learned to scavenge some from the land, as they do. Though now Rohan harvests every oasis in our vicinity, we march on.

Yet, still, he does not face me. They are as gnats in the night, never cutting deep enough to do more than sting. But this cannot last forever. I must draw him into battle. If he shall sting me, then I shall do the same. Rufinus and his men can no longer be our shield alone. It is time to let loose the hounds of war.

Jai felt proud of his father in that moment. He set the book aside, and leaned back, stretching his arms.

It had felt so long since he had been clean. He was almost feeling himself again. Jai sank further into the water, its roiling surface reflecting the dim light, creating a pattern of ripples on the canvas roof above.

Winter, her scales glimmering in the steam, slid into the wide tub with serpentine languor, the water rising and pouring over the edges at her arrival.

Jai shifted to make room, and she stretched curled from rim to rim, her belly resting over his lap. A rumbling purr vibrated from her, the comforting sound reverberating deep in Jai's chest.

Jai tilted his head back, letting the water wash over his face. He held his breath, and let his thoughts drift. For soon . . . he would have to stake his claim. Speak for himself, among the nobility of the Kidara.

He could not change their growing avarice, fueled by Nazeem's rumours. But perhaps he could redirect it, use it as a means to ensure their survival. The details were murky. His uncle wanted peace, and with that, the promise of trade and prosperity. But . . . with war too came opportunity. Jai just had to show them where it lay.

His mind summoned half-formed speeches in the heat, espousing his claim to the throne. His sore lips mouthed the cut and jab of imagined arguments, of snappy retorts and rousing calls to action.

It wasn't he who heard it, but Winter – the soft, sibilant tearing of fabric yielding to a blade. He emerged from the water, marvelling that his bond with Winter had grown so strong that he could hear what she did, or at least the feeling of hearing it. He listened, and looked. And there . . . a blade, in the darkness. Sawing a hole in the tent.

Jai's heart hammered a sudden staccato rhythm as he rose from the water. Winter was already scaling the central pole of the tent, her form disappearing into the inky gloom above.

He cast around for a weapon, but the tent was as empty as it had been before. Jai dove into the water, gathering stones into his hands, and tucking them in the folds of his waiting towel. The rhythm of the blade persisted. Already, it was a foot lower than it had started.

He slipped from the bathtub as quietly as he could. The oil bottle was nearby, its amber liquid gleaming under the dim lantern light. He doused his body, a slick coat against grasping hands.

With a soft splash, a handful of crumbled soap joined the foam gathered on the tub's surface. Retreating into the tent's darkest corner, Jai hunkered down, listening intently. He focused, letting his mind drift, pulsing what mana he had through his body. He dared not use a fireball, for he could hear the laughter of children outside and it would pass right through if he missed.

He could hear the laboured breaths of the intruders. Three. Maybe more. And the scrape, scrape, scrape of the blade. Then . . . the scraping stopped.

With moments to spare, Jai cast the shade spell on himself, cursing the flash of green that revealed his place.

It was a hungry spell, and with what he had saved, it would

last less than the span of a held breath. Jai thought to call out, but who could help him? Even if Feng were near, it was not worth sacrificing the element of surprise.

Poised in a low crouch, Jai's gaze flickered to the lone lantern, its light painting a warm halo below Winter's hiding place. With a mental nudge, he signalled her. She knew what to do.

Out from the darkness, five men emerged, like phantoms born from its shadows. They were taking no chances, each one holding a blade, and armoured in steel and leather. Their faces were obscured by cloth bound over the nose, but Jai deduced they were not Sithian. Too pale for that. Their eyes . . . almost looked like Feng's.

The five paused, seeing the tub empty, only for one to raise a hand, and beckon the others to follow. Together, they surrounded the foamy water, and raised their blades high.

With an infusion of mana to his arm, Jai launched the first stone from his arsenal. A *thock* accompanied its collision with the back of an assassin's head, along with a fine mist of blood. The man fell, and the others spun, shouting in alarm.

'Wei!' one cried out, the name loud in the hushed confines of the tent.

Jai's second missile missed its mark, yet it landed a blow to the abdomen that doubled one over. A third stone connected with a crunch, breaking the same man's collarbone, and swiftly followed by a fourth that struck true, spinning him away in a spray of crimson.

Three men remained.

The leader yelled in an unknown tongue, stabbing his blade at Jai's side of the tent. The spell was still active, but he had seconds to spare.

Now. Jai willed his desire to Winter.

There was a roar from above, turning the assassin's gaze long enough for Jai to hurl one last rock, before the lantern fell. It shattered upon the floor, its candle leaving but a sputtering flame that plunged the tent into murky half-light.

Jai's soulbound eyes could see better than most, and they had adjusted to the dark of his corner. With the men slashing blindly, he launched himself from the shadows, leaping to land a stone-weighted punch to an assassin's jaw.

The man's neck snapped like a marionette; Jai's hand sung with pain, as another man yelled, charging Jai's shrouded figure by sound alone. Jai ducked a wild sword swing, then another stab at his belly, until Winter plunged from above, slamming the man to his knees before tumbling to the ground, awkward in her landing. Her tail lanced at his eyes, claws slashing across his belly as the man wailed, his blade falling nerveless from his hands.

The man screeched and staggered back, scrabbling at Winter with his fingernails. He fell into the tub, Winter with him, and the water bloomed red.

The final man, their leader, spun and slashed blindly. Suddenly, a light penetrated the tent, as someone new ducked into the tent, a lantern held high.

The assassin hurled his sword at Jai, even as a woman screamed, and Jai's opponent sprinted for the tent's exit. Jai dove, but his desperate lunge barely grazed the man's retreating form, Jai's fingers ripping a swathe of fabric from his back.

There was a thud, and Jai saw the assassin fall. The man rose, only for a boot to his head to snap him back, onto the floor. He began to snore, and twitch horribly, until the boot came down once more.

Winter erupted from the water, screeching her displeasure, hackles raised as the new arrival picked up a fallen lantern, and then sparked a flint.

Lai's face appeared in the gloom, as she blew the candlewick back into life. She held up Jai's blue shirt, even as she nudged the assassin with her boot. A fleck of blood had landed upon the silk, and she licked a thumb and rubbed it gingerly with a sigh.

'You're still paying for this,' she said.

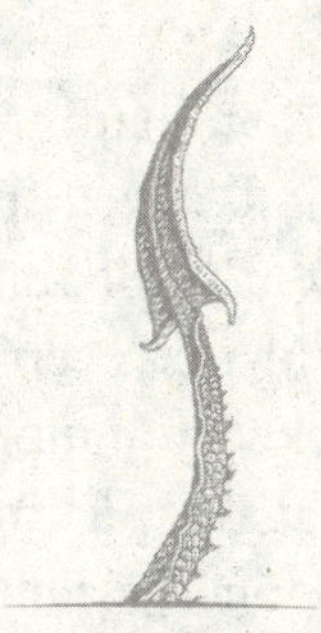

Chapter 29

Jai panted on the floor, more from adrenaline than any true exertion. It had all happened so fast, it could have been less than thirty seconds before the floor was littered with corpses.

Lai nudged at the man she had killed, her face inscrutable. Jai knew the life of a steppe trader was a treacherous one, but even he was surprised by her cold indifference.

'I know this man,' she said.

'Who are they?' Jai demanded.

Lai gave him a look that told him he should watch his manners, and Jai relented, taking a deep breath.

'Please,' he said. 'I heard one of them was called Wei.'

She shook her head, and hunkered down, bringing the lantern close. Winter snarled nearby, as if Lai were stealing her food.

'These are traders. This is Wei's brother, Bao. There were five of them?'

Jai nodded, reaching out to Winter and laying a calming hand on her head. She snorted, and shook it off, prowling to the place where the men had cut their way in.

'Your uncle must've offered a fortune to get this cowardly lot to risk their necks here,' she said. 'They're no assassins. Just bullies.'

'You know about my uncle?' Jai asked.

Lai shrugged.

'I knew the Kidaran prince had arrived back when you and Feng approached me, but I never thought you were who he said. Not least because you're of mixed blood – the rumours said you were Arjun. I did not even know you existed. More fool me – should have asked for more money for this shirt.'

She sniffed, and stood again, picking her way over the bodies to replace Jai's lantern upon the tent pole. As she passed him by, she handed him a towel.

Jai realised he was still entirely naked. He swiftly wiped himself dry, scraping off as much of the oil as he could. Then he pulled on his trousers, nearly falling over in his haste.

It was just in time too, for Jai heard the approach of footsteps, and snatched up a blade, even as Feng burst into the tent.

Feng stared, wide-eyed, and began to curse.

'It's all right, Feng,' Jai said.

Feng's eyes bulged.

'What . . . ? They dared . . .'

'It's okay, Feng,' Jai said again.

Feng took a deep breath, closing his eyes from the bodies. 'Jai, the Great Council is starting earlier than they said. I should never have trusted the messenger – it's happening right now.'

Jai took the shirt from where Lai had left it, and shrugged it on, along with his father's armour. He didn't bother to button it, for his chest was red with blood. He tugged on his socks, hopping from one foot to the next.

'Listen,' Feng said. 'You have to delay. You're half-dressed, and your hair isn't braided. We can use this. I just need time to—'

'We do this now,' Jai snapped, pulling on his boots. 'While the blood is still wet.'

He turned to Lai, and bowed, as was the custom of their people.

'When this is all over, come to me. I owe you a debt.'

She smiled at him. 'You can count on it.'

Jai ducked down, and picked up the man who had been called Wei. He humped the body onto his back, and called Winter with a thought.

'You can come with me,' Jai said to Feng. 'Or go with Lai. I don't know how tonight is going to end.'

Feng's throat bobbed as he gulped, and he knelt and clutched Sum close.

'Be good,' he whispered. 'Stay with Auntie Lai.'

Sum nodded, and he gave her a kiss upon the forehead. Feng set his jaw, and straightened his tunic, before scooping up Leonid's diary from Jai's rucksack.

'I'm ready.'

THE JOURNEY TO TEJI'S grand abode was not far, yet Jai chose the long way, ensuring his grim cargo was displayed for all to witness. The dead assassin bore the weight of his stark message, slung over his shoulder in a morbid display of the dangers of crossing the returned khan.

The guards at the entrance blanched at the sight of him, but neither barred his way as he strode through, Feng and Winter on his heels.

Within, Teji's bedchamber had been cleared away, leaving an enormous space filled with what looked like every Kidaran man and woman worth their salt. Heads turned upon his arrival, and Jai could see their kohl-darkened eyes widen at the sight of him, a bloodied, open-shirted ruffian striding down the red-carpeted corridor towards a raised throne.

Each of the Kidaran nobility was dressed in their most ostentatious finery, decadence on full display. Jewels, both precious and semiprecious, glittered from earlobes and necklines, catching the torchlight. Gold and silver bracelets encircled wrists and fingers, and every one bore the sigil and colours of their house, a menagerie of animals, flowering plants and the natural world embossed upon their attire.

A pregnant silence hung over them, the rush of murmured conversations and whispered intrigues cut short, replaced by a palpable tension that seemed to choke the air. Jai could feel their eyes boring into him, questioning his audacity, some excited, others grim and troubled.

Jai came to a halt at the end of the pathway, where the great horns of the Kidaran throne cast shadows across his face. Teji reclined there, a leg draped nonchalantly over its arm, making no move to greet him.

The Kidaran king was a picture of controlled power and inscrutable calm, fingers steepled against his lips as he watched Jai, the bloodied interloper, draw closer. His clothing was a sight to behold, all draped swathes of embroidered silks, and a crown made of khiroi teeth resting upon his head. A blue jewel of enormous size nestled in his ear, glittering in the torches arrayed behind him.

And there, beside him, was Nazeem. His hands were in constant motion, fussing with a sheaf of parchment, another adjusting the robes of his master. A silver chain hung from his neck, supporting a pendulous amulet that bore the great horned Alkhara, the crest of the Kidara tribe. At the sight of Jai, Nazeem leaned closer to Teji, a sense of urgency in his hushed whispers. His dark eyes flickered with calculation, underlined by a faint hint of trepidation.

Jai let the corpse fall, the grim thud against the rug all the greeting he offered. The audience rippled with gasps, the grisly sight breaking the decorum of the regal gathering.

'You do not kneel for your khan?' Nazeem demanded, his voice like slick oil.

'Whom do you ask?' Jai replied. 'Our dear regent? Or the true heir, returned?'

Nazeem faltered, his eyes bulging at Jai's forthright words. The devious man had once again underestimated him it seemed.

'So kind of my uncle to greet me so,' he called to Teji, for the benefit of the onlookers. 'He sent five men to warmly welcome me during my bath, unarmed and unprepared.'

He looked directly at Teji now.

'Only five?'

With a defiant lift of his chin, he slapped his chest.

'It will take more than that, Uncle, to usurp my throne.'

Teji finally rose, his hands raised in an attempt to quell the rising chaos. His command was met with almost instantaneous silence. It was clear, Jai's uncle still held sway in this court.

'Which men?' Teji asked, his voice strangely different without the booze slurring his tongue. 'This is the first I hear of it.'

'Who else would want me dead?' Jai called out. 'The Sabines? So soon, after my arrival? Perhaps a little bird flew to Latium and back, to tell of it?'

'Quite,' Nazeem said, nodding gravely.

There was laughter in the audience, enough for Nazeem to cast a glare until it silenced.

'I have come for my throne,' Jai called out. 'My claim is greater than yours. Everyone here knows it. Do you deny it?'

Teji responded with a hearty laugh, throwing his head back in apparent amusement. 'Oh, what an entertaining spectacle this boy has arranged,' he commented, rising to his feet with Nazeem's assistance. 'I can only apologise to my esteemed guests for this diversion.'

Jai stood in silence, crossing his arms. Blood pooled at Jai's feet, and Teji wrinkled his nose in distaste.

'What you see before you is an imposter. Bought and paid for by the Sabines.' He turned his gaze to Feng. 'No more my brother's son than this lapdog, who lied to us so prettily in his audience.'

Feng stiffened at the accusation, but remained silent as Jai laid a calming hand. He sent a thought to Winter, and the dragon let out a deep rumble, enough to quell the murmuring of the nobles behind. A reminder of the lies that dripped from Teji's tongue, for Winter might be strange, but she was evidence enough that Jai was no imposter.

Jai turned, and pulled his shirt wide, displaying his father's breastplate upon his bloodied chest.

'My uncle would paint me as Emperor Titus's pawn, sent

here to usurp him. Why, pray tell, would Titus need another pawn when he already commands one? Do enlighten us, dear Uncle. Tell them of our peace mission with the Sabines.'

The tent was still as a grave then. Teji cleared his throat, his mouth forming and reforming words, until Nazeem stepped forward, raising his hands for a silence that was already there.

'A breastplate, even one of Damantine steel, is an easy forgery. Your dragon is simply proof of payment for your crimes. Your brothers hardly knew you. We've heard of you here, though. Leonid's arsewiper. A preening peacock. Is that who you would call upon to be your khan?'

This last question, he addressed to the crowd, and Jai knew Nazeem had struck a chord. Yet Jai stood proud, letting Winter's growl show his displeasure.

'Who do you call khan now? Is it the one who sent my brothers and I there?' Jai demanded. 'Who agreed to the so-called peace terms that left tens of thousands of our brothers and sisters in fetters? *This* coward. A traitor to my father's name.'

Nazeem derisively spat to the side at Jai's words, and now it was Jai who held up a hand for quiet as the uproar began again. It came slowly, but it came. He had them. They were listening.

'Let me get this straight,' Jai uttered, letting disdain colour his words. 'Titus allowed me to slay Leonid and abscond with his bride and a rare dragon. All to take a throne that is already mine by right?'

'And murdered your own brothers,' Teji interjected. 'Beloved Arjun, and Samar. An exchange of life for life. You cleared his path to the throne, and he cleared yours.'

Jai responded with a hollow laugh, 'And then this supposed puppet master sends assassins after me? Isn't that your implication?'

He nudged the lifeless assassin with his foot, leaving Teji flustered. With false conviction he murmured, 'The Sabines know I am reasonable. You . . . you are nothing but a rabid dog.'

'Which is it?' Jai demanded. 'A preening peacock or a rabid dog? A Sabine target or their puppet? Why send me all this way, only to have me murdered?'

This even Nazeem had no answer for.

But Jai did.

'I have bled, and fought, and killed to be here. I have clawed my way out of the dark pit you threw me into. Watched my brothers choke on their own blood, watched the life drain from their eyes. Killed the Lion of the Sabines, our people's greatest nemesis. Travelled the length and breadth of an empire, broken the chains of the great gaol of Porticus. Survived captivity, survived assassins sent by my own kin, with nowt but my bare hands.'

He mounted the throne's raised platform, and turned to address his people.

'I am your king, by blood, by oath and by right. I bring you the body of my would-be killer, the diaries of our age-old foe, the breastplate that still bears my father's blood, and a dragon from our allies in the next Great War. What does Teji give you? Lies, nothing more.'

Nazeem held up a finger.

'But you are riteless,' he said. 'No more a man than a babe on his mother's teat.'

To Jai's surprise, this drew consternation. Feng joined Jai on the platform, as if sensing Jai's confidence wavering.

'And what chance has he had to be rited?' Feng called out. 'Was he supposed to Rite into the Tainted tribe that broke the Pact to capture him?'

Now men and women stood at the back of the tribe. Shouts of 'nay' and 'no' were audible, even amid the tumult of voices.

'He will lead you to ruin!' Teji bellowed, bringing his fists crashing down on the throne armrests. 'This riteless pup is a warmonger, drunk on revenge. As if he does not already have enough blood on his hands. I will not stand by, and let our people suffer.'

'Drunk?' Jai spat. 'Careful, Uncle. Lest you call the kettle black.'

A murmur of agreement rippled through the crowd.

Teji rose, levelling a pudgy finger at Jai, then swung his gaze towards Nazeem, as if seeking approval. The vizier gave a barely perceptible nod.

'If you wish to follow him into war, then I will abide by the rules of our people,' he said. 'But I have no desire to see the Kidara die for a lost cause. I renounce you, Jai, and whoever would follow you.'

And with that he stood, and allowed Nazeem to hand him the paper the vizier had been holding.

Teji straightened and accepted the parchment Nazeem proffered. With a flourish, he struck off his crown, allowing it to clatter upon the floor.

'I hereby announce my severance from the Kidara tribe. I will depart, as is my right, establishing my own tribe, as permitted by the Pact. All those who wish to accompany me are welcome. But before you choose, think carefully. Remember, my khiroi and wealth go with me. It was Rohan who left this tribe in a state of frailty and penury. Claim your inheritance then, boy. What is *mine* leaves with me.'

And just like that . . . the council descended into chaos.

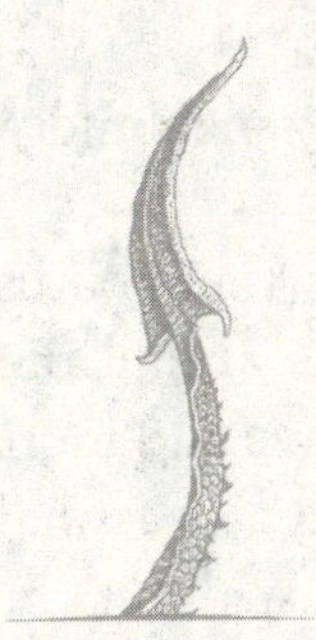

Chapter 30

'Can he do that?' Jai demanded, his voice barely audible above the burgeoning chaos.

'I don't know if we can stop him,' Feng shouted back.

With a commanding whistle, Teji summoned his staunchest allies, men and women dressed in the most regal of finery, whose loyalties must lie more in gold than in blood.

As one, they followed Teji as he stomped towards the tent's exit, clearly well prepared for what was about to take place. Contingencies in contingencies . . .

Nazeem flashed Jai a sly smile as he caught his gaze, following Teji's procession out of the room. Jai knew this could not have been planned in a day. This was what had awaited Arjun had he lived to return.

The vizier was a cunning schemer.

Still more followed Teji, leaving their places like soldiers routing from battle. At the sight of the exodus, nobility formed clusters around their peers, raising their banners and roaring commands. Voices escalated to shouts, and shouting devolved into skirmishes, fists flying. Had weapons been allowed, it might have become a bloodbath.

'Winter!' Jai called, leaping onto the throne. 'Now!'

Winter's chest expanded as she drew a deep breath . . . and then she let it out in an earth-shattering roar, one that quietened the room, save for the few men and women still wrestling upon the ground.

'Do the Kidara forget their oaths so swiftly?' Jai shamed. 'Let the traitors leave. We are all the stronger without them.'

'They will take their leave and more besides!' a noble shouted. 'Teji and his loyalists own at least half the khiroi! What chance have we against a legion without them?'

'We will find more,' Jai called out, even as voices were raised once more. 'I swear it. We are the Kidara. We will endure, and we will overcome.'

His words echoed in the tent, and still they stared at him. By now, the scuffles had ended, leaving several with bloody noses, shaking themselves free of the hands that sought to keep them there. Their resentment was evident in the flare of their nostrils and the glare in their eyes. Jai took his place on the throne, feeling the cool press of the large horns against his back.

He knew he could not keep them here. They would steal away in the night, and take more than their belongings with them.

'Anyone who wishes to leave is free to do so. No one will stop you,' Jai said, his voice clear and cold. 'But know this – by leaving, you betray your tribe and join a traitor. You, and all those who follow Teji, will be branded oath breakers, traitors and cowards. All the Sithia will know what your new tribe stands for.'

His proclamation was met with a stunned silence, followed by a flurry of movement as several tore away from their peers and stormed out of the tent. Their departure thinned the crowd, leaving the final count less than half as full than when the council had begun.

Feng stood, and cleared his throat.

'All hail, Jai, son of Rohan, khan of the Kidara, first of his name!'

'Hail!' came the resounding reply.

Feng lifted the crown from where it lay, and lowered it onto Jai's head. It was heavy, a reminder of the responsibility now bestowed upon him. Jai knew this night was not done yet. He surveyed those that remained.

Among them, he recognised Harleen, Gurveer and others. His remaining supporters were mainly the elderly and the young, their attire less ostentatious than those who had departed.

They were waiting. Waiting for his command.

'Go, protect your khiroi!' Jai ordered. 'Make sure Teji takes only what is his. Avoid bloodshed wherever possible, but keep what is ours!'

Harleen gave a deep bow, then addressed the others.

'Gurveer, lead our warriors and secure our khiroi in the plaza. They'll have difficulty seizing them there. Everyone else, gather what's left and join us. If they intend to plunder us, there will be blood. My lads, stay outside the tent. Protect your khan.'

She turned to Jai, and bowed once more.

'With your permission, my king.'

'Go,' he said. With that, Jai gave a small nod, triggering a flurry of action as his followers rushed out of the tent. He moved to join them, but Harleen subtly motioned him to wait, until it was only the two of them left. Outside, the air was filled with the noise of raised voices but no screams of battle – at least, not yet. Jai itched to go and observe, but for now, Harleen had something to share.

'Please,' she said. 'Let your warriors do their work. You are far easier to protect here. Out there, you will be too great a distraction.'

Jai acquiesced, settling back into his chair. She then went to take her leave, but faltered in her step.

'Tell me,' Jai said, raising his hand. 'What's on your mind?'

'You did well,' she said, her head still bowed. 'But know, we have hard days ahead.'

Jai nodded gravely, and summoned her closer with a beckoning hand.

'I will not pretend to know our tribe as you do, or what must be done. I appoint Feng as my vizier for his wisdom and loyalty. And you, Harleen, will serve as my steward.'

Harleen bowed deeply.

'I thank you. But that is not what I have stayed to discuss.'

'Then speak freely,' Jai said. 'And you can look me in the eye, Harleen. I will not stand on ceremony in my court.'

She hesitated, then straightened.

'I will be frank. We walk a razor's edge. Teji is correct – by our laws, a royal's sibling has every right to leave this tribe and form his own. The stink of this betrayal will follow his lackeys, for they *have* broken our laws – Teji's attempt to usurp the crown precludes his right to form his own tribe. I have long suspected they were planning this for when Arjun returned from exile. But I had thought I had years left to prepare for it. You were right to let them leave. Had you not . . . the tribe would have torn itself apart this very night – and on a night they seem to have us at a disadvantage.'

Jai nodded, feeling some relief. He had not been sure of the decision.

'But it is not tonight that concerns me. It is in the days to come.'

She looked behind her, checking for eavesdroppers, and approached the throne.

'By our laws, there is an amnesty when a tribe divides. But three days hence, Teji may treat us as any other tribe. And to keep this pretence of lawfulness, of following the Pact . . . he will wait.'

Jai stared at her, trying to understand.

So she explained. 'He will come for us in three days. To take back what he left behind, and return his followers' honour.'

Jai felt his palms grow slick with sweat. There was so much about this world he did not know.

'Thank you for your stewardship,' Jai said, trying hard, but failing ever so slightly, to keep his voice steady. 'Please, tell me what course you would advise me take?'

She gathered herself, turning away from him.

'Tomorrow,' she said, 'we run.'

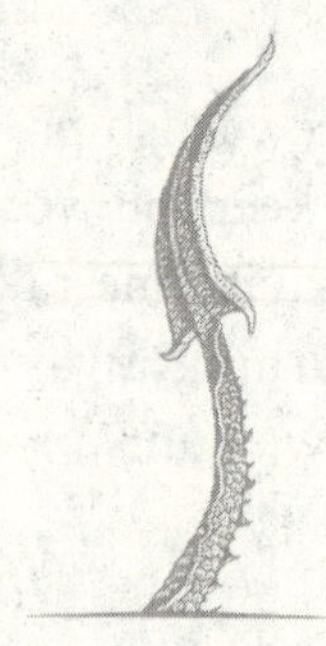

Chapter 31

Jai sat, alone in the tent, his hand absently rubbing Winter's head. The little dragon nuzzled up to him, nudging at the throne, annoyed that it got in the way of her draping herself over his lap.

The tent was so large, and so empty. Outside, the noise had fallen away, leaving him in its muffled silence. At his feet, the corpse of Wei stared through him, a look of shock upon his face.

Jai's stomach turned, and he looked away.

'You did it,' Feng said, smiling broadly at Jai. 'You're . . . you're khan!'

Jai tried to return the smile, but it was but a shadow.

'Then why do I feel . . .' He trailed off, struggling to articulate the turmoil within him. '. . . Like I've just lost?'

Feng gave a heavy sigh, and let his head drop to his chest.

'You've weathered worse storms,' he remarked. 'Could you imagine you would be here someday, when you hung from the poles of Porticus?'

At that, Jai chuckled, but it was tinged with bitterness.

'Yes, but this time, if I stumble, it's not just my life that's at stake . . . but the legacy of my father, of Arjun and Samar, everyone that stayed behind . . . All could be lost.'

Seeing Feng's troubled gaze, Jai gathered himself. Now was

the time for action, tired though he was. Three days was not a long time. Decisions had to be made.

'What can we expect from Teji?' Jai asked.

'As Harleen said—'

'Beyond that.'

'They'll need at least the night,' Feng said after a moment's thought. 'Just as we will. Some of his supporters may have been privy to his plans, but for most, this is a shock. They'll be angry that Teji forced this upon them. Some may even be regretting their choice.'

'We're in the same boat, then,' Jai replied with a rueful grin. 'At least there's that.'

'Nazeem will keep them in line,' Feng said. 'He will have something on every one of them. He trades in secrets and lies.'

'How do you know this?' Jai asked.

'Many who trade with the Kidara do, including my parents. He is a treacherous viper. Did you know, he was once your father's most favoured man? He was also born Tainted.'

'And yet still he joined a tribe like the Kidara?' Jai asked.

Feng nodded.

'How?' Jai asked. 'I thought the Tainted were banished.'

Feng nodded. 'It is rare, but possible – just like your ransom. Only a khan can make it so, declaring them cleansed of their sin – but they will often remain Tainted in the eyes of all but the tribe that welcomed them. It was a controversial decision, and Nazeem never managed to shake off the stigma.'

'And yet?' Jai asked.

'And nothing.' Feng shrugged. 'He is loyal to no one. Only the coin in his pocket, and the power it commands.'

'I had no idea,' Jai said.

'Rohan risked his reputation just to bring Nazeem into the fold. Shielded him, promoted him. Now look at him. Plotting against the man's last remaining heir. You think your opponent is Teji, but he is but a sotted fool, content to spend his days in a haze of wine, poppy and concubines. Nazeem is your true opponent. And mine.'

Feng turned and lifted his shirt, revealing to Jai a crisscrossing of red welts. Jai's hand rose unbidden to his mouth, horrified. The sight churned his stomach. He couldn't fathom how Feng managed to stand, let alone walk, in such a condition.

'This was what he did to me, after I demanded your ransom. To extract the truth of your claim. Thank the Mother he believed my lies.'

'Feng, you must . . . I don't know. I have little mana to spare. Is there a healer here?'

Feng lowered the shirt, and shook his head.

'If there is one, they'll be busy securing their own belongings tonight and will spare no time for me, even if the khan commands it. It's of no matter, though. Tonight . . . we must make a plan.'

Jai hissed out a breath, feeling a wave of exhaustion sweep over him. The hour had grown late, and the adrenaline that kept him alert and focused was gradually ebbing away. Despite the aid of mana, he'd used much of it in the fight, and the crushing need for slumber was settling in – with little mana, he knew couldn't stave off the necessity of sleep for long.

But now, he realised . . . he could help Feng. For he knew the healing spell – more or less. He knew it was one that was complex, and required a good deal of practice to perfect. He had rarely attempted it himself, for it was a hungry spell, and he had only trained on the lesser majicking of flame. But then, he had succeeded in Balbir's shade spell, and that was no easy thing.

'Come closer,' Jai said. 'Please, Feng. Sit here in front of me.'

Feng complied, a sigh of relief escaping his lips. Jai then lifted his hand, modelling his gesture after the healing technique he had observed Erica and Rufus use. He formed a closed fist, fingers slightly raised and flexed just so.

Gritting his teeth, Jai forced mana through his hand, and out in the direction of Feng's back. To his surprise, a sputtering golden light emerged. His form was not perfect, and the spell was wasteful, casting sparks and offshoots that fizzled into nothingness.

But miraculously, it had some effect. The angry wounds turned from raw red to pink, the few scabs sloughing away to fall like a bleeder's leeches upon the floor.

When he finally withdrew, he found his mana reserves down to all but nothing. The wounds remained too, but at least they no longer wept. It was an inefficient casting, but worth every mote of mana expended. Jai refused to mirror Nazeem's ruthless tactics. He firmly believed in the principle that loyalty begot loyalty – a creed he vowed to uphold.

Exhausted yet determined, Jai rose from his throne. Feng looked over his shoulder, tracing the now-healing scabs with his fingers, astonishment clear on his face.

'I . . . I don't know what to say, Jai,' he stammered, 'I thank you.'

'No need for that,' Jai responded. 'You're not just my vizier, Feng. You're my friend. We look out for each other.'

His resolve then hardened, returning to the issue at hand.

'Let's focus on what's next,' Jai continued. 'Teji and Nazeem may hold off until the three-day amnesty is over for the sake of their reputations, but we should not assume they will play fair. They will follow us, though not so close that they would lose the element of surprise. The first question is . . . where do we go?'

Feng nodded in agreement, standing to join Jai. He cast about, and his eyes lit up. The page Teji had read from earlier lay discarded on the ground. He picked it up, flipped it over to the blank side and grabbed a piece of charcoal from the remnants of the dismantled bedchamber's hearth.

He drew an arrow pointing north in the corner, and then made a rough sketch of the Kidaran sigil in the centre.

'We are here, the Kidara,' he said, pointing to the sigil. Then, pursing his lips, he scribbled a crude representation of a phallus on the paper, flashing a quick grin at Jai. 'And here are Teji and Nazeem.'

Jai couldn't help but let out a snort. His newly appointed vizier, it seemed, had retained his sense of humour at least.

'This is the Great Steppe,' Jai said. 'It's all a vast expanse, nothing but open space.'

Feng tapped his nose, a wry smile playing on his lips.

'That may be, but even in a barren desert, there are waypoints for those who know where to look. While you were in the bath, I made a few enquiries with the Kidaran scouts. It took some silver, but they were willing to share knowledge about this area.'

Jai looked at Feng in astonishment, and Feng's grin widened.

'I had to know where to run with Sum if things turned sour.'

Jai started.

'Sum!' he said. 'We should make sure she's safe.'

'Trust me – that was foremost on my mind. The traders are the safest place for her right now,' he said. 'Now, let me focus. I need to remember.'

He closed his eyes, his brow furrowing as he concentrated before continuing.

'The Valor took a path less trodden to get here, but we are now in one of the main migration routes of the khiroi. There are oases around here – that should help us shore up our supplies.'

Feng marked the map with a symbol that looked like a cross between a leaf and a water droplet, in a scattered fashion around the crude map.

Jai furrowed his brow.

'Why should we need supplies?' he asked. 'Don't the Kidara live off the land as the Valor do?'

Feng shrugged.

'Some,' he said. 'But there are thousands here. Less now, of course. The tribe would have to spread out much further than the Valor to harvest enough for everyone. It leaves larger tribes vulnerable to attack, and that is something we can ill afford, now more than ever. But the oases – they're a treasure trove. Where do you think the bamboo grows, or the fruits come from? Most of the large tribes bounce between them and buy the rest.

'We have at least a dozen oases within reach,' Feng said. 'When we know where we're headed, we'll chart a route through as many as we can.'

Lost in thought, Jai leaned over the impromptu map, tracing invisible paths with his fingers. He recalled Leonid, in those early days, poring over his own maps on a grand table that now lay somewhere collecting dust.

Vivid memories surfaced, of receiving a hiding for meddling with the intricately carved figures that represented the legions and the formations of adversaries. To Jai, they had been but toys. Now he would likely seek his own.

The old man had seemed to question every battle, every strategic move he'd made, even after the victories had been won. As if he was constantly seeking a better, more efficient path.

In those days, Jai had found such activities tedious. He'd preferred diving into the antiquated scrolls that chronicled the exploits of Leonid's predecessors, or the young king, hardly older than himself, beset from all sides, before developing the greatest army the world had ever known, and carving an empire the like of which had never been seen.

But sitting upon the throne, with the weight of his people on his shoulders, he began to comprehend the value in Leonid's method. The need for planning, for strategic thought, was all too clear.

'What else?' Jai asked.

Feng sketched the crossed lupins of the Valor, some way east of the Kidara.

'They'll be moving hell for leather,' Feng muttered, 'but they're there.'

Jai rubbed the stubble upon his chin, thinking.

'Magnus's legion is to the west, and we know that is where Teji headed before,' he said. 'The Valor may be useful to us yet. Let's do Teji no favours. We head east, at daybreak.'

Chapter 32

There is heathen blood in the grass now. A dozen Gryphon Guard can take out a small tribe in the dead of night, before they can even mount their khiroi. These herders know only to look to the horizon, never thinking to turn their eyes to loftier heights. There is more than one lesson in that, I think.

But this war will not be won by striking these pitiful bands that scratch out an existence in this barren place. Hell, most did not even know we were here before the gryphons ripped their livers out.

Now they do more than harry my supply trains. Twice now, we have awaited replenishment, only to be greeted by the smoke of their smouldering wagons in the skies. They are as jackals; but they know not the lion lies in wait.

We have not enough Gryphon Knights to both protect our supply lines and hunt the smaller tribes of the Great Steppe. So I have spoken with the traders that have experience in these matters. Fine wine loosened their lips, and I have gleaned much.

There is a second caste among these so-called Sithians, though few use that name in parlance, preferring the banner of their tribe to identify their peoples. Indeed, it appears my Gryphon Knights have laid waste to this second caste, for they travel in smaller groups, rejected from any society but their own. Tainted, the Sithians call them.

These Tainted tribes follow no laws but their own, and will rob the traders that frequent this place. So these traders have devised a way to defend themselves, alongside the Phoenixian mercenaries that accompany them.

Their wagon trains form a square, such that their khiroi cannot ride through, slaughtering with their blades as they are wont to. Within, the traders form a circle, where every man, woman and child that can hold a pole brandish pike, or halberd, or spear. Wherever a rider might penetrate, swinging with their long blades, a row of sharp points greets them.

This tactic has improved things, and given the Gryphon Guard time to hunt. Rufinus's nephew, Magnus, has made a name for himself already. He bandies around with a string of bloodied ears about his neck. Even I can see that some are no smaller than an infant's. Such brutality is a necessary antagonism of my enemy, but I cannot say I am glad of it.

Even Rufinus cannot stomach such slaughter, for his men kill them by the hundreds. Only time will tell if Rohan's can stomach the same.

'Form up, form up!' Harleen's command echoed across the bustling plaza, cutting the morning air. Men, women and children darted to their designated spots – the able-bodied members of the tribe taking the front in a neat formation, the elders and little ones filling in behind in haphazard fashion.

Jai oversaw the proceedings from a platform cobbled together from crates and draped with cloths bearing his house's sigils. It was a makeshift affair, reflecting their current state. Teji had stripped them of everything else.

Feng and Jai's remaining nobles stood alongside them, surveying their tribe the morning after the split. Many of these nobles Jai had met already, for they had accompanied Harleen and Gurveer into his tent that first day. But the multitude of new faces among them heartened him; the Kidaran nobles did not betray their khan so easily.

As the Kidaran subjects gathered in what remained of the plaza, Jai couldn't help but compare them against his uncle's new tribe, who were gathered a few hundred feet from the edge of camp. Their numbers looked to be the same as his – roughly two thousand each, according to Harleen's estimation – but Jai knew that much of the wealth of the tribe was with Teji.

Even now, his uncle's followers milled about, sorting through furniture piled high. In truth, he was glad of it. Teji had been foolish, taking everything that could not be nailed down. Sure, it meant more riches, but it also meant more to be carried by their khiroi. Harleen, in her wisdom, had focused on retaining those above all else and her efforts were rewarded, for she had reported they had succeeded in retaining two hundred of them, along with a glut of doe calves. Teji had a hundred more, but considering the disparities in the herds' burdens between the two factions, Jai felt they had come out the better in that exchange.

Even now, Jai's tribe's khiroi stood, lowing loudly, unhappy to have their herd divided in two. Despite them being split up, Jai had still never seen so many, particularly up close. The grooms were visibly on edge, striving to keep the massive animals from breaking away to join their brethren in Teji's camp. Across the way, Jai was certain Teji's grooms did the same.

It was clear they would soon need to embark on their journey.

'Khan Jai of the Kidara, first of his name!'

Jai started at Harleen's words. Last night, he had thought he'd spend it tossing and turning, meticulously crafting his speech. Instead, he'd been jostled awake by Feng from the Kidaran throne, with little more than a sore back to show for it.

Now there was no applause, nor had he expected it. The mood was sombre, and there was a chill to the spring air.

He cleared his throat, his mind a blank. He looked to Feng and Harleen, and both subtly nodded.

'I know I am not the returned khan you expected,' Jai called out. 'Nor was this how I intended to start my reign. But I promise you this: we are the stronger for it.'

The crowd was restless, but silent. He could feel the weight of their eyes upon him, and still more words tripped from his mouth unbidden.

'We have cast out the traitors,' he called out, stabbing a finger in Teji's direction. 'And you see what kind they are. They took everything they could. Not from me. From *us*. From their brothers and sisters.'

He paused. There was anger in their eyes. But he could not tell where it was directed, even if those eyes stared at him now. He was in it now, though, and pressed on.

'Too long, Teji has hidden in his chamber. He cares only for the wine in his belly, and the gold in his coffers. When did he last walk among you?' Jai demanded.

He could sense it now. That simmering resentment. Almost smell it.

'He has not ruled you in years, not truly. No, he sits upon the throne like a child upon a calf. And lets a snake in the grass, Nazeem, take the reins.'

'Tainted prick!' a woman screamed.

Jai winced at that, but stilled his tongue, because he could sense others held the same sentiment as that woman. The crowd began to stir, their passion ignited. It was time to steer the course of their burgeoning fury.

'*We* are the true tribe. We, who bear the khiroi's mark. Who know our strength is in the blood of our khiroi, in the arms of our kin, in the unity of our tribe. We do not follow the ways of the Sabines. We do not crawl towards the wealth of the Phoenixians. We are Sithians. We are the Kidara!'

Their cheers responded to his rallying cry. It was not a deafening roar, but it was enough.

'We ride east,' Jai bellowed. 'Steward! Give the command.'

Harleen leaped into action, her words cracking like a whip. The camp dissolved into a frenzy of activity, though the khiroi had long been loaded up for the journey. Already, the grooms were clucking their beasts into position, as men and women vaulted into saddles. Still more khiroi, mostly the old and the calves, were already loaded up with the belongings of the Kidara, but they were not overburdened. They would travel light . . . and that was how Jai liked it.

'Your ride, my king,' Harleen's voice interrupted his thoughts.

Jai turned to see an enormous Alkhara, one so tall he'd have to leap from the crates to get into the saddle. Winter could pass beneath its belly, and not even have to duck. His dragon chirred from his feet, as if she heard him thinking of her.

'Have no fear,' she reassured. 'He is an old soul. No bucking to worry of.'

Indeed, the giant khiro was an ancient thing, almost as old as Navi, if he had to guess. And as scarred to boot, though these were not the crisscrosses of a cruel man with a whip. Its face and shoulders were etched with the legacy of swords, and uneven sutures. It was a beast that had ridden into battle, many times before. A charger. A war khiro.

'I couldn't take the Alkhara of another,' Jai said.

Harleen smiled.

'He belonged to your father, Jai,' she said. 'This is Chak. Even Teji could not lay claim to him, try as his men did last night. He is your Alkhara, by right. No khan of the Kidara should be without one.'

A surge of pride filled Jai as he rested a hand on Chak's saddle. Even Winter's pang of envy couldn't dampen his exhilaration.

Jai mounted his khiro – their one remaining Alkhara, Chak – climbing what might well have been a small rope ladder down the great beast's side. He knew Teji had three such animals: Priya's, his own and Nazeem's, but it was no matter. One was enough . . . for now. The other khiroi followed it, and soon the Kidara were on the move, leaving behind nothing but the flattened grass, and the detritus of Teji's leaving. Beyond, Jai could see Teji's khiroi straining to join, and one calf broke free, scampering to join its mother within their herd.

Jai smiled to himself, his gaze lingering on the scene. Teji could pursue with his warriors, but it would leave their tribe and supply train vulnerable. And as the thought crossed his mind, he found himself laughing. He kicked his heels, riding to the head of the tribe, Winter scampering alongside him. Behind, he could hear the thunder of his tribe's khiroi, smell the fresh scent of broken grass.

Jai felt the Alkhara shuddering beneath him, the rising sun kissing his face, the wind lifting his hair. Ahead, the Great Steppe stretched out, in an endless sea of green.

Khan Jai rode east. And his tribe followed.

JAI WAS PLEASED TO see Feng riding up by his side upon Navi's back, with a sleeping Sum cradled to his chest by a curled arm. Jai had been worried for the little girl, but there had been no time that morning to check on her. He was glad to see she was okay.

'She suits you well,' Jai said, nodding to the khiro.

Ahead, Chak paused in his lumbering to inspect a flowering plant. Navi snuffled, and nudged Chak aside, chomping down.

The old khiro let out a grumble, and waited for her to finish before ripping the whole plant from the earth, swallowing it down, soil and all.

'I'm sorry,' Feng said hurriedly. 'I only thought to bring her to you.'

Jai shook his head, and gave Feng a smile. 'You misunderstand me. She's yours. I can think of no better an owner,' Jai said. 'You checked on her last night, did you not? I didn't ask you to do that. And after all, what vizier can be without a steed of their own?'

Feng looked at Jai in astonishment and let out a stream of thanks. Jai had to hold up a hand, embarrassed.

'You just take good care of her,' he said. 'And me. That's all the thanks I need.'

Feng turned away from Jai, his eyes welling with tears.

Jai looked down to Sum, and smiled.

'Lai look after her, then?'

Feng sniffed, and wiped at his face before turning back. 'That she did,' he said.

Behind Jai, some hundred Kidaran warriors rode their khiroi, each armed with a falx and lamellar armour made up of metal or leather squares. At their head, the nobles who had chosen to follow him rode, resplendent in the respective emblems of their houses, but all upon the rich blues of his lineage. It was a sight to behold, and Jai was honoured by it. He doubted the Kidara typically travelled outfitted in all their war regalia, and appreciated the show of force.

Seeing Harleen at their head, Jai beckoned for her to join him, and she clucked her khiro nearer with a gentle knock of her heels.

'My khan,' she said, keeping her head low, and her gaze to the ground.

'Harleen,' Jai said softly, 'I am not my uncle. I have said this before and I will not say it again. When I am not on the throne, we will not stand on ceremony.'

She glanced up, a smile touching the corners of her lips, and spurred her khiro to ride alongside him.

'When we make camp tonight, I wish to summon my nobles,' Jai said. 'Just leaders of the great houses, and their heirs.'

'The Small Council,' Feng muttered.

'As you wish,' Harleen said. 'It will be good for you to meet them and I think they will in turn be happy by your call.'

'Why do you say that?'

'You will find, most of those who came with us were never privy to Teji's Small Councils.'

'Something I am sure he regrets. Let them know I will hear all voices, so long as they wait their turn to speak.'

'I will make it so,' Harleen said, turning. She smiled suddenly, and motioned with her head.

'Looks like you've made a friend . . . or three.'

Jai turned to see that they were not alone in their journey across the steppe. A half-dozen wagons were trailing behind them, their horses picking their way over the flattened grass.

Jai had not given the traders much thought, for it had seemed the vast majority of them had remained with Teji. So it was a surprise to see some coming with them.

And yet maybe it wasn't so surprising, as he could see Lai was among the trade caravan, Jai recognising the rich multi-colours of her caravan.

'I wish to speak with them,' Jai said. 'If I leave the head of the column, the tribe won't stop, will they?'

Harleen shook her head with a wry smile, as if surprised by Jai's ignorance, and switched her gaze to a young squire, riding a few steps back from Jai.

'Keep on,' she barked.

The groom was swift to respond, ripping a coloured cloth of green, and binding it with practised speed to a bamboo pole. He raised it high above his head and bellowed.

'Keep on!'

The pennant fluttered in the breeze, and Jai grinned. Leonid had used much the same to control his armies, back when his legions had marched in their tens of thousands, and battlefields spanned many miles. It was interesting to see the Kidara use the same.

'You tell your flag bearer what you wish, and it will be so,' Harleen said.

'Thank you,' Jai said, surprised to learn he had a flag bearer. Then he started turning Chak with a flick of his reins. 'Will you both join me?'

Jai chose to loop around the tribe rather than ride through it. It felt strange to be up so high upon his Alkhara's back. Stranger still to have the great horn bisecting his view, like a captain at the wheel, staring through the mast of his ship.

As he passed, those men and women would stop and bow. Jai could only incline his head, unsure of how to respond.

He still wore his bloodstained shirt, and he wished he'd had time to change. He imagined he looked a fierce, wild man, and he knew this could not continue.

'What more have I inherited?' Jai asked of Harleen, as they began to near the traders. 'Do I have any gold?'

Harleen grimaced, as if she had been dreading that question.

'Teji took the treasury,' she said. 'It was the first thing he did. None of us knew how much Rohan had left, when the Great War ended. Certainly, we had very little. When we confronted his men, they claimed it was all his, and there was a lot of it. But we took what we could, before they drew their blades.'

She withdrew a heavy sack from her saddlebags and handed it to Feng.

Jai looked surprised, and Feng caught his expression.

'The vizier is also the treasurer,' Feng said hastily, holding it out to Jai.

Jai shrugged and waved the bag away.

'It is no wonder Nazeem was drawn to that role,' he said wryly. 'I wonder how much of Teji's gold made its way into his pockets.'

'Not Teji's,' Feng reminded. 'The Kidara's. Yours.'

By now, they had reached the back of the tribe, where sleds

attached to calves dragged much of the tribe's belongings, as well as the old, the young and the infirm – few of whom Teji had taken with him from the Kidara. Many were empty, testament to just how much Teji's tribe had taken from them.

In the distance, Jai could still see Teji's tribe, as yet immobile. Jai wondered now if he'd done the right thing, remaining in his tent while Teji had robbed them of everything of worth. But it was too late now.

He found Lai sitting upon the driver's seat of her wagon, and she drew her conveyance to a halt. For some reason, she looked apprehensive, her eyes wide in the face of the enormous Alkhara.

'Teji's gold not to your liking?' Jai joked.

Her face broke into a smile.

'Just common sense,' she said, stabbing a thumb over her shoulder. 'Shows what they know about trade.'

'She's right,' Feng said. 'I'm surprised more didn't come with you, Lai.'

'Oh?' Jai asked.

'You think Teji wants to buy *more* stuff, with hardly enough khiroi to carry what they have?' she asked. 'It's the Kidara who will wish to replenish what was taken.'

She looked around, as the other traders trundled by, calling out greetings and tipping their hats to Jai.

He waved, before a look from Feng lowered his hand. Not the most kingly of behaviour, he realised.

'I have something for you,' Lai said, 'but mind, I hope you'll repay the favour in kind.'

She turned and withdrew a heavy sack from the canvas behind her. It jingled, and she tossed it to Jai.

He caught it, and almost dropped it, for it was as heavy as a sack of bricks, though smaller than the one Feng had tried to hand to him. He looked within, only to see gold glinting there.

'What is this?' Jai asked.

'Your uncle's payment for your assassination,' she said. 'I

took it from Wei's wagon, while all the ruckus was going on. And their wagon too, truth be told.'

She pointed at another wagon passing them by, one driven by a young woman who bore a striking resemblance to Lai. Even from a distance, Jai could see arms and armour piled in the back.

'Why would you give me this?' Jai asked, handing it to Feng, whose eyes boggled at the weight of it.

Lai sighed, and pulled open her shirt, revealing the Samarion tattoo just below her collarbone, saying: 'I cannot lie. Nor steal. Teji would have found out who had taken it eventually. So, I ask you. May I keep the wagon?'

Jai understood as soon as he saw the tattoo. Lai taking the wagon would be stealing, under the laws of her religion. But by bringing it to him, it would be *he* taking it. Then he could give it to her as thanks, and her conscience would be clear.

'Fine,' Jai said. 'But you can sell back what my tribe needs for half the market price – and I know you won't lie about that. Feng will be doing the buying.'

Lai broke into a smile, and clapped her hand.

'Very generous of you, Khan Jai,' she said. 'Of course.'

'And . . . I have need of more clothing,' Jai said, looking down at the bloodied top he still wore. 'I'll have those at half-price too, fair?'

'Fair,' Lai said, nodding profusely. 'You'll have an outfit fit for the king you are, and more to spare!'

'Later, then,' Jai said. 'If you can have something ready before the Small Council tonight, though, I would be grateful.'

He looked to Harleen and Feng, whose faces were a picture of bemusement at his generosity – perhaps a strange concept to the guileful tradesfolk. He might not know the value of the coin in his purse, but he had to trust someone, at some point. Harleen and Feng had given him no reason to doubt them – in fact, they had risked a lot for him already.

That settled, it was time to make sure his people were protected.

'Make an inventory of the weapons we need,' Jai instructed. 'We will arm my warriors. It is time to repay their loyalty in kind.'

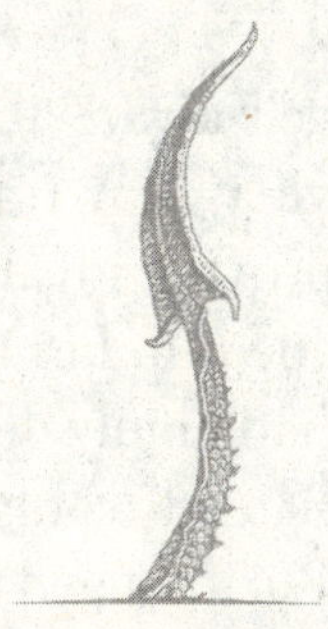

Chapter 33

Jai ached as the sun began to set, so he allowed some mana to leak from his core, letting the golden light soothe his pains. He was even tempted to form a healing spell, but knew it was not worth the mana. He had so little to spare, and his brief bursts of soulbreathing in his tent that day had not filled the well.

Now he sat upon his throne, as groomsmen and servants scurried to create a partitioned bedchamber within the back confines of the royal tent. Jai rested his elbows upon a round table of heat-flattened bamboo, one that spanned half the room.

Set around this imposing centrepiece were twelve vacant cushions, each silently awaiting the presence of their intended occupants. The seats were reserved for the leading figures of the Kidara's most esteemed houses. As Jai watched the transformation of his quarters, the tent began to resemble a powerful council chamber.

It had been a hard day's ride, and he was glad to see it draw to an end. Harleen had urged him to maintain a punishing pace, despite the obvious toll it was taking, not just on him, but on some of the less hardy of the tribe.

His Kidaran scouts reported that Teji's vanguard was maintaining their distance, yet never quite slipping from their sights. Though Jai himself had not caught sight of them from his elevated perch, he was well aware that their passage through the grasslands would leave a clear trail to follow.

Already, Harleen was proving invaluable as his steward. Her constant diligence was evident in her actions, keeping the court functioning smoothly. Jai had kindly dismissed the young women who had been assigned to tend to his hands and feet, a lavish treatment he had learned Teji indulged in during courtly proceedings – forcing the fettered women he had purchased to do so. However, Jai had permitted them to groom his hair, arranging it in the braided style befitting of a king.

During his travels across the empire with Rufus and Erica, and then his captivity with the Valor, his hair had grown out, reaching a length that now fell to his shoulders. This was slightly shorter than most Steppemen, but not remarkably so. And now, thanks to the careful attention of his groomers, his hair was tightly plaited into five distinct braids that converged into a thick knot at his back, the meaning of which he'd been too embarrassed to ask.

His fledgling beard had been similarly tended to, skilfully fashioned into a distinguished fork. He raked his fingers through the rough hairs of his seat, for it was draped in a soft khiro pelt. The luxurious fur was a welcome relief against his aching rear, a discomfort he attributed to the broad-backed Alkhara that he was still adjusting to.

The bargain Jai had struck with Lai had paid off, resulting in an ensemble of regal attire that Feng had insisted he wear, if only to not be upstaged by his nobles. His boots remained, for they were hardy, practical things, but he now wore silken trousers, shirt and robe that put him in mind of Leonid's pyjamas.

Still, they sat light upon his frame, and were cool against his skin, even if the fine gold and silver threads that etched the symbols of his house and tribe were gaudier than he would have liked.

As for the khiroi tooth crown, it sat heavy on his head, a jagged, uncomfortable thing he looked forward to removing. A fragrant touch of rosewater, paired with the smoky intensity of kohl around his eyes, completed the regal ensemble. It felt more a costume than anything else, but Jai would play his part. He had to.

He glanced at the weapons, his gift to his nobles, stacked high in the corner. His purse – already lean to begin with – was all the lighter as a consequence. But it had been worth it. If there was a battle to be fought, they would have what they needed. And a little something to get things off on the right foot.

In addition to overseeing the weapons' purchase, Feng had also organised for the services of a Kidaran cartographer, a former apprentice who hadn't chosen to follow his master. The map was laid out upon the table. It was made from a large, carefully stretched hide, dyed a vibrant green. Instead of traditional illustrations, the geography was represented by carved game pieces, reminiscent of the tablus game Jai used to play with Leonid.

'Sire.' Harleen approached, her voice respectfully low, and head bowed even lower. 'Your nobles have gathered. Shall I summon them?'

She stood resplendent in her own robes, eyes boldly outlined with kohl, gleaming with an intensity that complemented her fierce beauty. Her hawk-like nose was the only blemish on an otherwise striking visage.

Jai offered a silent nod in response, his throat too parched to speak. This was to be his inaugural assembly with his people as their khan, his first real test. They had already sacrificed much in his name; he could only hope to live up to their expectations.

They took their places around the circular table, some subtly vying for positions closer to the king – a silent power play unfolding in the dim-lit chamber. Jai longed to ease the tension, but Feng and Harleen's guidance echoed in his mind.

He remained silent, allowing them to settle, his eyes meeting each of theirs in turn. The seriousness etched on their faces did little to still the anxious fluttering in his stomach.

He couldn't help but note the youth among them. Many who had paid him a visit that first day in his tent were present now, Gurveer among them. They were not the seasoned elders he had expected, but individuals of his own age, thrust prematurely into positions of power and authority. It was a sobering realisation – many of their predecessors had fallen in service to his father, and these were the heirs, the new generation taking up the mantle of leadership.

'Be seated,' he instructed, his voice firm as he could make it.

Compliance was immediate. They claimed their designated seats, and as they did, every pair of eyes swivelled to focus on him – expectant, almost beseeching.

'Firstly, I extend my gratitude,' Jai said; his gaze travelled the room, meeting each pair of eyes, ensuring that his sincerity was well noted. 'Your loyalty, your courage – it fills me with honour. I am privileged to be leading such dedicated leaders, such devoted sons and daughters of our tribe.'

He motioned towards the stack of weapons in the corner of the room.

'These arms are my gifts to you, a token of my thanks,' Jai continued. 'These are the tools we will wield in the face of adversities that lie ahead. I trust they will serve you well in preparation for the battles we may face together, and allow you to arm more bannermen to our cause.'

A ripple of grateful murmurs washed over the room. One man, a tall figure with an air of quiet authority, rose from his seat.

'I am Aman, my king,' he introduced himself, his voice carrying an unassuming gravity. 'I am the patriarch of clan Gujara. Let me express our collective gratitude for your magnanimous gesture and wise leadership. We stand by you, Khan Jai, as we stood by Khan Rohan. Today, tomorrow and for all the days to come.'

The gathered nobles thudded their fists on the table, a firm affirmation of this vow of loyalty. Jai felt his anxiety fade, if only a little.

'Harleen,' Jai began, feeling the confidence grow in his voice. 'Please brief the lords on our current situation.'

Harleen inclined her head in assent and rose with grace. A servant instantly stepped forward to present her with a long bamboo pole, ready to trace the course of their present and future on the map laid out on the table.

'The Kidara stand two hundred knights strong,' she began, her pole tapping lightly on the Kidaran symbol, the large statue of an Alkhara. It was surrounded by twenty smaller figures of khiroi, stationed in formation behind it in the heart of the map. One of these khiroi was a shade larger than its counterparts, symbolising the gargantuan Alkhara that Jai now rode.

A new piece sat not far behind this ensemble, this one identical to that of the Kidara, but blackened with soot. It too had the khiroi miniatures.

'Trailing us, we have Teji's tribe. He calls them, the Tejinder,' she continued, her tone carrying an underlying note of derision. A ripple of laughter eased the tension in the room, and Harleen allowed a wry smile.

'But he comes with formidable strength,' Harleen allowed, her face growing serious again. 'Three hundred riders, all told. And three Alkharas to our one, even if we *do* have a young dragon.'

The jesting light in the eyes of the nobles dimmed at this, replaced by grim concern once more.

'The Valor lies one day's journey to our east,' Harleen went on, her pole guiding their gazes to the symbolic crossed lupin flowers etched into the map. 'Our scouts have ventured as close as they could without rousing suspicion. It seems, however, they remain unaware of our pursuit. Their scouts are focused on what lies ahead, rather than what follows them. They have sixty war-ready khiroi, if you stretch the definition, after Jai's ransom.'

Intrigued murmurs fluttered through the chamber at this revelation. Harleen silenced them with a sharp look before continuing her briefing.

'We have oases here, here, here . . .'

She went on, until Jai interjected with a gentle raise of his hand.

'That will be sufficient, Harleen. Thank you.'

Almost immediately, a servant advanced to offer Jai the bamboo pointer. As Jai accepted it, all eyes in the room focused on him in expectant silence, awaiting his next words.

'Have we widened the distance from Teji?' Jai asked.

'One of my finest scouts kept an eye on them,' Harleen responded with assurance. 'He lingered till the last possible moment before detection forced him to retreat. He reported back just a while ago. From his account, Teji's group has been busy preparing, spending most of the day and night. It appears our hard ride has paid off – we have secured at least two *kiris* distance from them, maybe more.'

The chamber came alive as the nobles drummed their fists against the wooden table.

'That is heartening.' Jai nodded, the corner of his mouth twitching into a brief, triumphant smile. 'But they *will* come for us. We must be ready when they do. To bring more numbers to bear, we must take the Valor. Can we catch them?'

Jai saw Gurveer roll his eyes, and understood the answer might seem obvious. Still, Harleen answered readily enough.

'Our tribe is lighter than before, it's true. However, the moment the Valor realise we're on their heels, they'll quicken their pace. Our warriors, on their own, could close the distance in two days, but it won't be feasible for the entire tribe without leaving behind the weakest among us.'

A hiss slipped between Jai's clenched teeth as he absorbed the information, thinking.

'What say the Small Council?' he asked.

The nobles looked surprised. It seemed they were not accustomed to giving their opinions here, if they had been privy to the Small Council before.

'Come now,' Jai said, keeping his voice steady and warm. 'What is the Small Council, if not to give me your counsel. I encourage you to voice your thoughts freely. Simply raise your hand and I will call upon you.'

The tent was silent, and still. Jai steepled his fingers, letting his eyes move along the table.

It was Feng who first ventured to break the quiet, lifting a hesitant hand. The flickers of irritation that flashed across some faces did not escape Jai's notice. He held his tongue, if for now. Feng would have to prove himself.

Feng, taking a moment to gather his thoughts, spoke in a measured tone. 'If we were to ride hard through the night, we could reach the Valor by dawn, just as they are preparing to depart. However, I lived among them for a time and can attest that they won't surrender lightly. They are well aware of the dire consequences of defeat.'

Gurveer, ever the warrior, responded with a grit in his voice.

'Then we fight them.'

Jai fixed a steady gaze on Gurveer who, under the weight of it, averted his eyes and muttered a hasty apology.

'A fight could leave us all the weaker,' Jai said. 'How many knights might we lose? How many khiroi? We might not have more than when we started, after the dust settles. It would be a flip of a coin.' He turned to Feng. 'Elaborate. What fate would they suffer?'

'They are Tainted. If they were to be caught by a tribe like ours, they would expect to be captured and sold as fettered to the traders. That is the way it has been since . . .'

He trailed off, his confidence shrinking beneath the gaze of the nobility.

Jai chewed his lip, thinking on it.

'And what if we didn't?'

'A wise choice, sire,' Harleen said. 'We parlay, offer to take only their khiroi and let them go free.'

'And where would that leave them?' Jai asked. 'Marooned in the midst of the Great Steppe, there to fall prey to any tribe that might pass them by, which – at this point – would almost certainly be the Tejinder. That fate is little better. They would not surrender to those terms either.'

The others sat there, silent, their faces blank. How could they not see it?

'What other choice do we have?' Harleen said. 'We take half? That's not enough.'

'We could leave them the calves,' suggested Gurveer, 'and perhaps some of the older ones. Like your . . . vizier's.'

The brief pause was hardly noticeable, but Feng seemed to pick up on the slight.

'An aged khiroi and a battle-ready one appear the same from afar, my . . . lord,' Feng retorted, his own pause far more pronounced. 'There's utility in that illusion. Teji would be expecting a surrender. If our forces appear equal, we can hold our ground.'

At this, Gurveer threw up his hands in exasperation. 'Well then, what is your fine idea?' he said. 'You're supposed to advise your king, so advise him. Unless you are better suited to holding his purse . . .'

His voice trailed off, followed by a quiet mutter, 'A Nazeem in the making . . .'

Feng rose to his feet, quickly followed by Gurveer, and the room descended into chaos. It took a few tense moments and multiple hands to pull them back into their seats. Jai finally intervened, his fist slamming on the table, releasing a pulse of mana that splintered the wood with a resounding crack.

'I will not tolerate petty pissing contests in my Small Council,' he growled, shocked faces surprised into silence by his sudden aggression. 'Hear me *now*.'

He paused, letting the silence stretch until he had their undivided attention.

'What we need are not just khiroi, but warriors – hard men and women willing to hold the line. I've lived among the Valor. Many of you have seen their courage first-hand. I can think of none better suited than they.'

'Sire,' Gurveer said, his head in his hands as he started to understand what Jai was implying. 'You cannot be serious. Mercenaries?'

'We do not truck with the Tainted,' Harleen said. 'So it is, and so it will always be.'

'Yes. But *why*?' Jai demanded. 'Can anyone actually tell me why? What wrong have they done? And I don't want fairy tales or rumour or superstition. *Tell* me. Prove it to me.'

His question was met with silence.

'That's what I thought. My father, who you so loved, trucked with the Tainted. If what I have heard is true, he wanted to unite *all* of the Sithia. Every tribe. Tainted included.'

'And look where that got him,' Gurveer hissed. 'Everyone knows it was Nazeem who betrayed him at the—'

'That was never proven,' Harleen snapped. 'I will be the last to defend that snake, but I will not have lies bandied about.'

She waited for the murmuring to die down, before continuing.

'Perhaps an alliance of convenience is worth exploring,' she said.

'I speak not of alliance,' Jai said. 'We may face down Teji once with them at our side, perhaps even twice. But the Valor will not ride with us forever.'

'Then what—'

'Not unless they join us.'

Harleen held up a hand, quelling the sudden intake of breath. She turned to Jai, and softened her tone.

'Jai, your people have been asked a lot of. To ask them now to welcome Tainted as their own . . . you may lose them in the very act of trying to save them.'

'Thank you for that advice,' Jai said. 'I do welcome it, and hope you know I need you to feel you can be candid with me. Believe me when I say, I understand how things once were . . . but we do not live in the past.'

His gaze swept the room, meeting each eye in turn.

'We are here now, facing threats the likes of which haven't

been seen in a generation. The Sabines once more march our lands, and an army of traitors hunt us. My father was the man he was because he was willing to break with tradition, unite the Sithia under one banner. We must adapt, or we will be swept away.'

His words hung heavy in the air. He could almost see the thoughts churning in their heads. His gaze shifted to Feng, who gave him an imperceptible nod.

'There will be no vote – this is happening. You know where to go if you disagree.'

Gurveer leaped to his feet, storming from the tent. A few looked to follow, their hesitation dragging on until the moment has passed.

'Think on this,' Jai said, his voice harsher than he meant it to be. 'You know Nazeem. You know Teji. That is your other choice. Yet you've never truly met these so-called Tainted. Never spoken with them, nor broken bread. Have you ever thought this was by design? Ask yourself, which is better?'

He sighed, sinking into his throne, glad of the soft cushion the pelt provided. He waved his hand, dismissing them.

'Make the khiroi battle ready,' Jai ordered. 'We ride within the hour.'

Chapter 34

Jai plunged through the darkness, a borrowed blade at his hip, and Winter perched behind him. His soulbound eyes could see well enough, the grass turned silver by the crescent moon, a subtle glow shrouded by an overcast sky.

His soldiers followed. Two hundred riders, blinded by the night, placing their trust in their surefooted mounts. Even Gurveer had joined, his mouth pinched into a grim line, yet resolute in his refusal to abandon his tribe to face the unknown alone.

Beneath Jai, Chak's snorting breaths were like great bellows, a rhythmic breathing Jai matched as he soulbreathed from where he sat.

Jai had never felt more alive. This was what it was to be a Steppeman. To feel his mount shifting beneath his thighs, the sharp sting of the wind against his cheeks. The stark beauty of it all made his spirit soar. This was not just living. It was freedom.

By now, the Valor's campfires were within sight, flickering like far-off stars. They had pushed deep into the night, but the sun's first tender blush was already staining the horizon, urging Jai and his force onward.

Yet even as the lights grew brighter, they flickered out, one by one, until all was dark where they had once been. It was obvious why.

'Harleen,' Jai called out. 'Feng! Zayn has heard the thunder of our mounts.'

The duo rode up alongside him, their weariness visible in the harsh moonlight. Their eyes, underscored by deep circles, mirrored his own fatigue. They were exhausted, as was he. Yet fatigue must yield to necessity. Now was the moment of reckoning.

'They will ride out to face us,' Jai declared, raising his voice against the wind. 'They won't risk their camp. Be prepared!'

His flag bearer, forever listening, signalled, though Jai doubted many could discern it in the veiled darkness. Still, they pressed on, Jai flexing his free hand and pulsing mana through.

He focused, and he sculpted a glintlight at his fingertip. He released it, letting the thin, invisible thread of mana control its movements. It hung above like a second moon, and his soldiers roared their approval, not knowing how much it was costing him.

Ahead, Jai saw the Valor in the distance. Their silhouettes surged in shifting shadow, and despite the solid wall of two hundred warriors at his back, a rush of fear coiled in his stomach. He set his teeth, and let out a cry of his own, ululating as they did.

A responding cry echoed back, and now he could see the distinctive outline of Zayn's humped Alkhara leading the enemy.

No, not the enemy. Not if this goes the way I hope . . .

'Slow!' Jai bellowed. The flag bearer flapped his flag, now visible in the ethereal light. He yanked on Chak's reins, straining against the Alkhara's combative spirit. It took a moment of wrestling for Chak to comply, and even then, Jai could see the unquenchable desire for battle flickering in the aged beast's wild eyes.

'Halt!' The order flew from Jai's lips, as the flag bearer nearly fumbled his ensign in response. The command echoed down the ranks, and gradually, the thundering momentum of the warriors behind him slowed until Chak stood nearly motionless, save for the excited pawing of its feet.

'Sire,' Harleen's voice rang out through the tense silence. 'They're still advancing.'

'They must think this their only chance,' Feng added, his voice desperate. 'We must meet their charge, or be swept aside.'

Jai spat out a curse, sawing at Chak's reins and manoeuvring to the side of his flag bearer. 'Parlay,' he snarled. 'Now.'

The boy scrambled to obey, his hands trembling, nearly dropping it. As soon as the new message was hoisted, Jai snatched the banner from his hands.

'Hold here,' Jai called out.

'Jai!' Feng yelled. 'You can't—'

Feng's protest was swallowed by the night as Jai spurred Chak forward, the Alkhara letting out a low moan of excitement as they raced ahead of the milling Kidara. Jai's glintlight drifting above, casting him in a circle of light, even as Winter dismounted, leaping in bounds, her scales blazing white in the glow.

Fifty yards.

Still the Valor came, and Jai swept the banner back and forth, even as the war cries of their warriors rang in his ears.

Thirty.

Zayn's Alkhara led the pack, far ahead of the rest, and Jai could do nothing but wave his flag as the two great khiroi charged head-on. Zayn was now in sight, his beast pounding the earth, its silver-streaked back a ghostly blur under the spectral glow. Zayn's blade was held high, glinting ominously in the light.

Ten . . .

Zayn's mount twisted away at the sawing of its reins, its rider's eyes wide and staring, shock upon Zayn's face at the sight of Jai. The Valor rode on, parting like water around a stone. Jai looked behind, and was relieved to see the Kidara had not followed, though Harleen rode the line, blade bare, holding back their soldiers.

'You dare ride on us?' Sindri screamed.

Jai wheeled, confronting a fuming, disordered Sindri, her face a taut mask of fury. Her blade whipped up, but a foot from his neck, and Chak reared, snorting his displeasure. A screech from Winter set Jai's teeth on edge, and he held up his free hand in peace.

Warily, Sindri lowered her blade.

'I knew you do not follow the Pact,' Jai said. 'But what Sithian rejects the rules of parlay?'

'Those who have no other choice,' Sindri snarled. 'What have we to discuss? You are a fool, Jai, to come here. Now you are our hostage once more.'

'Not so,' Jai said. 'I come to talk, and I give you one more chance to honour it. I promise you, I come not for war.'

'What, then?' Zayn called, keeping a wide berth. 'Trade? We have nothing you could wish for, and our khiroi are not for sale.'

The two Alkharas' eyes were fixed upon each other's, pawing at the ground. Chak was larger by several hands, but Zayn's was younger, more muscular. Jai had to use all his strength to keep the great khiro under his control, letting his flag tumble, heaving at his reins with a white-knuckled grip.

'That is where you are wrong,' Jai said, twisting Chak around. 'Come, let us discuss it where ears cannot pry.'

He did not wait for an answer, instead spurring back towards the thin strip of no man's land between the two armies, keeping his pace slow so as not to startle Sindri's blade through his throat. It was so close, the two armies could have spoken with but a weak shout.

He saw Kiran try to intercept him, but she thought better of it as Chak jerked past, as if she saw something in his eyes.

Soon enough, he discerned the rumble of hooves behind him as Sindri and Zayn followed his lead. When he finally halted, he was just out of earshot, but not too far that the Valor couldn't chase him down should he dare attempt an escape.

Trust begot trust. This was a gamble. And he'd stake his life to win it.

'What, then?' Sindri spat, her voice low as she cantered up to him, Zayn trailing by her side.

Jai straightened his back, and met her gaze.

'I come here not as an heir, but a khan. And I come with an offer. Allow me to anoint you as the lord and lady of the esteemed clan of Valor, under my banner. Join us. You are Tainted no longer. Join the Kidara.'

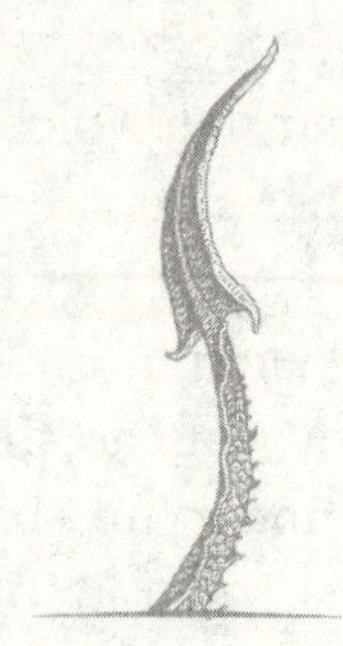

Chapter 35

'Why?' Sindri said.

The question came before he'd even finished his speech, her arms crossed in stubborn defiance.

'It is a trap,' Zayn scoffed. 'And a feeble one at that. They will fall upon us the moment we approach in peace.'

Jai retorted, 'Isn't that what *I* just did? I stand here, putting myself at your mercy. If this were a trap, it's poorly planned on my part.' He gestured expansively towards the warriors behind him. 'What you see here is the entirety of the Kidaran forces. Teji has formed his own tribe, pulling away much of our strength. Now they follow us.'

He locked eyes with both Sindri and Zayn, whose own had widened at his words.

'I hold nothing back. So I won't hold this back as well: I need your warriors. In return, I offer you a new chance. To be of the Kidara, and ride with us as equals under my rule. Your khiroi will be granted access to our bloodlines; my mount, Chak himself, will rut with your does.'

Perhaps more than anything, the mention of the pairing between the beasts seemed to pique their interest, for older as he was, Jai's Alkhara was a veritable giant, a mountain beside a hilltop.

'You will share in the spoils of our victories, as our brothers and sisters,' Jai pressed.

Still, they were silent, and so he held his tongue, letting the gravity of his offer sink in. This would be a first, Jai knew. When his father had faced the Sabines, a few Tainted tribes had fought alongside him, and those fought under their own banners, seeking both profit and vengeance. To integrate a Tainted and untainted tribe, let alone with one of the Great Tribes . . . it was almost unthinkable.

No – it was *unthinkable.*

Until I thought it.

This wasn't hubris, but rather survival. There was a problem that needed to be solved, and Jai was not so bigoted that he was blind to the solution. He could only hope Sindri and Zayn – not to mention his own tribe – would see the same.

'We can reshape our tribes, our people's future, together.' Jai extended his hand towards them, his gaze steady. 'I do not offer domination, but alliance. Do not kneel before me. Stand *with* me.'

He waited. Finally, Zayn spat, ignoring Jai's hand until Jai dropped it.

'We have no need of your acceptance,' Zayn said. 'Nor your aged beast's loins. Your bloodlines are ours already. These does are Chak's offspring, are they not?'

He motioned behind him, where Jai could easily pick out the khiroi that had been the Valor's ransom. Of course, a bull like Chak was far more valuable than a doe for breeding purposes, but the man was not wrong.

Except that wasn't the issue. Because while Jai knew little of the ins and outs of the bloodlines of the khiroi, even he had seen the difference between those of the Kidara and the Valor. And his own tribe's beasts were broad of chest and long of horn, bright eyed and thick furred. They were the product of generations of rigorous breeding, and to compare them to that of the Valor was akin to weighing a prized stallion against a mule.

The Kidaran khiroi were revered among all tribes for their

strength and size, the symbol of Jai's house a testament to their fame long before Rohan had taken the throne. Chak, in particular, was a prime specimen of this lineage, his sheer enormity unrivalled even by Zayn's own beast.

But he knew, more than anything, Zayn's ambition. Only the love of his sister prevented him from declaring himself king.

His disappointment mounted, but he held it in check. For Jai had tried the carrot.

Now the stick.

'You said you had no choice,' Jai said. 'Now you have one. Accept it, or we can all die here. The Kidara conquer the Valor, Teji conquers the Kidara, and our souls can bicker in the great beyond.'

'Or we take you now,' Zayn growled, pointing his blade at Jai. 'And negotiate free passage.'

Jai let out a bitter laugh, even as he gripped Winter by the nape, where she remained perched on the rump of his enormous mount. She had not forgiven Zayn his trespasses against her, and even Jai's mental urging could not keep her from hissing her displeasure.

'What do you think these Kidarans abandoned Teji for?' Jai said. 'It was for the hate of him, not love for me. After all, am I not a Sabine half-breed, hardly Sithian at all?'

Zayn grunted at his words, but Jai saw he had struck a chord.

'Take me, and they will charge. I will likely die, and so will you. Without me to stop them, your people, your families, will be given the same treatment as any of the Great Tribes would do to the Tainted: fettering, a fate I would not wish upon anyone.'

Sindri chewed her lip.

'I must discuss it with my council,' she said.

Jai shook his head.

'We don't have time. We must ride immediately if we are to

reach my tribe by nightfall. They travel as fast as they can, using the oldest and youngest of our khiroi, but Teji will whip his own beasts bloody to catch up when his spies report we are divided.'

'Then we have you at an advantage.' Zayn grinned. 'What more can you offer us than the favour of being subservient?'

'I have little gold,' Jai said. 'And the only khiro of mine you see before you. I will not command my people to give you what is theirs.'

'Then I will take your Alkhara,' Zayn growled. 'And you must give me the right to leave, and form my own tribe, with those that would follow. No tax of blood, or gold, or flesh. I *will* be khan in this lifetime.'

Jai felt a pang of dread at the thought of parting with Chak. He could feel his father's soul in the great beast. And he had barely had him but a day. But the old bull was past his prime, and Jai knew Chak had sired half the khiroi in his camp. And he had no choice.

Sindri began to speak, but Zayn silenced her with a curse and a raised hand. She averted her gaze. Only now did Jai see the bruise beneath her eye, half obscured by a thick rim of kohl.

A rift between the two had formed, he could see that now. Zayn must have been planning for this, just as Teji had. The familial politics of the steppe were no less cutthroat than that of the Sabines, it seemed. He hated Zayn, in that moment. But he needed him.

'You may have him when you leave,' Jai said, swallowing down the bitter lump in his throat. 'And you may not leave until my tribe is safe from Teji. And remember . . . until then . . . I am your khan.'

Jai extended his hand again, his resolve decided. It was a high price to pay, but he had little choice. The next few days would determine his tribe's fate, and he would play every card he had.

The sun was rising slow over the horizon, casting its soft glow over the vast plains, as if to seal the peace with its beauty.

Zayn reached out and seized Jai's hand, a twisted grin upon his face.

And even as he rejoiced at bringing the Valor into his fold, he couldn't help wondering if he had just made a terrible, terrible mistake.

Chapter 36

Jai's heart soared as the Kidaran camp drew into sight, Harleen's scouts accompanying them the last few miles, cheering the exhausted army.

They had ridden through the day in grim silence, for though the going was easier with the grass already flattened, the Kidaran warriors had been overburdened with the Valor's citizens and baggage train.

Indeed, sunset was well and truly begun, with the cooking fires wafting the now familiar scents of Kidaran dinner. Riders slid from their mounts, leaving the grooms to their work, before staggering to their tents.

Jai himself was yearning for a moment's respite – if nothing else, he needed to soulbreathe. But as he dismounted Chak, the excited chatter of the Kidaran citizens swiftly turned into alarmed cries. The reality of their new companions – the Valor – struck the camp.

It had all happened so fast, last night. He'd had Harleen inform the warriors of his plans to integrate the Valor, briefly, before the journey. Their reaction had been one of grudging acceptance, or so he'd been told, though he wondered if Harleen had sugared that pill.

So too had the general populace of the Kidara been informed in turn, though not by announcement. Even now, they stared at the Valor, children hiding behind their mothers' skirts.

Jai knew he could not rest. Not when there was still so much to do, bonds to be forged and fears to be eased. The first step in weaving the two tribes together had been taken, but the path ahead remained long and arduous.

His eyes sought out Sindri, finding her amid the flurry of activity as the Valor began to erect their tents. As much as the Valor helped sell the Kidaran numbers, it was still striking to see how Sindri's tribe was dwarfed by the Kidara, their camp but a sapling shadowed by a mighty oak.

For a while, he simply observed, caught in the whirlwind of his thoughts. There worked the Valor, their bodies sweat-stained with exhaustion, as they hammered stakes into the earth.

On the periphery of the Kidaran camp, his people had gathered, their numbers swelling into the thousands. Their initial alarm, as palpable as a gust of wind against his face, had begun to ebb, replaced now by a curious murmuring. His weary warriors started to mingle, sharing tales of their journey, and slowly, curiosity began to supplant fear.

For many of the Kidara, this was their maiden encounter with the Tainted. Unlike other tribes, the Kidara did not habitually hunt them to sell as fettered. In this, at least, Teji and Nazeem had taken a path of wisdom, focusing more on trade. The sight of the Tainted now, living and breathing amid them, was a strange reality they had to grapple with.

A flash of white caught Jai's eye, as Winter darted from her perch behind him, where she had snoozed for much of the journey back. She darted among the Valor children she had once befriended, her lithe body weaving between their legs. At one point, she leaped upon a stack of wooden chests, flapping her wings for balance before it toppled with a crash, earning her a shaken fist from the elder they belonged to.

The Kidara, warming to her, began to laugh at the little dragon's antics. The sight of the fearsome beast playing like an oversized pet had lightened the mood, soothing their unease like a warm hearth on a winter's night.

In the midst of the laughter, a Kidaran boy extended a trembling hand towards her, emboldened by the example of the others. Winter, basking in all the attention, leaned into his touch, nuzzling against his palm with a soft purr. The boy's fear melted away into a laugh of delight, and the crowd roared with laughter at his startled face when Winter lapped his face.

The tribes were united, if only for a brief moment. They were simply people, joined in shared mirth.

Jai could feel slumber calling, but he resisted. With a surge of energy, he rode over to Sindri, who was barking orders at her people.

'Why do you camp apart?' Jai demanded. 'The Tejinder might arrive at any moment.'

'It is only out of respect,' Sindri explained, her eyes downcast. Nearby, Zayn gave his own instructions, sending scared tribesfolk scurrying to and fro.

'Your people are Kidara, and mine the Valor,' Jai said. 'Bring them closer. And have your warriors form up in full regalia.'

'To what end?' asked Sindri.

He paused. 'Let our people see your warriors in all their glory,' he said. 'This is the birth of a new people and they must see what this alliance has wrought. Meet their new family.'

'As you wish, my king,' Sindri said, the words stilted on her tongue. It must have been strange for her, to kowtow to the boy she herself had once held captive but a few days earlier.

Still, she was swift to give the orders, and the Valor, to their credit, reacted enthusiastically. For they too had likely never seen a tribe such as the Kidara, and they wished to impress. Truly, the ancient laws of the steppe had kept these two peoples apart.

Yet not all appeared pleased to be in the Kidara's midst. Zayn and his close-knit band stood apart, arms folded, eyeing the onlookers with undisguised ill humour, leaning close to speak. It was well that they only made up a score or so, though they were made up of the best of the Valor's warriors – Kiran among them, her face inscrutable.

Tents were taken down and then re-pitched with efficient haste and the air filled with the sound of excitement as the Valor rummaged for fresh garments. Amid the flurry of activity, Sindri stood tall, making her will known.

Jai couldn't help but feel a pang of gratitude for Sindri's strength and leadership. A lesser leader might have balked at the situation, but she had taken it in stride. He doubted she would leave with Zayn, when the time came. When all was said and done, he was fairly sure the Valor would be another of the great houses under his banner, and she their leader.

However, his gaze kept drifting back to Zayn and his group. Their discontent was palpable, a dark cloud that loomed large. Jai knew he would have to fix this sooner rather than later. Discord had a way of spreading like wildfire, and he had his own sparks – like Gurveer – he needed to douse. He spurred Chak closer.

'Zayn,' Jai called out as he neared the group, the chatter among them coming to a sudden halt. He was met with stony silence and a circle of wary eyes.

'Yes, my khan?' Zayn asked, giving an exaggerated bow.

With a sigh, Jai swung down from Chak's back, his boots sinking into the soft earth. He could feel the weight of their gazes on him, some openly hostile, others merely curious. But Jai had learned by now to confront challenges head-on, and speaking imperiously down to them from his mount would earn no friendships.

'We are all of the steppe,' Jai began, his voice carrying over the growing quiet. 'Sons and daughters of the Mother, all. And now we are of the same tribe. But have no fear: you remain Valor, as a great house under the Kidaran banner.'

Zayn's eyes hardened at his words, but Jai did not falter.

'I know that trust is earned, not given. I ask not for your trust tonight, but your patience. Give this union time, and it will show its worth.'

There was a pause as his words hung in the air. Then, slowly, one of Zayn's companions, a grizzled warrior with a battle-scarred face, spoke up.

'And if it doesn't?' he asked, his voice gravelly.

'Then you may leave, with Zayn,' Jai said, forcing the words, for they were sour on his tongue. 'Freely, when the threat of the Tejinder is passed.'

The warriors nodded, apparently satisfied, even if Zayn spat off to the side. No matter. Right now, Jai needed the man's blade, and his Alkhara, and these twenty or so warriors. Not his loving adoration.

Soon enough, the Valor were ready to ride into camp, for their belongings were few and far between, a consequence of the few khiroi they were accustomed to.

Yet even as Jai summoned his weary nobles, his flag bearer signalling at his command, the difference between the two tribes was all the more obvious. For even in all their finery, their hair braided with their jewellery, the symbols of the Valor emblazoned upon their garments, the Kidara were still the richer and more numerous, their clothing a deep blue while the Valor's were the browns and greys of furs and leathers, punctuated only with flashes of purple.

'With me!' Jai called, as the Valor formed up behind him, a haphazard train of khiroi, sleds and bone-weary men, women and children.

He nudged Chak forward, heading for the central passage down the heart of the Kidaran camp. A ripple of uncertainty passed through the Kidara as the Valor approached, parting the crowd. The citizens watched in awe, as the Valor walked and rode, tall and resolute, even as onlookers shrunk away. They looked fearsome, each khiro rider a warrior in full battledress.

'Jai, is this wise?' Feng asked, spurring alongside him.

Jai wasn't sure. He could feel the tension, and it was only growing.

The central plaza, one made for cooking, music and laughter, felt eerily silent as Jai and his party neared. Eyes followed them as they moved by the onlookers, their passage marked by a trail of quiet whispers and the soft wind rustles of flapping canvas and furs.

Close by, a Kidaran child babbled a few words of song, careless of the silence around him. His mother hushed him. But Jai recognised the melody.

It was a walking song, one he recognised not from his brief time with the Kidara, but from the Valor. A shared song, one that had survived the hundreds of generations of separation.

He found himself mouthing the tune. Then chanting. Perhaps singing, in his own way. His voice was weak at first, high and tremulous in the hushed air. Then Sindri, her voice lilting and soft, the first notes so surprising Jai turned to look at her.

A rich baritone joined him – Gurveer, nodding to Jai. Their voices rose together, as more joined, the Valor one by one lending him their voices.

A few Kidara joined, children at first, then adults, elders. They sang with different words, different tunes, but the melody was strikingly similar. The resulting chorus was wondrously discordant, and Jai allowed himself a small shred of hope.

And then, too soon, it ended, leaving the plaza silent as the last words faded, the air still, but eased of tension.

All eyes turned towards Jai. He knew they expected him to speak. To make a rousing speech he had to summon from his very soul, because he'd certainly had no time to think of one. Yet as he looked out at the sea of watching eyes, the rich scent of the stew in the air, he had a simpler idea.

There was one thing that had always brought people together, more than any speech or song. He grinned and clapped his hands, shouting but two words.

'Let's eat!'

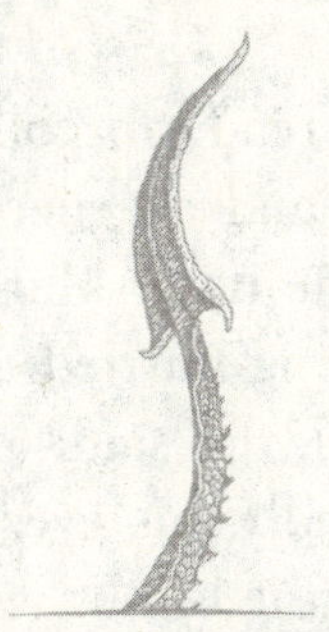

Chapter 37

It was not all peace and unity, for few Kidara sat amid the Valor, nor vice versa. Yet the food was doled out easily enough, and to Jai's great surprise, the Valor distributed their own foods to the Kidara, sharing in the rich exchange that was the cuisines of the differing tribes.

Expressions of pleasure and gestures of approval began to replace the tense silence, as the delicious dishes made their way to grateful mouths. The disquieted whispers faded, replaced by the sounds of eager chewing and contented swallowing.

The younger Valor children, quick to finish their meals, raced away to explore their new surroundings. They made a beeline for the bathhouses, their laughter and the sound of splashing water soon filling the air. Yet the watchful eyes of the mothers, trailing the excited youngsters, cast an uneasy pall over the jubilation.

There was no denying the reality. There would be disagreements in the days to come, resentments to address, disputes to mediate. But for the moment, the situation was better than Jai could have hoped.

The Kidaran citizenry surprised him, in fact. He supposed the looming threat of battle with those who had once been their brethren had a way of smoothing past prejudices.

As Jai dismounted, a groom stood ready to take his weary mount, Chak. The old creature, worn out from two days of relentless travel, seemed ready to collapse on the spot. It took a good deal of coaxing and a generous serving of dumplings to entice Chak to join the other khiroi in the grazing field.

Jai was grinning as Feng hurried up to him.

'Things are going well,' Jai said.

Feng nodded distractedly, his eyes wide and anxious. 'Well enough,' he said, 'well enough. But we have hardly any time to spare. I've ordered our warriors to rest as soon as they have eaten, and for the khiroi to be fed the last of our fermented grain – it will help with their recovery.'

Jai nodded, his own exhaustion making it hard to listen. The adrenaline of the last moments was fading, and he swayed, even as Winter slipped beside him to nudge him upright.

'I think I should follow your advice,' he muttered. 'I need rest.'

Feng shook his head.

'Teji's army will be moving fast now,' Feng said. 'We need to make a plan.'

Jai, his mind wrestling between the demands of his growling stomach and the pull of sleep, managed a dull nod. He staggered over to a nearby cooking fire, gratefully accepting a bowl of piping hot soup. Despite the steaming heat, he swallowed it quickly, his soulbound throat able to resist the heat. Soon after, a handful of dumplings followed the same path.

'Shall I convene the Small Council?' Feng asked.

Jai looked to Harleen, still upon her horse, exhausted yet still giving orders. If she could keep this up . . . so too could he.

'Do it,' Jai said. 'But grant us a few hours' rest. I think we've all earned it.'

THE RELIEF OF SLEEP was fleeting for Jai. It felt as though he'd only just closed his eyes, sinking into the comforting furs that lined his bedchamber with Winter curled up against his belly, when the soft chime of a bell pierced the tranquillity. He jolted awake, his heart pounding in the sudden wakefulness.

Feng appeared between the parted curtains, his face a picture of exhaustion. He had clearly not slept at all.

'The Small Council are here,' he said. 'Zayn and Sindri too.'

Jai got wearily to his feet, and made his way through the partition to sit upon his throne. It was warm in his chamber, and already sleep tugged at his eyelids once more. He shook himself awake.

'Let them in.'

One by one, the nobles entered, the soft fall of their steps stirring the air. Feng had taken it upon himself to arrange the round table at the foot of his throne, and the nobles took their seats in respectful silence.

Zayn and Sindri were among the last to enter, and there was an awkward moment, for only one cushion had been arranged for them. Zayn took it swiftly, leaving Sindri to hover until another was provided.

Harleen rapped the table with her hands, tearing their eyes away from Jai.

'It has been a busy few days,' she said. 'And it is high time we *all* swear our fealty to our king. Let us make the blood oath.'

There was a short burst of applause as the Small Council got to their feet, kneeling beside their chairs. All but one.

The room was still as everyone turned their gaze to Zayn, who remained standing, his face impassive. There was a tension in the room, a silence filled with anticipation as they waited for Zayn to move.

For a moment, it seemed he would refuse. He stood there, defiant, his gaze locked with Jai's. Then, with a slow nod, he bent on one knee, and bowed his head in a show of fealty.

'Under the gaze of our ancestors and the all-seeing Mother, we pledge our loyalty to Jai of the Kidara, first of his name,' Harleen said, the other voices echoing her speech. 'Our strength is his shield, our courage his sword. From this day forth, only gold, blood or flesh may release us from our vow. So do we speak, and so do we swear.'

The words hung in the air, and Jai, unsure of what to say, uttered thanks, before the sighs of relief as the nobles were seated once more.

While they did, Feng had taken the liberty of arranging the map upon the table. Jai was surprised to find it was different from last time. Now small banners had been attached to the khiroi that represented the Kidaran military strength, and Jai could see that now the Valor were the largest of his divisions. This was not lost upon his gathered nobles, most of whom had no more than ten khiroi apiece under them.

Zayn's Alkhara had now joined his own, and Jai found their numbers were close to that of Teji's tribe, if short by forty men and an Alkhara. He'd faced worse odds . . . though never on this scale. The Tejinder's carvings had been placed not far from his own, and even taking into account the relative nature of the map, he could see that they were perilously close.

He glanced up, and realised the entire table was staring at him, waiting for him to speak. For all he had read about warfare, the battles he knew were mostly that of legions against hordes of disorganised men. He wished he had read more of Leonid's diary now, seen how he had dealt with battling against khiroi.

'Answer this,' Jai said, after a moment's thought. 'Are we all agreed to ride out and face Teji's men, spare our people the bloodshed?'

There were nods and 'ayes' around the table.

'Humour me,' Jai said. 'Why so?'

Zayn scoffed, but it was Sindri who spoke first.

'To protect them,' she said. 'The enemy might fire our tents, slaughter the innocent. Take our families hostage, put blades to their throats.'

Jai tapped his jaw, musing.

'Teji wishes to take back the tribe,' Jai said. 'As do his nobles. And I do not believe they are so evil as to kill their innocent friends by the thousand. Tell me, then, why will the common soldiers fight for him?'

The nobles stared at him, confused at what must have seemed a rhetorical question.

'Their oaths,' Harleen said, after a moment's pause. 'Each man and woman is sworn to their noble house first, and their khan second. It is why our own warriors will fight for you, when their time comes. Because *we* will it.'

Jai raised a finger.

'Now, we get to the heart of it,' Jai said. 'The men and women we face do not wish to fight us.'

'How do you know this?'

'Because did they not fight beside you all, in times past? Feasted with you, laughed with you? This schism between my uncle and I is not of their making. They are but pawns bound by blood and oath.'

Harleen nodded gravely.

'You speak truth. But I don't see—'

Her words were interrupted by a grunt of amusement from Zayn.

'Something to say?' Jai asked.

Zayn stood, and sniffed.

'We ride, we face them, and if they charge, we meet it,' he grunted. 'We should be resting, and sharpening our blades. This is foolish talk.'

Jai stood himself, slamming his hands upon the armrests.

'Sit, and be quiet.' He stabbed a finger at Zayn's seat, and the man's face darkened. Yet he did as asked.

Jai let out a breath to calm himself, feeling every bit of the weight of his exhaustion. Still, he closed his eyes, and spoke as his thoughts gathered.

'This is no common battle,' Jai said. 'It is a conflict most of the participants do not wish to fight. Do you truly expect the warriors who have fought and bled beside each other will now slaughter the families of their old comrades?'

The others slowly shook their heads.

'Will they fire the tents of their friends? Slaughter their cousins, their nieces and nephews?'

'They would not,' Gurveer grunted.

'So why fight them in an open field, where their numbers are to their advantage?' Jai demanded. 'Let us face them at our camp.'

Jai let the murmurs of the Small Council swirl as he turned his attention to the map. There had to be some landmark they could use to their advantage. All he saw were oases.

'The map shows our riders,' Jai mused. 'But how many warriors have we?'

They stared at him, confused.

'Grooms,' Jai said. 'Men and women of fighting age. To attack, one must use your khiroi to catch up to those that flee. But to defend . . .'

'Another hundred,' Harleen said, starting to catch on to his line of thinking. 'Maybe fifty more that can hold a blade. But—'

'Hang on a moment,' Jai said, holding up a hand and furrowing his brow.

Maybe he *had* read enough of Leonid's diary. How his supply trains had defended themselves against his father's raiders.

'Do we have spears?' Jai asked.

Harleen looked at him with raised brows.

'Some,' she said. 'Our groomsmen carry them in case of direwolves, sabretooths, manticores. All hunt the grasslands here. But those are usually only a problem in winter.'

Winter perked up at hearing her name, letting out a deep rumble that made Aman jerk away. Jai smiled, letting the small moment of levity take some of the anxiety from where it coiled in his belly.

'Sindri,' Jai said. 'You will have fought with traders. They use spears, do they not?'

He spoke the words casually, and winced as he saw the expression on Feng's face. Of course. He had almost forgotten his vizier's parents had met their demise in much the same way. It was no wonder he hated Zayn so bitterly.

An apology for another time, he thought. He had to focus on the battle at hand.

'Some,' Sindri allowed quietly, after a moment's pause.

Jai saw he had been further thoughtless, for now he saw the dark looks of the Kidaran nobles. They clearly did not approve of Sindri's past betrayal of the Pact.

'Under my rule,' Jai said, eager to settle the matter, 'we will follow the Pact. But there are lessons to be learned from the past, and we cannot afford to ignore them. Agreed?'

The men and women around the table nodded. Turning his attention back to Sindri, he asked, 'They square their wagons, do they not? And crowd the gaps with spears.'

Sindri nodded, although she was clearly taken aback by the line of questioning.

'A coward's tactic,' Zayn said.

'Did it *work*?' Jai asked.

'We never tried,' Sindri said, interrupting Zayn before he could speak. 'They were not worth the trouble.'

'Exactly,' Jai said, pointing at Sindri.

'I do not understand,' Aman said.

'We need to make this not worth the trouble. That is what we need Teji's men to think, at least. That a confrontation with us will only leave them the weaker. Or did you want to fight this battle?'

There was murmuring around the table, until Gurveer caught Jai's stare.

'My khan . . . it is just not how we do things.'

Jai steepled his fingers, looking at them with a steady gaze, leaden though his eyelids were.

'The warriors that are coming broke their oaths to my father and his house when they joined the traitor Teji, and with every day that goes by that Teji has not taken back the Kidara, their shame grows. They outnumber us – if we face them in open battle, they may well risk it all to regain their honour. They will say, if they win, it was the Mother's will. But if—'

Before Jai could go further, though, there was an outcry from outside. Jai stood, and guards rushed to his side.

A man staggered into the tent, held up by two royal guards. He was bloodied from a deep wound in his shoulder. He uttered a few words, but even Jai's soulbound ears could not discern them.

As servants rushed to bind his wounds, Jai shooed them aside. He brought up a hand, concentrating, the healing spell crooked upon his hand.

He gritted his teeth, and let out a burst of white light, the spell sputtering from his inexpert fingers. But it was enough.

The man's wounds closed beneath the flowing light, turning pink, then tan with skin once more.

Jai released the spell, cursing and shaking out his hand. It burned with pain, a consequence of his amateurish form. Rufus had been a good teacher, but Jai had not been powerful enough then to practise much spellcraft.

Water was brought to the man, who was still weak from blood loss, careening back in the chair brought for him, gulping the water as it flowed over his chin.

'Word from the rearguard,' he finally said, sputtering, dizzy. 'They are coming.'

Chapter 38

Jai waited with his men in the darkness, listening for movement. It was still and silent, as if the whole of the steppe were holding its breath.

Then a rumble. Low at first, but growing ever louder, until even the Kidara could hear it. Jai could tell by the quickening of their breaths, the subtle rasp of metal sliding against leather as swords eased from their scabbards.

Jai was glad of his soulbound eyes, though he cursed the mana he had wasted, even if it had saved a man's life. Who knew if that mana would be the difference between victory and defeat tonight?

'Steady,' Jai muttered, half to himself. 'Stick to the plan.'

'Steady!' the order travelled down the line, and Jai bit his tongue.

Leather creaked, and khiroi grumbled, their lowing almost mournful as they voiced their displeasure at being awake at this early hour. Jai had let them all sleep as long as he could, mounts included. But Harleen's scouts watched for the approaching enemy, and had updated him every hour. Teji had slowed, it seemed, since the wounded Kidaran scout had escaped them. He kept coming, though, and at a certain point, Jai needed to make sure his warriors were ready.

At least, he mused, the fatigue would be mutual.

Jai's uncle must have ridden day and night to catch them.

Sunset had been and gone an hour ago, and Jai knew this battle would occur in the black of night.

This was by design, Jai was sure of it. In the darkness, where strategy played a smaller part, numbers had the advantage.

'Will they parlay?' Jai asked, looking down the line.

His companions – Gurveer, Aman and Harleen – waited, silent ahead of their respective troops, their faces etched with grim determination. It was Feng, the stalwart presence at his side, who responded.

'I predict they will dispatch a messenger bearing their ultimatum. There will be no negotiations, however.'

Winter chirred from her perch on the saddle behind him, and Jai reached out, calming her with a hand.

Still, Jai could see them now. Even in the waning moonlight, he could spot the silver glint of their weapons and armour, and the blue tinge of their clothing and banners. The cowards still dared to wear his father's colours. Jai tried to picture if he could ever have done the same. The idea that he'd do such a thing to Arjun or Samar . . . his mind revolted at such a thought.

And yet that's exactly what Teji had done to the memory of his brother, Rohan.

He snapped back to attention as a man rode at their head, resplendent in such finery, Jai was almost surprised it could be called battledress. As he neared, Jai made out the face of the man, the white flag clutched awkwardly in his grip.

Nazeem. The man had grown rich of late, it seemed. *Rich off* my *people – the people he* stole *from.* So much silver and gold dripped from him that it was a wonder he did not jingle like a wind chime.

The man rode the line, his khiro snorting. His face was a picture of quiet satisfaction, as if all was as he expected. Jai looked forward to wiping the grin from the man's face.

Pulling up at the head of Jai's formation, Nazeem cast aside the flag, its purpose served. 'You all know why I am here,' he declared, his voice thick with condescension. 'Surely, you all saw this confrontation coming. It was foolish of you to align with this pretender.'

Gurveer's retort was cut off as Harleen's hand clamped down on his shoulder, a silent order for restraint.

'Yes – watch your tongue, boy.' Nazeem chuckled unpleasantly in the night air. 'You may regret your words come dawn.'

Jai spat to the side in a display of contempt. A momentary flicker of distaste crossing Nazeem's features.

'Teji is magnanimous,' he proclaimed loudly, his voice carrying clearly in the still night air. 'Surrender now, and all will be forgiven. Your only penalty will be a tax, a small reparation for our pain and suffering. A fair deal, don't you think?'

His words slithered through the quiet like oil, slick and unctuous, yet met with resolute silence. In response, Jai spurred Chak forward, staring Nazeem down with cold eyes. For a fleeting moment, the man's complacency faltered as his eyes darted towards the discarded banner.

'Your offer is rejected,' Jai said quietly. 'Prepare for battle.'

He pivoted Chak around, presenting his back to the man.

'Oh, I was *hoping* you would say that,' Nazeem chuckled again. 'I am rather looking forward to some private time with you. Feng, I am sure, can attest to my . . . welcoming nature.'

Jai waited for the rumble of Nazeem riding away, then swept his gaze up and down the battle lines.

'Remember!' Jai called. 'You are the true bearers of the Kidaran legacy. Oath keepers, every single one of you. The Mother smiles upon us!'

He thrust his blade high, a beacon for his warriors as they cheered. And then, as the distant drumming of Tejinder's approaching forces grew, Jai wheeled about, steeling himself.

Jai's fingers tightened around the hilt of his blade. He waited, counted the heartbeats.

'Harleen!' His voice was steel edged. 'Fall back.'

With a curt nod, Harleen relayed the command. Her warriors

retreated swiftly, streaming through the lines in a disorganised mass.

'Gurveer – now,' he commanded, and Gurveer's warriors melted back as well, their swift departure echoing Harleen's unit.

'Aman,' Jai called. His soldiers joined the retreating ranks, leaving Jaï alone with half his men.

He could hear the cheers of the oncoming cavalry. They sensed victory, thinking Jai already abandoned by his lords.

Let them cheer at this, then.

'Full retreat!'

His command rippled down the lines, setting the first phase of their plan into motion. Their forces turned and ran; the Tejinder, a tidal wave crashing after them.

Now they were engulfed in a breathless race. Beneath Jai, Chak bellowed, leading Jai's contingent with a speed that belied his years. Ahead, the detachments of Harleen and Gurveer coursed through the central artery of their camp.

The encampment closed in around them as they raced down the makeshift corridor, a canopy of tents narrowing their world to a singular point.

Behind him, he could hear the yips and ululations of their enemy, plunging after them in wild abandon, even as Jai's men spilled into the central plaza, the wide-open space bathed in moonlight. Jai pulled up at the edge of it, turning back to see his men pouring into the clearing, a stream of silhouettes. His heart pounded a harsh rhythm in his chest, but he steadied himself, clearing his throat.

'Onward!' he called, his voice lost across the open space. 'Press on!'

His forces kept forward, pouring into the corridor on the other side where Harleen and Gurveer had positioned themselves. Turning in his saddle, he took in the spectacle of the Tejinder army flooding into the central square, catching up fast.

But not fast enough.

'Not yet,' he breathed. 'Not yet.'

He could see the blades rising, battle cries rending the air.

'Now!' he roared, the word repeated, rippling through his ranks. 'Close the trap!'

Kidaran citizens burst out from the tents at the plaza's edges, plugging the gaps and escape routes between them. Each held a spear in their hands, some of wood and steel, but most simple lengths of bamboo, sharpened and hardened over fire.

The Tejinder wheeled in disarray within the plaza's centre, cut off from escape. In the midst of the tumult, Jai saw Teji, bellowing commands from atop his Alkhara, Nazeem's screeching voice piercing the din alongside him. But unless you were near either man – both of whom had conflicting orders – it was probably impossible to hear over the chaos.

Torches were lit by Jai's foot soldiers, and Jai added his own glintlights to the sky, mana surging in a flick of his fingers, bathing the plaza in the cold light.

Jai spurred Chak forward, summoning his flag bearer to follow.

'Parlay,' Jai shouted at Teji, his spearmen parting to allow him by. 'Parlay!'

He knew he could not yet be heard above the din, for the Tejinder were in a panic, but eventually one of them would relay the news to either Teji or Nazeem. In the meantime, he charged forward, even as some of the Tejinder charged at the spearpoints, but none dared meet the bristling wall. Those skirting the edges could find no way out, their curses colouring the night.

Seconds stretched as the clamour dwindled, Teji's flag bearer casting about for the white banner Nazeem had left in the dirt. Jai could not help but grin as he saw Nazeem say something to his master, and receive a slap in return.

Finally, a strip of canvas was tied to a pole, and there was a momentary respite. And now Teji approached, Nazeem and a handful of nobles riding in his wake.

'Small Council!' Jai called. 'With me!'

He waited until they flanked him. Then he drew a deep breath, and trotted forward to meet the man he had once hoped to call family.

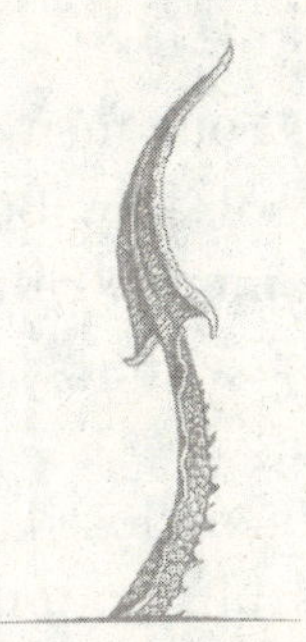

Chapter 39

'Well played,' Teji conceded, clapping as he approached, his applause slow and patronising. 'Quite the performance.'

'I am my father's son,' Jai replied.

The retort took Teji aback, a flicker of surprise crossing his features before his expression hardened.

'Should you expect any concessions, you are gravely mistaken,' Nazeem interjected, usurping Teji's attempt at a retort. 'We can breach this . . . this mockery of a blockade.'

'I eagerly anticipate your attempt,' Jai replied, casting a nonchalant gesture towards his assembled forces behind him. 'In the unlikely event that you manage to breach our spear walls and then turn in time to meet our charge, my knights will ride you down. Are you willing to take such a risk here, in the midst of our encampment?' He paused, gesturing towards the labyrinthine network of tents. 'Observe, even now, my forces secure your avenues of escape.'

It was true. The corridors that had been used to enter were now a maze of fabrics, some little more than a fur stretched between two stakes . . . but impediment enough for cavalry trying to manoeuvre.

'We'll cut them down,' Teji hissed. 'And any who try to stop us.'

'I think not,' Jai said. 'Your men may be willing to combat mine. That is the nature of war. But see who surround you. Will they cut through common citizens? Through the people who had, until a few days ago, been their friends and family and neighbours?'

Teji's mouth flapped, then closed.

'So the serpent's game suits you, then?' Nazeem sneered, his words laced with an acrid bitterness. 'Hiding behind innocents?'

Now Jai felt his blood rise. There was accuracy in that statement. For it was true. Those clutching spears were not trained soldiers but ordinary men and women. But coming from Nazeem . . .

'You're one to talk. As if you've ever had the people's well-being in the mind.'

'How dare—'

'Only a desperate man resorts to trickery,' Teji finally blurted, cutting off Nazeem.

'In my experience,' Jai retorted coolly, 'it's not trickery if it's in plain sight. Did my father not use the feigned retreat upon Leonid, in our first major victory in the War of the Steppe? For someone so concerned with legacy, you seem to know little of our family's history.'

Teji spat in Jai's direction, but the gesture was feeble, the spittle landing harmlessly somewhere between them. His nobles bristled and Winter let out a deep, resonant growl, but Jai held up his hand. A moment of tense silence ensued.

'Our khiroi outnumber yours, three to two,' Teji declared, in an attempt to fill the disquieting silence, a dismissive wave accompanying his words. 'I'll allow you it will be a bloody affair, but that will be on *your* head.'

Jai was not sure if enraging Teji was a good idea, for he still wished to end this without bloodshed. But it seemed his uncle could not see what was plain. So poor was his understanding of battle, he still thought he had the upper hand.

It was time to shatter that illusion.

'I'm not the one who attacked, am I? I let you and your people go, yet you're the ones who chased us down after your treachery. So the Mother knows whose hands the blood will be on. But that's all of no matter.

'Sound the horn,' Jai called out.

His flag bearer already had the horn in his hands, and now he lifted it, and let out three short bursts.

The sound echoed around the square. Then, in the distance, came three notes back.

It hung long in the air, before being returned in kind from the distance, as if it echoed from a distant mountain. Then silence. A hushed murmur floated on the wind, soon replaced by resounding battle cries and the ominous rumble of approaching cavalry.

They came then, the Valor streaming in, cutting a circuitous path through the tents to gather in a predesignated clearing, behind the Tejinder knights. Jai knew the Valor numbers had been inflated by grooms from both camps riding the leftover khiroi, untrained, or too young or old for battle – but Teji didn't know that. All he saw were the riders, their blades raised high, mounts surging en masse.

'Fight your way through that,' Jai said, forming the lie on his lips. 'Our forces are at least evenly matched, if not tipping in our favour. And our men have not been ridden hard, day and night to reach here.'

Now Teji's eyes widened.

'You . . . you ally with the Tainted?' he demanded. 'Never have I . . . that you would stoop so low.'

Jai merely shrugged, a twinge of conflicted pity twisting inside him as Nazeem averted his gaze.

'No, you stooped much lower, in that you enriched yourself at the expense of the Kidara. Again, though, that's of no matter. Because you look through a prejudiced lens. I see no Tainted here,' Jai said, his voice steel. 'Only seasoned warriors. More, I know your men fear them, whatever their provenance.'

He turned to the nobles flanking Teji, his gaze hard.

'These men behind you are loyal to their oaths, which is more than can be said of you. They will question now whether they owe loyalty to one who would betray his own blood. To die for your lie. So I ask you: are you sure they will shed the blood of their brethren for it?'

The Tejinder nobles' eyes flickered uneasily, some bristling, others averting their gazes. Shame lurked within many of their eyes.

'It's not too late,' Jai added softly, such that only those close might hear. 'You were given an impossible choice, ensnared by the lies of a usurper. I can forgive that. I offer you what Teji pretends to offer me, but with no demands. No tax, no punishments. All will be as it was.'

'He lies,' Teji snapped. 'He'll cut you down where you stand. Would you join a tribe that rubs shoulders with the Tainted? You would be . . . you would be Tainted like the rest of them!'

Nazeem laid a hand on Teji's shoulder, and leaned in to whisper, cupping a hand around his king's ear. Even to Jai's soulbound ears, it was a serpent's breath, too soft for him to hear.

'What are your terms?' Nazeem asked, after Teji gave a curt nod.

'You vow never to wage war against me again,' Jai said, his words slicing through the tension. 'You leave your weapons and khiroi here. You can retain your banners and your battle garb. Those nobles that wish to rejoin me can remain and retain all that is theirs. We will send riders ahead of you, to return their families and belongings.'

'You expect us to *walk* back?' Teji snapped. 'In all our armour? Your offer is laughable.'

'We'll give you thirty khiroi,' Jai allowed, after a moment's thought. 'Of our choice. To carry your belongings. I'm sure you can buy more.'

'Never,' Teji snarled.

'Then you can meet your end here,' Jai said. 'Or wait it out. I doubt the mountain of gold you abandoned would attract any unwanted attention. Perhaps I should dispatch some men to retrieve it instead, while you ponder. It seems I have riders to spare.'

Teji faltered. Jai watched as the old lecher's mind turned. The mention of gold had sparked something within the man, exposing the corrupt core that had consumed him.

'We keep the gold?' he asked.

'My word is my bond,' Jai said. 'That is more than I can say of you.'

Teji thought on it. His eyes swivelled in their sockets, as he surreptitiously looked at the enemy surrounding him. For a long time, he had basked in a life of extravagant luxuries, offloading the burden of decision-making onto Nazeem's shoulders. But now, faced with an uncertain future, something in Teji had been dislodged. The thought of losing his amassed gold seemed to have done the trick.

Squaring his shoulders, he finally said, 'A hundred khiroi. My camp is extensive. We will be stranded with any less.'

In response, Jai's gaze hardened. He was not about to be swindled, but to walk away with a bloodless victory was beyond tempting.

'Fifty,' he countered. 'I'm sure the traders will be happy to take some of your baggage off your hands. And you keep two Alkharas too.'

A moment of silence lingered before Teji replied, his bitter voice barely a whisper.

'Done.'

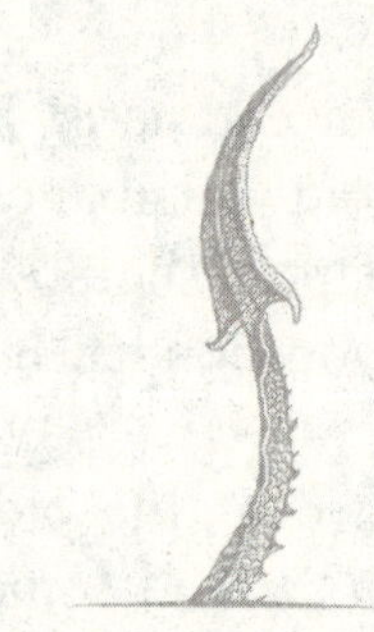

Chapter 40

A jeering throng of Jai's followers sent the Tejinder army off as they filed out of the camp. Teji and Nazeem shared the saddle of Teji's Alkhara, while the remaining mounts were piled high with glistening armour. Bereft of their steeds, the Tejinder soldiers would face the humiliating task of marching back on foot, their elaborate battle regalia strapped to their encumbered mounts' backs.

By the time the sun painted the horizon with hues of blush, the departing enemy had diminished to a speck on the horizon. They were considerably fewer than they once had been, for several nobles – and their men – had elected to remain with the Kidara.

Jai knew it was not out of new-found loyalty, for they would surely be bitter at the loss of their standing. Rather, they knew Teji would not conquer the Kidara anytime soon, and they and their followers could not stomach a future as a tribe of oath breakers. That, and Jai let those who stayed keep their khiroi. That, above all else, moved them to break with the Tejinder.

Still, Jai *was* ready to forgive. Already, he had sent his scouts ahead to fetch the families and belongings of the newcomers. None of those staying trusted Teji to send the latter.

Sitting upon Chak's back, with his Small Council by his side, Jai only now began to let his worries ease a fraction. The legion still marched free, but finally, so did he. He breathed easy, petting Winter in silent contemplation, as the sounds of celebration roiled around him.

Feng had managed to secure Jai's rights to the khiroi and weapons that were his personal property. As the khan, Jai was entitled to half the spoils, leaving him with a considerably heavier purse; a consequence of Feng's horse-trading with the Valor for his newly acquired khiroi. It was a lucrative affair, strengthening his army and his personal wealth in equal measure. The realisation was sobering – war, indeed, was profitable.

He wasn't sure he liked the feeling, but it was the reality – and a necessary one – for now.

Spurring away from his men, Jai rode Chak through the great herd of khiroi, lowing pleasantly in their joy of being reunited. Many of the Valor's smaller, weaker khiroi had been the fifty left with Teji, swapped by Feng for the Tejinder's well-bred specimens.

In all, Jai's cavalry was well over five hundred strong, if he could find the warriors to ride them. And he would need them soon enough. For while he scrabbled in the grass with his uncle, the Sabine legion marched deeper into their heartlands.

Based on those first entries in Leonid's diary, he imagined the current legion plagued with the same problems as those of the past, and would inevitably seek the same solutions. Which meant it would not be long before the Gryphon Guard were unleashed upon the Great Steppe, to goad the Sithia into war. That was, if they weren't busy with the dragons of the Dansk already.

Still, reading the diary was becoming more tedious. After those initial entries, he'd found that the bulk of the scattered scribblings were ration lists, salary pay and other such administrative notes. Which left him even more troubled, because he couldn't fully figure out a way to beat back Titus's incursion.

His father had only managed to best the Sabines by forming

alliances with other Great Tribes, and even then, it was a close fight. Now, facing a legion five thousand strong, Jai understood the daunting odds. And he was under no illusion that this legion was just the beginning. Once the Sabines resolved their skirmishes with the Dansk, they would send more legions, turning the tide overwhelmingly in their favour.

'Jai,' Feng said. 'May I have a moment?'

Jai turned, wincing at the disturbance. He'd been just moments away from retreating to the quiet of his bedchamber, where he could marshal his thoughts in solitude.

'Yes, Feng,' Jai said, allowing himself a smile as Feng's steed, Navi, playfully nudged Chak, eliciting a long-suffering grumble.

'We have much to discuss,' his vizier said.

'Teji is toothless now,' Jai said, waving away Feng's concerns. 'What could possibly be the matter now?'

Feng let out a long breath . . . then drew another of the same. Finally, 'Well . . . *everything*.'

Jai looked at him, weariness warring with wariness.

'To start,' Feng said, 'rancour brews among the nobles. Sindri demands an audience while Zayn stirs his warriors to abandon our cause. The populace clamours for their share of the spoils. And the traders swindle the Valor, while the Valor are only beginning to sense the deceit . . .'

He gulped another breath, but Jai raised his hand, forestalling him.

'Where's the booze,' Jai said. 'The khymis.'

Feng glared at him.

'You want a drink at a time like this? Did you not see what that stuff did to Teji?'

Jai stared at him, until he answered.

'Most of it is with the elders, brewing in the plaza.'

'Seize it,' Jai commanded. 'At least for the day. Encourage everyone back to their tents to rest, and enforce a curfew at dusk. If a reason is required, say we're rooting out spies. We probably should be doing that, anyway – have Harleen arrange a watch.'

Feng's eyes widened.

'Lying to your people already, Jai?'

Jai returned the surprise with a wry smile, his eyes reflecting a stark pragmatism. 'There's no lie. But call it a half-truth, if it comforts you. Either way, it's necessary. Leonid always said that liquor was the fertile ground from which mutiny and discord are sown. It emboldens the foolish, fuels the rash and blunts good judgement. Whispers become accusations, and understanding frays at its seams. By dawn, a drunken brawl could turn this camp to chaos. Seize the liquor, Feng. The people might resent me for it, but better that than regret tomorrow.'

Feng nodded. 'What else?' he asked.

'Ask Lai to assemble the traders and work out a fair payment to the Valor. Make it clear to the traders that if they don't abide by her decision, I'll let the Valor loose on them – their fear of the Tainted will do the rest.'

Feng chewed on his lip, before giving a curt nod of agreement.

'Share out half of my remaining gold among the citizenry and ensure they know who it's coming from.'

'Half!' Feng protested in disbelief. 'Do you intend to be a pauper khan?'

Jai shrugged.

'What have I need of money for, if not to keep the loyalty of my people, and the strength of my army? I already have the latter. Will gold buy me khiroi? More men? No. So let us tend to the people now. They risked their lives just as we did, didn't they? They deserve their share.'

Feng looked like he was not ready to drop it, but he bowed in reluctant agreement.

'What about Sindri and Zayn?' Feng asked, moving to more pressing matters.

'Zayn can wait – he can't leave without my approval. Although it would be difficult to convince him that Teji still poses a threat . . .'

Jai paused, trying to think. With a sigh, he clucked Chak forward.

'As for Sindri,' he said over his shoulder, 'invite her to my tent. I'll grant her wish.'

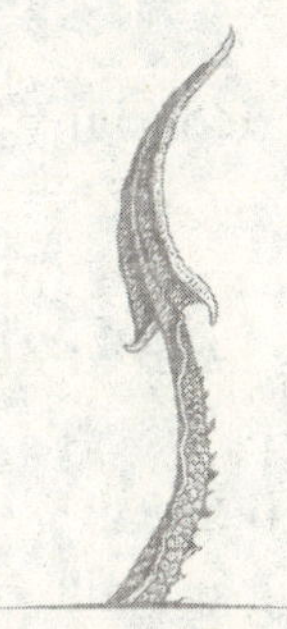

Chapter 41

Weary from the day's events, Jai slumped into his throne with a heavy groan. An increasing familiarity was creeping into these long hours of rulership, and he found himself pining for the peace and solitude of his scarcely used bedchamber. Winter had already absconded there, and was snoozing.

His moment of quiet awaited Sindri's arrival. Her banners represented nearly one-sixth of his entire army, even if her civilian followers formed a far smaller proportion of his peoples. It was crucial to keep her happy, especially because if Zayn chose to leave, there was no telling how many Valor would follow him.

Feng poked his head through the tent entrance. 'Sindri is here.'

'Enter,' Jai said.

Sindri stepped in, her eyes widening in awe as she took in the grandeur of Jai's chamber, for he had forgotten to shut the curtain behind the throne. It occurred to him that many among the Tainted had never seen the inside of another Great Tribe's camp, let alone a royal tent.

She walked closer to him, her eyes downcast, head bowed. She looked . . . different. Her hair had been oiled and she had clearly made use of the baths. Her face was made up, not just with kohl, but other intricate designs, dotted and curling around her eyes with red henna.

It was alluring, and beautiful, more detail emerging with every second he stared. He averted his gaze, realising he'd been fixated for too long.

'My khan, permission to speak?'

Jai put on as comforting a smile as he could.

'Speak freely, Sindri,' Jai said. 'And please, no need for such formality.'

She glanced up at him, hesitant. Then matched his smile with a weak one of her own. Feng coughed, and she nodded.

'I thank you for settling our dispute with the traders,' she said.

'They brought it on themselves,' Jai said. 'But I hope your warriors have not been selling their share of the weapons. They will have need of them yet.'

Sindri's brow creased as she struggled to understand.

'Teji is a neutered bull, without his khiroi,' she said. 'You need not fear him.'

Jai shook his head.

'I speak of the Sabines.'

Her laughter resounded in the tent, followed by a dismissive shake of her head.

'Fighting them . . . that's madness.'

'Watch how you speak to your khan,' Feng admonished sharply.

Sindri's jaw tensed, her gaze lowered once more in a show of deference. 'My apologies, my khan,' she uttered.

An uncomfortable silence filled the room until Jai broke it.

'Just call me Jai, Sindri, unless we are in public.'

She looked up, offering a nod in response. His casual address seemed to ease her slightly, yet she appeared reluctant to speak further. The abrupt shift in their relationship was, undoubtedly, hard to reconcile.

Feng cleared his throat, and she glanced over to him.

'I . . . it's about Zayn,' she said. 'May we speak alone?'

Feng bristled at that, but waited for Jai to speak.

'Feng is my trusted adviser, Sindri. His disdain for Zayn is well known, but he is first and foremost loyal to me. You can trust him.'

After another moment of hesitation, she blurted her truth.

'He plans to leave – tonight if you allow it. Now that I am no longer a queen . . . his men . . . they will not follow me.'

Jai chewed his lip, confused. He had always thought the Sithia had as many female khans as they did men, by way of primogenitor. Yet he remembered Zayn's camaraderie with his warriors in the bathhouse, a bonding that Sindri couldn't partake in.

'How many are loyal to him?' Jai asked.

'Twenty,' she said. 'But as many again will follow them, out of kinship, blood bonds or marriage.'

Jai cursed beneath his breath. That was half the Valor's warriors. And almost a tenth of his entire force.

'What do you suggest?' Jai asked.

She hesitated yet again.

'My lord, we must speak privately.'

Jai puffed with annoyance, but caught Feng's eye. He gave Feng a reluctant smile, and shrugged. His vizier sighed, and inclined his head.

'Call out if you need me,' Feng said, bowing and backing away.

'He won't,' Sindri snapped.

Feng shrugged himself. 'I'll be right outside.'

No sooner had Feng left, she stepped closer to the throne, Jai assumed in case they were overheard. He leaned out to listen, only to find her hand cup his face.

She kissed him, her lips soft on Jai's own, pushing him into the back of his seat. He felt her hands rake his chest, and for a moment, he was lost in the bliss of it, feeling her hard body, with all the deliciously soft parts, pressing closer to his own.

He pulled away suddenly, the movement jerking Sindri back. Temptation to draw her close once more filled him, but he pushed it away, thoughts of Erica's face steeling his resolve.

Sindri touched her face, her eyes wide with hurt.

'Do I not please you?'

Jai stood. She was beautiful, true, but this . . . it felt wrong.

'What is this?' Jai asked.

'I would make a strong queen,' she responded. 'Marry me, and I'll reclaim my title. The men will stay for a Valor queen.'

Jai stared, horrified. 'I hardly know you,' he said. 'How can you ask this of me?'

She lowered her gaze, locks of hair cascading to hide her face, but not before a solitary tear betrayed her anguish. It struck Jai then, the depth of her pain. Overthrown by her own brother, robbed of her legacy – her heartache was palpable.

And Zayn had struck her. More than once. A brute, through and through.

She straightened, lifting her chin, and pawed the wet from her face where it had streaked her henna.

'A concubine, then,' she bargained. 'Queen consort.'

It made sense, in its horrible way. This was politics, not love, and it secured something for both Sindri and him. But it wasn't the way. For one thing, he did not love her, and – perhaps naively – that mattered to him. More, though, it didn't actually solve the problem of Zayn. If anything, it could exacerbate the issue.

Jai shook his head slowly, and took her hand. It was shaking. Behind that hard facade, there was a sensitive heart.

'What else can I do?' Jai said.

She sniffed. Pulled back her hand, and stared away, as if she could see through the tent wall, and deep into the very steppe itself.

'Those men follow Zayn because of his ambition. They want to be famed warriors. Scourges of the Great Steppe. Some even wish to become soulbound, as he is.'

Jai nodded, slowly.

'Well, there will be plenty of battle with the Sab—'

'No,' Sindri said, cutting him off. She caught herself, though, and softened her tone.

'Even if your five hundred could prevail over five thousand. They covet . . . all this.'

She gestured expansively at the grandeur of the tent, the throne – their present surroundings.

'The Sabines lack khiroi and everything our people prize. Even Sabine weapons are ill-suited for khiro-back, and they would rather be stabbed than shoulder the disgrace of donning Sabine armour.'

'The legion will have gold,' Jai said. 'Wages for the soldiers.'

Sindri threw her hands up, her frustration evident.

'What use is gold?'

'Every possible use,' Jai retorted, his own irritation mounting. 'Enough to purchase whatever they could desire.'

'Did the incident with the traders earlier today escape your notice?' Sindri questioned, her voice soothing. 'They are ignorant of its value. Just ask Feng . . . he fleeced them worse than the traders did.'

Jai grimaced, knowing it to be true. He conceded the point, burying his face in his hand and giving a reluctant nod.

'You want to confront the Sabines?' she queried. 'Then you need more warriors. Which means conquering other tribes.'

Jai gritted his teeth. His father had not been a conqueror, even in the face of Leonid. Jai wished to follow in his father's footsteps. To earn alliances, unite the tribes.

Leonid was the conqueror. Jai would not become what he hated most.

'How do you think the Valor became what it is today?'

Jai looked up.

'Pull up a seat,' he begrudged.

Sindri did so, dragging a cushion over, and wiping off the

makeup with her sleeve – which told him all he needed to know about how much she had wanted to be married too.

At least that's something we can agree on.

'Zayn and I began with nothing,' she began, her voice steady. 'We were just two fettered escapees from a Phoenixian trader, sold there by a rival Tainted tribe before I could even form memories. Zayn recalls it – he was already a boy, but I was barely more than an infant. He does not speak of it.'

Jai listened intently. Even Feng did not know the whole story of the Valor. But now he knew why the Valor raided traders, ignoring the Pact.

'We had but one khiro, an old nag we stole from our master. It could barely hold our weight, but it let us travel the steppe. We scavenged, scratched out a life. Zayn . . . he . . .'

She sniffed, and then composed herself.

'He was big, even then. And he'd tended our master's khiroi, knew their ways. So when we escaped, and the nag fell sick, he went out, alone. Left me in an oasis. For months, I waited, eating what our forebears had planted for me. And then he came back, soulbound to his Alkhara.'

Now she had Jai's full attention.

'Don't you see, Jai. Strength begets strength. Whenever we encountered Tainted, they would join our cause. These were the outcasts of the outcasts. They wanted Zayn's strength. His power.'

'So I let other tribes join me,' Jai said. 'Is that not what we did with you?'

Sindri shook her head.

'Just listen.'

She inhaled deeply, as if revisiting the memories was a struggle in itself.

'We hunted khiroi with them. That's how it started. Turned two khiroi into five, into ten, twenty. And then they came. The Valor.'

Jai stared at her, not understanding.

'We lost many people that day. King Harpal, he abandoned those he deemed worthless. The children, the wounded. He tossed them aside like spoiled fruit.

'But we swore our oaths. And we followed him. He married me, Jai. And Zayn became his right-hand man. When Harpal died of fever, I became their queen.'

'What are you trying to tell me?' Jai said.

'That what happened to us was inevitable,' she said. 'The bigger tribes absorb the weak. It is the way of the steppe. We understood that. So too will the tribes you conquer. An alliance is a fragile thing, subject to the changing whims of those who make them. Oaths and khiroi, Jai. That is the true currency of the steppe.'

It was hard not to see the truth in these words. But it was easy to know this was not what he wanted.

'The Valor had nearly a third of your army's khiroi count when you met us in the field. That is because we understood this principle. We confronted our adversaries, vanquished those we could and held our ground against those we couldn't. You must do the same.'

'I have no need to,' Jai snapped.

'You are one of the so-called Great Tribes, diminished though your people have become over the years,' she snapped. 'That means your army is the weakest among them. Teji was a coward king, everybody knew it. The riteless did not flock to him. Traders circled him like vultures. What little your father left behind, he squandered in petty dealings and baubles.'

She sniffed, then stood.

'You are not even rited. And that stands for something, even among the untainted, I'm told. I know for sure the Valor will never follow a riteless king.

'As I said, Zayn will come in the morning, and demand his release, with many among the Valor at his back. I shall speak my case, but it will only carry so much weight.'

'Again, I ask you: what do you propose I do?' Jai asked.

Other than marry you, he thought.

'I suggest you give them a reason to stay.'

Jai meant to reply, but she had already turned her back, stalking out with a feline air. He sighed, and called for Feng.

Sleep would have to wait a little longer.

Chapter 42

Jai waited, his Great Council assembled before him. Every household had a representative here, filling the tent. Even outside, hundreds gathered, their ears pressed to the canvas. He felt like a doll, upon that throne. Feng and Harleen asked Teji's old servants to his tent, and they had worked through the night. So much had they hated the old khan, they had refused payment.

Now Jai was as primped and gaudy as a pleasure garden's peacock, down to the royal blues that draped him, and the whorls of red henna upon his face and hands. It all felt ostentatious, a puppet show of grandeur, but it was a show he had to perform nonetheless.

Before him, the assembled council watched in expectant silence. Old and young, men and women, each member was a leader in their own right, representatives of the diverse banners under Jai's rule. In this way, every family had a voice, and Jai could address all his people from the confines of his tent. Their eyes weighed heavy on him, gazes filled with expectation.

Few among them knew more than what they had heard. Rumours abounded, and Harleen had given him an overview from what her people had told her.

They had done all he'd asked, and they'd seen the profit in it. There had been anger, even calls to usurp him, when the Valor had arrived. But now, after Teji's defeat, and having celebrated with some of these so-called Tainted, who had saved them from a bitter civil war, the tide was turning.

True, there were some discontents, but Jai knew they would come around. They'd have to. Now he had to focus on the task at hand. It was a risk to do this so publicly. Indeed, Feng had hoped to keep this quiet. But Jai knew that this was the only place that he could speak with the Valor without weapons drawn on either side.

And then they came. Sindri and Zayn, walking in together, most of the Valor along with them. Zayn walked with confidence and an unmistakable air of authority, all eyes on him as he ducked into the tent.

Sindri, on the other hand, moved with quiet determination, her eyes meeting Jai's in a silent promise, almost apologetic in their bearing. They made their way to the front of the council, the sea of representatives parting to allow them passage.

'Sindri and Zayn of the Valor,' Feng said, his voice resonating throughout the tent. 'You stand before the Kidaran Great Council. You have asked for this audience. It is so granted.'

Zayn did not stand on ceremony, ignoring Feng and speaking directly to Jai.

'We had an agreement that once Teji was no longer a danger, I could leave, and take any who would follow me, without blood, or flesh, or gold as payment.'

Jai steepled his fingers, and nodded.

'I did.'

'Teji is vanquished,' Zayn said. 'So I take my leave.'

He began to turn his back, to gasps from the watching Kidara. Turning your back upon a khan was an insult, let alone in the Great Council.

'Stop,' Jai snapped, before the insult was complete. 'That is for me to decide.'

Jai saw the man's jaw flexing as he turned back, a finger in the air.

'Will you deny it?' Zayn growled.

'Watch your tone,' Jai said. 'I am your khan until I release you. If you will hold me to your terms, then I will hold you to mine.'

Zayn let his finger fall, and crossed his arms.

'Teji may rise again,' Jai said. 'He has the gold, and the people. Why, there is nothing stopping him from hiring five hundred mercenaries and returning here. Or buying as many khiroi from some gold-hungry tribe, and mounting another attack.'

There was murmuring from the onlookers, and Jai cursed his loose tongue. He did not want to sow fear, but he had to speak the truth.

'That is your doing,' Zayn snarled back. 'You had him in your grasp, yet you chose to let him go. All to keep me in bondage.'

Jai could practically feel the spittle against his face as Zayn sprayed the final words, but he held his nerve. The man had worked himself into a rage, and Jai intended to use it.

'Oh yes,' Jai said, letting the sarcasm drip from his words. 'When I was winning us an army's worth of khiroi and blades and the return of half my nobles, without a drop of blood spilled, I was really thinking about keeping *you*, Zayn. You think much of yourself.'

'Bastard!' Zayn snarled. 'Half-blooded, riteless cur.'

Jai's guards stepped forward, hands upon their blades, but Jai held up a hand.

'Did you swear loyalty to me?' Jai said, addressing not just Zayn, but his men behind him. 'Or do you not keep your oaths?'

Zayn looked around him, breathing deeply, and realising he had stepped too far. Had Teji been khan, Jai was sure Zayn would have been cut down where he stood. As it was, the Valor's fingers strayed to their empty scabbards.

'I did,' Zayn allowed. 'And I expect you to keep yours.'

'The Tejinder threat is in hand,' Jai said. 'Even if he returned, we have more than enough khiroi, blades and fighting men to defeat him.'

'So you admit it!' Zayn said, triumphant.

'I do,' Jai said. 'But I have a question.'

'Ask it,' Zayn said.

'It is not to you, but to the people of the Valor.'

Jai almost stood, but held himself back. The throne was a powerful symbol and he would use it to its full effect.

'You stand here, today, richer. Every one of you rides a Kidaran khiro, bred from the bloodstocks denied you for centuries.'

He could see nods from the Valor, some grinning at his acknowledgement of their gain. Just as he could sense the anger from the Kidara.

One thing at a time.

'Your purses are heavy with gold, now that you can trade freely. Do not forget my intervention to make sure you were paid fairly.'

Zayn stared at Jai, his brow furrowed. He could not yet see Jai's strategy. Good.

'In one night, you were given everything you ever wanted, and more. Not a drop of Valor blood was spilled. You are now part of a Great Tribe, and none but our enemies will call you Tainted. I ask you . . . why are you so desperate to leave?'

'Because we are Valor,' Zayn snapped. 'Because we kneel for no man!'

But Jai's words were having an effect. He could see men and women murmuring. *Zayn* may kneel for no man, but his soldiers . . . they had something to consider now.

'Therein lies the heart of it!' Jai retorted. 'Zayn would be khan. His choice is to serve his own ambitions. And you follow, because you know no other way.'

'Lies,' Zayn said, fingers curling into fists.

'You all know me!' Jai called, above the rising voices. 'And I know you. Sindri has led you well, but I know you live in fear of tribes that hunt you, like the Keldar. Any day, you might be subsumed by a larger tribe, or sold as fettered to the Phoenix Empire. Tell me that isn't what you've lived with your entire lives?'

None could deny it, and so he pressed.

'With me, *you* are the hunters.'

Zayn was turning now, trying to quell the tide of dissent behind him.

'He is a riteless coward,' he crowed. 'Come begging for us to save him, in the dead of night. He shirks the glory of battle.' He spun back around. 'Tell us then, my so-called khan. Who shall we hunt?'

It was cleverly done, and Jai cursed beneath his breath, such that Winter, crouched by his side, lay a head upon his lap. But she didn't know that while this wasn't exactly how he wanted to announce this, he *did* have an answer.

All the room looked to him, expectant. Sindri, her gaze fixed upon his own, nodded ever so slightly.

'The Keldar,' Jai announced.

Zayn clearly didn't expect him to have an answer. The rest of the tent clearly didn't know what to make of it. Jai ploughed on in the wake of the confused silence.

'They are among the largest tribes of the Tainted, are they not?' Jai said. 'Long rivals of the Valor. It was not so long ago that they hunted you. I remember, because I held the line along with you, standing in your front ranks.'

Zayn scoffed. 'The Valor need not become your servants to defeat the Keldar.'

He thumped his chest, turning to his warriors. 'We will thrash them ourselves!' he bellowed.

'How?' Jai asked swiftly, curtailing any response from the Valor. 'What will you become, if you leave with Zayn?' he gestured beyond to the families crowded there. 'Twenty, thirty riders? Easy prey for even the smallest of tribes. How many years will it take for you to become the force you once were?'

'You jest,' Zayn said, letting out an exaggerated laugh. 'All of the Valor will come with me.'

'You seem quite sure of that. And yet you do not speak for them,' Jai retorted. 'You are not their khan, nor ever were. Their oaths are to Sindri. Sindri, what say you?'

Sindri now met Jai's eyes, her gaze almost meek, but what came out of her mouth were words of confidence.

'I will remain with Jai and the Kidara. I care little for the title of khan. I care only for the betterment of those beneath my banner.'

Zayn turned upon her, his hands clenched. But Sindri stood firm, met his gaze.

'If you wish to leave, then do so, brother,' Sindri said, her voice high and clear. 'Long have you allowed your ambition to cloud the love you hold for our people. For *me*. So leave. But know I will not come with you. And I will implore my people to follow my example.'

Jai held his breath, as Zayn trembled with rage. Only the gaze of the onlookers seemed to prevent him from striking.

'Go,' Jai commanded.

His words seemed to snap Zayn into action.

'Those who stay are dead to me,' he growled. 'Those who follow shall ride to glory.'

It was a weak finish. But as the big man pushed his way through, out of the tent, some twenty men and women followed, even as their comrades pulled on their clothing, imploring they remain.

In the final moments, some ten more followed, regretful, still calling to their friends, their families. Jai's heart hurt at the sight. But this was not of his making.

Thirty warriors. Fewer than Jai had dared hope. But still more than he could afford.

'Kneel!' Feng said, his voice ringing out across the crowded room.

The Valor stared, until Sindri led by example, falling to one knee with her head bowed. In the sight of the Kidara, Feng began to recite the blood oath that would bind Sindri, and the Valor to his cause.

Another bloodless victory.

This one felt much more hollow, though.

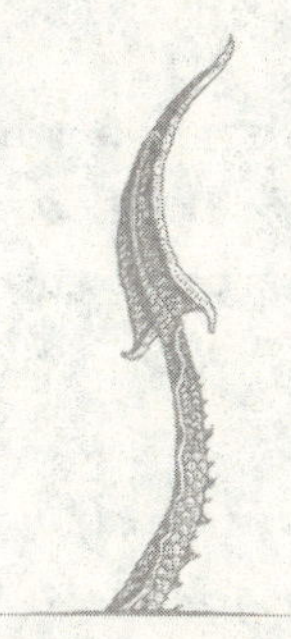

Chapter 43

Our expedition into the ocean of green is over. Now we reap the maelstrom we have summoned.

They came. Twenty thousand strong, riding the outskirts of our camp. My supply trains are but burned-out husks left in our wake. It is a siege, now.

We outnumber them, but every sally is met with retreat. Without cavalry, we have no hope of catching them. I have lost too many men pursuing these ghosts of the grasslands. Let them ride – it bothers me none.

Because who besieges whom? Night and day, our Gryphon Guard fly, furious to be relegated to carriers of grain. Little do they know, therein lies our salvation. For while our men sit, and bathe in the sun, awaiting their wing-bound repast, Rohan's soldiers ravage their own land. It is picked bare, twenty leagues all around.

It is said that a Sithian rider can range the Great Steppe with nary a crumb in their pocket, let alone grain; for their so-called 'khiroi' need nothing but grass. As for the heathens, they gather their herbs on the move, and bleed and milk their beasts when that will not do.

But there is only so much blood to be had, and teats run dry, the khiroi's winter calves already weaned. So we wait. Let us see if this Rohan is the terror they say he is when all around him is hunger and privation.

Jai rode at the head of the column, the open steppe an endless expanse before him. Near four hundred warriors rode at his back, as he led the ancient tribe of his ancestors east.

For that was where their prey lay. The Keldar.

His scouts had said as much, aided by Kiran and the remainder of the Valor. Her soulbound eyes and nose were well attuned to the passing of other tribes, such that she could oft tell which tribe had passed simply by the smell of their cuisines.

Kiran was now Sindri's new right-hand woman, stepping into Zayn's shoes. It was strange to give orders to her and her soldiers that morning, when a few weeks prior, she'd been beating him black and blue.

Still, those Valor that remained seemed all the more loyal to him, now that they had made their choice. They believed in him, and what he had promised. He just had to deliver.

In order to do that, he had to prepare his own people. Because the Kidara of Teji's reign were not used to this kind of hunt. Yet it was also his uncle that made such a transition to hunters possible; Teji's pillaging of the camp was a blessing in disguise. For while the Tejinder nobles had been busy loading fine-carved furniture, silks and tapestries, they had left behind what Jai considered all the more valuable: the tools, the furs, the heavy ingots of steel.

More, Jai's uncle had left behind a people that was lean in possessions and hungry in ambition. He had left them as their ancestors had once been. How Jai's father had led them. No longer would they spend every other day sitting idle. No longer would they covet the petty trinkets of the east.

They would learn to be Sithian again, as he had.

'Jai.'

It was Sindri. She wore all the regalia of her house, and it was clear the traders had lightened her purse. The Valor's crossed symbol flowers were all over her, from the garlands braided into her hair to the embroidery on her silken battle-robes.

He nodded in acknowledgement, and she rode closer. It felt strange not to tower over his fellow riders as he once had, for he no longer rode Chak. This, Navi could attest, as she had discovered this morning. The old doe had turned her horn up at her paramour's replacement – Baal, a smaller, more unruly Alkhara – the one that Nazeem had been forced to leave behind.

Jai had not had the heart to see Chak go, for Zayn had taken him, as was his right. Another piece of Jai's father had gone, and he still felt bereft.

'Sire,' Sindri said. 'May I have a private word?'

Jai spurred Baal out of earshot, the beast reluctantly edging ahead of the herd, fighting him all the way. Sindri raised her brows as she neared, giving the snorting Alkhara a wider berth than she needed.

'Jai, you are riteless still,' she said. 'For now, it is tolerated. But until it is done, your rule will be forever questioned.'

There it was again.

'I am told a great feat can serve as a Rite. Surely my return to our people was feat enough?' Jai demanded.

Sindri shook her head.

'There is a ceremony to it. And there must be witnesses, when you leave.'

'Feng!' Jai called, earning an eye roll from Sindri.

His vizier was not long to reach them, Navi somehow managing to sulk while she trotted, her head low, her eyes mournful.

'Sindri says I need to be rited, and soon.'

'It is not uncommon for an unrited heir to replace their fallen khan. Why, Teji was riteless when your father fell. But it is a circumstance that is tolerated, and expected to be resolved.'

'So you agree with her,' he pressed.

'I do.'

'I don't have time for this,' Jai groaned. 'We are at war.'

'Perhaps to you,' Sindri said. 'But your people do not even acknowledge it is your intent to face the legion, for it seems so far out of reach. For them, you have returned to the old ways, hunting the smaller tribes to bring them under your banner, or take what is theirs if they won't. If anything, they expect it more. It is not merely a tradition, Jai. It is . . . a necessity.'

'Did Teji eventually do it, then?' Jai asked.

Feng thought for a moment, then turned and rode back, calling for Harleen.

'Might as well call a Small Council at this rate,' Jai muttered.

Sindri gave him a blank stare.

'Never mind. About the other night . . .' Jai said, while Feng was out of earshot. 'I thank you. It cannot have been easy, casting your brother out. And for your offer . . . no easier too.'

She sniffed. 'He is my brother no longer. That man is gone.' She thought on it for a second. 'Maybe he'd been gone for a long time,' she finished quietly.

Jai opened his mouth to comfort her, but Harleen and Feng's arrival closed it again.

'For a king to be rited in wartime is a risky thing,' Harleen said, before Jai could even speak. 'To ride or walk the Great Steppe, alone. The Pact is not held sacred by all, as well we know.'

She gave Sindri a pointed glance, but the former queen did not react.

Jai didn't understand. Clearly, that was evident upon his face, as Harleen apologised and spoke again.

'But risk is not all there is to consider. Until you are rited . . . with my apologies . . . you are not yet a man,' she said.

'Even as khan?' he asked.

'Many think Teji ended the war, so he could rite himself,' Harleen said. 'That is why he did not use the fact you are riteless against you in his speech.'

'If you seek to ally with another tribe, as your father once did,' Feng said, 'they will not lend their swords to a riteless young prince. There are many marks against your name already, but being riteless is perhaps the greatest.'

'If I lead my tribe,' Jai said, 'who is it I am to swear loyalty to?'

Harleen gave him a forced smile.

'Your ancestors.'

'We ride to take the Keldar,' Jai said. 'As you said, Harleen, we cannot stop for me to hunt and break a wild khiro.'

'There are other things you can do,' Feng said. 'Blood. Or flesh. If you can kill an enemy of the tribe, alone or with other riteless, you will be rited too. Or gold, taken from them – alone or with other riteless.'

'What would you have me do?' Jai asked.

He waited for an answer, but all that came was the chirring of insects in the grass. He shook his head, and spurred Baal ahead.

'We ride on!' he called, mind churning. 'I want to see their campfires when we camp for the night.'

Chapter 44

To be khan was a lonely thing. Jai sat, brooding in his great tent, listening to his hearth's fire crackle. Had he not Winter, her heavy head in his lap, he might have despaired.

He had always thought of himself as being alone. But now, he realised that Leonid, for better or worse, had been his constant companion. Even in the dead of night, all those years ago, he could hear the old man snoring through the thin walls of his makeshift wardrobe chamber.

With Winter asleep, and unable to offer much more than silent feelings of love and encouragement, he longed for companionship.

For Rufus's ribald jokes. Even his nudging, and prodding, at Jai's reddening face.

And Erica. With her wild beauty, and hidden depths. The kind heart behind steel walls, where only thoughts of her people were allowed to enter.

Where could she be now?

Yet no sooner did their faces swim to the surface, he pushed them down. He knew he had more pressing things to consider. How could he help them, when he was still drowning himself? For now, they would have to wait.

He yawned, glad he had allowed himself and the rest of the tribe the afternoon and night to rest, after Zayn's departure.

But the time to think had allowed tongues to wag, and he knew his riteless status was the topic of the day.

The Rite. He cursed the practice, even as he knew it was the great equaliser. Pauper or prince, every Sithian that belonged to a tribe had gone through it. Though, he knew, most made far more paltry offerings. Stolen oxen from a trader, or pilfered gold from the same. Perhaps a wild old khiro, near dead on its feet, or a calf, abandoned by its mother. Others might bring other animals, grass eaters of the plains, or their carcasses to be eaten.

These, according to Feng, were the most common offerings. More often than not, it was the ceremony that was important.

But not for him, lest the shame of his pathetic offering to the tribe follow him the rest of his life. He, the son of Rohan, soulbound to a dragon. To bring back anything but a wild, fresh-broken khiro or the heads of a handful of legionaries would be paltry.

He might also perform an act of daring. Like crossing the Great Steppe without a khiro. Or kidnapping the heir of another tribe. Fat chance of doing that, soulbound or not.

The only thing worse was to be riteless forever.

He knew that he could cheat. So many did, if the tales Harleen told were true. Even Teji had been dogged with rumours.

Still, even Sindri said that he had a few weeks yet before it became a worry. His people knew his purpose. But whatever Tainted tribe they hunted, whether Keldar or not, once that was done, he'd be out of excuses.

Worst of all, he had another conundrum. Because Harleen had reported there were no Keldar campfires on the horizon that night, though the smoke of others stained the far skies. Lean as they were, they were still too slow.

Hunting another tribe meant riding out again, leaving his tribe exposed. Already, the rumours of his split with Teji would have spread throughout the Great Steppe – traders often profited more from their news than their wares. Many had peeled away from his own, remoras in seek of another shark to follow. Soon it would spread that a Great Tribe was vulnerable.

More enemies would come, for both he and Teji. And with many tribes moving east in fear of the Sabines, there would be more close by than usual. This was not the time to play cat and mouse games, alone or with his army.

Yet that was what he had been forced to do, one after the other. Was it right to make war on the Keldar? They had never done him any harm. And yet he knew, they would easily have fallen on the Valor, had they shown weakness.

He had no choice. This was the way of things. For now, he must ride the Great Steppe's tide. Only when he had crested might he make his own way.

To hunt the Keldar, he would need to leave a sizeable force behind to protect his people. Three hundred, at least. Few tribes could field more than that number, and those that could would not force a battle with the same.

Scouts and outriders aside, that left him with some hundred and eighty knights to spare. Hardly much greater than the Keldar's numbers, if Sindri's estimate was accurate. He had not enough to force a surrender and it was too many to face in a fair fight.

Jai wondered if his father had suffered such evenings. Alone, in his tent, weighing the fate of the Kidara. If Samar and Arjun could see him now. Jai raised a horn of wine, where the servants had left it for him. They were still used to how Teji had liked things, and for once, he was grateful.

He looked up to where the smoke from the hearth drifted through the tent's opening. There, he could spy the stars. The self-same stars he and his brothers had looked up at, dreaming of the world they had left behind.

He gave them silent toast, letting the bitter fruit of the wine slip down. Hoping they were watching him, from the Mother's bosom, somewhere out there.

It was only now, as his thoughts turned to family, that he remembered. Though both his brothers' mother and his own had died, he wondered if Arjun and Samar had aunts, or cousins among his people.

Even as he knew he would have none of his own. For his mother . . . she had been a concubine. Not even queen consort, as Samar and Arjun's mother had been.

And he realised then. That here, now, he might find the answers to the questions Balbir could never give him. To know of his mother. Even . . . her name.

He put aside the drink, and called out.

'Guard.'

An armoured man ducked into the tent, his head bowed. 'Sire?'

'What elder might remember my father's time?' Jai asked.

'My khan, Meera is the memory keeper of the tribe. Now she shall be asleep, but her disciples are young and can be roused.'

'Memory keeper?' Jai asked.

The man reddened, and Jai winced as he realised he had revealed how little he knew of the Sithia's ways once more. He hoped the guard understood discretion.

'An elder who holds the memories of the tribe,' the guard said tactfully. 'They remember the victories and defeats, the oaths. The bloodlines of the herd. The bloodlines of the nobility . . .'

Jai held up a hand.

'You said a disciple could come?' he asked.

'Yes, my khan,' the guard said. 'She has two of them, listening to her stories, until they know them too. That way, it is not forgotten.'

Jai almost let out a chuckle. It sounded like he'd been Leonid's inadvertent memory-keeping disciple. But for it to be their entire purpose . . . they must be as patient as the Sabines' saints.

Jai knew it would be proper to wait until morning. But by then, the problems of the morrow would be upon him. He allowed himself to be selfish.

'Please,' Jai said. 'Summon one of her disciples.'

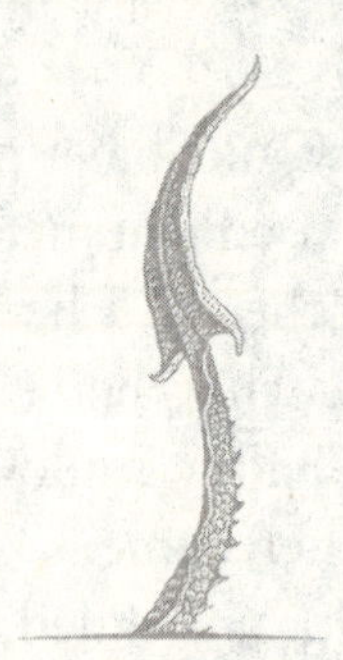

Chapter 45

It took a while for the guard to return. Jai paced, brimming with anticipation, such that Winter had been stirred from her sleep, and watched him with a bewildered gaze from his throne.

Finally, they came. Jai saw the guard helping a wizened old lady through the door, even as she belaboured him with her walking stick.

'Let me go! I'll walk before my khan, unhand me, you imbecile . . .'

The guard abandoned his efforts, as a young girl followed behind him, her eyes wide as she saw the grandeur of the tent.

'Meera,' Jai said, hastening to the old crone's side. 'I had not meant to wake . . .'

'You think the Kidara's memory keeper would miss a chance for an audience with the khan?' she asked, waving away Jai's help much the same as she did the guard. 'I would not dream of it.'

Meera struggled with the next few steps, and this time allowed her disciple, with some grumbling, to help her to the audience cushion at the foot of Jai's throne.

Jai hastened back to his seat, and caught the disciple motioning at her ear, even as Meera pulled an ivory ear trumpet, one as white as her hair, from the folds of her moth-eaten robes.

Understanding, Jai took a seat opposite her, the pale orbs

that were her eyes boring into him. He smiled at her, and took her hands.

Her face was more wrinkle than anything, creasing in a toothless smile as she leaned closer. Her wizened hands reached out to feel him, tugging at his hair, brushing his lips and nose.

'Rohan's boy,' she said, nodding with approval. 'You have his bearing.'

'Thank . . . thank you,' Jai said, taken aback. This had not been how he'd pictured the conversation.

'Meera, do you remember the old times?' Jai asked, speaking into the earpiece.

'Wouldn't be a good memory keeper if I didn't!' she cackled, before her laughter turned into a hacking cough.

Her disciple smiled awkwardly at Jai, as she patted Meera's back.

'My little birds tell me . . . all the goings-on of this . . . place,' Meera said, still coughing. 'I say, good! A return to the old ways. Why, it has been so long since Teji brought me here, even if it was only to hear his petty woes and foibles . . .'

'I—' Jai tried to interject.

'It's a dark day indeed when the memory keeper must rely on the prattling of her khan's concubines instead of his testimony. A memory keeper's as much a secret keep—'

'Mistress, please,' her disciple said loudly.

'What?' Meera said, turning her trumpet. Her voice had a slurping, slurring quality, a consequence of her lack of teeth.

Jai took his chance to speak.

'Meera, do you remember my mother?' he asked loudly.

Meera turned back, and nodded sagely.

'A captive, from a Sabine baggage train,' she said. 'Near the middle of the war, after your father drove Leonid back west. A pretty one, or so I'm told. My eyes were never good, even then.'

Meera snapped her fingers, and the disciple hastened to a pouch at her waist, and stuffed a handful of jerky into her own mouth. Jai stared, confused, as the girl's jaws worked busily.

'What was her name?' Jai asked. 'Tell me everything you know.'

Meera snapped her fingers again, and the girl spat into her hand, before handing it to Meera. The old lady masticated thoughtfully with her gums, letting out a hum as her eyes rolled back.

Jai leaned forward. He had never dared think that he would know who his mother was. And while there was so much pressing in all around him, he found this was the only thing that mattered at this moment. Finally, Meera swallowed, and cocked her head.

'Rohan,' she said, raising a finger. 'He was . . . well . . . he never gave much thought to captives back then. All men of war, you see. He kept them, traded them for the return of his own captives. All part of the game.'

Jai resisted the urge to simply demand his mother's name. That would come. He'd waited this long . . .

'Then, one time . . . it was all women. Concubines for the legions. A reprieve for the soldiers, sent for by Leonid himself. Rohan said the legionaries must have been close to mutiny, to attempt such an expedition. Hell, there had been so many Gryphon Knights and cavalry protecting that baggage train, your father lost a hundred men to capture it. Imagine his fury at his reward – no weapons, no gold or food. A bunch of frightened women, press-ganged into a perilous fate.'

Jai's gaze drifted to Leonid's diary, where it sat upon the armrest of his throne. He wondered if Leonid would have cared enough to mention this shipment's capture.

'Your mother . . . she was Leonid's concubine first,' she said. 'Or one of his generals'. That was what Rohan thought. She rode in her own carriage, with her elderly mother. And your father knew more than most: lusty loins loosen lips.'

She savoured the last phrase, a devilish grin tugging at her lips as she nudged her protégé. The nudges persisted until a forced, weak chuckle slipped past the girl's mouth, her eyes offering an apologetic smile to Jai.

'Thus, he would summon her to his private quarters, questioning her about the man who was his adversary. Striving to know how he thought . . . how he fucked,' she said, tapping her temple with a wink.

Jai cleared his throat, sick of hearing what seemed tantamount to gossip – particularly about his own mother. Then Meera caught herself, and lowered her head respectfully.

'Rohan learned all too well,' she said, after Jai allowed a few moments of silence. 'A seducer of kings, that one. Wasn't long before she was Rohan's concubine too.'

'Her name,' Jai said.

'Miranda, her name was,' Meera said, closing her eyes as if straining to remember. 'He only let her name slip once in my presence. He forbade it spoken, you see. Kept her secret. Arjun and Samar's mother . . . she was a jealous one, even then. His interrogations became more intimate. He loved her, and she him – that's all he told me.'

She sighed, and gathered her robe closer about her.

'Who can say if a love can spring between captor and captive? The poor girl must have been frightened to death. But even with her last breath, she called for him. For you. I hope that gives you some solace.'

Jai sat back. He didn't know what he had expected to hear. Certainly, he had known some of it. But . . . he had never known she had been a captive. That she had once known Leonid.

To hear of her death . . . that she had wanted him. That perhaps she had loved his father. That meant something. He could feel it in his chest, the unwinding of something coiled tight.

'I know this is not what you wish to hear,' Meera said, perhaps taking Jai's silence as anger. 'But she was a secret, even to me. Your birth too was hidden. It was only when your father died, and Teji negotiated terms, that your existence came to light. By then, your mother was dead, and you were just another chip to trade, another hostage for peace. That's how Leonid wanted it.'

Jai wiped at his eyes, for they pricked and watered. He had always wondered why Balbir had known so little of his mother. Even believed her to be lying. Now he knew.

'How did she die?' Jai asked.

Meera sniffed deeply, and then lowered her chin into her hands, huffing.

'The Crimson Death,' she said. 'It came from the east. Took your mother, and her mother too. Arjun and Samar's mother. And many, many others. Some say, it was the Crimson Death that forced Rohan's hand to fight the final battle. He knew, in time, the plague would reach his armies.'

Jai stared, digesting the news. So much kept from him. So many years.

'I hear it made its way west, years later. Perhaps you remember it.'

Jai well remembered the terrible disease that had wracked Latium when he had been a young boy. That red rash that crept up people's bodies, sucking the life from them until their ravaged bodies fell where they stood.

'Anything else?' Jai asked, his voice hoarse as he pushed himself to his feet.

'She was pale of hair, skin and eye,' Meera croaked, reading Jai's cue and grasping at her disciple's arm to struggle to her feet. 'Her mother too. But Miranda is a Sabine name. Mayhap some Dansk in her, I saw. Or Samarion.'

Jai turned, so that the disciple could not see the tears that now readily messed his face, running down the henna that still dried there.

'If that's all, then,' Jai said.

He heard the thud, thud, thud of Meera leaving.

'We buried her, as we guessed was her people's custom,' Meera called. 'Her grave lies in the Blue Mesa. She said . . . it reminded her of home.'

Chapter 46

Finally able to sleep, Jai dreamed of his mother's face. Or rather, the lack of it. He followed her, through the tall grass, seeing golden hair flashing through the stems. She called his name, even as she ran from him.

And behind, the rumble of a khiro, and the ululation of a warrior. His father, calling his name. Calling him back . . .

'—We must break away now! Before the Tejinder regroup. They *will* come for us.'

Gurveer was adamant, leaning over the table, his hands spread. His voice broke through Jai's remembered dream, and he rubbed his eyes, returning to the task at hand. The Small Council.

Another week. Another empty horizon. Their passage was too slow.

If they stopped now, his people would know that the pursuit was abandoned. A weak move, if there ever was one.

But so too could they not keep up this punishing pace. The tribe was not used to it, and the old and infirm could not bear it much longer. Not to mention, it was getting them nowhere. They were just too slow.

By now, the Keldar knew they were being followed. No matter how hard he pushed his tribe, they could not catch up to the smaller one, only keep pace with it. Already, they were nearing the Phoenix Empire's borders, though they would have to travel weeks longer to try and trap them there. Weeks he could ill afford.

'We leave two hundred with the tribe,' Harleen said, snatching at the pointer stick in Gurveer's hand. He held it out of reach, and she abandoned the effort, instead stabbing a finger at the map in front of them. 'The same and eighty more follow the Keldar. Three days there, two days back.'

'Two days back?' Jai asked.

'The tribe will have caught up by then,' Feng explained. Jai caught Gurveer's eye roll, and realised once again, he had shown his ignorance.

But the question had sparked an idea. He let it percolate, then asked, 'They are that far?'

'Kiran is now sure of it,' Sindri said. 'Three days' ride – including riding through the last night – and we'll have them.'

'There must be more than this,' Jai muttered.

'How do you mean, my khan?' Harleen asked, catching his words.

Jai gestured to the map, pointing at the oases that scattered it. Already, they had stopped at one, replenishing their fast-dwindling supplies, a small detour that put them even further behind. He'd had little time to enjoy the beauty of their placid pools, nor the forests of bamboo and fruit that sprang up around it, instead bathing where it was safe in his room.

The duties of a khan were never done, as dispute after dispute were brought to his chamber, many between the Valor and the Kidara. Some nights, the queue would be longer than it had started by the time he had finished, collapsing upon his bed only for the queue to be waiting again in the morning.

Every choice seemed to make an ally and an enemy. Half the time, he couldn't decide either way, choosing based on gut instinct more than anything. It was a thankless task, and without Harleen and Feng in his ear, he might have collapsed beneath the stress of it.

'My khan?' Harleen asked, interrupting his thoughts.

'A good general uses the terrain to his advantage,' Jai said. 'We have not the wood to build walls, as the legions do. And the little trick we used upon Teji would never work against a different enemy – they would not hesitate to put the camp to fire and slaughter.'

He lowered his chin to his hands, staring at the table as if something might leap out at him.

'Is there *anything* in the vicinity that isn't an oasis or more grassland?' he said.

All eyes turned to their newly minted cartographer, a young, timid-looking man named Sony who had stayed with them during the tribe's division more out of indecision than anything else.

'My lord, by now, we near the Phoenix Empire's edge,' Sony said, his voice high and querulous. 'Another few weeks east, and we will reach their borders. The Kashmere Road lies south, not far from your throne, as the roq flies.'

He flashed a smile, but saw Jai's expectant eyes.

Tapping his chin, Sony hurried to clear the table, his hands shaking as he swept aside the game pieces. This time, he piled rocks along the edge of the map, huffing as he carried armful after armful, apologising as the Small Council shifted back to make room for him. He arranged them as swiftly as he dared, closing his eyes at times to try to remember.

'To the north are the Yaltai Mountains,' he finally said, pointing to the rocks. 'They stretch from the east to the west, where they join the Petrus Mountain Range that divides the Sabine Empire from the Great Steppe.'

Jai steepled his fingers, looking closely.

'And beyond?'

'They are impassable from the steppe,' the cartographer said, motioning at where much of the Small Council sat, beyond the map's edge. 'The Frostweald. Ice, and more ice. Nothing to hunt, nothing to grow. Even the Dansk leave it alone.'

'So we hide our vulnerable in the mountains,' Jai said. 'Get our people where enemy khiroi cannot manoeuvre, while we hunt down the Keldar.'

Sony's Adam's apple bobbed as he swallowed, and he stuttered until Harleen held up a hand and spoke.

'The Yaltai Mountains are not the Great Steppe,' Harleen said. 'There are still tribes there. Our cousins. Sithians, true, but of a different kind.'

'Oh?' Jai asked.

'The Mahmut tribe, and their mammoths, call its eastern ranges home,' she said. 'And the Caelite tribe too, further west, in the mountains themselves.'

Jai perked up at that. Even he had heard of the Caelite, though they had long faded into obscurity, unseen or heard of since his father's War of the Steppe.

The mammoth riders of the Mahmut were legend too, their great beasts breaking the walls of Leonid's camp in a bloody battle that had left no victor, but forced Leonid to end his siege. Jai had only seen one, slaughtered for entertainment in Latium's Colosseum.

It had been far bigger than even Chak.

But a Caelite . . . he knew only that they too had done their part in the war.

They were bird-folk. Terror birds, native to the mountains' lowlands, were what they rode into battle. But their soul-bound . . . they flew. Riding the great roqs, eagle-like beasts, as large as gryphons, such that they might snatch a khiro calf from the ground. In time, they had helped Rohan resist Leonid's dominance of the skies.

'The Caelite allied with my father once,' Jai said, screwing up his eyes as he tried to remember. 'Both of them. I am not their enemy.'

Leonid had rarely spoken of the War of the Steppe, for he knew how it upset Jai. But he had heard the Gryphon Guard speak of them, those times he had served them in their mess halls. They were but snatches of conversation, half-heard tales from grizzled knights who had long since retired. But it was enough, now, to spark hope.

Harleen nodded, though she looked hesitant.

'An alliance is perhaps too strong a word,' she said. 'I was still a young woman then, but I remember it was Leonid that brought their ire upon himself. His Gryphon Guard . . . they were a terror. Thousands of innocents, slaughtered across the lands. They left every tribe no choice, no choice at all. But when Rohan followed Leonid back into the empire, to defeat him once and for all . . . they did not follow. Too many dead, so the tale goes.'

Jai sighed, letting his head thud against the throne as he leaned back. Rohan's name seemed worth little, in the aftermath of his defeat. Jai had hoped the tribes of the steppe would flock to him, to fight this returned threat. Instead, they flocked east, hoping the problem would go away, in time.

Politics. He was sick of this game. What must he do to convince the Sithia of Titus's danger?

Jai rubbed his eyes, turning back to the task at hand.

'How many days to the mountains?' he asked.

The cartographer stared, wide-eyed, but answered readily enough.

'Two days. Perhaps one, if we ride through the night.'

Jai stared at where the young man had pointed, a rocky outcrop jutting into the Great Steppe. And between, an oasis.

'Do the Great Tribes range the Yaltai Mountains?' Jai asked.

'No, my khan,' he said, bowing his head. 'The grasses are poor there, and the danger of roqs carrying away calves is far greater. There are more predators there too, direwolves, sabretooths. They hunt the ibex that call the mountains their home.'

Jai leaned forward, staring.

'How much bamboo have we left?' Jai asked.

At this, even the Small Council looked surprised.

'Hardly any,' Feng allowed, checking through papers piled

upon his lap. 'We used most of it for the spears, and the barricades.'

Jai chewed his lip, thinking.

'The tribe will head for the Yaltai Mountains,' Jai said. 'Two hundred and fifty warriors will go with them. They will camp with their backs to the cliffs, in this hollow here. They will stop at the oases here, and here, gather as much bamboo as they can. This, and earthworks, will be used to build a wall, here.'

Jai used the pointer to cut across a valley between two jutting cliffs.

Then he turned to the Keldar, their game pieces forlorn, far ahead of them.

'I will take two hundred riders,' Jai said. 'Thirty shall scout for the tribe, keep an eye for enemies that approach, send word to us. If they lay siege or are spotted soon enough, we might return in time.

'Harleen?' Jai said, prompting her to take up the idea.

'We will need to strip the oasis bare to have even half of what we need for a wall such as this,' she said. 'Most of what we had was used for the spears.'

'Make do,' Jai said. 'Use the tent poles if you have to, sleep under the stars.'

'A wall such as you describe will do little to stop the Mahmut, or the Caelite from attacking,' Sindri noted. 'Only khiroi might be stopped. *Might*.'

'What have we that they desire?' Jai asked. 'Such that they would break down our walls and face the two hundred and fifty riders we left behind, and spear-armed citizenry? They have no use for our khiroi, nor do we have much gold for trade.'

He saw understanding spark in their eyes, and even Gurveer uncrossed his arms to look more closely at the map.

'It is the Great Tribes of the steppe we must fear,' Jai said. 'So let us go where they will not follow. I'm sure the Yaltai's tribes will not begrudge us a visit for . . . what, six days?'

'Seven,' the cartographer said, eyeing the map carefully.

'Even three hundred would not be enough,' Sindri said. 'They have a hundred and fifty warriors by my estimation. They would never surrender to a force hardly larger than their own.'

'Perhaps for surrender,' Jai said. 'But I will offer them the same deal I offered the Valor. Join me, or be crushed. You will come with me. Make them see reason.'

He settled back, his mind made up as the chaos of dissent descended once more around the table.

No matter. The dance of rulers required a sure foot. And he was sure.

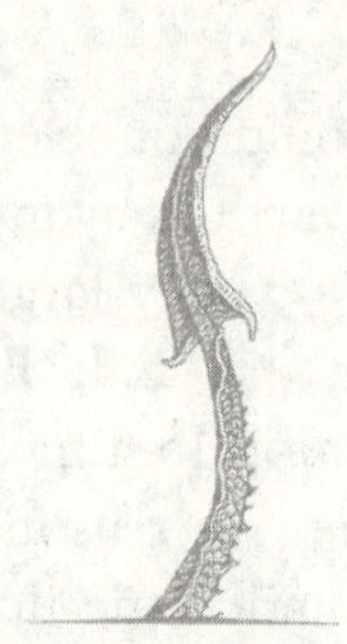

Chapter 47

At first, it was but smoke upon the horizon. Then flames, orange where green grass met blue sky.

Jai's scouts had spotted it in the late afternoon, on their third day riding out in pursuit of the Keldar. Now they followed it. It would only cost them a few hours to investigate.

These were not campfires, made of old bamboo and dried khiroi dung. There was too much smoke for that. Jai knew that, even before he could smell the blood on the wind.

Winter raced ahead, her lithe body spearing through the grass, and Jai urged Baal onwards, for she would not slow. Behind, he could hear the thunder of a thousand khiroi feet. Two hundred warriors, at his back. Hunting for prey upon the steppe.

It was strange to see the scene unfolding as they drew near. The oxen, lowing mournfully, cropping at the grass. The burned-out husks of the caravans, and the men and women, strung up like marionettes from what remained of them.

These were traders, of that there was no doubt. But what had happened to them . . . Jai could not yet say.

There were no dead khiroi nearby. The goods within the caravans, such as there were left of them, were burned with the rest of it. Silks, fine furniture, exotic fruits from the east. None of it had been taken.

Just left to burn, haphazardly. Stranger still were the oxen.

Some, true, had been killed. But more still remained, some hundred by his count. This had been a large caravan, likely one that had followed a Great Tribe and were now on their way home.

'These were not Sithian hands that did this,' Sindri croaked, her throat parched from the windswept ride. She gulped from her waterskin, and spoke again. 'This is mindless slaughter. Torture too.'

She motioned at the bodies, still hanging from the makeshift gibbets of their caravans' burned-out rafters. Men and women both. Phoenixian, by their attire, though their faces were a ruin.

Sindri was right. They *had* been tortured. Their limbs had been hacked off, while others were a mess of crossbow bolts. As if they'd been used as living target practice.

But it was their limb stumps that made Jai stop, and stare. He'd seen this before. Back in the tavern, after Rufus had used his whytblade to sever a robber's limb. Cauterised perfectly, and sliced easy as a slow-cooked ham.

He knelt, and picked up a tawny feather, from where it lay. He swallowed, and raised it, letting his voice carry to the hundreds milling behind him.

'Sabines!' he cried out. 'Gryphon Guard!'

His warriors' eyes turned to the skies in fear, blades drawn, khiroi spinning and rearing. But he held up his hands, calling for calm.

'This is what awaits all the Sithia!' he called out. 'This is what they *do*!'

He hoped this would strengthen their resolve, but all he saw was fear in their eyes. Everyone knew of the great slaughter Rufus's men had brought upon the Great Steppe. Anything to force the High Khan into a decisive battle.

Jai sighed, and dismounted. He felt the weight of guilt, settling heavy upon his shoulders. Because he knew, in his heart of hearts, he was to blame for this tragedy.

Traders were the messengers of the Great Steppe. The gossipmongers, purveyors of information. It might be that the legion had wanted the lay of the land, and had ravaged these traders in that pursuit.

But Magnus had been here, Jai was sure of it. And Jai knew, he and Erica could not be far from the man's thoughts. Jai knew his name had been uttered in this place.

He felt Winter brushing against his waist. By now, she was able to lap at his chin with only a stretching of her neck. Her growth spurt was coming in fits and starts, but it would not be long before she rivalled Navi in size. Already she'd made her way through a good portion of the jerky in the Kidaran reserves, but the people fed her freely. Often, she would slip out while Jai was occupied, returning with a bellyful of rich meat.

As for her wings, they were no longer the paltry things laid flat along her back. More and more, she unfurled them, and even now she held them wide, soaking in the last of the sun. The wingspan was so great, it stretched from Baal's horn to his tail.

'We make camp here!' Jai called, scratching his erstwhile dragon under her chin. 'Take what you can, and double the watch.'

'Sire,' Harleen said, riding up to him. 'Is this wise? To camp among all this?'

Jai held her gaze.

'We must bury the dead. And they,' he said, indicating the Kidaran warriors, 'must know death. Know their enemy. For all Gurveer's bluster, he and most of the men have not been tested in real battle. This is as close to the reality of it as we can give him before it is upon us.'

Sindri, trotting up beside her, was for once in agreement with Harleen.

'This will sow fear,' she said. 'We should keep on. There is still light in the day yet.'

'A measure of fear is useful,' Jai said, a little unkindly. 'It will keep the men from charging when they should not. These warriors, for all their weapons, armour and khiroi flesh, are but boys and girls playing dress-up.

'Have the Valor speak of battle,' Jai said to Sindri. 'Of facing down an enemy, and standing firm in the face of their charge. Let my soldiers know the truth of it. When the time comes, they will be champing at the bit. Temper the flames of their youth with the wisdom of your experience.'

'As you wish,' Sindri said, spurring her charge away.

Harleen looked to speak, then thought better of it. She too left him then. Jai wished Feng had come with him to offer his guidance, but the vizier was no warrior by his own admission. No, he had stayed with the others, there to look after the affairs of state.

Jai turned to Winter.

'I guess it's just you and me again, eh, girl?' Jai said.

She chirred happily, glad of the attention. Beyond sleeping, curled at the top of his bed, with Jai's head resting upon her belly, they'd had little chance to be together. Luckily, the bed had been reinforced to satisfy many occupants, a legacy of Teji's salacious tastes. It held up well enough beneath her growing weight.

Jai remembered when they'd had all the time in the world, making camp in the forest with Erica and Rufus. Where he would watch her hunt bugs among the trees, her tail lashing with excitement.

She was his beating heart, the second piece of his soul. And he had neglected her. He crouched among the ash and ruin, and hugged her tight.

'Stay close, my heart,' Jai whispered. 'We sail in troubled waters.'

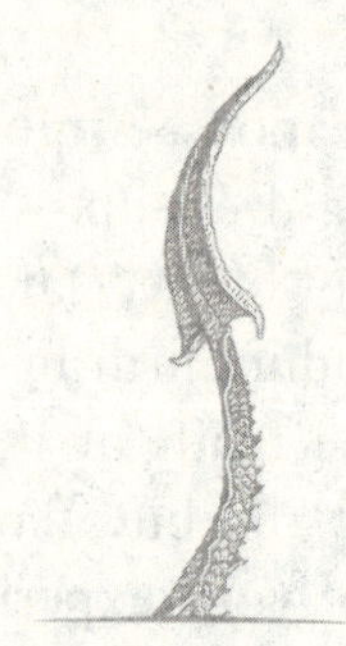

Chapter 48

They brought the oxen. It was too great a treasure to abandon, and the beasts followed them readily enough. Indeed, they could hardly stop them, for they were used to humans.

Lucky for Jai's men, their path was easy, for the trail Jai's knights carved had already been beaten by their quarry.

The Keldar. The grass in their path was yet to reclaim its domain, and he could see the footprints of shoe and khiro in the mud.

By now, his eye was accustomed to picking out the useful plants, hidden in among the leaves. He could see few had been harvested at the edges of their path. This was a tribe in flight.

They spurred themselves on. Into the night. So it was not long after the sun had set, and the moon but a silver glow behind an overcast sky, that they at last saw the fires of the Keldar, growing larger on the horizon.

But as they drew closer, consternation began among his riders. He signalled a general halt, to hear the whispers, even as he called back the eager Winter with a thought.

'They didn't know we were coming,' Harleen said, catching up to him, Sindri hot on her heels.

'What does that matter,' Jai said. 'Isn't that a good thing?'

'No,' Sindri snapped, stabbing a finger towards the horizon. 'Look.'

Jai furrowed his brow. And saw other, more distant lights. Many of them, now that he looked. Sindri summoned Kiran, and the soulbound knight spurred closer to them, her mount snorting, white foam gathered on its hoary lips.

In that time, Jai realised his folly. He voiced it.

'That is another Great Tribe?' Jai asked, and received a nod in return. 'So they travel fast, but in plain sight, even with a Great Tribe close enough to see them. Yet they continue, dangerously close. Why aren't they scared of them? And what were they rushing for?'

'Mayhap they are late,' Harleen jested.

The two Valor gave her unamused looks, but Jai caught the meaning behind it.

'Sindri,' Jai whispered. 'How many riders do the Keldar have?'

'One hundred and fifty,' she said.

'You're sure?' Jai asked.

'You think I am their regular guest, counting their warriors?' Sindri snapped back. 'You think we truck with traders as often as you Kidara, shooting the breeze about our rival's forces? I don't know, Jai. If they sent half their force to meet us that day, then that is my prediction.'

Kiran raised a hesitant hand.

'They may . . . be closer to two hundred,' she said. 'Judging from the tracks.'

Jai cursed.

'They must have left more than half behind, when they rode out to face us,' Jai said. 'Riders to protect their families. Scouts, perhaps a small force in case of a band of riteless. Perhaps they are not the marauders you think they are, Sindri.'

Now it was Sindri's turn to curse.

'So we only match their number,' Sindri said.

'No,' Jai said. 'More.'

They stared at him, and Jai rubbed his eyes.

'Even if they have fifty more knights than we expected, it is still not enough to warrant fires this close to a Great Tribe. Too great a risk.'

Harleen sniffed, and nodded.

'We've followed them for days, yet only see their fires tonight. Wherever they were headed . . . I think they have arrived.'

'So what is this?' Harleen asked.

'We've a few hours of light left,' Jai said. 'If we move any closer now, they will see us. Kiran and I will go on foot. The rest of you . . . dismount, and keep your khiroi's heads low.'

'Alone?' Sindri asked.

'We are soulbound,' Jai said. 'You'll only slow us down.'

He leaped down, wincing as his stiff legs came to life once more.

'Ready?' Jai asked.

Kiran nodded, leaping down with far more grace. She kissed her khiro goodbye, huffing her breath into the beast's nose. It calmed the whickering khiro. And then, with a few steps . . . she was gone, into the underbrush.

Jai followed without a second thought, glad he was tall enough that grass did not reach his face. Still, it snatched at his body. He could make out Kiran, her head just visible. Soon, they were in parallel, and Jai felt the mana surge in his muscles as he forced himself through the tangling, grasping strands.

It was hard work to move among this. This was what Leonid's legionaries must have faced, as a horde of khiroi and screaming warriors charged at them. He did not envy it.

They pushed on, together, Winter winding a sinuous path at their front, leading them ever closer to their destination.

Soon enough, Kiran held up a fist, stopping him in his tracks. She drew her blade, holding it low and kneeling to rub mud upon it, dulling its shine.

Next, she cut the grass around them with great sweeps of her blade, before knotting and stacking it with practised hands.

Before long, there was a small, tight mound of grass, which she used as a stepping stone to peer at the enemy. Jai tiptoed and did the same.

Beyond, he could see the Keldar camp, now far more clearly than before. They were close. Dangerously so, and he was glad that the wind was against them. He could smell the cooking fires wafting, and the animal scent of khiroi.

But most of all, it was the voices. He ducked down, and concentrated, listening to the words. It was hard to make out, especially in the accented sithosi that he was not yet used to.

'A wedding,' Kiran whispered. 'Big one.'

Jai stared at her. 'How do you know?' he hissed.

She crouched beside him, and motioned the camp's way with her chin.

'They cook with saffron,' she mused aloud. 'That is only for special occasions – marriages or royal births.'

Jai sniffed deep, and caught the tang of it. And something else.

'Fresh blood,' he said, scrunching his eyes tight. 'And booze . . . khymis.'

Kiran straightened, leaping a foot off the ground before ducking once more.

'There are khiroi,' she said. 'Many of them. This is the union of two tribes.'

Jai bit back a curse, and rubbed his eyes.

'How many?' he asked.

She rubbed her chin, thinking.

'Three hundred.'

He was right. They outnumbered him.

'How do you know?'

'Rare for tribes of unequal powers to join. I would say four hundred, but the Keldar are the largest of the Tainted tribes. They have no equal.'

This time, he did curse. Long and loud enough that even Kiran glanced nervously at the enemy camp.

'We retreat,' she said. 'Fight another day.'

Jai did not reply. He was thinking.

'If we do that, I have placed my people in danger for nothing,' Jai said. 'There is only so long we can hide in the Yaltai. We won't get another chance like this. We'll be chasing our tails across the steppes, warring with lesser tribes for scraps. While the gryphons lay waste, and my people die.'

Jai chewed his lip.

'Will they have time to meet us in the field?' he asked, suddenly. 'If we charge now?'

Even from where they lay, Jai could hear the music and laughter clearly. But there were scouts, dotted along the edges of the camp. Watching.

'They will be taking no chances with a Great Tribe on the horizon,' Kiran whispered. 'The warriors will be ready to run for their khiroi at a moment's notice.'

'Why not defend from the camp?' Jai asked. 'Why rush to meet us in the open?'

She looked at him, confused.

'To protect their elders, their children,' she said. 'When a tribe rides into the other's camp, victory soon follows. They would never dare risk it.'

Jai let her words sit for a while. The inklings of an idea were forming in his mind.

'We've seen enough,' Jai breathed. 'Let's get back to the others.'

'You have a plan.' It was almost an accusation.

'I do.' And he found that he was smiling.

Chapter 49

They waited. Two hundred warriors, blades sheathed and mudded, faces blackened by clods of earth. They lay low upon the backs of their khiroi, and their chargers' horns were tied to the fur of their chest, such that they could not raise their horns above the grass line.

It had taken them much of the night to manoeuvre, for Jai had been meticulous in his preparations. They would get one chance at this.

Harleen and Sindri had fought him every step of the way. This was not how things were done on the Great Steppe, they said. But he wasn't here to do things the way they had always been done.

This was about more than another victory under his belt. The Sabines would wreak a devastation upon this land the likes of which had never been seen. Already, they had but a taste of it at the caravan. The Gryphon Guard acted with impunity. Flying above, out of sight. Able to descend upon any and all. Even he, ensconced in the middle of his tribe, secure in his tent, could be a target.

He did not know how he would stop it. But he knew driving the legion from their Great Steppe was a good start. And he could not do that with his paltry army of some five hundred.

His father had crafted a legend. He would now do the same, and secure his place as khan.

'What is taking them so long,' Jai hissed.

Harleen and Sindri lay flat upon their mounts beside him, as did all the warriors at his back. All stared not at the Keldar camp, but into the darkness beside it, back the way they had come.

How confident he had been, when he'd set this plan in motion. Now, in the cold of night, it felt like stupidity. Had Leonid felt this way, when he had risked all?

Yet it had been Leonid that had inspired this folly. Jai had read about it, all those years ago. The Siege of Damantine.

There, the emperor, in his youth, had bluffed the collective armies of the Southern Kingdoms before they had been subsumed into the empire. How Leonid, outnumbered and hunted, surprised by the alliance, had lit campfires as far as the eye could see, such that the enemy's scouts thought he had ten times his number.

The armies stopped to reform, giving Leonid time to escape, and fight another day.

Now Jai too would use the same trick. And finally . . . he saw them.

Torches, lit one after the other, flickering into existence as if by majick. Floating, above the grass line. Soon, more than a hundred lights burned merrily in the distance, close enough that Jai could see the black forms shifting beneath.

Though from this distance it was impossible to tell, he knew what they were. Oxen, with torches bound to their horns. And a half-dozen of Harleen's fastest riders, lighting these torches as fast as they could.

If he had not known the truth of it, he too might have believed an army waited there. He only hoped the Keldar would think the same.

Already, the music in the Keldar camp had ceased. Cries could be heard, at first of alarm, then excitement and anger. For the Keldar had seen the torches too.

Jai was amazed at the speed at which the enemy warriors

were mounted. It was as if one moment the camp's edges were milling with running figures, and the next a host of mounted, screaming cavalry was charging, ululating into the dark.

Away from Jai. Towards the decoy.

But still some remained. Stragglers, mounted up but too late to join the charge. At least fifty by Jai's count, many swaying drunk in their saddles.

'Jai,' Sindri hissed.

'Not yet,' he said. 'Let the noose tighten.'

He could see the torches retreating, the oxen following Harleen's outriders, and the Keldar's own, bobbing in pursuit.

'Wait,' Jai hissed, hearing the rasp of blades in their scabbards.

Jai's heart pounded in his ears. He drew his own blade, hearing the scrape of soil that dulled its shine. Beneath him, Baal let out a low rumble, pawing the ground.

Jai did not shout the order. No, he simply spurred his Alkhara, and the others followed. No battle cries. No ululation, or clattering swords. Just the rumble of their mounts, slow at first, then picking up speed as the first yells were heard, his army finally spotted.

The world surged back as Baal increased his pace, the song of battle loud in Jai's ears. It was the wind tearing at him, the battle cries of his men, and the *thrum*, *thrum*, *thrum* of Baal leaping and bounding through the whispering grass.

Jai led the way, ahead of Winter, ahead of his entire army, but he could not stop Baal if he tried. He could see the enemy, turning towards them. Terror, stamped across their faces, threescore men and women milling upon their mounts, grooms stumbling at their sides. And beyond, the camp filled with families, celebrants and their ilk.

The wind tugged at Jai's blade as he hefted it, his arm outstretched. The other, he raised. Summoned his mana, crooking his hand.

Baal lowered his head, the great horn aimed plum at a half-turned knight at the camp's edge. Twenty feet.

Hesitation, as he saw the faces lit up by the roiling ball of flame gathering about his hand. Terrified.

Ten.

Jai let his mana fly, the flames fanning out in a roiling wave of fire. It was blinding in its brilliance, in the dark of the edge of camp.

Keldar warriors twisted away, some dropping their blades, clutching at their eyes. Jai felt his core emptying, emptying, and dropped his hand. Then he was sweeping his blade, cutting his target deep along his chest.

And then . . . he was among them. He swung, two-handed, too fast to see the damage he wrought, near losing his sword to the suck of flesh, a groom clutching at his face.

Jai was now cutting left, then right. Baal was a true war beast, prancing close, then away, swerving through the scattered enemy, and Jai felt the rhythm of the fight still his shaking hands.

A groom came at him, yelling. A boy, hardly older than Sum, the blade almost comical in his hands, but pointed with intent at his belly. At least, until a blur of white hit him from the side: Winter, clawing at his chest before ripping out his throat with a single lunge of her head.

Jai could taste the blood upon her tongue. Feel her excitement, even as his belly roiled at the sight of the gurgling boy. Warriors, such as could see him, spurred their mounts to face him.

Only to be swallowed by what followed.

Kidaran warriors tore through the scattered enemy, a devastating maelstrom of chopping blades. One khiro stumbled, an impaled groom dangling from its horn. Another struggled, its head buried in the side of another, its rider lost.

It was child's play. And butchery. All at the same time.

Jai saw Keldar faces, drunk and blind and scared and shocked. Baal came to a stop, rearing, as Jai turned to call upon his soldiers.

And suddenly, Jai could hear the screams. It had all been a

dull buzz, the blood rushing in his ears. But now . . . just the chop and thud of weapons, and the cries of agony.

'To me!' Jai called. 'To me!'

The butchery hardly stopped. Men and women glanced up at him, turned their mounts to face him. Some even rallied to him, a dozen making their way through the mess of death. But for most, this was the work of war. And it could not be reasoned with until it was done.

'Jai!' Sindri bellowed. 'We must take the camp!'

Jai did not know what this meant, only saw her riding with her bodyguard deep into the tents, her blade rising and falling. He followed, lifting his sword once more.

'On, Baal! On!'

Baal pranced beneath Jai's tight rein, eager to turn back to the screams they had left behind. But that battle was all but done. Now they had to finish it.

Sindri's soldiers seemed to have taken over, for they were used to this work, if on a smaller scale. The civilians were corralled into the plaza at the camp's centre, an easy enough task considering the festivities.

He could see the tear-streaked faces. The bride, a young girl barely past her first blood, crying softly. The children, wailing, despite their parents' hushing. Food lay out on sitting mats, and crockery shattered and spilled, food spraying as the Kidaran mounts crashed around the plaza.

'Quickly!' Sindri screamed. 'All nobles. At the front, now.'

They emerged, at first hesitant, then faster as Sindri struck a slow-moving man with the flat of her blade. There were perhaps two dozen of them, marked by their fine attire, and some by the fat of their bellies. The bride too was dragged to the front, even as the women of her family screamed and clawed at the Kidaran invaders.

Soon enough, they were all kneeling, lined up in the direction the Keldar army had gone. Valor knights had dismounted beside them, blades at their throats.

Jai could see the contrasting colours among them. Kiran had been right. This was a wedding after all. Two tribes, in one.

And two armies . . . about to return.

Jai did not know how this would go. Sindri had been so sure the enemy would surrender. But what if they didn't? What if they just attacked?

He spun, and found his flag bearer. The young man was white as a sheet, and half his flags seemed to be missing. He had a cut to his thigh, and he was staring at it.

'Manu,' Jai called to the young man. 'Rally the knights. Sound the horn.'

Manu nodded, and did as he was bidden, the note faltering. The boy turned, and vomited over his khiro's side, then returned to blowing.

By now, much of Jai's army had already begun to follow, and it was not long before Jai found himself surrounded by scores of khiroi, unable to manoeuvre in the midst of the Keldar camp.

'Cut down the tents!' Jai ordered, glad his soulbound lungs allowed him to project over the mess of screams, wails and shouts.

His will was done, though most were simply trampled, even as hiding occupants wailed within. This . . . was horror. He had known, and yet he had not known, what would happen this night.

Only here, hearing the screams, could he fathom the consequences of his actions. For he knew he had lost himself to the lust of warfare. He looked to see two boys, the spitting images of Arjun and Samar, kneeling alongside the others. Young Sithian princes. And now Jai held the blade.

He was no better than Titus. He was a coward.

'They're coming!' Harleen called out, somewhere behind him. 'Form up, form up!'

Jai found himself jostled into place, as the khiroi massed, shoulder to shoulder, the hundreds of sobbing Keldar behind them. A score of seasoned Valor circled their captives, keeping them in place.

Baal used his considerable size to bully his way to the front, Winter ducking and dodging between the forest of khiroi feet below.

Then silence, but for the crackling of the cooking fires. There was the stench of blood on the wind. Even the Keldar were near quiet, but for the sobs of babes and children. They, like Jai, were listening.

His soulbound ears could hear it now. The rumble of a charge. The ululation, fading in and out as the wind ebbed and flowed. But growing ever louder.

'Torches!' Jai ordered, raising a hand.

The last dregs of his mana allowed a single glintlight, spinning like a glowing apple above them. Its path was aimless as Jai lost concentration, his hand trembling. Still, torch poles were hurriedly stabbed into the ground around the line of kneeling enemy nobles, who were now in a row, shoulder to shoulder, across the entrance to the plaza. If the enemy were to charge, they would trample their own in the process.

He could feel the vibrations through Baal's body, and see the dust rising from the ravaged ground.

'Hold,' Sindri called. 'Hold!'

Jai parroted her cry, and it was taken up by the line, until it was a mantra, chanted by his soldiers. Now they could hear the cries of the enemy in earnest.

A high, keening ululation, such that they put his teeth on edge. And then the dark forms, rolling into the camp. Enemy knights, charging in their gold and red finery.

'Hold!' Jai cried out.

He could see the whites of their eyes, the steam of their charges' snorts misting the air. And then . . . just like that . . . they began to slow.

Horns blared, flags swept back and forth. The momentum drove them onwards, khiroi bellowing as they dug in their heels. Until, finally, but a few feet from where the Keldar nobles knelt, they ground to a stop.

The lead rider leaped from his mount, his face a rictus of despair and rage. He held his blade aloft, before stabbing it into the ground and kneeling. His eyes met that of his bride, and Jai could see the crown upon his head and the ceremonial henna that adorned his face.

Still more leaped down. A man that might have been the groom's father. Women too, battle-scarred matriarchs in the golden colours of the bride's house. They dared not come closer, but their blades were all grounded, their chargers' reins tied there.

'Sindri,' the groom hissed bitterly, staring at her with hatred. 'You treacherous bitch.'

'Hold your tongue, Devin,' Sindri retorted. 'Lest you say something you'll regret.'

'You are a traitor to your people,' Devin muttered, though in a lower voice. 'Allying the Valor with . . .'

Devin stopped himself, and shook his head. He reached out, whispering reassurance to his bride, whose tears fell silently to water the churned earth.

Sindri remained silent too, in the face of these fresh insults. In fact, everyone did. It took a few beats before Jai realised all eyes were upon *him*. This time, there was no Feng to speak for him.

'Do you surrender?' Jai asked, his voice as loud as he dared make it, without risking the trembling he felt in his throat.

It might seem he was asking the obvious, but Devin replied by letting his blade topple from its seat, and bowing his head low. He swayed, a little. Drunk, it seemed, from the celebration of his marriage. The young man was reeling.

To go from drunken joy, to the rage of battle, to the misery of defeat, and the fear of its consequence. All in a matter of minutes. Jai felt guilty, shame burning his face, incredulous of the steel in Devin's spine as the young man lifted his chin.

'Great Khan, I will surrender without more bloodshed. But only if you do not fetter us,' he said, almost as if in prayer.

'Take what you will, and let us go. Or at least . . . let my bride free, and her family.'

Jai realised then that Devin had seen he was untainted – a khan among the Great Tribes of the steppe. And when the Great Tribes hunted the Tainted . . . their fate was always fettering. To be sold to whichever empire was closest, be it the Phoenixian or Sabine.

That was what Devin thought would happen. Indeed, he could see the bristling of the men behind, ready to turn tail and run. To abandon their nobles to that fate.

Jai cleared his throat. It was time to dissuade them of that notion.

'You are in no position to make demands. But there will be no fettering this day. Such practice is an abomination.'

Devin dared to look up at him, his eyes red-rimmed, his face tear-streaked where the henna had run. He was a young man, by all accounts, with a noble bearing, a high forehead and a forked, almost piratical beard not dissimilar to Jai's own.

He seemed confused. Suspicious too, behind those piercing eyes. Jai had accepted his terms, but this was not the way of the steppe. Only now, it seemed, did the man notice Winter, for she sat upon her haunches at Jai's side.

'I am Jai, son of Rohan, khan of the Kidara tribe,' Jai called out, letting his soulbound lungs carry his words. 'Know this: none of you shall be fettered, if you let fall your blades.'

He waited, until Devin's father, or so Jai guessed, stood and barked an order.

There was the clatter of metal, as their swords and other weapons fell to the ground. No doubt, they could be snatched up again, but Jai was glad of it. For now at least, he had their attention.

'You called the Valor traitors,' Jai barked. 'They are no such thing. We are one tribe, beneath the Kidaran banner.'

At this, the silence was broken, as the Keldar muttered, the news spreading up and down the line. This too was unheard of. But so too had they also heard of his name, his tribe. Rohan had broken the mould. Jai hoped they might believe he too would do the same.

'You want your freedom?' Jai asked. 'To keep your lives, your weapons, your banners? I ask only one thing of you.'

Devin stared up at him, disbelieving. But within his eyes too, Jai saw a flicker of hope.

'Name it,' he breathed.

Jai took a deep breath. This, all must hear.

'Join me,' Jai roared. 'Become my bannermen. Take the blood oath!'

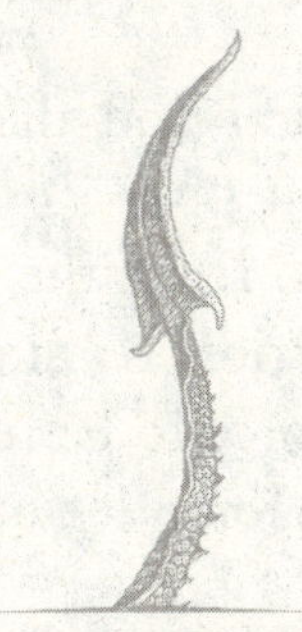

Chapter 50

Jai crouched in the grass, stroking Winter's head as he watched over his camp, unseen. It was alive with the sound of laughter, and merriment. What a difference a week had made.

In the morning, they would finally reach the Kidaran camp once more. The going had been slow, for the wounded could not take the gruelling pace Jai had hoped to set.

And there had been many casualties. That, Jai regretted. But one more wounded was one less dead, and it was the latter that weighed the heaviest upon his heart.

He had sacrificed two khiroi in their honour, old, infertile does bought with coin from the Keldar. They all had mourned, together. For he and the Kidara too had suffered losses. In all, fifty. Jai did not distinguish between sides.

He wondered, still, if the Keldar would have accepted his terms had he approached under a banner of peace. Unlikely, he knew. This was the way of the steppe, and Jai could only be thankful they had been spared more bloodshed. Indeed, the Keldar had joined him as was the manner of any conquered tribe in the Great Steppe, ceding half of their belongings.

It had surprised Jai how civilly this had been done, but it was apparent by now that such conquests were not uncommon among the Sithians. And for the Keldar, who had conquered others by this method themselves and thought their fate was to become fettered, this union and their tithe was a welcomed alternative.

Now Jai only needed to reach the Kidaran camp once more. With his five hundred warriors reunited with their two hundred and fifty, he would be a force to be reckoned with. Perhaps not enough yet to defeat a Sabine legion, but enough to make a start.

Jai turned to stare out at the mountains behind him. They were tall as anything he'd seen before, even the Petrus Mountains he had been imprisoned within at Porticus. It was strange to finally see something other than endless horizon.

Beneath them, he could make out the orange lights of the Kidaran camp. So close, he'd been near to ordering a march through the night. But the wounded needed their rest. Jai, though, had decided he could not wait. And if he was to be rited anytime soon, he would have to get used to riding the steppe alone.

Jai turned to Winter, and scratched her beneath her chin. He was tempted to go back to his tent, but he was tired of the interruptions and politics of the camp, where he'd found a stoic, mysterious silence was all that kept him from revealing his tentative grasp of Sithian customs or speaking words he still struggled to pronounce. This night, he was itching to be away.

'Wanna go for a ride, girl?' Jai asked.

She yipped in agreement, and Jai grinned. He went to Baal, saddled nearby, and mounted up. By now, Jai was used to the broad-backed beast, and so too had Baal changed since the battle. It seemed Jai had earned his spurs in Baal's eyes, for whereas before he had fought Jai's pull on the reins, he now responded as docile as a lamb.

Jai kicked his heels, and they rode on through the grass, headed for one of the scouts keeping watch. He needed to let Harleen know where he was, lest they find his tent empty and panic.

To Jai's surprise, Jai found Devin, seated upon his Alkhara, staring at the Kidaran campfires.

'A fine night,' Jai said, trotting up to him.

Devin started, then allowed Jai a smile and motioned for Jai to join him.

'A fine night indeed,' Devin said. 'I welcome the morrow, where I might greet the rest of my tribe.'

Jai knew Devin was laying it on thick, but he appreciated the sentiment.

'I am glad you feel that way,' Jai said. 'Mother knows I might not were I in your shoes.'

Devin shook his head ruefully.

'To keep my people safe,' he said, 'I would do anything. Even marry a woman I had not yet met.'

Jai looked at him, surprised. Devin shrugged.

'It is our way.' He sighed wistfully. 'Never had I seen so many Tainted in one place,' he said. 'We were the two largest Tainted tribes on the Great Steppe. We would have become almost a Great Tribe of our own. Imagine that . . . a Tainted Great Tribe.'

'Now you *are* part of a Great Tribe,' Jai said. 'Untainted, Tainted – it no longer matters. Your people are safer than they ever were, even if I rule above you.'

Devin uncorked a skin, and offered it to Jai.

'That you do,' Devin allowed, motioning for Jai to swig.

Jai smelled the acrid scent of khymis, and braced himself, letting the cloying, sweet liquid burn its way down his throat. He choked back a splutter, and followed Devin's contemplative gaze towards the horizon.

'We have sold our fair share of fettered,' Devin confessed. 'I hold no grudge against you. I am only grateful we were spared the same fate.'

Jai shook his head.

'How could you do it?' Jai asked, handing back the drink. 'When it is the fate you fear most yourselves? The Valor avoided it where they could, and they do not even honour the Pact.'

Devin shrugged. 'We do,' he said. 'And we never sold Sithians. Tainted or not.'

'That is cold comfort,' Jai replied. 'There will be no fettering in my tribe. Is that understood?'

Devin held his hands up in peace.

'I regret my part in it,' he said. 'But when a bunch of foreigners fall into your lap . . . if it wasn't us, it would be someone else.'

'I would not call a band of traders going about their business falling into your lap,' Jai snapped.

'Nothing like that,' Devin said hastily. 'As I said, we follow the Pact. It was just a bunch of Huddites, seeking refuge in the east.'

Jai froze. Then his hand had seized the man's collar, pulling him closer.

'Was there a girl?' Jai asked. 'A Dansk one?'

Devin's brows furrowed.

'How did you—?'

'What did you do with them?' Jai demanded. He realised he was yelling, and Devin's eyes were wide with fear. The Keldar prince's Alkhara shuddered, and Jai released him, taking a deep breath to calm himself.

'Where did you sell them?' Jai demanded once more.

Devin was breathing heavily, his hand upon the hilt of his blade. Winter snarled at him, and he raised his hand away slowly.

'Answer me!' Jai bellowed.

'To the Caelite,' Devin blurted. 'I'm sorry. Please, my khan, I did not mean . . .'

'Why?' Jai asked. 'Why them?'

Devin was too terrified to speak, and Jai realised his own hand was on his hilt.

Twin spots of light had appeared on Devin's chest, and Jai realised that in his rage, he had allowed his mana to roil through his body. His eyes were glowing.

Jai took a shuddering breath and closed his eyes, sucking his mana back to his core.

'Devin, this girl is important to me,' Jai said, feeling his heart rate begin to settle. 'I need to know what happened to her.'

Finally, Devin spoke, stammering.

'We sent her together with the Huddites to the Caelite two weeks ago,' he said. 'To fund the bride price, nothing more, I swear it.'

'Why them?' Jai demanded once more. 'Why not to a fettered trader?'

'Because the fettered traders are all west,' Devin uttered, his face still pale with shock. 'They go to buy captive Dansk to sell to the Phoenixians – there's a war there.'

'And what use have the Caelite for fettered?' Jai hissed, his suspicion plain.

'Who can say? We only know they pay for fettered, though their prices are so low, most choose to make the journey to the east or west. She was a noble, ripe for ransom, and only the Caelite can fly their roqs to negotiate terms. Can you imagine one of us, trying to reach the Dansk, or Sabines, in the midst of this war? Better it be their problem. We were poorly compensated, if that helps.'

'It does not,' Jai uttered, feeling the blood drain from his face.

He rubbed his eyes, trying to come up with a plan. From what he'd learned in the Kidara's approach to the Yaltai Mountains, the Caelite kept to themselves, but were known too for trading in rare goods, for their winged members flew far afield, seeking the secrets of the universe.

It made sense, now, why the Keldar had come this way. Not knowing what to do with Erica and the band of Huddites, they had taken her to the only people that might be able to negotiate a ransom in the fog of war. He realised had the Caelite been closer than the Kidara when he'd been a Valor captive, Sindri might well have traded him to the Caelite too.

Either way, the answers would not lie here.

'I ride for the Kidaran camp,' Jai announced, startling Devin. 'Let Harleen and Sindri know.'

'Yes, sire,' Devin said, lowering his head. Beneath, Winter growled from the grass, making him shudder.

Jai clucked his tongue, giving Baal free rein. The beast trembled with anticipation, and then Jai lurched forward, riding for his home.

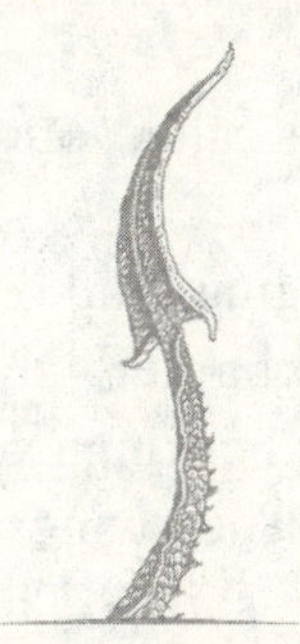

Chapter 51

A cool breeze tore at Jai's hair as he rode through the darkness, the lights on the horizon growing ever brighter. He breathed in tandem with Baal, entering the half-trance, letting the mana flow through his body.

Across the Great Steppe, Jai could now see a hurricane of mana, countless motes drifting on an unseen, unfelt wind. This was the sight that greeted him every morning when he soul-breathed. There was so much more mana here. Just as when he'd been in the forest. As if the plants themselves produced it, like a golden rain falling in reverse.

He thanked the heavens for it, as it had been far easier to refill his core here, when compared to the barren lands of Porticus.

Beside him, Winter leaped and chittered, her wings flapping with every bound. With one great leap, she glided for a few moments, before they drew to a trembling close, and she was back to racing through the grass once more. By now, she was tall enough that her head breached the top of the grass, for she was as large as a pony.

Jai looked on in wonder. He had dared to wish that one day, he could ride upon her back. Much as he had come to love riding through the steppe, he dreamed of dancing amid the clouds, the great expanse of the grasslands beneath him, like a swathe of emerald rug.

'Come on, Winter!' Jai called out. 'Let's see who gets there first.'

He kicked his heels, urging Baal on, and the beast responded in kind. Jai held onto his charger's shaggy mane as they hurtled over the grassland, Winter barking excitedly as she bound beside him. Each time she flared her wings, gliding on the wind, she caught up to him, and he shouted his encouragement, pulsing his feeling down the invisible cord that bound them.

'On!' Jai cheered. 'On, on!'

He had to get back home. Feng would know what to do.

Jai was a khan of a Great Tribe for Mother's sake. And right on the Caelite's doorstep. Surely he could buy her freedom, and that of the Huddites.

The problem was time. Who knew how long it would take for the Caelite to find buyers for Erica? Two weeks was a lifetime. He'd been sold to the Kidara, retaken his throne, joined his clan with the Valor *and* Keldar and staved off the threat of the Tejinder in less than two weeks—

Jai's stomach plunged, the world turning dark as he fell. Pain ripped through him as he slammed onto stone, Baal's great weight choking him.

He stared up, at a circle of dark sky above him. And Winter's head, peering out from its edge. His mind caught up with him. He was in a pit.

Pain. Deep and aching, coming from his legs. He heaved, pulsing mana into his arms as he shifted Baal off his chest, hearing the splintering of wood as he did so.

He sat up, gasping like a beached fish, unable to fathom what he was seeing.

Baal was dead. Speared through his body in a half-dozen places, from the sharpened stakes at the pit's bottom.

Jai's leg was skewered through the thigh, the broken spar of wood jutting out from it. He stared at it, unbelieving, pain screaming so loud he could hardly think.

He gripped the stake, and pulled. Blood spurted, thick and

fast, and Jai could hardly stop it as he pressed his hand over the wound. With shaking fingers, he managed to burst some of the healing spell's golden light upon the jagged hole, enough to seal it, and stem the flow of blood. If he'd had any less mana, he would have surely bled to death.

That was little comfort as Jai fell back from the effort, feeling the dregs of his mana that were all that was left in his core. He groaned with pain, feeling his other injured leg beneath him. It had not been speared through, but crushed beneath Baal's weight. He used a sputtering of the healing spell to heal that too. It was fragile, but the pain faded to a dull ache for now.

Jai cursed, and struggled to his feet, groaning. There was little space within the pit, for it was narrow. He cursed again, and cut Baal's saddlebags free, tying them about his waist. Then he turned to the wall, as Winter wailed down at him.

The walls were sheer, and lined with a strange combination of clay, mortar and flat slate, seemingly to keep the pit from filling with water. Baal's body too was covered in clumps of desiccated grass, and the shattered remains of a mat of woven reeds.

A simple trap – one he should have spotted from the yellowing colour of the grass they had used to cover it. If only he'd been paying attention rather than fretting about Erica. How was he going to—?

Clumps of soil rained down from above, and Jai looked up.

'Winter, no!'

But it was too late, the dragon leaped down, her wings flapping frantically, filling the air with dust as she scrabbled from wall to wall, before reaching the bottom.

Now Jai was sandwiched between khiro and dragon, coughing and choking on the dust-filled air. He tucked his face into his shirt, waiting for it to settle.

He groaned, and pulled Winter close to him.

'A fine mess we find ourselves in,' Jai whispered, knuckling her where she liked it, just behind her ever-growing horns. 'What bastard put this thing here, eh?'

He knew it could not be one of the khiroi-riding tribes. They would never hunt khiroi this way. Nor would any that respected the beasts of the steppe, the way they did.

No, this would be the work of the Caelite or the Mahmut, Jai was sure of it. Their beasts lived not in the grasslands, but in the lower ranges of the mountains. This was meat for terror birds. They cared not where it came from.

Winter purred with consternation, peering upwards, and Jai followed her gaze. And there . . . he saw them. A face, staring down at them, shrouded by the dark of night.

Then . . . the patter of feet. A squawking sound, not unlike the noises Winter made. And then the tearing of grass, receding.

'Winter, help me up,' Jai growled.

He pushed his fingers into the walls of the pit, his soulbound grip making short work of the mortar there. Water seeped from where he wormed his fingers in, but he was able to haul himself up by his arms alone.

It was hard work, even with his soulbound strength and Winter pressing her head against his rump. Soon enough, though – his face a mess of soil and dust – he emerged from the pit.

He drew his blade, staring at the broken strands of grass as Winter scrambled out behind him. He wanted to follow, but the trail headed away from the Kidara.

Jai swallowed down the temptation. He took a step and almost collapsed. His leg could hardly bear his weight. Winter nudged her nose beneath his arm, and he leaned upon her.

He hopped on his leg and even that was agony. And it would stay that way, until he had enough mana to heal himself. Hours and hours of soulbreathing.

He could not afford that. Not with whoever he'd seen looking down at him, running off for help. Jai needed to get out of there. Fast.

Except fast wasn't an option.

Chapter 52

Jai hopped another step. Another, and another. One leg hurt to move, the other to put weight on. He alternated between the two, leaning heavily on Winter in the meantime.

She was so big now, he had no need to stoop as they battled their way through the thick grass. Winter had unsheathed her claws, and slashed them a path, but the going was still slow. Jai was only glad that they had the mountains to head for – without Baal, he'd have only had the sun to guide him.

By now, the sun had begun its first rays on the horizon, and the mountains stretched higher above them. The light was heartening, but didn't lend him any more strength. Even an ascended soulbound had their limits, and with two wounded legs, and agony ravaging him with every step, he was not sure how much longer he could continue like this.

And then . . . a rustle. A whispering of grass. Sounds Jai had learned to pick up on, in his months in the Great Steppe.

Winter too had heard it. She could smell something as well, so that Jai could almost taste it. Like the inside of a henhouse, but less potent, more . . . animal.

He spun, catching a glimpse of a half-dozen dark shapes, and then ducked down into the tall grass. Winter growled, and ducked down as well. Jai, already leaning and twisted away, sprawled across her back. He sensed her intent, and had but a second to throw his leg over her tail, his sternum complaining from the blunt horns studding her spine.

Then she was off. Jai seized two horns, clapping his legs tight against her sides. Grass ripped at his face, and he could hear the sounds of pursuit. Rustling, squawking, hissing beasts and the *yip*, *yip*, *yip* of human voices, trilling and whistling in excitement. He was being hunted. Jai tried to think, to plan, even lifting his head to breach the green forest. But his thoughts seemed snatched away, barely managing to wrap an arm about Winter's neck, as she lunged and leaped through the grasses.

He could feel her wings, trying to open, but his legs trapped them to her sides, for he was too far back on her body. It was a foot race, now. Ahead, he could see the smoke of the cooking fires, stark against the white stone of the mountains.

They were close. So close.

He snatched a glance behind them. Now he saw them in earnest.

Hunters for sure. Beaked skulls adorned their helms – spear-wielding warriors, all. But it was their beasts that burned their sight into his memory as he turned and urged Winter on.

Tangerine beaks, cruelly hooked, with a feathered crest above. Their necks held perfectly still as they zigzagged through the grass behind him. Terror birds.

'On!' Jai yelled. 'Come on, girl.'

Winter renewed her efforts, leaping ever higher, such that Jai's ribs slammed into the horns upon her back, tears springing to his eyes. He could not help it. He was in agony, and he could do nothing but urge Winter to ignore his pain, his fear, to push harder, run faster, leap higher.

All while there were terror birds on either side. Spears levelled, voices shouting, counting down. A horn sounded. And then, just like that, they broke away. Turned back in a wide arc, their cries fading.

Jai raised his head, to see a Sithian boy riding towards them, a horn clutched to his lips. A young Kidaran groom on an old doe, but armed and armoured. One of his thirty scouts, dutifully on his watch.

Still more were coming, riding towards the alarm, but Jai urged Winter only to slow, breathing relief as he lifted his chest away from her back. She continued on, past the scout, even as Jai shouted a hoarse thanks. The grass began to recede, until they were riding into the camp itself, children chasing him, riders following in his wake.

'Victory!' Jai called, his voice hoarse. 'Spread the news!'

The cries were echoed behind him as he rode, and grinned through the pain. To return alone, bloodied and without his Alkhara, would be deadly for his legitimacy. He had to play this off as best he could. It was fortunate the day was still young, and the morning reveille had not yet been blown.

He pushed himself to sit upright, glad that the grass had wiped away much of the grime and soil that had coated him in the pit. Wincing, he ran a hand along his torso, as Winter finally slowed to a walk, panting and coughing. He rubbed her head, sending thanks, even as he smiled and nodded as his people turned to stare.

Soon enough, Winter had found her way to his tent. He dismounted from her, patting her side. By now, he was a wreck of pain, and it took everything he had to wipe the tears from his eyes, and walk stiffly between the guards, nodding to them as he did so.

'Send for Feng, please,' Jai asked, wondering just how strange the fake smile he'd fixed upon his face was.

Still, one hurried away, leaving Jai to shuffle through the tent's partition and collapse to the fur-lined floors. This, at last, allowed Winter to drag him to his bed, careless of the silk of his robes as it stretched and ripped between her teeth.

He lay there, on his back, staring at the ceiling. Water. He needed water, but the jug seemed so far away. Jai closed his eyes . . .

* * *

AND OPENED THEM AGAIN. He knew he had slept, but with Feng's anxious face swimming into view, he knew it could have been no longer than a few minutes. Despite this, it seemed his aches had begun in earnest, and his legs were seized and stiff as he shuffled himself upright, resting his back against the headboard and a well-placed pillow.

'What happened?' Feng said, staring at him. 'They . . . Is this your blood?'

Jai waved away his concerns, motioning for the water jug. Feng gave it to him, and Jai flooded his face as he gulped it down.

'Jai,' Feng said. 'Talk to me.'

'The Keldar prince was marrying with the Maues tribe. We ambushed them both, and they swore the blood oath to my banner.'

Feng pumped his fist, but Jai found little joy in it. His guilt still weighed heavy on his soul. He remembered the triumph he had felt, when he had made his first cut. And the shame, when he saw the dead man's eyes.

'So . . . what is this?' Feng asked. 'What happened?'

'I rode out alone,' Jai said. 'Fell into a pit. Barely got away – Winter got me out of there.'

He let a hand flop onto Winter's side. She was already sleeping, poor thing. Exhausted. If only he could do the same.

'Are Harleen and the others back yet?' Jai asked.

Feng nodded.

'Our scouts are already leading them back here. I confess, they rode out upon your arrival. They feared the worst.'

Jai closed his eyes. He hoped rumours would not spread of this. His loss of an Alkhara to a simple trap like that one . . . it smacked of inexperience.

'I did not know there are traps like that in the Great Steppe,' Jai muttered. 'Send word to Harleen; there must be more of them nearby. Pits and hunters and terror birds. Be discreet.'

Feng did as asked, running to instruct the guards before

returning to Jai's side.

'These traps, they are only common near the mountains,' Feng said. 'It must have been the Caelite. They value the khiroi only for their meat.'

'At least they had the decency to wait nearby, put whatever they caught out of its misery. Only they didn't expect to find me there.'

Feng inclined his head. Jai sighed, and groaned.

'When they arrive, I want Kiran and every other soulbound we have brought to me.'

'As you wish,' Feng said.

Jai thanked him, and closed his eyes, waiting for Feng's footsteps to recede. He wrapped himself around Winter, letting the smooth warmth of her belly be his blanket.

He wasn't alone. All he needed was Winter. He breathed her breath, and let sleep take his pain away.

Chapter 53

Both Feng and Winter helped Jai to hobble past the partition, and take a seat in his throne. There was no need to hide his pain now. Because he was going to ask them to heal him.

To Jai's surprise, Kiran was accompanied by six other men and women of varying ages. Most wore the colours of the Keldar and the Maues tribes, revealing that Teji had managed to take most of the soulbound of the Kidara with him in the split; only one bore the Kidaran colours. And Jai was surprised to see he recognised her. It was Meera the memory keeper.

'Thank you for coming,' Jai said.

They replied with nods and smiles, too nervous to speak. All but Meera and Kiran, who looked at his dishevelled appearance with raised brows.

'Are you all soulbound to khiroi?' Jai asked, too impatient to stand on ceremony. 'No Alkhara?'

They replied in a jumble of yeses. Jai nodded slowly.

'Are any of you ascended?' Jai asked.

None replied. Most were terrified of him. This bloodied, dirtied prince, with his enormous dragon curled about his feet. Jai knew this was a long time coming. He had neglected the path for far too long. The second half of Winter's gift had saved him more than once. And he'd squandered it with sleep, with thumbing through an ancient diary.

'Who here knows the healing spell?'

Meera raised her hand, as well as Kiran.

'Good,' Jai said. 'You first, then. My legs. Please.'

Kiran helped Meera hobble closer, and the old crone aimed her hand at his lower half. There was a brief flash, and Jai felt the light run through his legs, like cool water in his veins.

'Better?' Meera asked. 'You should find yourself a woman, my khan. Give you something else to do than go gallivanting off on your own.'

So the word was already out. Of course, she would know. Her disciples would have found out for her.

'Come,' Jai said, calling the others, ignoring her jibe. 'Please, do the same, if you have the mana to spare.'

The remainder came closer, and Meera helped them achieve the correct forms with the help of a few whacks with her cane. More flashes, relieving his pain like splashes of ice. Most were dull and momentary, though Kiran's was the brightest of all. All were too brief, too weak. None of these warriors could do more than a few spells, before they ran dry of mana. And what they used now might well have taken them all month to accumulate.

Yet it was enough. By the end of it, Jai shook out his leg. It was not quite good as new, but he could walk unaided.

'Thank you, all,' Jai said.

They all nodded, nervous, one even bowing in the fashion of the Phoenixians.

'Tell me,' Jai said, 'how you came to be soulbound?'

Kiran was first to speak.

'It is the old way. We bleed the khiro, bleed the acolyte. Wait until they are close to death. If the bond does not happen, we hope they survive. Many do not.'

Jai nodded slowly. It seemed almost all methods of soulbonding required a near-death experience of some kind.

'Have any of you heard of Balbir?' he said. 'Her khiro's name was Samara.'

Meera held up a hand.

'I am now bound to Samara. When Balbir passed, we all knew of it. Samara almost died of sorrow where she stood. I bonded with her, for my own khiro had passed too; as is our custom.'

Jai stared at her, surprised.

'Speak freely,' he said. 'Tell me all you know.'

She bowed her head.

'Balbir was my acolyte once. There were but a few of us, among the Kidara. Soulbound, I mean. Apart from your father, of course.'

Jai's eyes widened, and he leaned closer.

'How did my father become soulbound?' Jai asked.

Meera chuckled, and tapped her chin.

'He bonded with his Alkhara when he rode out to blood himself. Battled Chak with rope and spear to bring him home to the tribe. The both of them almost bled out. Only they soulbonded instead. Not unlike that Zayn, or so my little birds tell me.'

Jai bristled at the comparison to a man he had grown to loathe, but knew the old woman was careless with her words when she wanted to be.

'And Balbir?' Jai asked. 'Do you know why she came with us?'

'It was Teji that arranged it. She could have run away, but she went because your father would have wanted her to. She said as much.'

Jai closed his eyes, and offered silent thanks to the woman that had been as close to a mother as he'd ever known. To know, at least, that she'd gone willingly was a debt created than he could ever pay. But at least now, he could pass on what she had taught him, as she'd asked him to.

He lifted his hand, and contorted the fingers. It was a complex move, the positions unnatural and hard to hold still, especially under the weight of Jai's exhaustion.

'This is the shade spell,' Jai said. 'Balbir asked me to teach it to our people. Share it freely, and make sure it is not forgotten.'

Meera scuttled closer, and eyed his hand. She peered so close, he could feel her whiskers upon his palm. She hummed and nodded, before beckoning the others forward.

'I will remember,' she assured him. 'That's my calling, after all.'

Jai sighed, relieved that it was done. A small piece of his debt paid.

Still, there was more to do. Even ascended as he was, he knew fewer spells than he would wish.

The shade spell was chief among them, and the most common, fire. Healing too. And some other tricks he had been taught. The glintlight, perhaps the most useful spell of all. The keep-fast charm, to tighten knots, and the reverse to loosen them. And lastly, the frost spell, one that used more mana than it was worth, certainly not enough to be used offensively, but handy on a hot day – or when Rufus wanted his booze chilled.

That was it. More than most would know, for spells were rare things, and kept secret by those that discovered them. Still, he'd missed out on much, for Rufus had known the full gamut of spells known to the Gryphon Guard, and more besides. But the man had been far more concerned with Jai's progress along the path, to become ascended – to become powerful enough to actually use the spells properly than to focus on the individual spells. Their training had been cut short by Jai's capture, however, and that had been the end of his learning.

He thought back to then. To his time with Rufus and Erica. They'd thought they had all the time in the world.

Yet another bit of foolishness on my part, he thought bitterly.

I won't take it for granted again.

'What other spells have the Sithia?' Jai asked.

He voiced the spells he knew, and found the frost spell was new to all of them, though Meera knew most of the others. And, he learned, she had another to teach him.

'The shield spell,' she breathed. 'And lightning, though my god, that's a hungry one.'

She extended her hoary hands, and grunted as her arthritic fingers shifted into position. They waited patiently, until she was satisfied.

'Look well, children,' she chuckled. 'It seems we will soon need it!'

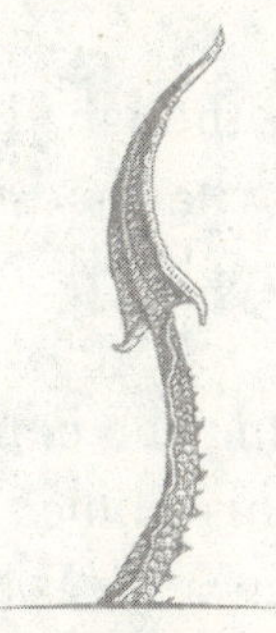

Chapter 54

Feng had summoned the Small Council no sooner had the soulbound left. Jai had tried not to complain. Feng had taken the liberty of claiming Jai's share of the spoils from the battle, small though they were – taken from the dead, as was custom. He was making arrangements to welcome the new tribe too, a feast included, though once again the khymis would be under strict supervision.

There was still much to be done, and the Kidara might be surprised to find another tribe of over a thousand people joining them. Or rather, two tribes. He'd had no idea if Devin now led both the Keldar and the Maues.

So when the Small Council was filled once again, Jai had not been surprised to find it a little more crowded. Devin had brought his bride, resplendent in her golden battle armour, to join him. She was introduced as Anita. It appeared the two would rule jointly over their respective houses.

The map was once more stretched along the crowded table, and Jai was glad of the height of his throne, so that he could see it from above.

Now the table was a rash of discussions, and none of them suggested heading west to fight the Sabines. Or even considered that as a goal. Still, exhaustion did not give him leave to tune out of the discussions. Ultimately, the decision lay with him.

He wasn't unprepared, though. He'd had time to rest and heal, and to ruminate on what had made him ride out, rushed and alone in the dead of night.

Erica.

'Devin,' Jai said, stopping the conversation dead.

The man blanched at his name, and Jai remembered their last exchange had not been a pleasant one.

'You say you traded some captives to the Caelite, a little over two weeks ago. Is this true?'

He nodded slowly.

'How?'

Devin stared at him, brows furrowed, until a prod from Anita set his tongue loose.

'Every month, they send a trading party to a meeting place, perhaps two *kiris* from here. We do not know if that is where their stronghold is.'

Jai cursed beneath his breath. A day's ride, but weeks to wait. His tribe could ill afford to remain here.

'And if you need to see them sooner?'

Devin extended his palms.

'I'm sorry, we have never needed to. We waited there, for the appointed time. They came, we traded. They left.'

Jai sighed, and rubbed his temples. This was not the answer he had wanted. But he knew they were out here. Hunting, with their birds. Would they entertain the flag of truce, if he used it?

Feng had said earlier, none knew, though rumour said they had once followed the Pact. Jai's encounter that early morning seemed to fly in the face of that, but he supposed he did not look like a riteless boy, seeking a khiro to tame, treasure to loot or enemies to conquer.

They truly did keep to themselves, their customs a mystery to most of the Great Steppe, who cared little for their strange neighbours. Nobody even knew how Jai's father had convinced them to join his cause.

He wanted to ask more of Devin, but the conversation had already moved on.

'—You didn't see what we did,' Sindri said. 'The Gryphon Guard plague the Great Steppe. They might descend here any minute and take Jai in his sleep. Begging your pardon, my khan.'

'I will sleep in a smaller tent,' Jai said. 'A different place, every night. Have our best warriors pitch their tent close to this one, and have the guard watch the skies. Should the Gryphon Guard attack, they will find an empty bed, and a ring of swords to greet them.'

It seemed weak to accept their helplessness to the Gryphon Guard's power of flight. Bows would be a reasonable counter, but as far as he knew, few Sithians hunted, for they got all the meat, milk, grain and herb they needed from their khiroi and the grasslands themselves.

Knowing this, the traders had no bows to sell either, of those that remained. Most of the caravans had abandoned them when they stopped for so long at the mountainside.

The table had fallen to an uneasy silence.

'It's only a temporary solution, of course. What we must do is deal with the threat at its source,' Jai said. 'These Gryphon Guard, they sally from the legion, which we must assume is working its way deeper into the Great Steppe.'

More silence. Even more uneasiness.

Jai understood why. He had been thinking on this very problem, while the table had debated. There was no profit in them risking blood and treasure to defeat the legion, for they had nothing the Kidara wanted. Perhaps they could melt down the steel, forge new blades. Take the gold meant for the legion's pay. All that was hardly worth the risk. After all, even in victory, they would lose many warriors. Any other tribe might take advantage of their weakened state then. It was why all the Small Council tacitly avoided the subject.

It was why it was up to him to press it.

'We must seek alliances,' Jai said. 'It was how Leonid was defeated in the past. So too must he be again.'

It was the only answer he could think of. Still, nobody would meet his gaze.

'Right now, the Gryphon Guard wreak havoc, and it will not be long before smaller tribes will begin to suffer. I know Magnus. If he has been unleashed on the Great Steppe . . . it will be a bloody business. Surely they will see this is the only course of action?'

'If they even grant us an audience,' Feng muttered.

'We have won victories, twice over,' Jai said. 'Great ones. I am the son of Rohan, the last of the high khans. I lead an army that any would fear. Why would they reject my envoy?'

'Sire,' Sindri said. 'In our eyes, you are khan. We will follow you into battle, stand beside you to the last. But . . . you are not rited.'

There were nods from the table, particularly from Devin, and to Jai's surprise, many of the Kidaran nobles. At her words, the tension in the room lifted. As if it was an unspoken secret, one Jai had not realised until this moment. Feng had warned him of this, and Sindri too. He thought he had time. He thought they all saw themselves at war, as he did. Clearly, to them at least, the war was over.

Now, it seemed, he must face it.

'How long can we wait here?' Jai asked, interrupting the debate. 'How much food have we?'

Eyes turned to Feng, and his Adam's apple bobbed.

'We cannot remain here much longer,' he said, confused. 'But now we have enough warriors to stand against any of the other Great Tribes. Why would we stay?'

'Because if you say I must be rited to be considered a true khan, then that is what I have to do,' Jai said. 'If we don't have enough food to remain here, I understand – I'd just like to know where to find you then, and know that you're safe in my absence.'

The table erupted in argument, but what were they actually arguing about? They'd said it themselves: he wasn't rited and until that happened, there was no true path forwards, no matter what path was chosen. So he let them argue as he leaned back, letting the words wash over him. *His* path was set.

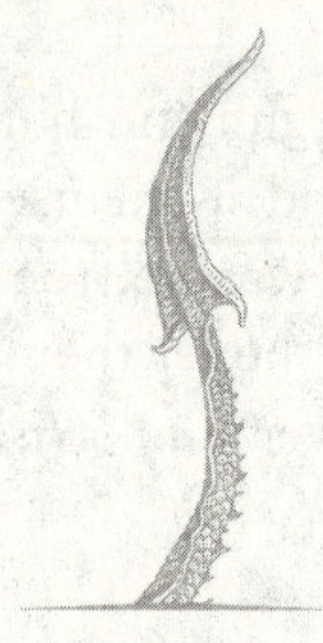

Chapter 55

If a tortoise is challenged by a hare, it should select a battle of patience as its chosen contest. I am the tortoise. Rohan the hare. We played at patience. He is no silly bunny, though, and he seeks a new game.

Now my Gryphon Guard suffer ambushes in the skies. No longer can they range in small bands, to raid as they will between charging their cores. Great birds, and their riders, descend upon them. These beasts are cousins to the gryphons and the chamrosh, or so Rufus believes, but who rides them is a mystery.

We know little of this new foe's origin, or their motives. But they take no risks, attack only when the odds are in their favour. They have the feel of mercenaries, in that regard. We have tried to send envoys, to outbid my erstwhile nemesis, though we know not where they are. None have returned.

So it is a new game. With Rufus's gryphons forced to travel in teams of ten or more, and wary of venturing too far, I must choose between food, or my raids.

For now, I choose the former. We persevere.

Jai watched the sun rise, breathing in the morning air. The steppe was an amalgam of scents, changing throughout the day. This was perhaps his favourite time, when the dew beaded, and the air was fresh and verdant.

His sleep was out of sorts, and he had woken in the early hours, having slept through the rest of yesterday. He'd spent much of the morning soulbreathing, recovering what mana he could.

He wished he had more, so he could practise the shield spell, but he had none to spare. Even the dozen hours spent curled against Winter's belly in the small tent he had moved to had yielded only a tenth of a full core.

But he could not wait much longer. Every day was another the Gryphon Guard rampaged through the Great Steppe, slaughtering the innocent. And Erica needed him. If he could meet the Caelite tribe, under his protected status as an unrited, he might be able to purchase her freedom. And if he had to steal her himself, all alone . . . it might be a feat of sufficient daring to pass his Rite.

Of course, he knew he could send out his army to range the mountainside, attempt to make contact. But he knew this was their territory – they'd disappear, and his chance would be gone forever.

Before leaving, he'd asked the guards to wake his Small Council at first horn, and bring them to see him off. He wanted no suspicions of cheating on his Rite, and wished for them to see him begin his quest alone.

He was brushing out Navi's coat before they set off. She was the only khiro Jai trusted, after his fall with Baal, and Feng had been kind enough to offer her use. Navi was sure of foot, and after all her years of hauling wagons up and down the Kashmere Road, her stamina was legendary despite her age. Certainly, she'd had no trouble keeping up with Chak, when he and Feng had ridden out together.

The old doe was shuddering beneath his touch, and though

he was sure his technique was rough, she appeared to be enjoying the attention.

She seemed a little sad too, and Jai knew she must miss Chak. Hell, he missed the old bull too. Still, Navi seemed to have made a new friend. Another doe was nudging his behind, eager for her own brushing. He sighed as a wet nose once again dragged up his shirt, cold against his back, and gave Navi one last scratch.

He turned to the other, and was surprised to find a khiro even older than Navi. In fact, it was so old now he saw it up close, Jai could hardly believe she had not yet been sacrificed to feed the tribe. The aged beast was nearly entirely grey, its eyes so deep in wrinkles that he had to lower himself to look into them.

They were deep and black, fixed upon him with an intensity that forced him to stare. To his surprise, the beast pressed closer, gently pressing its snout to his forehead. It was a strange moment, but one Jai relished. It was rare for a khiro to hold another's gaze, and was a sign of a deep trust.

What he'd done to earn it in the elderly beast's eyes, he had no idea. Perhaps its good nature was what had kept it from the chopping block.

'I see you've met Samara,' Meera's voice called.

Jai jumped, for the old lady had crept up on him. There the memory keeper stood, a world-weary disciple supporting her arm.

He turned to stare at the old beast. Of course. That was why she was still around. She was Meera's soulbound beast, inherited from Balbir.

'She remembers you,' Meera said, shuffling closer.

'I've never met her . . .' Jai uttered, reaching out a hand. The beast rested her snout in his hand, and Jai saw a tear running down the beast's face.

'She knows she has,' Meera said gently, reaching out to brush the tear away. 'I feel it.'

Jai felt tears spring to his own eyes, and he let them run freely. This was all that was left of Balbir. He remembered her end. Magnus. Titus. Her ragged corpse, lying without her dear face.

'They say,' Meera said, her voice soft, 'that for soulbound, a piece of those gone remains, if their other survives. Sometimes, I think I can hear her voice. As if I listen just hard enough . . . I might . . .'

She trailed off, and moved closer to her soulbound beast, pressing herself against Samara's side.

'Soon enough, our time too will pass,' she said. 'All we can do is keep the memory alive, yes?'

Jai nodded.

'So you teach your disciples our people's history?' Jai asked. 'So it's not forgotten?'

She nodded.

'Whether they like it or not,' she said, the joke weak in the sombre shroud that had fallen.

He wanted to ask more. His father, he knew, had been a secretive man. But surely Meera knew more than most.

'Then let this be taught,' Jai said, an idea coming to him. 'Here, take this.'

He fished the tattered diary from his satchel, and handed it to her. She peered at it closely.

'Feng will help translate it while I'm away,' Jai said.

'Pah,' she spat dismissively. 'The boy has other priorities. Twice I've sent my disciples to him, to record the happenings. He refused us – too focused on the future to think of the past. My acolyte can speak the language, for she was once a fettered in the provinces. She will do.'

I'll need to change that when I get back, Jai thought.

She paused, seeing the proffered mess of pages, loosely bound by string and glue.

'What is this?'

'Leonid's diary,' Jai said. 'Of his wars against my father – you have to look carefully, for it is mixed with his field notes, and other administrative papers. I dare not take it with me before it is recorded, for I don't know if I'll return.'

'You will.'

'Then I will want it back.'

Meera clutched the diary close to her chest, thanking him in a surprisingly soft voice.

'I will treasure it, my khan,' she said, breathless. 'And remember its contents.'

There were hurried footsteps behind them, as Feng, Harleen, Sindri and most of the Small Council approached. Winter let off a low growl, as if she could sense the impending argument.

'Sire,' Feng said. 'I still think this is folly. There are few wild khiroi this far north, and the Caelite hunt the area by your own account. At least let us send some of our riteless with you. There are a few young men and women among us now that have not yet passed the Rite. You're allowed to work together.'

Jai shook his head.

'I will not drag others into this,' he said. 'Let them pass their Rite where the khiroi are plentiful for them to capture, and our enemies do not surround us.'

'All the more reason to stay,' Harleen urged. 'There is time yet.'

But Jai could see that many others held their tongues, looking at Jai with expectant eyes. Every one of them had gone through this Rite, in the flower of their own youths. Hell, many would have been younger than him. Despite all he had achieved, he knew that he would not be true khan in their eyes, until this was done.

'Are you sure I can borrow Navi?' Jai asked of Feng. 'We are used to each other, and she makes up with experience what she lacks in speed.'

Feng sighed in defeat.

'It would be my honour, my khan,' he said.

* * *

HE HAD NEVER SEEN Winter so happy. To be alone with him once more, riding out into the unknown. The dragon was leaping through the grass, chirring contentedly, and occasionally rubbing herself against Navi's side.

Jai smiled, allowing himself this brief moment of peace before the storm. Because he knew the storm was coming.

He had a plan, of sorts. Having extracted all the Small Council and indeed Meera knew of the Caelite the day before, he was fairly sure they honoured the Pact. After all, the traders of the Great Steppe did not live in fear of dark shadows flitting from high above to raid and steal their belongings. At least, not until they met the Gryphon Guard.

So he hoped he was safe if he rode alone. Still, as Navi trudged through the tall grass, Jai found his eyes darting to the sky, trusting the old doe to avoid any traps in the light of day.

They were headed back to Baal's corpse, if there was any of it left. Jai knew that was his best chance of finding the Caelite, and seeking a trade with them without waiting two more weeks. By then, the area would be stripped of all food, and the tribe would have to move on.

Even without Erica in the mix, having read the latest passage from Leonid's diary, he knew he would need to meet with them eventually. Clearly, his father had made some sort of alliance with them. Jai wished to follow in those footsteps.

It did not take long for Jai to reach the pit. Indeed, Winter led him straight there, her tail lashing back and forth as she ploughed ahead of them. Jai knew her sense of smell was far better than his own.

The grass surrounding the pit had been flattened, and there was blood everywhere. Worst of all, a giant pile of guts steamed in the sun, the thousands of flies swarming it, twitching and lifting with the breeze. The stench was overwhelming, such that Jai could hardly smell anything else.

Even Winter was confused, her nostrils filled with the metal of blood, and the ammonium of rot. The pit had been reset too, the stakes fresh sharpened and fire hardened, the walls repaired and a thin layer of woven reed covered fresh clumps of grass. Lifting its edge with care, he could see the shallow puddle at the pit's bottom, and the red that stained the mortar.

So Jai looked to the ground. There were claw marks, in the ground, not dissimilar from Winter's own. But they were smaller, and thinner. Terror birds.

He followed their direction as best he could, and after a few false starts, found the beginnings of what looked like a path. Jai cursed the speed of the grass's return, for whatever wound the terror birds' trail had wrought on the land was fast healing, leaving only a broken stem here, a leaning tuft there to mark their route.

Still, after a minute, the stench had cleared, and Winter had picked up their scent. Jai could almost taste the echo down the thin umbilical cord of soul that bound them. That same birdcage scent remembered from when he'd had to clean the bedding of Leonid's pet finches. Fainter now, but there.

'That's right, girl.' Jai grinned as Winter yipped and picked up her pace. 'Let's see where they headed.'

She was hunting now, and Jai smiled as he remembered watching her tumble about the woods, seeking out squirrels. How far they had come, in but a single season. She was growing fast, and Jai dreamed of flying with her, high in the skies where he could see the edges of the world.

But she made a poor mount. He had seen how close the Caelite had come to them when they had given chase. The terror birds were faster than Winter in the grass, not to mention the fast-healing bruises upon his chest – no time to make a saddle that would sit amid her horns. Navi would have to be his ride for now – she would outpace anything that was not on the wing, or another younger khiro.

Winter yawped, her tail standing on end. Now she had picked up the scent in earnest. Jai let Navi take the reins, following her old companion more or less the direction they had come, but taking a wide arc around the far reaches of the Kidaran camp.

Headed back, towards the mountains.

Soon enough, they were tearing over the grassland at high speed, and Jai's heart was in his mouth, for he knew more traps might be near. But Winter could not be slowed, and Jai was relieved when they finally fell into the shadow of the mountains, where the grass was shorter, and the going tough as turf turned to rock and rubble.

Now Jai could see the scratches in the rock, where the three toes of the terror birds had made their marks there. They were on the right track; he was sure of it. Even if Winter had slowed, and was leading them in circles, her nose whipping to and fro as she snuffled at the ground.

So it was some surprise to Jai when Winter halted at a sheer cliff face. She snuffled a little longer, before sitting at its base, staring up at the enormous structure.

Jai crouched beside her, noting the claw marks in the ground, and on the cliff itself. It seemed incredible to him that two-legged birds could climb such a thing. But sure enough, the tell-tale tri-clawed marks were there, going all the way up the side of the mountain, concentrated around the small, rocky outcrops that studded the face of the cliff.

Winter let out a low rumble, her wings unfurling. Jai could feel her gathering herself as she leaned back on her haunches. Then she launched herself up the side of the cliff, her great wings flapping.

She made it a stone's throw up before her claws lost purchase, and she slid back down. Winter let out a yap of annoyance, flapping her wings a few more times. Close, but not quite there.

He could feel her frustration, and it mirrored his own. He had hoped to find the Caelite and begin negotiations. Instead, it seemed he had reached a dead end.

Jai sighed and dismounted, staring up the cliff face. He would camp out nearby, and hope for their return. With any luck, he could catch them on their descent.

JAI HUDDLED CLOSER TO Winter, resting his back against the furry hump that was Navi, the loyal khiro dozing on her side.

It may have been spring, but the nights on the steppe were still bitterly cold on occasion, and tonight was one of them. And Jai dared not start a fire, not with the grey rock to reflect the light, and let the steppe know he was there.

It had been two days now. Two days soulbreathing, true, but they were days he could hardly spare. For while he languished here, Erica's ransom could be on its way, or indeed the Kidara ranged further afield for food. Soon enough, they would have to move on, following the spine of the mountains east as instructed, leaving Jai the hard task of catching up to them.

Already, the sloping wall was furrowed with the markings of Winter's claws, who had, in her boredom, decided that this was the perfect time to attempt flight.

Of course, she could quite easily climb ahead, following the path of the terror birds, one Jai had mapped out as far as he could see. But she wanted to fly unaided, not leave him alone in the grasslands. Indeed, after Jai's near miss in the pit, she had been glued to his side. Not that he minded it at all.

Jai lay in the dim light, staring at the stars. Somewhere up there, the Mother was looking down upon him. He could feel her, in the soil, in the grass. He had never been religious, for he knew the so-called god emperors too well to believe in the Sabine pantheon that Leonid was now a part of.

He felt a stir, though, now that he was at home with his people. Having seen the thanks offered to the Mother, he had never felt closer to belief in a greater power. There was a pulse, in this ancient land. He could sense it, when he let the half-trance take him – in the eddies of the dusty currents, swirling to an unknown force.

And then . . . he saw it. Not the Mother, but a flicker across the clouds. Dark shapes, hardly visible but for his soulbound eyes. A burst of mana, carefully meted out from his precious supply, gave him a brief glimpse of a V shape before they were out of sight.

A flock of geese, perhaps. But in his heart of hearts, he knew they were the Caelite. This was no hunting ground, far from their camp. For now, at least, he could assume there were still some there, camping near the mountaintops.

Winter, oblivious to what he had seen, stirred at the excitement that pulsed through him. He calmed her with a stroke, and breathed deep. His mind was made up. Tomorrow, he would make the climb.

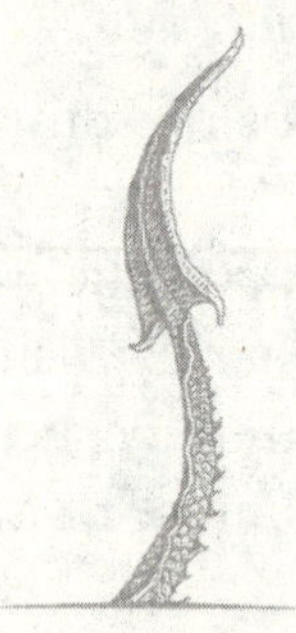

Chapter 56

Morning could not come soon enough, for Jai could hardly sleep for the nerves. Fortunately, he'd used the time to soulbreathe, topping up what he had acquired in his two days of waiting. By now, his core was over half full, and he was feeling far less vulnerable than before. Winter had been kindly sending him every bit of it that she had, and he was grateful to her for it.

It was a chill dawn, the sky dark and foreboding with clouds. If a rainstorm were to hit him on his ascent, Jai knew he might find himself on a fast descent to the bottom.

He spat upon his hands, then rubbed them in the dust at his feet. He looked up the rock face, pressing his face close. It was angled in his favour, but he knew he could not follow the terror birds' path so easily – the distances between each outcrop were too great for him to leap between them as they must have.

No, Jai would have to climb between each ledge, using them as stopgaps to catch his breath. Winter was watching him with growing alarm, for though she had sensed his intentions, she disagreed with his plan entirely. Even now, she nipped at his breeches, and a word, or intention, was pulsed down to him at regular intervals.

No. No. No.

Jai sent a pulse of disagreement back, insistent, sending her images of Erica in danger, until at last, he was blessed with silence, if not the depth of her unhappiness that he could sense regardless of her intent. By now, Navi had been freed of her saddlebags, and the same, alongside his blade, were strapped to his belt.

He had a small, curved blade, one used for eating and other such needs, that he had tied to a long leather strip harvested from Navi's reins. In a pinch, he hoped to drive it into cracks in the rock, with the other end tied about his waist.

A poor anchor, all told, but he had to make do. He had wasted enough time, waiting in the shadow of the mountain.

With no wild khiroi to tame, he could only hope that in the process of rescuing Erica, he would encounter an enemy worth enough of his Rite. One whose head would serve as proof of his success. The reason, he now knew, his people were known as headhunters.

He kissed Navi's snout goodbye, for she could not follow him. He dared not leave her tied and helpless, for a predator might easily take her. Instead, he had tucked a scribbled note into her saddle, so his people would know his plans.

'You get home safe, old girl,' Jai whispered, letting her hoary lips nuzzle his palm. 'I won't be needing you where I'm going.'

He slapped her rump, sending her off, back to the Kidaran camp. It was visible at a distance, and after a few hesitant looks, Navi trundled on towards the grasses, eager for a meal.

Jai turned back to the wall.

'Ready, Winter?' Jai asked.

He received only a remonstrative look back. Sighing, Jai lifted a foot, resting his boot on a hump within the rock, and levering himself upwards. He jammed his fingers into a crack that had been out of reach, and grunted as he lifted himself upwards, finding purchase.

Winter shoved at him from below, and Jai stretched out another hand. And began the long climb upwards.

* * *

JAI'S ARMS BURNED LIKE fire. He panted, and shifted his weight to his feet, only for one to slip away, sending a jolt of terror through his gut. His straining fingers held their grip, crying out in protest as his full weight was thrust onto them. He clung to his precarious hold, the precipice yawning beneath him.

Breath came in ragged bursts, harsh pants in a rhythm that struggled to keep pace with the heartbeat pounding in his ears.

Even as a soulbound, he was struggling. For someone who had spent much of his short life cooped up in a single chamber, this was far beyond anything he had ever attempted.

With a grunt of exertion and a litany of curses, he slid his wayward foot back onto the shallow indentation in the cliff face. Leaning into the cold, unforgiving stone, he used the meagre foothold to push himself upwards, letting his battered fingers claw their way to the next sanctuary.

With a final surge, he clambered over the edge and onto the narrow strip of safety, pressing himself against the rock as if attempting to melt into the mountain itself.

Beneath him, Winter's call echoed off the stone walls, the worry and admonishment clear. Only by pulsing thoughts of Erica's rescue did he give the dragon pause, a reprieve from her ire.

Joining him on the slim ledge, Winter pressed her sleek form flat as she went, her belly pushed against the rock. The space was narrow, a mere two feet wide, just enough for her to perch precariously without falling into oblivion.

Jai took deep, sobbing breaths, letting a pulse of mana soothe the muscles of his arms. He wanted to drop his blade, and the contents of his pack, now cinched to his belt. But he could not bring himself to just yet. He needed the water and food. And the blade would be his only defence when his mana ran out.

Jai jammed the smaller blade into the rock, though its purchase was unlikely to hold his weight. But the leather line about his waist was chafing him, and he'd be damned if he didn't make use of it. The tenuous lifeline was all that might keep him from falling should the ledge crumble, or he lose his balance on the precarious precipice.

As he rested, he found his gaze drawn downwards to the deadly plunge that awaited a single misstep. A vertiginous abyss yawned beneath, a stark reminder that failure was not an option.

In the distance, Jai could see an ominous clot of storm clouds darkening the horizon, their melding shapes riven with streaks of lightning. The tranquillity of the steppe below would soon be shattered by the furious might of the heavens. He could already hear the distant grumble of thunder, as if the Mother was angry at his antics.

It was here, high above the world, that he resolved this was what he sought to preserve. The way of life he had come to love. The fierce people that were his family, with their deep connection to the land they inhabited. So deeply rooted in the soil that its flora and fauna depended on their stewardship, trusting them to disseminate life-giving seeds and vital oases before the voracious grasses claimed their bounty anew.

There would always be that anger deep within, like an ember in his heart that seared the names of his brothers, of Balbir, over and over again. But the wound it made had scarred, and he could bear the thought of them now without that rage overwhelming him.

He had a higher purpose now. To continue his father's legacy. Finish what he'd started. Taking several profound breaths to still his heart and steel his resolve, Jai turned back to the wall. He had climbed through the heat of the day, the sheen of sweat so thick that encrusted salts shone stark against his skin. The grit of dust had long been replaced by a slick sheen on his palms.

He dried them as best he could, and looked up the wall. It was impossible to tell from here just how far he had to go, but based on the number of ledges he'd reached, he was a little over halfway.

Another rumble. Closer this time. There was an ill wind in the air, the first gusts of the coming storm.

A sense of urgency seized him. He could not afford to be clinging to a stone wall when the deluge hit. With a surge of adrenaline, he pressed himself closer to the wall, his fingertips seeking the next hold above, the other hand yanking the blade from its anchor.

Swiftly, he began his ascent, no longer pausing to consider each movement. He called upon every ounce of his strength, propelling himself with a burst of effort that left his muscles screaming for respite, and his lungs burning.

Ledge after ledge slipped by beneath him as he climbed, Winter in his wake, her mind a maelstrom of rising panic. His sweat, once hot with exertion, was now chilled by the initial rain spatters licking the nape of his neck.

'Come on!' Jai hissed between his teeth, pulsing more mana to recover his strength, sapping his reserves.

He found a good hold, and dared glance behind him. The storm had drawn nearer, its dark heart pulsating with delayed rumbles of menace. By now, the time between flash and rumble was momentary. Lightning forked across the sky, casting the landscape in a surreal tableau of blinking light and shadow. Wind whipped around him, tugging at his clothes and sending small pebbles scattering down from above.

Even Winter, her form pressed to the rock beneath him, seemed to sense the urgency. Her claws scrambled against the rock, the sound adding to the cacophony of the encroaching storm.

Time lost all meaning as Jai willed himself higher.

By now, he had no idea if it was night or day. The sky grew ever darker and the wind stronger, until it was a savage animal, howling and tugging at him with relentless fury. The rain came in torrents now, a stinging lash against his skin, the wall becoming a slick, treacherous adversary.

Winter too clung for her life, her cries of concern lost to the storm's symphony. Yet, despite her own plight, her concern for

Jai echoed loudly in his mind, such that he was forced to close her from it. Her terror was a palpable force that compounded his own, leaving him in doubt of every move he made.

As the storm raged around him, Jai roared his defiance, pushing on in the face of the heavens themselves. Each boom of thunder was a call to arms, each lightning flash a beacon guiding his path. This was a trial, a brutal baptism by wind and rain, and he was determined to endure.

Finally, he saw it. The summit. It loomed ahead, tantalisingly within reach. His heart pounded with renewed hope. He could do this.

Jai's fingers slipped. For a single, heart-stopping moment, he scrabbled for purchase. Found none. Then he was falling, into the dark.

WINTER'S BODY SLAMMED INTO him, and for a moment, they hung in the void, suspended in a cruel mimicry of flight.

Then she too was falling, their bodies entangled, her claws seizing his arms. The grip was harsh, sudden, her talons digging into his flesh.

Her wings flared, their spread enormous against the canopy of the storm. Jai felt her strain against the wild winds. Somehow, she managed only to temper their swift descent into a slower, spiralling tumble, but still they spun in the heart of the tempest, a leaf in the gale, the ground rapidly rushing to greet them.

Blind panic surged within Jai, his vision reduced to a mess of flashing light and relentless rain. The world spun, his senses engulfed by the tumultuous descent, swamped in a disarray of frantic thoughts. He clung to Winter's claws, her body a lifeline in the chaos.

Jai willed her strength. And mana. For the first time, going to her, and not the other way around. It pulsed down their umbilical, sent unthinking, in silent prayer. The effect was immediate, her wings thrashing with renewed vigour. Their descent slowed, the howling winds serving to buoy them rather than cast them down. They were no longer falling . . . but gliding.

The storm's fury was no longer their enemy, as the winds swept them up, higher and higher. With a triumphant roar, Winter soared, buoyed by the mana Jai forced to her with panicked abandon. Beneath them, the unforgiving ground receded, replaced by an expanse of storm-wracked night.

The respite was fleeting. The storm, momentarily tamed, was far from a benign ally. Winter struggled to maintain control amid the turbulent gusts and savage torrents of rain. The tempest tossed them about like ragdolls, every violent swerve and sudden drop a cruel reminder of their precarious balance upon the tide of wind they rode.

Jai could only cling tighter to Winter's legs, his heart pounding out of his chest, his racing pulse echoing in his ears over the roar of the storm. Blinded by rain, he pressed his eyes shut, the flashes of lightning casting silhouettes through his eyelids.

A sudden gust drove them sideways, smashing them into the mountain. Pain wracked Jai's body as his back made contact with the unyielding surface. He dared release a hand, flailing to find a hold upon the slick rock. His fingers slid over cracks and crevices, but the deluge made the wall treacherous, and he found no purchase in its deceitful promise.

Again, they tumbled, until Winter managed to right them once more, her wings battering against the gusts as she sought some semblance of control. By now, Jai's mana was reaching its dregs, and Winter's own reserves were spent.

Blinded both, they were as a single, flailing entity, clawing for survival in a world that had turned against them. Amid the wild dance of the storm, Jai held onto what shreds of hope he had, praying to the Mother as Winter forced her way upwards, her great chest heaving with every beat of her wings.

Jai could see his mana ebbing away, the golden liquid within his core fading fast. This was going to end soon, whether he wanted it or not.

Blinking through the onslaught and the boiling darkness, he could see the ghostly outline of the mountaintop, and the distant carpet of the grasslands below. He could just as easily be dashed against the ground in a descent. He had to choose . . . and he chose the summit.

His heart hammered as he willed more of his mana to Winter, hoping that the final infusion of energy could propel them to safety. It pulsed down their umbilical in a great bulge of blinding light, the effort enormous, such that Jai almost lost his grip.

Winter let out a hoarse roar, her wings redoubling their frantic beating, her sinews creaking beneath the strain. Their ascent became a desperate race against the storm and their dwindling reserves. Winter's breaths came in gasping, shuddering gulps as she strained against the tempest, her great wings beating against the torrent.

The world swayed and pitched in tandem with the storm's fury. But amid the madness, they were drawing ever closer to the top. Each agonising moment brought them nearer, and then, in a heart-stopping instant . . . they crested the heights. Jai's view filled with the white expanse of the tundra beyond.

They landed in an awkward tumble, Winter's claws skittering along the stone as she folded her great wings, their bodies rolling along the flat tableau of the mountain's peak. They scrabbled nail and claw against the rock, their bodies skidding along the slick, rain-pelted surface, seeking an anchor against the gale that sought to hurl them back into the abyss.

Jai's fingers curled about a rocky outcrop, his breath hitching as he gazed upon the tempest below them. The storm raged on, oblivious to their tiny victory.

But they held fast, clinging with numbed limbs to their fragile purchase, daring not to release and find better ground.

They had nothing left to give, but for now, it was enough.

They were alive. They were together. And they had conquered the mountain.

THE PASSAGE OF TIME became an indecipherable blur, as they curled together like frozen anchors, enduring the rage of the storm above. It was a time of misery, of cold, and perpetually tensed muscles, of soulbreathing through chattering teeth and a shaking that trembled through his entire body.

He had focused on survival, gasping in staccato bursts, absorbing the sparse wisps of mana he could draw from the storm-ravaged skies. The mana had been pulled high by the storm from the grasslands below, and wafts would pass Jai by, even as he leaned out, trying to sup at it.

Each breath, each shred of mana he managed to draw in was immediately used, a desperate gambit to keep him alive. These fleeting bursts provided but a fragmentary reprieve, instilling a temporary warmth, a transient surge that kept the biting cold at bay.

So it came as some surprise when he was stirred from his stupor by a growing stillness, an eerie calm that replaced the storm's riotous symphony, leaving only the distant rumble. A touch of warmth began to seep into his freezing extremities, tentative rays of the morning sun piercing the dispersing clouds above.

Winter stirred beneath him, her rough, forked tongue licking at his face. She had willed him every ounce of mana she'd had that night, for she could bear the cold without a second thought, though her greater size had left her twice as exposed to the wind that sought to dislodge them from the summit. Twice, she had slid away from him, and twice she had clawed her way back, never able to quite reach him until now.

Jai kissed her smooth snout, blinking tears from his eyes as he silently thanked her, pulsing his gratitude and love for the great beast. She pressed closer, finally able to share the warmth of her belly with him, and the pair clung to each other for a while longer, revelling in the life they still clung to, and the closeness of their loved one.

It was Winter that stirred first, giving his face a final affectionate lick before nudging him, almost as if to test if Jai could stand.

With a groan, Jai sat up, his stiff muscles protesting the movement. He forced himself to his feet, his legs trembling, leaning against Winter's side for balance. The storm had passed, soaring on into a landscape cloaked in white, the empty expanse that he had heard speak of. The Frostweald.

The mountain peak on which they stood was a ragged crest of rock and ice, the slopes on either side descending steeply. Adjacent, the mountains unfolded in a breathtaking range of jagged peaks and valleys, a cold, unyielding scape awakening under the touch of the morning sun.

Who could have thought that dragons required mana to fly? Winter had sent much of her mana to Jai since she'd matured into an adolescent dragon in these few short months, for she'd had little need of it. So too had she only just unfurled her wings from their usual tight-folded position at her sides.

Erica had never mentioned it, but then Winter had been so young, and their journey had been cut short. He supposed it was obvious, now he'd seen it in action.

In the cold light of day, neither had more mana than a few dregs, hardly enough for a small ball of flame. And he was far from the part of clifftop he had been climbing, following their inaugural flight. Jai leaned over the precipice as closely as he dared, trying not to grow nauseated at the sight of the great height he had almost fallen.

It all looked the same. If there were ledges cut into the rock, he could not see them. He was only glad to know that he would be in the vicinity, at least, of what was clearly a thoroughfare for the Caelite tribe. However, there was one tell-tale sign – his own tribe. Visible to his west, their tents like a diorama, though shrouded in morning mist.

It was just as well, for to the east, the crest of the mountain went ever higher, its path nearly as treacherous as the climb he'd made before. To the west was flatter, and wider. Enough room to walk, just about.

On trembling legs, and wishing he could curl back up against Winter's warm belly, Jai took a few hesitant steps, picking his way across the rubble-strewn ribbon of what passed for a trail along the ridge of the mountaintop.

It was hard going, and cold as anything. He was too disorientated to use the hummingbird technique, and secure a few motes of mana to warm him. So for now, he was forced to endure the cold and dizzying heights, and even his ascended soulbound body was feeling the strain of what it had been put through.

Worst still, he could not lean on Winter, for the path was too narrow and treacherous for that. Still, he let her squeeze past after a time and lead the way, offering him her spiked tail to hold. With each faltering step, his feet knocked treacherous pebbles to plummet soundlessly off the knife's edge he walked.

It was surreal to walk this high. On one side, the world was one of barren ice and dark skies. On the other, an expanse of fresh-watered verdant green and cloudless blue. It was incredible to see the eddies of the wind swaying the grass in great undulating waves, as far as the eye could see.

Jai had never been so high, nor seen so far.

He struggled on, along the barren mountaintop. It was no wonder the Caelite came down to the Great Steppe to secure food. Nothing could grow here. He was surprised anything could survive at all.

But he had to keep walking. To reach the Caelite, secure their alliance and buy Erica's freedom. As dusk cast its sombre cloak over the mountain, though, the last of the sun's glow seeping from the horizon, Jai found himself perched precariously on the brink of slumber, swaying with fatigue.

Even a soulbound body needed sleep, and Jai was worried he might fall from the top in his exhaustion.

The very thought of another night on the mountain filled him with dread, even without the wind and rain. But he knew, he had no choice.

The harsh mountainous terrain offered nothing of comfort or sustenance. There was no wood to burn, and his provisions had been lost in the tempest's fury. What remained were only a few morsels of once-dried jerky, now sodden from the rains. Half of it he had dutifully set aside for Winter, who had already swallowed it in a single lap of her tongue.

Casting his gaze back at the peak they had descended from, a sobering realisation struck him. Despite their gruelling efforts, they had made what seemed like scant progress.

Yet their journey had begun to bear some fruit. Now he could see the Kidaran camp in earnest, its campfires glowing in the fast-dimming light. This was near where the Caelite hunters had reached the mountaintop, he was sure of it.

Evidence of their presence was etched in the dried white splotches of the terror birds' droppings, though much of it had been washed away by the rains. Of the Caelite themselves, there was nary a trace.

With the light fading fast, and Winter's exhaustion compounding his own, Jai finally stopped, settling where the path widened slightly, and there was enough room for him and Winter to make some semblance of a camp.

Winter curled herself in a great semi-circle, and Jai lay against her, glad to have something solid between him and the steep fall behind. Her belly was hot, and Jai revelled in it, shedding his sodden, tattered shirt to bask, pressing himself skin to scale. Her belly was smooth, but softer and more pliant there, and had almost a pink sheen to it.

He closed his eyes, and began to soulbreathe. High up in the mountains, the mana was far more sparse. Still, it might be enough to begin warming his chilled limbs, and bring some strength back to his beleaguered body. If he only—

JAI WOKE TO HIS head thudding into the ground, Winter sitting up in panic. Winter had jerked upright, a wave of raw terror radiating through their bond. He was immediately on high alert, the adrenaline rush eradicating any remnants of drowsiness as he fumbled for the hilt of his sword.

Winter's growl reverberated through the cold night air in a primal warning. He was on his feet in an instant, eyes darting in every direction for signs of danger. It was only when he saw Winter's gaze, turned upwards, that he finally saw the threat.

Jai stared in horror. He could see the dark shapes spiralling against the dark sky, and he pulsed mana to discern feathered forms descending in the pall of night.

Winter, having managed to gather a precious smattering of mana, urged him to action. To leap upon her back, allow her to hurl themselves from their seat to glide down to the Kidaran camp far below.

Now! Now!

Jai shook his head, laying a calming hand upon Winter's side. For these were not Gryphon Guard. They were the Caelites.

Great birds of prey, their wingspans Winter's own size and half again. A dozen of them, swooping ever closer.

'Wait,' Jai said, shaking his head as if he could dislodge Winter's internal screaming.

They were vulnerable here. Out of their element, and out of mana. Weak in body and spirit both.

Yet Jai knew, he had no choice. He was here to speak with the Caelite. And here they were. It seemed his visit to their mountain home had not gone unnoticed.

The first of the great beasts alighted near him, then another and another, encircling him on all sides, their curved, yellow talons clicking as the birds danced for balance, furling their great wings. They were enormous – half again in wingspan compared to Winter.

And on their backs . . . were people. Sithians, yet not so. For they had no beards, no hair to speak of. Even their brows were shaved away, giving them strange, wide-eyed appearances.

Each held strange sickles in one hand, curved, hook-like blades. And about their wrists, there were coils of tight-wound rope. Their clothing, for want of a better word, was strange and pillow-like, as if they had stuffed their shirts with down.

And all across their bodies were rings upon rings, pierced into their earlobes, brows and lips. Many of these dangled feathers of all kinds, colourful as any on a palace painter's easel.

Now the sickles fell from their hands, only to stop short, for they were attached to the ropes. These, they swung in their hands, until they spun in glittering, thrumming circles that set Jai's teeth on edge.

The foremost of these strange figures slid off their mount, landing gracefully upon the icy ground with a soft crunch. They – or rather, he, as Jai could now discern – turned to face Jai, revealing a face made eerie by the lack of hair and the gleam of his metallic piercings. His eyes, wide and dark, bore into Jai's own, before they swept over Winter with an interested air.

He had the body of a warrior, lean and corded with muscle, and scarred in a dozen different ways. As for his mount, its piercing orange eyes almost glowed in the moonlight, its hooked beak digging amid its tawny plumage, seeking out ticks.

The man's gaze returned and held Jai's own, the silence hanging heavy between them, broken only by the soft murmur of the wind and the occasional flap of the roq's wings. Despite the blade in his hand, there was no hostility in his eyes, only an inscrutable curiosity that Jai found himself mirroring.

They remained in this impasse, the silence stretching. Finally, the man cleared his throat, and Jai realised they expected him to speak.

'I greet you,' Jai said, bowing his head with respect. 'I am Jai, son of Rohan, khan of the Kidara. I come for parlay.'

The response was subtle, a slight raise of the man's barren brows, his eyes flickering momentarily towards Winter.

'I—'

A raised palm stopped him in his tracks, and the man finally opened his mouth to speak.

'Parlay,' he muttered. He spat to the side, and stalked closer, careless of the low rumble of warning from Winter. He leaned close to her, letting her sniff him.

'You may follow us,' the man said. 'Or stay. Your choice.'

With that, he returned to his mount, a graceful, skipping leap taking him back atop his roq. The colossal wings unfurled, churning the frosty air in powerful gusts that whipped against Jai's face.

Within moments, the Caelite were airborne, heading west. Jai was alone, on the mountaintop. Without a glance, Winter lowered herself, and Jai eyed the stubby horns that studded her back. He gathered the remains of his tattered shirt, hastily mussing it into a makeshift cushion before perching atop her back, his limbs awkward, mind still reeling.

His legs curved around her sides, his body nearly horizontal against the front of her back, careful not to inhibit her expansive wings. Leaning forward, his fingers wrapped around the sturdy horns at her neck, a silent plea to the Mother whispered under his breath.

'Winter, I'm—'

Before the words could fully form, the world tilted as Winter propelled herself upwards, her muscular legs launching them into the open air. A single powerful beat of her wings, driven by the scarce mana she had stored, catapulted them aloft. And then . . . they were flying, the ground falling away beneath them as they joined the flying roqs in the starlit expanse of the night sky.

Jai clung tight to Winter as they careened through the vast heavens, embracing the wild pulse of the wind. They drifted on the generous gales that swept them on like an autumn leaf. It was just as well, for Winter had little mana to spare.

Jai could feel Winter's joy coursing through their bond, a heady sensation that was infectious and addictive in equal measure. Soon, he was no longer filled with fear, only the joy of his beast, his other half, discovering her primordial purpose.

This was no mere survival-driven scramble to surmount the rocky precipice. No, this was a different dance altogether. It was the ballet of unfettered spirit.

As they forged ahead, following the fleeting outlines of their hosts, the frost-capped peaks shimmered in pale moonlight – stark contrast to the black ravines beneath.

Already, they were catching up to the great birds ahead, and Winter let out a roar that turned their bald heads. Jai laughed aloud, snatched away though it was.

The formation of roqs veered away abruptly, and Jai's stomach seized as Winter banked with them. Yet, as the Caelite spiralled down, Jai saw their destination.

The mountainside lay strewn with caves – dark coves embedded into its face. An overhang of jutting rock made up the bulk of the tall peak, rendering a climb from the ground impossible.

Winter followed, awkward in her descent. Her wings struggled as she angled them, fighting against the wind.

Jai's knuckles whitened as he gripped her horns tighter, his eyes widening in turn with the expanding rock face below. They were limping towards one of the largest caves, the entrance looming dark.

The echo of the roqs' calls grew loud, eagles' shrieks that set Jai's teeth on edge, the sound reverberating as the formation tightened, straightened, and whipped into the cave in quick succession. The coordination was breathtaking, and Winter pulsed with competitive envy.

Her determination set, she dipped her wings, sending them into a deep swoop. Jai let out a gasp, unbidden. His world blurred, the rock rushing up to meet them.

With a final downstroke, Winter pulled them out of their dive. Her talons extended, straining.

A jolt, dust and loose stones erupting as Winter skidded to a halt, her talons scraping furrows into the hard rock. Jai was tossed from her back, wild momentum carrying him across the cave floor. A final jarring roll punched the breath out of his lungs.

For a moment he lay dizzy, hugging the ground, waiting for the nausea that suddenly beset him to subside.

Slowly, the world returned to normalcy, and Jai flopped onto his back, gasping for air. There was light above. Soft . . . and blue.

A lichen, mossy in its texture, furling along the cavern's vast ceiling like a carpet in reverse. It glowed with a gentle turquoise light.

Jai sat up to find scores of faces, staring at him, yammering in that same fluting, clicking language he could not understand. Their voices echoed around the cavern, putting Jai in mind of a service within a grand cathedral.

These people were similar to those riding the roqs, but with small, shaved caps of hair upon the tops of their heads, and all wearing the same pillowy clothing. The roqs were nowhere to be seen. Indeed, the people there seemed as shocked to see him as he was them.

Jai was in a cavern of enormous proportions. So large, the imperial palace could be built at its centre, and just about touch the sides.

The ceiling was so far, a strong man might throw a pebble with all his might and never hit it. At ground level, where Jai sat, was a circular space as large as an amphitheatre's arena. Within its centre lay a clear pool of water, dripping from the ceiling from a great array of lichenous stalactites.

And above all that put Jai in mind of a wasp's nest. Row

upon row of concentric ledges, and each peppered with caves and stairs.

He turned to check on Winter, and found her crouched low, her hackles raised. A score of spearmen surrounded her, their eyes full of fear, their communication whispered.

Already, a dozen more spear-wielding warriors were approaching Jai, shuffling forward with the same hushed trepidation. Jai raised his palms, and attempted a smile through his wind-numbed lips. It did little to help, and he could only shuffle backwards on his buttocks, until he and Winter were pressed together, staring down the forest of spears together.

No sign of those that had brought them. Had this all been a trick to capture him too? He dug into his pockets, finding the remains of a white kerchief. He flapped it weakly, but all that did was spur further whispers.

Then a shout. A burly man barged his way through, his voice deep and booming. Spearpoints lowered at the man's behest, slapped down by his meaty palms.

He approached Jai with a fixed smile, and lowered himself to Jai's level.

'Welcome, Jai, son of Rohan,' the man whispered, a light accented twang colouring his voice. 'Are you hungry?'

Chapter 57

Jai could smell food, a scent he did not recognise, yet one that strained his starving belly and watered his mouth despite its mildness. He had been ushered into a cave on the lower levels, Winter glued to his side. Now he sat opposite the man who had greeted them, unsure of what to say.

The man had introduced himself as Cyrus, but had refused to say more until Jai was settled within the cave, away from prying eyes. Even still, scores of faces peered past the row of spearmen guarding the entrance, eager for a glimpse of their visitor.

The interior was bare, and lacking in wooden furniture. Instead, ledges and alcoves had been carved precisely into the rock. There was no fire, but it was surprisingly warm within the cave.

'It has been a while since we last welcomed a Sithian royal to the Sanctum,' Cyrus said. 'Hardly a handful since your father.'

Jai stared, but before he could ask a question, a bowl of disappointing brown liquid was pressed into his hands. Winter, on the other hand, was presented with a bowl of chopped offal, fresh and stinking. She buried her face in it with relish, her fear of the onlookers momentarily forgotten in the face of shiny meat.

'You know the way to her heart,' Jai said, the joke lame, but breaching a smile upon Cyrus's face.

'Good,' he said, smiling and nodding. 'Please,' he then said, motioning to the gruel in Jai's hands. Lacking a spoon, Jai lifted the bowl to his lips. It had a mild, cloying smell, and Jai slurped a mouthful under Cyrus's watchful gaze.

A nutty, mushroom taste coated the interior of his mouth. It was cold, but not unpleasant, and soon he was gulping the mixture down.

Cyrus nodded appreciatively, waiting for Jai to finish before starting on his own. He quaffed it in a single gulp and smack of his lips. But to Jai's surprise, he said nothing, instead leaning back and looking at Jai with an appraising expression.

It was strange to face a man without a beard wrapped about his face, or braids in his hair. He was no warrior, of that Jai could tell, for a heavy paunch flopped from his belly, and his arms were skinny as a pike pole.

'Where are the men that brought me here?' Jai asked. 'Do you speak for them?'

Cyrus motioned upwards, though all Jai saw was the cave's ceiling, replete with the same soft-glowing lichen as before.

'All in good time,' he said. 'Come. We walk.'

He stood suddenly, and Jai could only follow as the man strode deeper into the gloom.

The deeper they went, the more expansive the cave became, an ever growing warren of tunnels, alcoves, stairs and chambers, many where Winter had to squeeze to make it through. Echoes of their footsteps bounced oddly around them, and he could see faces peeking out at him as they made their way.

Then the ravine opened into a wide, bustling space. The sight before Jai was unexpected, to say the least. In this subterranean world, young boys and girls were hard at work, their hands gently tending to a sprawling expanse of mushroom beds. In the dim, ethereal glow of the lichen above, the fungi sprung from the ground like fantastical miniature forests.

Every imaginable shape and size of mushroom blanketed the floor. Tall, stately red caps stretched above the rest, shadowing squat flat-topped browns. Delicate white mushrooms clumped together beneath, their thin stems reaching skyward and crowning in small, bulbous caps.

Fuzzy lion's manes with cascading yellow tendrils grew at ground level, alongside clusters of orange stubs. Strangest of all were the luminescent ones, grown at intervals along the way, green frilled and slimy, illuminating the children's concentrated faces.

The workers scattered handfuls of what looked like dried grass, while others plucked away with small hands, nimbly pruning the fungal harvest. The contents of that bowl were no longer a mystery.

Despite it all, more fascinating was above. For amid the glowing lichen of the ceiling . . . was movement. A seething mass of dark shapes, trembling in unison. Scores and scores of chittering bats, hanging and flitting back and forth along the ceilings. Every now and again, their guano would plop down onto the sprawling mounds, fertilising the fields below.

'The pride of the Sanctum,' Cyrus whispered, his voice reverent. 'The work of a thousand generations, a harvest of cultivars from all corners of our world.'

Cyrus ducked low, and plucked a cluster from the ground. He wiped it upon his puffy shirt, and proffered it to Jai. Glancing up at the bats, Jai politely declined, and the man popped it into his mouth with a smiling shrug.

'Come,' he said, striding on.

They followed, looping around the expanse until they reached another tunnel. From deep within, Jai could hear the squawking of birds, and the cries of men and women.

Emerging at the other end, Jai found them open to the elements once more, facing the wide-open expanse of Frostweald. And there . . . were the birds. Cawing and flouncing along a wide slope down into the tundra, their riders yelling as they wielded bladed lassos, practising their craft.

And above, high in the mountainside . . . were the roqs. He

could see their forms, perched high above the rest, their great nests peeking from their ledges high in the night sky. One glided in the sky, its dark outline just visible in the moonlight.

Winter let out a deep purr, as if appreciating the cool snow that stretched to the horizon, pale as her scales on a moonlit night. She stretched out her wings, and Jai heard calls as those below noticed their arrival.

He half expected the bald man that had led him there to approach him. But of the bald roq riders, none could be seen. Only those with the caps of hair, and the terror birds on the long, snowy slope to the Frostweald.

By now, Jai's fear had begun to subside. Whatever the Caelite's intentions, it seemed they meant him no harm.

'Where are the Huddites,' Jai asked, his patience worn thin. 'Where is the Dansk woman?'

Cyrus nodded solemnly, and nodded up, towards the tall peak of the mountain where the roqs appeared to reside.

'The woman is up there,' he said.

'And the others?' Jai asked.

Cyrus motioned with his chin, and Jai followed it to where a few dozen men in Caelite-styled clothing huddled, warming their hands around a small fire.

But with a flutter of Jai's hopeful heart, these were not the pate-headed folk Jai had seen. Their hair was long, and unkempt. And now Jai made out their features.

No guards keeping hostages captive. No prison cells, as there had been at Porticus.

Just the Huddites.

Jai tried to run, but found the snow up to his knees. Undeterred, he ploughed ahead, his boots sinking deep into the powdery carpet. Winter, agile as ever despite her larger form, effortlessly bounded through the snow ahead. She seemed to revel in the frosty playground, her large body carving a path.

Excited shouts and cries rang out from the gathered men as they caught sight of her, the dragon that had helped free them.

A buzz of recognition travelled through the group, their cries echoing from the surrounding snow-covered rocks. Jai's heart pounded in nervous anticipation as he recognised a figure stepping forth from the crowd – it was Hanebal.

The last time he had seen the man, he'd been little more than a skeletal frame, wasting away in the dank confines of Porticus, a prisoner in his own skin. But now there was a healthy glow about him, his cheeks flushed from the cold. His hair, once greasy and limp, now cascaded down his back. He was the picture of health, but his eyes still burned with the fierce intensity, a flame refusing to die.

The distance between them diminished, and Jai extended his hand in greeting. But Hanebal had other plans. With a booming laugh that rang out across the silent tundra, he swept Jai up into a bear hug, gripping so hard that even Jai's soulbound chest lost its breath.

Jai was lifted high off his feet, the cold wind whipping around them.

'I prayed you'd make it,' Hanebal growled. 'Who would have thought? Jai the Steppeman.'

He released Jai, even as the remaining Huddites thumped his back, their joy infectious as they welcomed him into their midst. The warmth of brotherhood was palpable in the harsh, frostbitten landscape, and more than Jai had ever experienced in his closeted life.

He felt himself shrink beneath the rough approbation, for some forty burly men were jostling him. It was only when Winter let out a deep growl of encouragement that he stood tall, squaring his shoulders and thumping Hanebal's back in return.

Finally, Hanebal barked an order, and the men sheepishly backed away. Another shout, and they moved further still, a few gathering close to Winter, who preened under their attention.

'How did you get here?' Hanebal asked. 'Traded too?'

'And Erica?' Jai asked, ignoring the question.

The name was strange on his tongue, and he realised it might have been only the second time he'd said it aloud since he had learned his friend's true identity.

'Don't you mean Frida?' Hanebal asked, giving Jai a meaningful look.

His message was clear. Erica had kept her name secret here, perhaps even from the other Huddites. Her identity was not yet known to the Caelite. Best to keep it that way.

'I . . . yes, sorry,' Jai said. 'Where is she?'

Hanebal sighed and rolled his eyes, and Jai waited a moment until he realised that was his answer. Above, like Cyrus had said.

'I had thought the worst,' Jai admitted, his voice barely audible over the blustering wind. 'That the Caelite were going to sell you as fettered.' He glanced back at Cyrus, whose patient gaze held a touch of bemusement. 'They are known for it.'

Shaking his head, Hanebal dismissed Jai's concern with a wave of his hand.

'These Caelite are no fetterers,' he asserted. 'Those they buy, they recruit.'

He motioned for Jai to follow him, a little away from the others. Winter reluctantly bounded away from her admirers and crouched close, raising her wings to shelter them from the wind, lest their words carry.

'Tell me,' Jai said. 'From the beginning.'

Hanebal took a deep breath, and clouded the frigid air with his words.

'For weeks we wandered the Great Steppe alone,' he said, his voice raw with remembered hardship. 'Water was scarce, and what we dug up was silty and foul. It turned our stomachs, made some of us sick. We scavenged for food, desperate enough to try what herbs we could find, foreign though they were. Those made us sicker still.'

A shadow crossed Hanebal's face as he spoke of those dire times, but then his features softened, adopting an air of reverence.

'Erica regained her strength. Soulbreathing through the cold nights, she nursed the sick back to health with her majicking, used the same to boil the water clean in the holes we dug. She was our lifeline in those bad days, the only thing keeping us from the touch of death.'

Hanebal paused, his gaze unfocused as he lost himself in the painful memories. He was silent for a moment before his voice, now tinged with a trace of resentment, resumed the tale.

'She navigated us by the stars, but that damned grass . . . Our going was slow. We had gone south, hoping to reach the Kashmere Road. Then the Keldar found us.'

He let out a sigh, and shrugged.

'In truth, we were grateful to them. Another few days, and even Erica could not keep us from dropping one by one. We were the walking dead.'

He shook his head.

'A few weeks with them, treated well enough, even if they kept Erica chained in Damantine. Then we find ourselves blindfolded at the bottom of a mountain, and flung over the backs of those stinking things. I dare to think how high I was dangling before we reached here.'

He spat between his teeth in the direction of the terror birds, whose harsh cries were constant in this far-flung place.

Jai made to interject, but Hanebal raised a hand, his eyes meeting Jai's.

'Don't worry,' he said, his voice steady despite the tremble in his hands. 'She's safe. We're all safe, in a way. The Caelite took us in, and for now, we are under their protection.'

Jai glanced back at Cyrus, who gave him a little wave.

'He's the guy in charge?' he asked.

Hanebal grinned.

'He's the quill pusher. The one in charge . . .'

He motioned again with his eyes.

'He's up there. With her.'

Chapter 58

'—So these bald brutes come out of nowhere and—'

'Khan,' Cyrus called. 'A word.'

Jai took a moment to realise Cyrus was referring to him, and turned, to find the man still waiting where Jai had left him. He had rather lost track of time in the swift recounting of his story to Hanebal, whose mouth had hung agape for much of it.

'We'll speak later,' Jai said.

With a sigh, Jai trudged back through the powdery snow towards Cyrus, feeling the mantle of duty returning to his shoulders. Cyrus greeted him with a congenial smile, his patting hand a silent invitation to join him upon a natural bench of rock. Its surface was weathered and smooth, bearing the wear of countless others who had looked out over the icy expanse from this spot before him.

'How do you know these Huddites?' Cyrus asked.

'We escaped Porticus together,' he admitted.

Cyrus nodded, a soft smile playing on his lips that suggested a level of knowledge Jai had not yet shared. His eyes, a steady, icy blue, held a sense of quiet understanding.

'I want to go see her,' Jai said. 'Now.'

Again, Cyrus nodded, but he was acknowledging the sentiment, not the demand.

'That is not up to me,' he said. 'The Caelite decide, and none are here.'

Jai was confused.

'Aren't you leader down here?'

Cyrus shook his head.

'I merely shepherd their flock here, below. We all serve them, and in doing so, find protection.'

Jai threw up his hands, turning to stare up at the peaks above. Now he noticed a steep staircase, one so sheer it could not be climbed by legs alone. It was not far, but not a single soul seemed to be using it. This did not surprise him – the route was treacherous, and a fall from it would unlikely be survived. The people who would go up there had other means, anyway.

'Then I will seek out the Caelite myself,' Jai snapped, determination igniting in his voice.

Cyrus held up his hands.

'Honoured Khan, I would counsel against such haste.'

'Why?' Jai said.

Cyrus smiled sympathetically. This perpetual lightheartedness was beginning to rankle Jai, in spite of Cyrus's generous hospitality.

'Most get one chance,' he said, holding up a finger. 'Take a moment to rest. Fill your belly, warm yourself. Soulbreathe.'

Rubbing his hands over his face, Jai felt the sapping weariness in his very bones. Despite Erica's safety from immediate ransom, each day that passed here was a day spent away from his tribe. Though he had faith in his tribe's leaders to maintain peace for a while longer, the luxury of time was not at his disposal. The Sabine legion continued their relentless advance, and the Gryphon Guard carried death on their wings.

'One chance to do what?' Jai asked, eager to focus on something other than the nagging worries tugging at his consciousness. A rest sounded so good, even if it were a moment of respite from his own thoughts.

'Why, to join them of course,' Cyrus revealed, a grand gesture emphasising his words. 'Many come here to join the Caelite's flock, finding contentment in life within the Sanctum here. We save others, purchasing fettered when our means allow. A select few, however, aspire to join the Caelite themselves. These devotees offer their service to the Caelite to prove their worth: they tame the terror birds, hunt meat from the steppe. All in the hopes of being deemed worthy of bonding with a roq of their own.'

He motioned at the men and women below, their cries and squawks colouring the air.

'What's so special about the Caelite?' Jai said. 'Their sect is scarcely spoken of.'

'Nor should it be,' Cyrus uttered. 'The Caelite do not recruit, nor share knowledge. They allow their flock to grow, certainly, for their mountain homes are vast and the land is bountiful. But only those who are deemed worthy they welcome as their own.'

He spoke as if in rote, giving an answer he had given many before.

'How long have they been here,' Jai asked.

'The Caelite are the oldest sect of the soulbound, predating even the Guild. Many have embarked on this journey only to be deemed unworthy. So I urge you to rest, Esteemed Khan.'

Jai stared up at the mountain.

'What if I don't want to join them?' he asked. 'What if I want to parlay, or barter?'

'They do not trade,' Cyrus said firmly. 'They do not accept envoys.'

He pointed back the way they had come.

'Traders meet down there,' he said. 'They meet with the flock, and the flock offers what they barter as gifts. There is no trade with the Caelite, only offerings.'

'Then what if I bring an offering?' Jai hissed, exasperated.

Cyrus pointed to a great spit, jutting away from the mountainside, beneath which the Huddites were gathered. Upon it,

Jai could see the piled remains of a khiro. Of course it was Baal. His Alkhara.

'We leave our offerings there,' Cyrus said. 'They are collected at their convenience.'

Anger welled up in Jai, threatening to spill over. Nevertheless, he held his rage in check, throwing a resentful glance at the devotees below. They continued their training, even under the relentless spring sun. Some had discarded most of their clothing, hoisting hefty rolls of compressed snow, their bodies glistening with perspiration.

'My father undertook this same journey,' Jai declared. 'I am certain of it. How did he establish contact with them?'

Cyrus bowed his head in acknowledgement.

'Your father once made the same ascent as you plan to do tomorrow. I assumed you were following in his footsteps.'

Mention of his father sent Jai's heart pounding. Could it be possible that Rohan had been a part of the Caelite's sect all along?

Jai lowered his face into his chin, and felt his resolve weaken. One more day, then. Surely he could allow himself that?

'What will I face, up there?' Jai asked.

As if he had sensed Jai's mind being made up, Cyrus clicked his fingers, summoning a young boy to his side.

'That I cannot tell you,' he said, that maddening smile touching his lips once more. 'Just know, you must be ready in body and spirit.'

The so-called shepherd turned his head, and muttered instructions in the language Jai had heard earlier.

'Enough,' he said, slapping the rock and getting to his feet. 'You need rest. We will speak more in the morning.'

He hated to wait. He hated more that Cyrus was right.

He hated that Erica was so close . . .

He hated, most of all, how much he looked forward to resting when there was so much to do and so little time to do it.

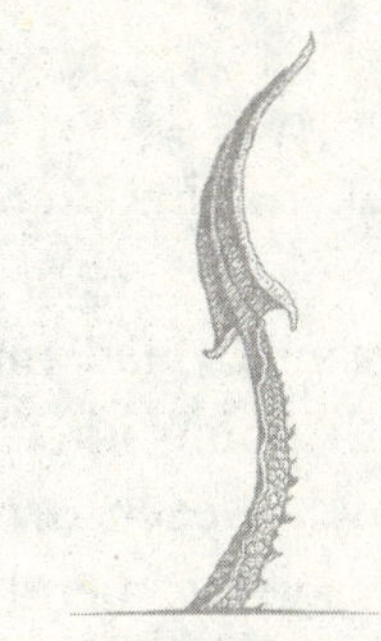

Chapter 59

It was strange to walk within the mountain. The room he had been given was large enough, with even a ledge for Winter, bedded with straw. Still, to be somehow deep within the earth, yet high above the ground, was a hard thing to parse, leaving Jai dizzy. It reminded him of his visit to Leonid's fabled whorehouse, and his journey down Latium's cliff to the plague pits.

With the day still his own, he soulbreathed, drawing in the mana that ebbed freely through the labyrinth of tunnels. A definite current of the life force was discernible, and Jai pursued it, ending up once again in the midst of the fungal fields. With Winter peacefully curled up below, Jai adopted a cross-legged posture, inviting the influx of mana. Whereas before, she'd freely given all she'd had to Jai, today she kept it for herself. He didn't blame her – the power of flight was addictive, it seemed.

This place . . . was special. The Great Steppe had been awash with mana, swirling up from the grasslands themselves. But here . . . the mana had a different source.

He could see mote after golden mote emerging from the furling, protruding fungi, larger and purer than any he'd seen before. Jai inhaled deeply, drawing the golden motes towards him. The tiny particles floated, almost suspended in the air before disappearing, absorbed through his skin, his nostrils, his very being. He felt them as they travelled, following the trajectory of his breath, a cool, tingling sensation making its way down to his core.

Here, the mana was transformed into a bright, gold-white liquid, slowly drip, drip, dripping into his innermost self.

He released some, allowing each drop to imbue a soothing energy coursing through his veins, mending his cuts and bruises. He dared not waste it with a healing spell, and was glad that his wounds were not greater than they were.

As the mana continued its work, Jai found himself losing track of time. The passage of hours seemed immaterial in this ethereal realm of quietude and growth. Cocooned in the dark, yet vibrantly alive, he knew now why the tunnels seemed to spiral up.

He knew too that this must be the source of the Caelite's power, a thick smog of mana that made soulbreathing easy for even the most untrained soulbound. This was why so many came to this place. This was the secret of the Caelite. Who knew how dense the mana became, as it swirled up to the top?

Around him, the fungal cornucopia maintained its ceaseless rhythm. He was amazed how this world was far from silent. He could hear the gentle creak of mushroom caps growing, audible to none but him and Winter, and the faint rhythm of his own heart beating. And somehow, in the distance, the chittering of bats, the delicate rustle of their wings, oblivious to it all.

He could feel his core filling, faster than it had ever before, and he felt an excitement, realising how much he longed to have it full once more. To follow his path, stretch his core so he could become more than just ascended, but a higher level of soulbound. He wasn't even sure if there was such a thing, but he could feel there had to be.

Just one more thing to strive for.

Engrossed in his reverie, Jai was abruptly jerked back to reality when something wet and slimy struck the back of his head. The unexpected sensation sent a jolt of surprise through him. He touched his head to find a green streak of bat guano upon his fingers.

He spun around, the vestiges of his peaceful meditation evaporating.

Standing before him were three devotees, their faces stern, their demeanour hostile. Each had a terror bird at their side, the large eyes unblinking and predatory, matching that of their handlers.

Jai instinctively rose to his feet, even as Winter let out a threatening rumble, uncurling from where she'd lain. The cold drip of bat guano slid down the back of his neck, and he brushed it off with a grimace, never breaking eye contact with the intruders.

His hand strayed to his empty belt, remembering he'd left his sword and scabbard in his chamber. Still, he raised his fingers in warning, contorting them in the ready position for majicking, as Rufus had told him to.

To his surprise, the trio did the same, fingers raised, their faces even angrier. So they had some training, then.

'What's all this?' Jai growled. 'You dare insult the khan of the Kidara?'

A surge of tension hung in the air, as thick as the mana that ebbed around them. The three devotees exchanged glances, their gazes only leaving him for a moment.

'Dare insult?' one of the three began, a sneer pulling at his lips. His head was shaved entirely, in the style of the roq riders Jai had seen earlier. 'It is you who trespass on the codes of the Caelite, khan or not.'

Jai was silent, trying to figure out if Winter could take the three beasts on her own. He looked closer, taking in the strange creatures that shared his opponents' lives and, apparently, their souls. The beasts were akin to giant ostriches, yet their appearance was far more intimidating. The terror birds stood taller than any man, their bodies dominated by a long, slender neck that ended in a sharp, hooked beak, as thick as a toucan's and twice as sharp. Their large orange eyes were piercing and alert, providing an eerie focus as they stared him down. What caught his attention, though, was the plumage around their eyes, a cascade of feathers in an array of garish colours – blues, greens, yellows, even hints of red. It was strangely beautiful against their otherwise drab plumage.

Their legs were thick and muscular, ending in large claws that rivalled Winter's own, splayed wide for gripping the unyielding rocky terrain that was their habitat. Their wings flapped with nervous energy, small things, but perhaps enough to allow them to slow a fall. More than anything, they were large – far larger than he'd guessed now they were up close. And despite their size, he could see a controlled grace to their movements, a deadly elegance that spoke of their predatory nature.

He wasn't sure he and Winter would be able to best these three pairs. For some reason, that made him angrier.

'Tell me, then,' Jai snapped. 'Clearly you hold some ill-judged grievance.'

His mana-charged fingers twitched, ready to snap into the fire-casting position at any moment. The trio shared another glance before the one in the middle, a woman with a streak of silver in her otherwise raven hair, spoke too. Her words were sharp, like the frosty peaks that towered above them.

'We did not fly here on the backs of dragons. We did not bypass the trials of the climb, nor did we shirk our duty to the Caelite. We stole a terror bird egg each, risking our lives in ravines of the sanctuary, as is the way of all devotees among the flock. Nursed them from hatchlings to adults. Bared our soul and shared in their spirit. We paid our dues. And yet now we hear you plan to make the climb alone, tomorrow. You only arrived today!'

Jai shrugged.

'You presume to judge me,' Jai said. 'You have no idea the trials I've gone through, for one thing. Yet you deign to speak on behalf of the Caelite? Then on behalf of myself, I say this: I shall not forget to relate this generous gesture, when I reach the top.'

The woman let out a gasp, as if shocked by his rudeness – as if it was *his* rudeness in question, not this trio's – but the third, a man little older than Jai, held her back before she could do something they all regretted.

'We do not prejudge,' he said, her previous words belying this statement. 'But know this. The Caelite welcome those that provide for them, and you bring them nothing.'

'My Alkhara lies on that slab outside,' Jai retorted. 'One of you cowards killed him, butchered him, brought him here. I thank you for the kind favour, but the claim to that gift is mine.'

Fire was now spurting from their hands, a trio of swirling balls of flame, hovering upon their fingers. Winter's rumble turned to a roar, and now Jai could see the Caelite's flock, hurrying towards them.

'You will lay no such claim!' the first man bellowed.

Jai flexed his fingers, feeling out the shield spell, letting the mana flow as he twitched them this way and that, feeling the resistance as he corrected his form.

He let a little spurt out, and a white, ethereal shape floated in a mass before him. He shaped it as Rufus had taught him to do with flame, leaving an opaque pane, seemingly fragile as the glass it mimicked. It moved with his hand, as if connected to his wrist by an invisible frame.

Even as he did this, he also lifted his right hand, this one less used to spellcraft, and prepared his own fireball. Not in time, though, as the first of his opponent's fireballs slammed against his shield, the pane cracking, heat flooding around its edges to sear his wrist. He'd been in battle, though, and while it surprised him, it wasn't enough for him to lose focus. He pumped more mana to his shield, new layers sloughing over, even as his fireball swelled.

And you don't have shields—

'You will stop this at once!'

The fireballs of the three before him winked out, one by one, and after a moment, Jai reabsorbed the mana of both his spells in response as well. Cyrus skidded to a halt between them, a dozen spearmen following. The soldiers looked terrified, the spears held awkwardly in their hands. The Caelite's flock were no fighters, that was becoming obvious.

'What are you doing?' Cyrus demanded.

The three devotees said nothing, just staring daggers at Jai. He thought about explaining what had happened to Cyrus, but then decided against it. He stood there, coolly looking back at the three who had attacked him.

'Fine,' Cyrus said, the anger mixed with what sounded like relief at this not escalating further. 'You three – go!'

The older man nodded curtly, taking the woman's arm to pull her away. Jai continued to make no move, and that seemed to be enough to antagonize the first man.

'You won't make the climb alone tomorrow,' he hissed, stabbing a finger at him. 'We'll see who claims the gift first.'

'I'm looking forward to it,' Jai finally said.

And as anxious as the prospect was, he realised a part of him *was* looking forward to the challenge, if only to show up these presumptuous bastards.

Chapter 60

Jai stood amid the Huddites, staring at the staircase. It was more a ladder than anything, its steepness such that the first three steps were as tall as he was.

Cyrus had told him that he could not circumvent it by riding Winter to its top. This was part of the so-called trial the Caelite expected of those that wished to join them.

And though Jai had no desire to become a member of this secretive sect, he knew arriving at their home through any other means would not earn their respect. Had they wished him to fly there, they would have led him to the top, rather than leaving him below with Cyrus.

The three devotees who had confronted him had left at first light, and he could see their small forms ahead of him, spread at intervals, a third of the way up the high staircase. He dreaded the thought of being so high once more, clutching the side of the mountain. One tip backwards . . . and he'd be dead.

He knew they'd left so soon, so they could claim Baal's sacrifice before he did.

'Erica did this?' Jai asked.

Hanebal shrugged.

'Didn't see her reach the top, lost sight of her at nightfall. But she left, sure enough, and she didn't fall down here.'

'Did she say why she went there?' Jai asked.

He shook his head.

'She said her people needed her, and the Caelite were the fastest way of getting back. We told her we'd accompany her back to her people if she failed. She told us not to wait for her.'

Jai turned to him, and gave him a smile.

'So you stayed and waited anyway?'

Hanebal chuckled ruefully.

'In all honesty, we've been hardly in a state to go anywhere else. Spent much of the first weeks just eating and sleeping. Cyrus has been kind to us, for one thing. And our homeland . . . it's not ours anymore. There's thirty-seven of us, true, and more among the flock. But it's not enough to make a difference. You tell me a better place to go, and we'll head there. For now . . . there's worse things than bat and mushroom soup every day.'

His face turned melancholy, and Jai squeezed his shoulder.

'You guys want to fight?' he asked. 'Make a difference?'

Hanebal nodded.

'Then you come with me, when I'm finished here,' Jai said. 'There's a legion to be dealt with, and I've the army to do it.'

Hanebal grinned. 'Then you hurry back from your powwow with the powers that be,' he said, motioning with his eyes above. 'We'll be waiting for you.'

Jai nodded. He could still taste the mushrooms, for his belly was full of them. But with a core that was now a quarter full, thanks in no small part to the thick mana within the mountain, he felt confident he would make it.

He turned to Winter, the dragon staring up at the great staircase with consternation, her claws scrunching tighter in the snow.

'You fly up there when I call,' Jai said, nuzzling her close. 'Or catch me if I fall,' he chuckled. Winter didn't reciprocate the humour, though. He sighed. 'It will be okay.'

She made a small sound, one of concern, but also one of trust.

And with that, he mounted the first step . . . and began to climb.

RAISE A HAND. GRIP. Push with the leg, grip with the other hand, raise other leg. Raise a hand. Grip.

Jai repeated the movements in his mind, methodical with every move. The staircase was crumbling, such that he had to test each step before surmounting the next. It was slow going.

Which was on purpose, he knew. It was meant to be hard. Meant to be dangerous. It seemed the Caelite never used this route, only the devotees who wished to join them. This was a challenge designed for soulbound; that much was obvious. Even he, ascended as he was with the innate strength and fortitude that came with it, still needed mana to help him.

He couldn't imagine that someone without majick would have even gotten as far as he already had . . . and he was still a ways from the top.

He could see the work of those that had come before – the work of those who clearly didn't want him to succeed. The fact that the three devotees were so malicious only furthered his resolve, even as he took in where a knife had been driven deep to loosen the shale, that it might come away in his hands. Or the oil slathered upon the step, such that he had to remove his shirt and wipe down the residue.

It wasn't just the sabotage, though. Those were sporadic, while the biting cold was a constant enemy, nipping at his exposed skin, his breath become clouds of mist in the thinning air. He wasted mana warming himself, a tradeoff against the stamina he siphoned it for.

So focused was he on the traps and cold that he had to remind himself he needed to keep observing his whole environment. Just in time too, because it was then that Jai heard the rumble. The scattering of stone, and a boulder thrummed by him, so close it tugged the cloth of his trousers on its way past. He cursed, pressing himself against the rock, folding over as much as he dared.

Dust and rubble fell in its wake, but only enough to make him cough, and feel a rattle of pain as pebbles pinged off his head and shoulders. Above, he heard laughter, drifting on the wind.

Earlier, he had wished Winter was climbing with him, even if to make him feel less alone, high on this windswept expanse. Now he was glad she had been left behind.

He looked behind – no, *below* – and felt the world stretch, the white desert blending seamlessly with the overcast sky. Jai focused on Winter, if only to find something to fix his gaze on, fighting the dizzying shock at the sight.

His dragon was waiting patiently, her blue eyes turned upwards, watching his every move with a worry that only served to compound his own. She wanted to help him, but knew this was his fight alone.

Shaking off the remaining dust, Jai continued his upwards journey. Every step he passed was a victory, each grip of his hand a new pledge to his commitment. Now the rock became icy and slick. Twice, his grasp had slipped, and only the rough bottoms of his boots had held him from toppling back.

Jai scraped with his fingernails, or dug handholds where the rock was too smooth to find a grip. The going was slow, and his heart felt like it would beat out of his chest.

There was no reprieve. No ledge to wait upon while he caught his breath, no safe alcove out of the high winds. Just the edges of the steps digging against his body, the friction of his boots and the grip of his fingernails were all that kept him from slipping away. He ground on, nothing but the sound of his hard breath and the whipping wind.

Until a scream, above.

Jai's head jerked upwards, his eyes widening as he watched the youngest of the devotees sliding down the steps. His hands scrabbled frantically at the icy rock, desperate to slow his fall. But the young man's efforts only seemed to swing him into a tumble, his body flipping backwards.

Before Jai could react, the boy plummeted past him. He felt sharp nails rake across his back, a searing pain that stole the breath from his lungs. The boy's hand found a hold on his leg, and for a moment Jai too was teetering back, before his outstretched hand pulled him back against the rock.

Jai looked down, the grip sliding down to his ankle. Terror-filled eyes stared up, a desperation in their depths.

'Hold on!' Jai shouted, reaching out, his fingers stretching. But it was too late. The boy slipped away, his screams echoing quieter and quieter, only to come to a sudden, gut-churning halt.

Jai stared after him, a wave of cold dread washing over him, his body shaking with shock. Far below, a forlorn figure. And crimson, slow spreading amid the white.

He allowed himself a single deep breath, before turning back.

Raise a hand. Grip the rock.

Another step up.

Chapter 61

Jai heaved himself over the edge, gasping like a beached fish. His tendons were on fire, his fingers crooked stiff, even as he shoved them down his trousers for warmth.

He rolled away from the ledge, choking down a few breaths, hugging the rock as if it were his dearest friend.

But it was not. This place was so inhospitable, Jai could not imagine why the Caelite chose to live here. The air was thin, such that no matter how much he gasped, he could never seem to catch his breath.

Still, there was a cold beauty here. For he had climbed through the clouds, to reach the high peak of the Yaltai Mountains. And above that grey blanket that covered the sky . . . was blue. A deep, bright blue, as if the firmament were made of lapis.

Beneath it, there was the sheer white of the mountains, spearing through the clouds like Winter's fangs. Among them, he could see the only source of life and movement – the great nests of the roqs, woven from twigs and dried grasses. Few were occupied.

Now he could make out the two devotees ahead of him, huddled together for warmth. At first, he had not seen them, for the snow coated them. The two were motionless, and Jai feared the worst.

He forced himself to his knees, his legs quivering. He could feel the cold seeping deep, his body shaking uncontrollably in the frigid air. His trembling hands were already purple from the cold.

Wherever he was, this peak was far higher than the one he had flown to with Winter. *Winter!*

He called out to her, the familiar connection soothing him when Winter's consciousness twitched, responding to his summons. She was already on her way, using her wings to beat her way up the steep incline. Jai could feel her struggle, the effort of her flight consuming her dwindling mana.

Jai staggered to the edge, looking down. The vista yawned out, an endless expanse of white. Below, he could see the cloud bank he had climbed through, and nothing more. Winter was somewhere below, battling the wind.

He could see the two terror birds, making their way up the stairs. It would be an hour at least before they reached their soulbound counterparts.

He watched as Winter finally broke through the clouds, her white scales gleaming. She flapped above him, the wind dragging her back, until she landed in a lopsided skip, her wings folding against her body. She panted heavily, her sides heaving, and Jai could tell that she had given everything to get there.

He rushed to her, wrapping his arms around her neck, the warmth of her scales a welcome relief against his freezing skin.

'There now, my darling,' he murmured into her neck.

Turning back to the two devotees, he shuffled closer. He was not their enemy, not now, not here. They were all just trying to survive.

Summoning his strength, Jai dragged the unconscious devotees towards Winter. The dragon grumbled, but did not protest, letting her body shield them against the biting wind. She curled around them, rumbling softly.

Jai ducked into the lee of her wings, crouched under her

heaving chest. His body screamed for rest, eyes growing heavy despite the bitter cold. He pulled Winter's wings tighter, creating a makeshift tent against the swirling gale around them.

The devotees were blue. He could see the older woman's face, eyes half-closed, expression a rictus of suffering. The other man was little better, though at least he still shuddered, while the woman's body was far too still.

Jai cursed the cold, trying to calm, to soulbreathe. He managed a few gulps of mana, but the golden motes were few and far between up here, just as the air was.

He struggled to spurt a small ball of flame, knowing it was a better use of his mana than the hungry healing spell. It was small, hanging in the air like an oscillating pinprick of sun. Any more, and he would not be able to sustain it, but the warmth was blessed.

He breathed in the half-trance, taking in what mana he could, fuelling his weak spell. Together with Winter, he waited, shuddering, his clothing growing sodden as the frost melted from his clothes. Their small cocoon warmed slowly, and he slapped at the older woman's flesh, glad to see her chest rising and falling in halting gasps, and the colour returning to her face.

A clap of palms. It was so faint, and Jai was not sure he heard it. Then another. And another.

He sucked in a breath, and let the spell sputter away. Pushed aside a wing, and poked his head out into the howling cold.

Jai looked around, unable to see the source of the noise.

Then a drift of snow moved from a flat rock, not far from where they lay. To Jai's surprise, he saw a man sitting upon the rocks. He had the same bald appearance as the roq-riding Caelite, his lack of eyebrows giving him a strange, emotionless expression.

He held a falx blade in his hand rather than the strange roped weapons Jai had seen earlier. He also wore almost no clothing, bare-chested as Jai was, seemingly unaffected by the cold.

Now Jai had caught his eye, the man shook the snow from his body and leaped down, facing Jai. He raised his blade, and held it out.

'What is this?' Jai said, his voice cracking after being silent for so long.

His opponent said nothing. Only stood his ground, blade outstretched.

'I have no wish to fight you,' Jai said, speaking loudly lest his words be snatched away by the howling wind.

Still, silence.

Jai stood as straight as he could, pulling the long blade of the falx from the scabbard on his back. The man remained, motionless.

'What do you want?' Jai repeated.

Nothing.

Jai pushed past Winter's wings, wading through powdery snow. He brought his falx up to meet its opposite, grinding his feet for purchase. It was not so different from fighting in the tall grass, if a little thicker, and lower.

The man darted, his falx smashing Jai's aside and lunging for his throat. Jai barely avoided it. No . . . he hadn't. A thin trail of warmth trickling down his neck where the blade had grazed him. Jai cut back in a wild swing, but the man had already danced out of reach.

He smiled, and bowed with a flourish. Winter let out a low growl, and the man's smile widened, wagging his finger at her.

'Winter, stay!' Jai yelled, feeling Winter stir.

The man had made it clear – this was a duel between them, and them alone.

Jai lunged, only to have his blade slapped down with the flat of his opponent's. The counter was swift, the sword flickering, and Jai felt another sting of pain along his chest, and blood warm for but a moment before freezing on his skin.

The man was playing with him. Dread pooled in Jai's belly, but he had no choice but to fight on.

Again and again, Jai struck and the man countered, always grazing, teasing. Jai barely managed to defend himself, let alone counterattack.

Jai's strength was waning, his falx heavier with every move. Meanwhile, the other man seemed undisturbed by any kind of exertion. His eyes tracked Jai's every movement, and never without a smile upon his face.

Desperate, Jai lunged, locking blades with the man, then turning in and low, sweeping his leg, the way Kiran had taught him.

It was like kicking a steel post, but it was enough. The man slipped, staggered.

Reacted.

Jai moved to counter, only for his enemy's hand to contort, as majicking fixed Jai's blade in the air, stopping it dead. Defenceless, Jai strained, fearing the next attack he wouldn't be able to counter . . .

Only for the man to bow low, his free hand folding over his chest in a show of respect.

Jai near tripped as the resistance fell away; his strange opponent stepped aside, gesturing towards the path beyond with his falx.

'And . . . these two?' he asked, breath ragged.

The man seemed to contemplate the question, then nodded.

As Jai sheathed his blade and moved past him, the man sat back down in the snow, crossing his legs beneath him. His bare skin seemed unaffected by the cold, his focus returning to the skyline before him. The man's gaze was already distant, as though he had forgotten Jai was there.

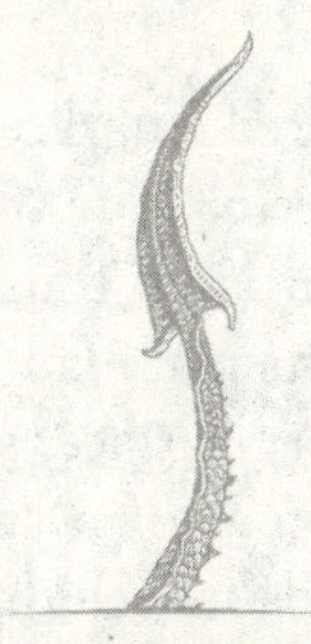

Chapter 62

Jai hefted the woman over his shoulder, letting Winter carry the male devotee, hanging by his shirt between her teeth, feet dragging in the snow. Jai took a moment to appreciate her beauty – she looked for all the world like a cat with her kitten 'twixt her teeth.

The trail indicated by the Caelite guardian was barely more than a knife's edge, flanked by sharp abysses on both sides. The path led unmistakably towards the grand summit that pierced the heavens.

It was terrifying to walk it, especially with this unfamiliar weight of the devotee on his back, and a thick layer of snow hiding what lay beneath. Each step, he felt out before putting down his weight, for what looked like a smooth ribbon of powdered path was likely treacherous beneath its frosting.

Now, though, he could see the roqs' nests in earnest, each one larger than his own royal chamber, the enormous birds silently watching him with piercing eyes. It seemed they were used to humans. Or at least, they simply had no reason to fear them. Both knew instinctively which could eat the other.

At the end of the long ridge, Jai saw an opening in the base of the tallest peak, and he staggered for it. He had envisioned a bustling enclave, teeming with the whispers of the Caelite, yet this realm was more desolate than any he had ever witnessed.

Stepping into the sheltered embrace of the cave's shadow, Jai beheld a wonder. The exterior bore the marks of the wind and snow's ravages, but within lay a touch of pure artistry. It was as if generations of craftsmen had dedicated their lives to perfecting every facet, every surface, sculpting the interior into an intricate helix reminiscent of a snail's shell. This spiralled chamber narrowed towards its zenith, tapering above an enigmatic abyss. At its heart lay a chasm, whose depths seemed to expand the longer Jai observed. At its bottom, countless tunnels spread in labyrinthine complexity, merging and converging in patterns that echoed a mathematical obsession.

For all that, there were no people here. Not plural, at least. Only a man. That same hairless man that had led him to the flock, adorned in nothing more than a simple cloth girded around his loins. With meditative repose, he sat near the precipice of the spiral on an ancient stone pedestal, his gaze lost in distant contemplation.

As Jai approached, dragging the weakened woman with him, he felt the weight of exhaustion, and dropped to his knees. Winter, with all the gentleness of a new mother, laid the male devotee beside him, who let out a pained whimper, curling in on himself in a ball.

'We've made it,' Jai said. 'You must help them. Their time grows short.'

The man snapped his eyes to Jai, a momentary ripple of irritation crossing his visage. With an agile motion that belied his serenity, he sprung to his feet, so fast Jai fell back in surprise. The Caeliteman leaned over and picked the pair up by the scruffs of their necks. His strength was immense, for he held them with arms outstretched, his face impassive.

Jai stared, aghast, as he turned to the edge.

'No!' Jai cried out, lunging.

But it was too late. The two forms were released, their descent eerily silent before making a muted impact against the slopes. Then their limp forms slid, twisting and bouncing in a grotesque dance, until they vanished into the gloom of the tunnels beneath.

'They'll live,' came a careless remark from the bald guardian. 'If they're worthy of another chance.'

Jai leaped to his feet, meeting the man's gaze. The Caeliteman's eyes were unnaturally dark, and Jai knew to fight him would be folly. Gradually, he calmed, and settled for spitting to the side to mark his displeasure.

'They had better,' Jai said, his threat weakened by the shaking in his voice. He was trembling uncontrollably, and Winter stepped forward unbidden, wrapping him in the warmth of her leathery wings once more, her great head resting warm upon his shoulder.

'They were tested,' the man said, almost confused by Jai's concern. 'And they failed.'

Jai crossed his arms, but bit back his retort. He was not here to throw away his people's future for the sake of two that had in all likelihood tried to kill him. But now he knew what this place was. Unforgiving of weakness. As cold and hard as the stone it was made of. And he didn't like it.

'I brought you an Alkhara,' Jai said finally, motioning down at the plinth far below. 'A gift, for the Caelite.'

The man sniffed, and gave a soft nod, as if forgiving Jai's trespass.

'A fine gift,' he said. 'Your father's symbol, sacrificed in our name. Yes . . .'

His eyes drifted, standing in his strange nakedness amid the snow.

'I must speak with your leader,' Jai said.

The man shook his head slowly.

'That is all for today.'

Jai resisted the urge to curse. He had clawed his way up here by his very nails, against all that nature and man could throw at him. And now . . . this?

'Who are you?' Jai asked, stepping in front of him.

'They call me the Speaker,' he said.

Jai waited, but the man remained silent, content to wait amid the freezing cold. Some speaker he was.

'I come as an envoy,' Jai said. 'Who will receive me?'

'We receive no envoys.'

'You lie,' Jai said. 'My father made a deal with you. I know it.'

The Speaker sniffed.

'You tread the same path as your father,' he said. 'But he was no envoy.'

Jai ground his feet into the snow, resisting the urge to punch the cryptic, strange man.

'What was he, then?' Jai demanded.

The Speaker bowed his head, wincing in soft admonishment.

'One of us, of course.'

Jai shook his head, disbelieving. His father, a member of this strange sect? The lie was so obvious, Jai could not understand why the man had made it.

'You may go,' the man said.

He leaped back into his sitting position, ignoring Jai completely. His eyes went blank, his face slack once more. He was soulbreathing . . . that much was obvious.

Jai clicked his fingers in the man's face, to no avail.

'So what, you expect me to just climb back down, after all that?' Jai shouted.

He knew he was letting the man get the better of him, but the rage was the only thing that seemed to be holding the freezing cold at bay.

The Speaker ignored him. Jai cursed, rubbing his hands together, a chill wind gusting through the gaps in Winter's makeshift shelter.

Jai entered the half-trance, ready to take a few hummingbird breaths, to let the mana warm his bones. Instead, his vision blazed golden white.

The cavern was *full* of mana. Swirling higher and higher, painting the world with such gilded brilliance that Jai staggered back, near blinded for the light.

Drawn like a moth, he stepped closer. Just a sip . . . a taste.

The Speaker's hand slapped Jai's chest, sending him tumbling back into Winter's side. The dragon let out a roar, the noise shattering the still silence, her open maw stippling the man's face with spit. He remained expressionless, locking eyes with her until she finally withdrew, letting out a final grumble of discontent.

'Only those deemed worthy may sample the bounty,' the Speaker said.

Jai grounded his feet, and took a deep breath to centre himself. That raw energy in the cavern, the tantalising lure of mana, had momentarily overwhelmed his senses.

'Where is the Dansk woman?' Jai asked. 'At least tell me that.'

'She endures,' the man said simply. 'As your father did.'

Jai cursed long and hard, such that he thought he saw the Speaker's lips twitch in response. Finally, he calmed himself. There was no going back.

'Then I will too,' Jai said, throwing caution to the swirling winds around them.

The first hint of an expression touched the man's face, a faint tugging of the corners of his lips.

'Come with me.'

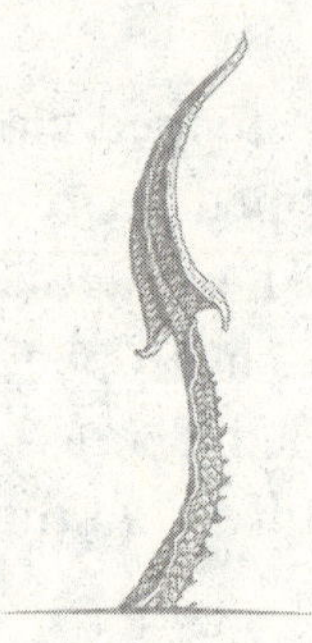

Chapter 63

Jai followed the Speaker, leaning against Winter as they travelled a serpentine trail that curled around the tall spar that made the Yaltai Mountains' highest peak. He used hummingbird breaths as he staggered, sucking in what mana he could to warm feet he could no longer feel.

The path was flanked by members of the Caelite, their figures statuesque, each settled upon stone plinths, soulbreathing or in deep trance. Despite the apparent paucity of mana in this area, here they were, lightly garbed against the freezing winds, a thin layer of snow frosting their bodies like a soft shroud. A closer examination revealed rough bands of cloth around many of their torsos, and Jai realised some of them were women. The pervasive baldness of most, reminiscent of the Speaker, seemed like a mark of age or seniority, while a few younger ones still sported hair.

It seemed an eternity before they reached the summit. The plateau at the mountain's zenith appeared almost unnaturally flat, as though a celestial hand had cleaved the tip for some grand purpose. All that marred the tableau's flatness was a series of perforations at its heart, among which sat a dozen people in contemplation.

In his half-trance, the world unfolded with heightened clarity for Jai. For now he knew where all the mana from the fungal forest went.

Here.

The mountaintop was awash with mana. It was like a swirling aureate fog, bursting through the small holes in a torrent of light, before dissipating high above their heads, becoming lost in the swirling eddies of the skies.

It was a great siphon, concentrating the golden dust that emerged from the fungal gardens into one lonely patch at the top of the world.

A man with jet-black skin towered above the others sitting amid the rushing mana, clearly hailing from the sun-soaked southern Sabine subjugated state of Shambalai. His presence debunked Jai's earlier notion of the Caelite being an exclusive sect of Sithians. They were, as Jai now realised, a tapestry of cultures and lineages from across the known world. Eagerly he looked at the others . . .

His heart leaped. For there, radiant amid the shimmering mana, was Erica. Her eyes closed, her oval face serene, ethereal in the glow, her hair a halo about her head. He wanted her to open her deep blue eyes, to see how far he had travelled to reach her. To see her smile. To hear her say his name.

Instead, he let the Speaker's grip upon his arm hold him in place, and watched as the man skilfully navigated around the seated soulbreathers. As the dark-skinned man rose at the Speaker's touch, he stood firm with an aura of regal command, and his penetrating gaze settled upon Jai, dissecting him.

In that gaze, Jai felt stripped bare, as exposed as he was to the unyielding chill of the mountaintop. The weight of the scrutiny was such that Winter, ever his protector, pressed closer, her snout seeking comfort in the crook of his shoulder. It was a small consolation, for the planar landscape provided no true shelter against the biting cold. With each heartbeat, the last remnants of Jai's mana threatened to evaporate, leaving him helpless. He dared not allow more than a minuscule trickle from his core, just enough to stave off the cold's embrace, if shuddering and numb.

Yet while he suffered the cold, Winter was in her element, taking well after her namesake. He could sense she longed for the freedom to soar amid the gusts and flurries, a desire Jai could feel simmering at the edge of her thoughts. And yet, despite her own wishes, she selflessly funnelled her reservoir of mana to him, a lifeline preventing him from succumbing entirely to the elements.

As the dark-skinned man approached, details emerged from the silhouette. Now Jai could see clearly the frosted sweat upon his chest, dusting enormous slabs of hard muscle. Yet he walked with a pardine grace that belied his great size and stature. His head, bald like the rest, looked almost small in comparison to the rest of his body.

The Speaker, in quiet reverence, trailed the giant with a bowed head.

The large man leaned forward, his breath hot in Jai's ear. A hot hand clamped upon the back of Jai's neck, and he shuddered awkwardly at the unnatural warmth.

He was drawn into a sitting position, his head still clamped beside the man's own, and Jai's ear was warmed as the man whispered.

'Jai, son of Rohan.'

The weight of his own name hung in the cold air, filling the space with a gravity that held him breathless.

'Yes,' Jai finally responded, his voice barely more than a sigh.

'Do you seek to join the Caelite, as your father did?'

A moment of hesitation clouded Jai's thoughts, the weight of his destiny pressing upon him. But the Speaker's earlier words echoed in his mind, leaving no room for dissent. This was a non-negotiable.

'Yes,' he affirmed once more, the word become a bond.

The towering figure pulled back, examining Jai with a gaze that seemed to pierce through the facade of his very soul. But just as swiftly, he leaned in once more, their foreheads nearly touching, the words shared between them a sacred covenant.

'Will you pledge to honour our code, abide by our tenets and accept the justice meted should you falter?'

The finality of the vow pressed upon Jai's tongue, yet he found the resolve to answer.

'Yes.'

Jai fell back, released from the iron grip. A moment of stillness lingered, and the man's gaze turned contemplative, as if glimpsing memories long past.

'I grant you the privilege of proving yourself.'

Jai rubbed the back of his neck. It had been like being pinched by steel tongs, the touch unyielding and hard.

The man's gaze then turned to Winter, meeting the dragon's eyes with strange understanding, and he reached out a hand. Jai had half expected Winter to snap at it, yet to his surprise, she instead lowered her head, and allowed him to run a hand along her brow. Even let him lift a lip to examine her teeth.

She trusted him . . . and feared him. Through her, Jai could sense a deep, simmering power behind his intense brown eyes. Like a dam, holding back a flood.

In an effortless motion, the man was on his feet, pulling Jai upright with him. He turned with a swift gesture to the Speaker, who ushered Jai back, the way they had come. Jai stood against the Speaker's pressures for a moment longer, watching Erica's pale face, willing her to open her eyes.

But soon the Speaker's grip turned steely, forcing Jai to follow. Back down the spiral path, past the seated soulbreathers, to the ravined path. They descended the winding trail, bypassing the meditative forms of the soulbreathers. The mountainside beckoned, not into its cavernous heart, but along its sheer face.

There, nestled among the craggy rocks, was an unassuming alcove, a humble indentation hardly spacious enough to shelter a man. There were dozens more beside it, though the place was so barren it was impossible to tell if they were occupied or not.

The Speaker motioned at Jai to enter, and Jai did so, leaving Winter to crouch in the snow outside.

'This is your place,' he said.

He went to leave, but Jai seized him by the wrist. Such was the man's strength, he nearly yanked Jai back out, hardly noticing the weight, but stopped and stared at Jai's hand.

'What about food?' Jai demanded, refusing to let him go. 'What about a bed, or a fire. How about just a door?'

He was angry. These people told him nothing, and spoke in riddles. The Speaker shrugged.

'We have no need of such trifles,' he said, prying Jai's fingers from his wrist with a force Jai could not even slow. 'Be patient, and keep your voice down. Speaking is my privilege, not yours.'

And with that, he turned, and leaped. A blur of wing and feather swooped, making Winter duck and growl in protest. The Speaker was borne away, leaving Jai sitting in a cold hollow, staring through a jagged, circular hole into blue sky.

Winter's head soon blocked his view, and she slid her sinuous neck through, plugging the gap from the cold of the wind.

'Trifles, huh,' Jai said bitterly. 'What am I supposed to live on, mana alone?'

And then, Jai realised, that was exactly what they expected. For he knew it could be done. Mana had kept him going, in those first days with Winter, traipsing through the forest.

But to do that . . . Jai would need a lot of it. And Rufus had told him that only powerful soulbound could live on mana alone. As one so early on the path, having only recently ascended no less, he would be hard-pressed to do so.

As fatigue and disappointment weighed him down, he found solace in the prospect of rest. But as he lay, his gaze was drawn to etchings overhead. Names, perhaps of predecessors or other aspirants, marred the stone. Many were crossed out, perhaps souls who couldn't meet the Caelite's exacting standards. One name, however, held his gaze, scratched deep, both in the rock and in Jai's heart.

Rohan.

Chapter 64

Jai lay in the relative warmth of his cocoon, tracing the lines of his father's writing. A sense of history washed over him: his father too had sought sanctuary in this very alcove, finding time among the elements to engrave his legacy.

Jai knew from Leonid's diaries that the Caelite had come suddenly, descending upon Rufus's Gryphon Guard during a protracted siege. Surely his father made this self-same journey during that time, leaving his tribe in the midst of war to . . . to bend the powerful sect to his will.

But had he become a member of the Caelite to do it? Jai pondered if he too would find a route back home if accepted into their ranks.

So many questions. But at least he was warm while contemplating them. With Winter plugging the hole of his cave, her hot breaths damp against his face – his body heat had gradually returned, and he was able to sit comfortably without using mana.

It was just as well, for Jai was as low as he had been in a long time. Winter let out a deep rumble of contentment, her head heavy in his lap. She was so big now, almost as large as a horse.

He imagined it a comical sight, her rump sticking out of the cave, bare to the elements, tail blocking the ledge around which the rest of the alcoves resided. But he cared not a jot.

For with Winter so close, he could soulbreathe in earnest. There was mana here, filtering through the pores in the rocks. The ambient mana, subtle but present, was enough to make it worth his time. Though not as abundant as the vast reservoirs of the Great Steppe, where the countless grasses offered limited potency in immense volume, it sufficed.

With every deep breath, he felt his core drip with the liquid gold so pure it was almost blinding white. It was hard work, pulling mana through the walls of the cave. He could almost sense it through the rock, blazing through the hollows on the other side. It was like pulling it through a heavy veil, tugging at the vibrant rush of power, shimmering just out of grasp.

It was strange, that so many soulbreathed around the edges of the great mana source, where you had to breathe deep just to catch your breath, and the cold sapped the mana from your core. Here, where the effervescence of mana evaporated into the skies above, so much potential felt squandered. A tantalising banquet of power, so close, yet held where he could hardly touch it. Could they not spare a mere morsel?

Jai knew now, it was this strange mechanism built into the mountain that must have drawn soulbound from far and wide. Such a nexus of power promised unparalleled growth on the winding path they trod. Perhaps it was this that drew his father here, seeking a solution to the Gryphon Guard that ravaged his peoples.

Jai was only a fourth-level soulbound. This was more than many on the path might achieve in their lifetimes, for having Winter as his totem had given him many advantages. Indeed, Erica had only been a fifth-level soulbound, or so Rufus had guessed. Few soulbound revealed their exact level, to keep their enemies in the dark about their true strength.

Yet, whether at the fourth or fifth level, Jai knew the vast gulf that separated him and Erica from the titans of majicking. If he faced Magnus or Rufus, he was little more than a mosquito to be swatted. There were far more powerful practitioners that walked the world. And it was places like these that made them.

Winter let out a deep rumble. A feeling of pleasure and familiarity suffused Jai's mind, like an itch being scratched. She lifted her head, and to Jai's disappointment, wriggled back. A voice . . .

'That's how you like it, girl. Did you think I forgot? That's it . . .'

The warm air wafted out, letting in cold that was like an ice bath. It invigorated him, and considering the small reserve of mana he had built over the hours, he ducked out.

Only to see Winter, flat on her back, wriggling like an excited puppy. And there, rubbing her belly . . . Erica.

Jai had hardly time to register the sight before he was knocked back a few paces by her embrace, so tight he could hardly breathe. She was alive with energy, such that his hair stood on end at her touch, and her eyes glowed. Erica was so full of mana it was leaking out of her.

'Jai!' she laughed, lifting him off his feet. 'What are you doing here?'

He managed a breathless retort.

'Trying to catch my breath, for one.'

Jai allowed himself to sink into her embrace, her body at once soft and hard. Only when she pulled away did he do the same, holding her shoulders at arm's length, looking at her in wonder. Somehow, she looked fuller in body than she had ever before, even in this barren place. Her lithe form was hardly covered but for a few swathes of cloth, but every bare inch of her was corded with smooth muscle.

She smiled at him, before touching her finger to her lips.

'We should keep our voices down. May I?' She nodded at Jai's cave, and ducked inside without waiting for an answer. Some things never changed.

Jai followed, and soon the two were squeezed together, heads pressed close. She was staring at him, still shaking her head in amazement.

'Really,' she said. 'Why are you here? Shouldn't you be finding your people?'

Jai cocked his head.

'I could ask you the same thing.'

'It seems we have a lot to talk about.'

They did. And yet, for the moment, they both seemed content to simply sit there, looking at each other.

They sat for a long time.

EVENTUALLY, JAI TOOK A moment, composing himself and his thoughts, the weight of their shared history and the intimacy of their closeness all at once making him feel slightly breathless.

Words tumbled, some coherent, others mired in his haste, for he had burning questions that only she could answer. Twice, Erica's laughter, light and teasing, broke through his narration, each time drawing from him a sheepish, almost boyish smile.

Erica was transformed. Yes, time had marked her with maturity, but it was more than that. While the iron determination he remembered was still evident in the set of her jaw and the flash of her eyes, there was now an underlying warmth, an infectious lightness of spirit. If past hardships had been a crucible, she had emerged not hardened, but glowing, refined. Some source of happiness had tempered the steel in her.

'Hanebal told me how you came to be here,' Jai said, breathlessly reaching the end of his hurried tale. 'But not why you stayed. Your turn, now. What is this place?'

With a heavy exhale, Erica reclined against the ancient stone, her eyes momentarily distant. 'This mountaintop . . . it's a realm apart. The energy here, Jai, is potent as anything I've ever seen. It's the kind of power that can tip the scales of the war.'

Jai nodded, enraptured. To see her speak with such passion filled him with the same, her expressive eyes pulling enough of his attention that Winter gave him an envious nip, until he rubbed her the way she liked it between the horns.

'When I came here, I thought the Caelite were my only hope of returning to my people safely. They could fly me through the enemies that block my path. So I climbed . . . and they gave me a choice. Join, or leave.'

'But at what cost?' Jai demanded. 'What is the weight of joining their sect?'

Erica's gaze, usually unwavering, flitted away momentarily.

'They demand no shackles, Jai; only a promise. Freedom, with a caveat.'

'And that caveat?' Jai pressed, his tone insistent.

She inhaled deeply, choosing her words with care.

'The core of it is a bond, an oath of protection. When summoned, members are bound to return, to stand and guard the mountain, to shield their brethren and this fortress.'

Jai laughed, though without much mirth.

'Who in their right mind would try to conquer this place? It's the greatest fortress on earth.'

Erica sighed.

'The Guild. Their ambition and greed know no bounds, coveting this place for centuries. They are two contrasting sects. While the Caelite champion self-mastery and simplicity, the Guild thirsts for dominance and wealth.'

Jai knew well the famed Guild, that secretive sect that spanned much of the known world. It had close ties to the Gryphon Guard, and many of their acolytes would serve a few years with the Guild before returning to the fold. Silas had been one such squire, who had condemned Jai and Erica to Porticus at the Guild's behest. The sect had hoped the prison would extract the secret to bonding with dragons from the supposed Dansk noble they had captive.

It was lucky Silas had not known who they truly were, or they'd likely have been ransomed back to the Sabines.

He wanted to ask more, but Erica had already moved on,

pointing at the bare stone behind Jai, where the mana flowed freely.

'It's extraordinary, isn't it? Every creature, every blade of grass, exudes mana. But the Caelite, in their endless quest for knowledge, have made an astounding discovery. The humble fungi, overlooked and trampled upon by many, is a veritable reservoir of mana. And then there are us – humans.'

Jai raised an eyebrow, intrigue lighting his eyes.

'Humans?'

Erica smirked. 'Why do you think the Gryphon Guard perched their Eyrie atop the bustling city of Latium? It's not just for the view. The very thrum of life, the collective energy of its inhabitants, becomes a source of power.'

Clarity dawned on Jai's face. The Caelite's dedication to their flock, their relentless endeavour to liberate the enchained from the world beyond, it was all about the mana. Harnessing it, amplifying it within the mountain's hollows and utilising its condensed force.

His brow furrowed. 'But what purpose does this vast reserve of mana serve them?'

Erica's voice dropped to a reverent whisper. 'To the Caelite, there's an allure that surpasses any worldly treasure: that of eternal life. They seek to uncover the universe's concealed secrets and to bask in its revelations for eternity. Through the path of the soulbound, they believe they can attain this.'

Jai stared, and shook his head.

'Impossible.'

Erica gave him a knowing smile.

'I had thought the same. But Eko is two hundred years old, and looks hardly older than my father once did. He is the man from Shambalai, with the dark skin. Some say he knew the first Caelite, before they were lost in the great War of the Steppe.'

Jai was stunned, still trying to digest this news.

'Who killed them?' he asked.

'Rufus, Magnus and his ilk,' Erica replied. 'The Caelite did not wish to fight. But your father forced their hand.'

'I wonder how he convinced them?' Jai whispered.

Erica nodded, her face grave.

'He is well known here, but far from beloved. Many here hold him responsible for the loss of their wisest members all those years ago. Peaceful men and women, dragged into a war not of their own making, or that is how the Speaker tells it. No – that's how they *all* tell it.'

Frustration welled within Jai, and he knocked his head against the cool stone behind him. So he was the son of a pariah, here to convince a tribe to repeat his father's so-called mistakes.

'How did he bring them into the fight?' Jai asked. 'Because the Caelite are all that kept the Gryphon Guard in check last time. And I need them to do it again.'

Erica sighed and shook her head.

'I wish I had the answer. But there's a tradition here. Upon joining the sect, you're granted the right to request a single favour from the sect leader. The choice to fulfil it lies with him. I've already made my plea.'

A contemplative silence settled between them for a heartbeat before Jai whispered:

'Eko?'

With a gentle nod, Erica sealed his despair.

He closed his eyes, letting the disappointment wash over him. There was much to learn here, and a favour from the Caelite would be worth something in the battles to come . . . even if they would not be willing to join the war as they had done for his father.

'Winter and I cannot fight the Gryphon Guard alone,' Jai said. 'She is but one dragon, and I hardly stronger than one of their squires. We need the Caelite.'

'You need allies,' Erica allowed. 'And you have them. And while the Caelite may be hesitant, know that you aren't alone. Upon my return, the dragons of the Dansk will rally to my banner. Rumours float through these corridors, messages from the Caelite's loyal spies, former members of the flock. The dragons of Dansk, although few, have fiercely guarded our territories against the relentless onslaught of the Gryphon Guard. So far, we hold our own.'

For a moment, Jai could do nothing but stare, a cascade of emotions threatening to overflow. 'You would stand with us? After everything?'

Her response was as firm as it was tender.

'There was a time I couldn't see past the clouds, Jai. But now the horizon is clear. The Kidara and the Dansk, we are bound by ties more profound than shared enemies. By the All-Mother, or as you revere her, the Mother, our destinies are interwoven.'

She looked at him.

'I'll stand with you, Jai.'

Jai grinned, and clasped her hand, looking her in the eyes.

'So be it,' Jai said. 'An oath, then.'

Two royals, orphaned both by the enemy they'd escaped, uniting their peoples high above the clouds. Jai might have thought it destiny had he not fought tooth and nail to get here.

'I grow more powerful here. Perhaps strong enough, someday, to beat Magnus himself,' she said. 'You will too. Even if you do not join, this place is special.'

'But how will your people hear of our alliance?' he asked. 'Will the Caelite risk war with the Sabines by returning Titus's enemy home?'

Erica grinned.

'Eko is still deciding. Though in truth, a few weeks more and I will not need it.'

Jai raised a brow, a question forming. But before the words could take shape, Erica, with a mischievous smirk, nudged Winter, prompting the majestic dragon to rise, casting off the blanket of snow that had gathered on her while she rested.

'Wh—'

Erica held up a finger and closed her eyes. Jai waited, unsure of what to expect. Then a shadow flitted past, darkening the alcove's entrance. He turned his eyes skyward, his vision blinded by the unyielding sun above.

Only for the light to be blotted by a swooping figure, one that landed with a thud and sent the white powder scattering as it folded its great, leathery wings.

Erica grinned, ducked out from the entrance and reached out her hand, her fingers tracing the silver-blue scales of the beast's horned head.

Her dragon's head.

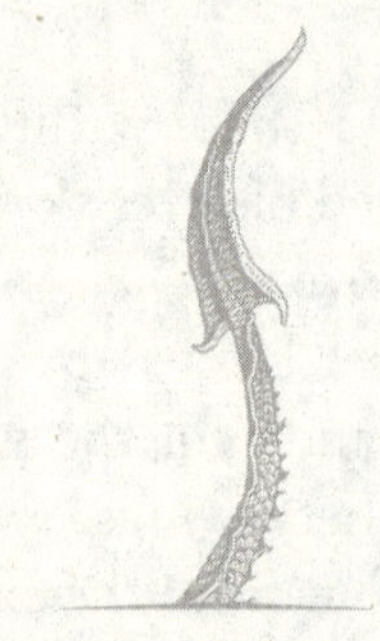

Chapter 65

Jai could hardly speak, not least because of the rush of sensations coming from Winter. She was mesmerised at the sight, and Jai could barely resist the heady rush of excitement and desire coming from the other half of their joined souls.

She yawped, then snapped her jaws shut at the involuntary sound. Jai sensed . . . embarrassment. The back of his neck warmed at the shared sensation, his hair standing up.

And truly, who could fault Winter for her captivation? The dragon before them was a paragon of its kind, as grand and proud as a stallion, draped in silver-blue scales that gleamed with each subtle movement. Its horns, regal and half curled, adorned a noble head beneath which lay eyes of vivid turquoise, gleaming with a wild intelligence. This creature was clearly older, more seasoned than Winter, who despite her own splendour was still but a fledgling by comparison, having been birthed before her time.

Winter was besotted. There was no other way to put it, some deep instinct within drawing her like a moth to a flame. Hell, the dragon even *smelled* good to her.

'Roqs aren't the only winged beasts that grace these mountains skies,' Erica said, the smile on her face ever more radiant. And Jai knew now the source of her great happiness.

It was not this place, or her new-found freedom. It was the dragon.

'Allow me to introduce Regin,' Erica said tenderly, her hand gently caressing the snout of the magnificent creature. 'Many a devotee has sought to forge a soulbond with him, to tame the wild tempest within. Most met their demise in the attempt. None succeeded.'

'Until you,' Jai breathed.

She smiled, and looked around, making sure they were alone. Even so, she lowered her voice in her reply.

'Cold enough up here for it. And it's always easier to bond with a new totem if you've done it before.'

'Right,' Jai said, his mind flashing back to the practices of the Gryphon Guard. The squires would forsake their chamrosh totems upon their knighthoods, pledging their souls anew to the fierce gryphons, severing their former bond in the process. A harsh transition, but one he surmised was mirrored in this place, where devotees would part from their loyal terror birds to embrace the mighty roqs.

The dragon, Regin, snorted, his curling nostrils wrinkling with disdain. In all his grandeur, he seemed to ignore Winter, as if her very presence was inconsequential. This apparent slight did not go unnoticed. Winter, ruffled and affronted, moved forth with deliberate steps, her wings unfurling in a display of silent challenge.

With a measured glance and another dismissive sniff, Regin paced backward, as if granting Winter some small acknowledgement. Then, with a grace belying his size, he sprang off the precipice, his form fading into the misted expanse below. Erica's gaze followed his graceful descent, a fond, almost wistful smile gracing her lips.

'He's an enigma,' Erica murmured, her voice tinged with wonder. 'My mother's dragon was my first bond. She had grown accustomed to the human touch, the shared emotions. But Regin? He knew only the wilds, the solitude. His heart still beats with the pulse of untamed nature. He hasn't yet granted me the honour of soaring the skies with him. But when that day comes,

I'll reclaim my place among my people, regardless of Eko's diktats.'

Jai looked at her in amazement, dizzied by Winter's desire to follow in Regin's footsteps. Her emotions, usually controlled for Jai's own benefit, were on raw display. Love-struck, poor thing.

Erica nodded, and turned her gaze skyward. Jai heard it then. The tolling of a bell, its mellow peals near lost in the ever-present gale that scoured the jutting peak.

'We should go,' she said. 'You're a devotee now, right? Come learn at the Speaker's feet.'

She did not wait for Jai, but her eagerness was infectious and Jai was hungry for mana. He was fast burning through what little he'd gathered, just to stand warm in the snow.

If he was to join this sect, and make the same sacrifice his father had, he might as well reap the benefits. After all, this was one of the most desirable places of learning for a soulbound in the world, such that even the great Guild coveted its secrets.

Winter let out a mournful mewl as Jai followed, and he turned back with a soft smile.

'Go on, then,' he said. 'But don't go far. This place is not safe, even for dragons.'

Her elation was infectious, and his smile turned to a grin as Winter let out as close to a whoop as a dragon could, a deep harrumph before leaping from the cliffside.

Jai's heart swelled into his throat at the sight – but his fears were soon allayed as her silhouette whipped back up again, and her feelings of exuberance drowned out lingering worry.

He followed Erica up the winding trail to the mountain's peak, past the frozen devotees in their strange meditation. At the path's zenith, Jai could see the dozen or so Caelite acolytes cross-legged at the centre, sucking in the mana therein.

It was fascinating, to see so many soulbreathing without their beasts. Certainly, Jai made sure to make physical contact with Winter wherever possible when he was soulbreathing.

To soulbreathe without one's beast was a sluggish affair, and he had pitied Rufus and Erica often on their journeys watching the pair soulbreathing alone. There was something about that touch that made the process faster, drawing the mana close and allowing it to flow freely through his channels.

But here, the mana was so abundant, Jai knew it likely made little difference to the many seated there. Jai had hoped to join the others, to find his place alongside Eko. Instead, Erica waved Jai goodbye, only to find himself alone.

'You are in luck, Jai,' the Speaker said.

Jai found himself tugged by the hand, as the Speaker appeared at his side, his movements so swift and silent Jai had heard nothing of it.

'How so?' Jai asked.

The man's hand thrummed the air, slapping Jai with such force he swayed dizzily. A swift finger to the Speaker's lips answered his question as to why.

'That's the only warning you get,' he said. 'I alone speak here.'

Jai resisted the urge to curse, instead touching his fingers to his lips and feeling the blood there. It seemed hardly fair, but he instead bowed his head in apology, clasping his hands in front of him.

The Speaker kissed his teeth, before pulling Jai away from the great font of golden mana. No, Jai would not replenish his mana that way. Instead, he was tugged to the edge of the plateau, where a few empty pedestals looked out over the Great Steppe.

There were gaps in the cloud bank, and through them he could see the great ocean of green, undulating as if brushed by the great invisible hand of the Mother, combing the knots in her child's hair. He felt a tug inside him, and realised . . . he missed it. Missed the scent of morning dew, the soughing of the breeze, the endless horizons.

It was strange to miss somewhere. The closest he had come

to that was his childhood desires to be tucked in his cot, the journals of a Sabine centurion waiting to be read by candlelight.

Both were a far cry from this desolate place. There was no green here, no warm sunsets to bathe his face. Only the cold blue of the sky, the black of rock, white of snow. Even the sun seemed paler here, sitting unimpeded as it was, high in the great blue above.

'Here, you sit,' the Speaker said. 'Soulbreathe, alone. No dragons.'

Jai stared at him, a question on his lips, and the Speaker grunted, at least pleased at Jai's acquiescence, and leaned in, gripping the back of Jai's neck in a way Jai was fast growing accustomed to.

Jai gestured at the air around them, where the mana was as scant as stars in daylight.

'To master the mana within you, you must learn to do much with little,' the Speaker muttered. 'The untrained body is wasteful. This is how we teach it not to be.'

He gave Jai a squeeze upon his shoulder, and Jai felt unnatural gratitude at the small hint of solidarity.

'I'll see you here in the morning,' he called. 'Or I won't see you at all.'

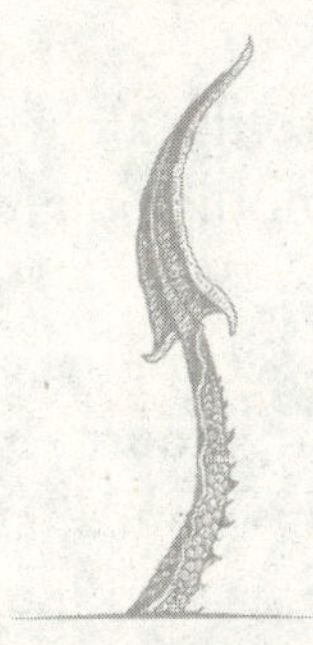

Chapter 66

Jai allowed himself a curse, as the last of the acolytes made their way down the trails. Jai breathed in, and out. He could almost taste each mote of mana as it passed between his lips.

He could *do* this. Hell, he'd already spent one night in the mountains, in the midst of a storm no less. But he'd had some mana to spare then, with Winter willing him her reserves no less, and it had been nothing compared to the cold of these heights.

Now, as night fell, and the moon but a sliver in the sky, Jai sat in frigid darkness, the howling of the winds his only companion. Even Erica had dared not disturb him, and Winter forced away from him, sealed from his pain as best he could.

Just another test. One that all those devotees on the mountaintop had to endure, before they were allowed the succour of the artery of mana within the mountain. Erica had managed it, it seemed. Those sitting along the trail had not.

It seemed unfair to Jai, for his competitors were sheltered in at least one direction, while he was most exposed of all. Had the Speaker singled him out to make things harder? Or make his triumph all the sweeter.

It mattered little – this was his lot. Still, the imbalance gave him some satisfaction as he watched one after the other stagger from their perches, down to the alcoves that offered a modicum of warmth and mana. Another night recovering, only to try again the next.

Jai could feel his body screaming at him. To do something, *anything*, but sit there and endure. Every instinct told him to jump up and down, clap his hands. He didn't have the time to waste, though. His people needed him. *All* the Sithians needed him. He couldn't spend day after day to pass this. Jai had to figure it out, and figure it out now. There was no second chance. Instead, he gulped down another enormous breath, sucking up the thin air and scattered mana in equal measure.

In truth, there was something to this challenge. He could track the passage of each mote of mana as it entered, feeling it dissolve into his body, trickling through his channels, those invisible pathways that scattered his body like blood vessels, sending impure mana in, and purified mana out to where it was needed.

These, he willed in faster, speeding them to his core before they dissolved, sucked away by a greedy body that would take weak, impure mana where it could get it, rather than wait for the more potent mana to return and do more good.

He sheltered his channels from that greed, sealing these invisible passageways in the labyrinth of his mind's eye, saving every mote of mana that travelled down their paths. Soon, he had secured a safe passage, a highway from lungs to the chamber that housed his core.

Only then would he see the tiny globules of mana finally settle upon the crystalline shell of his core, filtering through to become that golden liquid light. In his current state, he had no need to seal his core, letting the mana seep out of his core to extremities the sooner it passed through.

But freezing as he was, Jai had to prioritise. Before long, he did not simply let the mana seep out, but rather sent it to his extremities. It was far more useful, and by now Jai had become adept at willing the mana to and fro, sometimes circulating when he had some to spare around his channels to warm every part equally.

So it was in this deep state of concentration that Jai found himself when a large figure ducked out of the darkness behind him, and took a seat at his side.

At first, Jai thought it Erica, there to give him comfort. Instead, he saw the enormous hands folded in a dark lap. Jai turned his frozen head slowly, only for the man to lean close, and whisper.

'You are so like your father, Jai.'

Jai did not give him the satisfaction of an answer. Eko leaned forward, and placed a hand on Jai's chest. Jai started, but the man held him firm, staring into his eyes.

Jai felt strange. As if the man was staring into his very soul. And now, as Eko nodded in approval, his eyes flashing with a brief pulse of golden light, Jai realised he *was*. Analysing his core. Measuring it.

The eyes approached, Eko leaning closer.

'I know what you have come to ask of me. Our birds fly far, meet many. The traders of the steppe sing with rumours of an heir returned, hellbent on the destruction of an invading legion.'

He stopped. His tone changed, beseeching.

'I urge you, do not waste the Caelite's favour should you join our sect. Ask something that can be granted. We still wish to help you.'

Still Jai said nothing, although his eyes conveyed much. Eko nodded, as if Jai had passed yet another test.

'You may speak.'

Jai lunged then, gripping the man by the head and croaking between frozen lips.

'I ask it now, and I will ask it again. Protect the steppe from the Sabines.'

Eko gently pried Jai's fingers from him, and leaned close.

'The Caelite care only for the Caelite, and the flock,' he said. 'No favour is worth risking that.'

'Who will the Sabines turn on next when we are done with?' Jai uttered. 'When the grasslands burn and my people lie dead? Your refusal is a risk in itself.'

Eko stared silently into the abyss beyond. His breath puffed steam, but if he had sighed, it was lost to the winds. He turned his head. Whispered, his words hot in Jai's ear.

'The war was a terrible thing. The Gryphon Guard were warriors trained. We did not follow that path, then. We walked the one of peace, not the one of war, of violence. Many were lost. Your father's defeat was the end of it. A blessing, I thought.'

'What path do you follow now?' Jai demanded, careless to keep his voice a whisper in his anger.

Eko stiffened, but with the wind their raised whispers were but harshened speech anyway. He inclined his head.

'Now we follow both,' he said. 'Our acolytes are trained in Talvir. Majicking. More.'

They sat in silence a little longer.

'In honour of your father's memory, I will help you down that second path. Fight your war, Jai. But remember, it is yours alone.'

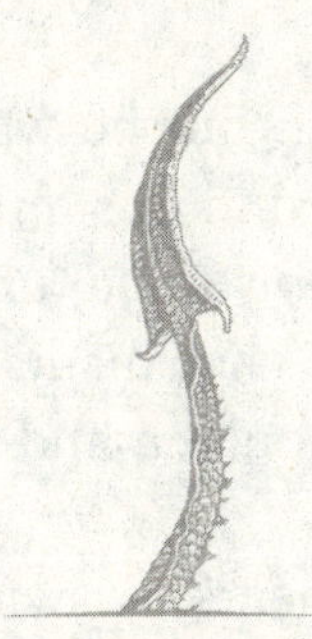

Chapter 67

The morning sun was like a blessing, soaking Jai in its light. He could feel the faint warmth upon his bare chest, see the orange behind his eyelids.

Jai was so deep in concentration, he had not opened his eyes since Eko had left him. But he could hear the Speaker's words, drifting like flotsam in the quiet ocean of his being. By now, the winds at the top of the world had settled, leaving a silence that was deafening.

Jai missed the susurration of grass. For all was still, but for that voice. At least now Jai understood their rules. It was this silence that they craved. Allowing the mind to do what it willed, without the distractions of the world beyond.

No distractions. No food. No sleep. No warmth. Just mana. It was their clay, and they the sculptors.

His heart pulsed in a slow beat, his breath bellowing in slow tandem, his body attuned to the world. Mana entered, and moved swiftly in its cycle to and from his core.

And Jai knew he had reached some new level of control, one he had only come close to once before. When the hemlock had ravaged him, he had been forced to do the very same, controlling the mana, fighting the spreading blossom of poison as he'd tossed and turned in the back of Silas's wagon.

This was a different battle, far more intense than the slow

siege the poison had been. But he was sure this was the same reason Erica had succeeded in this test too, for she had suffered a similar battle with the poison. Jai understood now that it was the suffering of this place that made the Caelite so powerful.

A hand touched his shoulder, and a voice whispered.

'Come.'

It took Jai a few moments to swim up from the depths of his subconscious. He felt the cold upon his skin again, and his core emptying out of the small reserve he had gathered.

He finally let the mana go where it willed, warming his feet such that he left glistening footsteps as he stood, sating the hunger that gnawed at his belly. He looked up to see the Speaker beckoning Jai to his side, where a dozen other acolytes sat, silhouetted amid the reverse waterfall of light. These were those who had passed the first test, and Erica was among them. He yearned to sit beside her, to let her see he had caught up to her, but she was in the midst of the pack, and he was realising such desires were not encouraged.

Indeed, the Speaker sat a little apart from the others, at the corner of where the great fountain of mana poured into the sky. Jai let himself abandon the half-trance, though, so he could not see it.

It was strange to switch between the two perspectives, one minute the whole world exploding with sparkling light, the next a windswept plain of frosted rock and snow.

Still, he settled where the Speaker pointed, just at the edge of the blazing mana. Jai sucked at it with hummingbird breaths, tasting the offshoots and letting it filter swiftly too, until his body steamed, and the cold of the night was well and truly purged from him.

If he just leaned a little closer . . .

A clicked finger turned his attention back.

The Speaker leaned forward, pressing a hand to Jai's chest, just as Eko had. He kept his voice low as he finally spoke, for the silence lay heavy over the mountaintop.

'You are a level-five soulbound now, Jai,' he said. 'No longer a devotee, but an acolyte. But we cannot allow you to join us until you reach the seventh level. The same as your enemies, the Gryphon Guard.'

Jai nodded slowly, for the Speaker was seated too far to whisper back. Not without disturbing the peace.

'Fifth-level soulbound can exercise control within their bodies. Look within, my boy. See what your night has wrought.'

Jai closed his eyes. Entered the meld, the full trance. Looked within, at his core. He grimaced, and shook his head. It all looked the same. He knew he had been doing something more, but that was just what he felt, not what he observed.

He felt a prod upon his chest, and the Speaker's voice, drifting as if from a great distance.

'The channels. Look to the channels.'

Jai did so. Looked closer, and closer, until all he saw was that thin network around his body. Still, nothing. There was frustration, but it was tempered by knowing all these tests had led him here, led him to a new accomplishment each time. So he kept looking . . . and then he saw it.

The passage he had sealed off from his body, such that the mana could pass through to his core for purification without being used up. It was different somehow. As if the walls had been smoothed, and shined. It was almost like there was a thin layer of crystal coating their sides, and as Jai explored further, he confirmed it.

The Speaker hummed in approval, perhaps seeing Jai's expression.

'As you learn to seal your channels more, they will become reinforced. You will use and harvest your mana more efficiently. Only a fifth-level soulbound can do this.'

Jai opened his eyes and caught the man smiling at him. It was disconcerting, for the man's browless face made his expression hard to read.

'Now you are ready for the sixth level,' the Speaker said.

'Where, first, you must soulwalk – see through your beast's eyes.'

Jai's heart jumped at that. For this was what he had secretly craved. To soar the skies as Winter did, only with more than the jagged row of spikes to hold on to. It was a technique even Balbir had known, one he should have learned long ago.

'I don't know how,' Jai whispered.

The Speaker heard him, and shook his head, a touch of disappointment.

'You are full of surprises, Jai, son of Rohan. Perhaps you will surprise yourself. Go now to your beast, and do not return until you have done so.'

'How?' Jai asked.

The man tutted.

'Never have I met an ascended soulbound who cannot soulwalk. It is a question of practice, nothing more. Go. Now.'

Chapter 68

A question of practice.

The man had sounded almost derisory as he'd said it, and stalked away before Jai could ask more. In his heart of hearts, Jai knew why.

He had neglected Winter. Neglected the path too, the journey every soulbound attempted to grow in their power. Many never even ascended. Some, little more than that. Few would go on to become so powerful as a Gryphon Knight, or a fully fledged member of the Caelite.

There was little excuse for his slow progress, even counting the shackles of his imprisonment, the weight of his father's legacy and his battle for his right to rule. He was bound to a *dragon*, one of the most powerful beasts associated with the soulbound. Yet he'd taken his good fortune for granted.

Taken *her* for granted.

He'd soulbreathed with her, true. Slept curled in her belly, made sure she was fed and cared for.

But he'd not explored their bond. Sought to know her, know her beyond her base needs and desires. And that was wrong of him.

He trudged back to his alcove, wishing he'd thought to do more than sip at the mana above. He felt the cold again, and yearned for the warmth of Winter's head in his lap.

Even now, he could sense her down their umbilical. The weighty cord of living soul that bound them together, the strands intertwined like a braid.

Along it, their stray thoughts and feelings pulsed. He could sense what she was doing. Feel her soaring on the wind, exhilarated at the path below.

But he could not see it in his mind's eye. Only picture it.

Now he called to her. He felt her hear it. More, felt her *ignore* it, until he called again.

She was as ever a stubborn thing, but she sensed his melancholy, how much he missed her. Perhaps too, she sensed his guilt . . . and his apology. Their connection was strong, he knew. Just . . . untested.

Winter flew. The exhilaration of it made him stagger. For to Winter, flying was like a fish that had lived its entire life in a shallow puddle, scraping its belly upon the sand, suddenly released into a great ocean.

It was a freedom like no other, as natural to her as the water for drinking, or meat for her belly. The skies were for flying, and she revelled in it, in the cold, high above the shadow of the mountains.

This was her natural place. Jai felt a pang of regret that she had lived so long upon the ground, sending Jai the mana she'd needed to break free of her earthly shackles.

She'd given everything, for him. Saved his life many times over, thrown herself in harm's way again and again. But it was more than that. She'd lost her way of life. Been tamed to live in his othering world, where she understood little that went on around her, where she found her small joys in the scraps that were fed her rather than ruling the skies above.

Erica's dragon, Regin, was everything she could have been. What she was supposed to be. Jai would not begrudge her it any longer – that he promised. And right now, he was gladdened by her freedom, and just wanted to see into her mind. Learn her deepest desires, whatever they might be.

Winter alighted with a flap of her wings, and a harrumph that told Jai just how she felt about his rude interruption. But behind it, he could sense the worry that had stained her night of freedom. Worry for him, alone on that mountain. Worry for herself that he'd sealed off her mind for focus, such that she could not know if he were alive or dead.

Anger, for how long it had taken for him to seek her out. Her reproaches hit him, one after the other, and he knelt at her feet, hugging her snout to his chest, kissing her growing horns, letting his tears freeze upon his cheeks.

'I'm sorry, my love,' Jai whispered.

It was as if the scales had been lifted from his eyes, in that one look from the Speaker. This had been too long a partnership of one.

Every bit of this realisation, he pulsed down their connection, letting her know his feelings even if they could not be explained. And in return, he felt . . . sorrow. For in the passing his regret of following that single, unyielding purpose, he had also shown her the great burden of his birthright. He had let slip the pain of his brothers' slaughter, of Balbir's brutal end, images flashing unbidden through his mind as he'd pondered what he'd done.

She let out another snort, and nudged him back, until he had been pressed safely into the cocoon of his alcove. His exit blocked, Jai sighed and settled into a cross-legged position, and began to soulbreathe.

It was amazing how much easier it was with Winter in his lap. She was like a weak magnet for mana, sapping it from the very walls of the cave, and from the thin air outside.

She stared up at him with her deep blue eyes, and Jai stared adoringly back. Her forgiveness was palpable, and Jai knew what she wanted in return.

Trust. To allow her to roam, to take the same risks as he did. To seek her own wants, her own needs. And Jai would give it to her. She was fast becoming an adolescent dragon, and he could feel the deepest drives, simmering beneath the surface. Her need to hunt. To eat.

And though she tried to hide it from him, he knew too that Regin was at the forefront of her mind. Another dragon. Another . . . her.

Jai felt, then, the loneliness. It was a feeling he knew all too well. To be one of her only kind, in a strange place. Where the wheels of the world turned without a care for what you wanted or needed. It had been much that way, in Leonid's chambers.

She hardly understood the reasons for why Jai did what he did. Only the strength of his convictions. That would have to change too.

Jai held her close, stroking her the way she liked, reassuring her with soft nothings. He wanted to tell her his story, from start to finish. To let her know who he *was*. And learn the same from her.

He stared into her eyes, seeking the connection they so rarely made. To explore the meld that joined their twin souls.

But he was asleep, a moment later.

Chapter 69

There was no food to fetch. No better source of mana that he was allowed. No place warmer, either. So when Jai started awake to find Winter snoozing on his lap, he did not shift her from her place, or attempt to go outside. Instead, he soulbreathed, and explored the meld.

She was dreaming. He could almost see it in his mind's eye. The cold cooling her from below, the sun warming her from above, the wind lifting her from beneath, tugging at her from the front. Flying was a mess of contradictions, and she revelled in it.

Still, there was no clear image in his head. Only the impression of what she saw. He knew he could do better. He needed to see through her eyes, as Erica could.

As if she sensed Jai's intrusion into her dreams, Winter stirred, yawning such that her great pink maw near enveloped his head. She was hungry, he knew. She too could subsist on mana for a short while, but her metabolism was far greater than his own.

'Go,' Jai whispered.

But she refused, stubbornly insisting on staying in their cocoon of warmth. Jai realised, they spent very little time this way. For usually, when he'd finished dealing with the affairs of state and they were both settled in his chamber, he was wont to fall straight to sleep. Hell, he hardly managed to read a few passages from the diary at a time before he was snoring.

Winter met his eyes, beseeching. Wanting more. Jai leaned forward, pressing his forehead between her horns, letting her deep breaths lull him. He entered the full-trance, and seized their melded umbilical.

Jai remembered.

THEY BOTH CRIED TEARS that day, nestled in their cocoon of warmth. Held each other close, and shared in their solace. It had been a different kind of pain, the kind Jai was not used to.

He had relived his life. From his earliest memories to this very day, the images pulsed down their connection.

Of his brief, happy infancy, with Balbir and his brothers. Of his move to Leonid's chambers, of the long years of solitude. The hatred he suffered, the derision, the fear of him and what he represented. The slaughter, and escape.

Her arrival into his life, that happy surprise. And more too, things that Winter had seen as well, even knew how Jai felt about, but did not understand.

Now Jai explained with pulses of emotion and meaning as best he could, hard though it was to explain geopolitics and the dark stain of fettering to a dragon.

It was not perfect, by any means. But was a bittersweet joy for her, to know him that way. She had known him in every other. Known his fears, his hates, his wants and loves. But not his history.

He himself had not relived it in that way. Gone over it in his mind, remembering who he was, where he had come from. It had always been too painful.

His tears were still hot upon his cheeks, the wet merging with Winter's own as she pressed herself closer, trying to soothe him.

For she too had flashed back her own history. This too, he knew intimately, for he had known her all her life. But now he understood far more. How she'd sensed the death of her own mother, trapped inside an egg within her belly, knowing she might die in darkness, having never seen the light.

Only for Jai to free her. To bond with her, to carry her with him across the wild lands. To care for her, and she him. She reminded him of their love.

It was when the tears had dried, and mana ran dry, that Winter finally moved. She lapped Jai's face, nudged his chest as if to keep him in place and pulled back to let the cold light in once more.

Jai took a few deep breaths, glad of the fresh air, before his heart somersaulted at the sight of Winter leaping from the precipice.

He wanted to soulbreathe, to fill his core once more. Instead, he closed his eyes. Let the world fade away, instead focusing on his connection to Winter. In truth, he had not once tried to soulwalk, as the Speaker had called it.

He'd never had a need, for since his escape, Winter had spent much of it at his side, and he had been more interested in how she was feeling than seeing the same world he could through her eyes. So it was strange to lean back and seek out the meld that joined them with new purpose, to seize upon it and draw all he could.

However, it was hard to grasp, in his mind's eye. He could sense their long, braided souls stretched into the darkness, but the glowing shard that was Winter's core felt far away, like a distant star. Still, he could see the light pulsing up and down their connection. At first, he knew not what to do, because he'd been told to *see*. What he realised, though, was that perhaps that hadn't been the right word, the right action. So he concentrated his efforts elsewhere, and *listened* to those pulses.

And they came. Bursts of sound in his mind. Fuzzy, and harsh. Such that at first, he thought he was doing it wrong.

It was only when Winter noticed what he was doing, and opened her mind to him, did Jai understand it was the roar of the wind in her ears, as she tore through the air below. With that window into her mind open, it slammed into him with a blow, and Jai found it hard to parse all the senses she sent him. Bursts of exhilaration dizzied him, and his sense of balance flipped and twisted as Winter did the same in the mountains' heights.

With all that, though, he saw nothing. Only sensed what she knew, that she was swooping through a ravine. But he could not see the shape of it.

He pulled his connection back and hugged Winter, wondering if those weeks of neglect were enough for this connection to be fully realised.

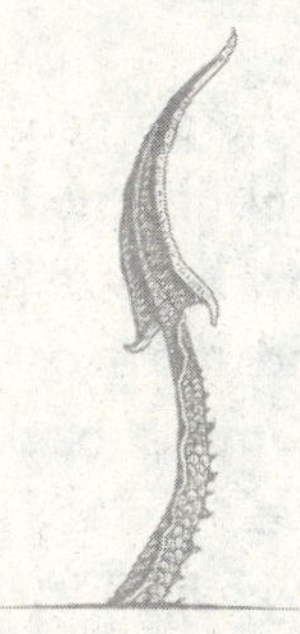

Chapter 70

Another night and then a day, alone in his cave. Jai craved to do something, anything, to make progress, but he knew forcing it would not do. So he ignored the pull of his responsibilities, even as his tribe drew ever further away, and the Sabine legion neared.

He stilled the hunger of his ambition, and rather let the curiosity of his soul interwind with that of its twin.

That first night, it had been hard. Dark hours, when the temperature dropped and icicles formed from the condensation of his breath upon the ceiling. It was all he could do to stave off the cold and hunger that would otherwise have wracked his body, let alone focus on Winter.

But this place was strange. In forcing the extremes, it taught him to perfect every aspect of soulbreathing, scaling up what he could manage as he became more adept. Even his body became attuned, the highway from lungs to core growing stronger with every breath, such that Jai could almost do it in his sleep.

For as morning came, he'd left his mind empty, riding the gale that was Winter's consciousness. He soared the skies he could not see. Wrestled with the wind itself, beating against its challenge, before turning to ride those same billowing buffs.

Winter had hunted wild goats upon the mountain, letting

her instinct take hold as she gorged upon their steaming flesh. Jai had tasted every morsel, listened to every crunch.

It irked him at how slow he was to figure this out. Such that now, with the sun set and the frost spreading, he once more released his umbilical, coming back to his own reality like surfacing from a deep dive.

He almost instinctively gasped for air, before groaning at his stiff body and discomfort of only smoothed rock for his bedding. Sleep seemed the next logical step, and he hoped he had accumulated enough mana that he would wake up to an empty core and a warm body.

But sleep eluded him now.

Perhaps Erica had come, and chosen not to disturb him. Or would she be offended he had not come to see her? Was it his turn?

Jai cursed his long years of solitude. Arjun would have known what to do. He had always been so jovial, so at ease with himself. Jai had always been jealous of that confidence, so natural it never strayed to arrogance.

Now he fretted. And knew sleep would elude him until he'd settled it. And the longer he waited, the more likely she'd be abed.

Jai emerged into the cold, hissing through his teeth as his feet crunched through the snow, its top layer frozen into an icy sheen. He ducked his head to look into alcoves, seeing some empty, their devotees beginning their next attempt to survive the night, in the hopes of becoming acolytes in the morning.

Others held men and women alone. Some had lit their spaces with glintlights, others had small balls of flame providing the dual purpose of light and warmth. Some lucky few had blankets, or had strung curtains to give them privacy.

So Jai was relieved when he spied Erica through one of these curtained entrances, reading upon her back by glintlight.

'Erica,' Jai whispered.

She turned, surprised, and Jai felt relief surge as she smiled at the sight of him.

'Come in,' she said. 'Get out of the cold.'

Jai ducked inside, closing the curtains behind him. It was tight in there, such that they had no choice but to squeeze opposite each other, their thighs pressed close, their heads near enough that he could make out the rare freckles beneath her eyes.

For once, he didn't mind their accommodation so much.

'You've been at it a while,' Erica said, her voice hushed after a quick glance at the curtains. 'I heard the Speaker. You've never soulwalked before?'

Jai rubbed the back of his neck, embarrassed.

'It's not that unusual,' Erica said, anticipating his answer. 'It takes a while. Most manage it after a year or two, but you had to ascend so quickly, with the hemlock and the soulgem and all . . . well. You picked a hell of a place to learn to do it.'

Jai nodded and allowed her a sheepish smile.

'That's why I'm here.'

Her face fell just a little and he immediately regretted his choice of words.

'I mean, I wanted to talk more. But I also . . .'

He trailed off.

'I can't see it, you know?' he said, keeping his voice down. 'I can hear it. Smell it. Taste it, even when I don't want to. But I can't see.'

He gave a grimace, and Erica's frown became a chuckle.

'Yeah, mountain goat takes some getting used to. Regin can't get enough of it.'

She tapped the side of her head.

'You need to . . . It's impossible to describe, you know?' she said.

'Can you try?'

'It's like . . . listening with your eyes.'

Jai chuckled, shaking his head. He might have given it more

thought, but it was hard to concentrate with her so close, the warmth of her soft thigh pressed to his, her hair grazing his shoulder. Her presence had always weighed heavy for Jai, but she had always been closed. Hiding herself. As if she were ashamed to be seen, in the throes of her grief for her father and her dragon.

Now he saw the woman behind the mask. A joy, and a passion for what she held dear, and a love for her people that he wished he could match. It made her radiant, even within this dim nook on the far crest of the world.

She ran her fingers along the roof of the cave, rubbing them along her lips where they had become chapped by the cold. They were pink, like petals in cardamon milk.

He had the urge to lean in and kiss them, but a fearful twist in his belly made him avert his gaze.

Even now, as she chewed her lip, thinking on soulwalking, Jai saw a spark behind those eyes that he had only seen a dim shadow of in their journey across the empire's expanse.

And Jai too knew he had changed since last they'd met. He had overcome so much, even since he had last seen her. Sometimes, he had felt an imposter. But today, he stood the victor of two battles, and was now leader of one of the greatest armies of the Great Steppe.

Now he felt her . . . equal. It gave him the right to risk that kiss, when the moment came. He dared see a world where a woman of her bearing would consider him a suitor.

'Let me try something,' she said. 'Let's soulbreathe together. Like you do with Winter. It should help with your mind's eye.'

Jai heard her, but the words did not register.

'Go on,' Erica said, and Jai realised he'd been staring. 'Close your eyes.'

Jai did so hurriedly, glad his complexion hid the heat of his cheeks. Erica placed a hand upon his sternum, mimicking the rise and fall of his chest.

'Together,' she said.

Jai settled into a steady rhythm, the cool of the wall unyielding until it numbed his back.

'I see you,' Erica said.

He felt her hand take his own, and Jai's fingers were pressed to the soft rise of her chest.

'Relax,' she said. 'Match my breath. My heartbeat.'

Jai could hear it. The dull boom of her pulse alongside his own. Slowly, his racing heart began to ease, as he focused on the sounds. The joining of their lungs, their hearts, in unison. It was unconscious, hard to do if he tried directly. He let his body adapt at its own accord, focusing on the breathing and letting his heart follow.

A stray subconscious thought flitted, Jai thought to do this with another person . . . it felt strangely intimate. But he pushed the thought away.

For a while, they stayed that way, and Jai sank deeper into the trance, the beat slowing, the breathing growing longer, softer. He could see his core's chamber, deep within himself. The first motes of mana dripped through its crystalline shell, a fierce glow in a dark cavern. With these in sight, he knew he had entered the full trance.

'Listen for the light,' Erica whispered.

Jai was too relaxed to try. He simply . . . allowed it. For his mind's eye to seek. And this time, he knew where to look. For the pulse, the music of Erica's life and soul, was coming from somewhere. At his front, he could see Winter's melded braid stretched from his core into the far darkness to her own, pulsing merrily with light.

He had seen it many times, but never so clearly.

But behind him . . . it was like his mind unfolding, slipping into another state. He could see the distant prick of light. Erica's soul. Glowing like a boreal star.

'Do you see me?' Erica asked.

'Yes,' Jai breathed.

'Come closer.'

Jai followed the instruction instinctively, his mind responding without knowing how. They were there. His core, and hers. Hanging like miniature suns.

But hers . . . it was strange. For while his own shard of core was a mass of jagged opaque crystal, her own core was pale and round as a white marble, with swirling, geometric patterns cut along its surface. It was glowing a near pure white, such that Jai could hardly make out the ornate beauty of its exterior – it was clearly filled to bursting with mana.

His own jagged lump looked drab and dull in comparison, filled with only a few drips of mana as it was. The sphere drifted closer, and Jai was compelled to match it, drifting his core closer.

'Jai, wait,' Erica said.

It was too late. His core brushed hers.

For a brief second, Jai saw his own face, eyes closed, brows furrowed. He almost looked . . . handsome.

A jolt slammed him back against the wall. He coughed, and rubbed the back of his head, dizzied by the crack he'd received.

He looked at Erica, who gave him an apologetic wince. She seemed none the worse for it.

'Sorry,' she said. 'You weren't supposed to touch.'

'What happened?' Jai mumbled.

He could feel his core had been emptied, for his body was beginning to chill.

'Forget it,' Erica said quickly. 'It seems you're pretty good with that mind's eye of yours. You just looked in the wrong place.'

Jai stared.

Realisation hit Jai. He'd spent so much time tugging and feeling at the cord that had bonded him to Winter, he'd not thought to follow its path, to seek out the source. No wonder he could only pick up a hint of what Winter was sharing with him.

'Long day tomorrow,' Erica said.

Jai was quick to take the hint.

'Thank you for the lesson,' Jai said. 'Sorry for . . . you know.'

She nodded hurriedly, and Jai ducked out into the cold before the awkwardness could draw on any longer. Still, as he hurried back to his own little hermitage, there was a bounce in his step, despite the prospect of a long night of soulbreathing to build up a reserve lest he freeze in his sleep.

For his mind was dwelling on other things. Because just for a moment, Jai had seen more than just Erica's gaze. He'd felt her *soul*.

It had been a brutal, intrusive thing, and he was glad it had only been for a moment. But he'd beheld himself in her eyes for the briefest flash of time. Felt the tug of care for him, of worry and even . . . something else. Of wanting to brush his own hair from his cheek.

A strange double feeling that had left him befuddled, and glad. Jai trudged frozen beneath a sea of stars, careless of the wind that burned him, a smile upon his lips. Tomorrow was another day.

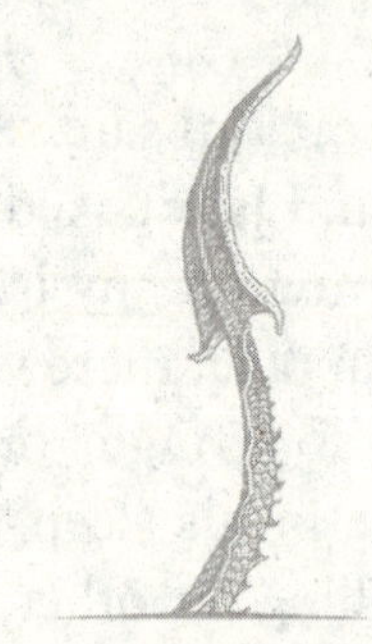

Chapter 71

It had taken him all morning to finally will his and Winter's cores close enough that he could discern the images she sent him. It seemed Winter had no control of her own core, and it drifted constantly.

Jai knew from Rufus's teachings that when he entered the full trance, his core could see beyond physical form to the ethereal world where souls alone resided. Where they roamed unawares in a dark abyss, where strange currents pulled them.

This was the world that they lived in in tandem with their own, invisible to all but the soulbound.

This was the place he had avoided, the place he was scared to look. For he knew, this path would be hard.

For now, he revelled in the simple pleasure of living in Winter's twin soul, letting his own worries fade away beneath the onslaught of her rushing senses.

The sky was an ocean, and Winter could hear its currents. It was like seeing with sound, in a way Jai could never do. She sensed the eddies of the airs, twisting her wings to catch each and every furl and dip.

Her belly was full, and he could taste the tangy salt of blood upon her tongue. She sought out Regin, whose scent was tantalising, and fleeting. Instinctively, she knew this was a game. In the world of dragons, it seemed it was the female that pursued.

And pursue she did, the mana in her core burning to be expended as she pushed for ever greater heights. Even now, she soared high above the tallest peak, and Jai watched in equal wonder. He could see the great spine of the mountains in earnest, a serrated knife's edge, dividing the green of the Great Steppe and the misted expanse of the Frostweald. Far to the east, the mountains shrunk, disappearing beneath the ground as the steppe met the borders of the Phoenix Empire. And to the west, Jai knew, far beyond where even Winter could see, beyond even where the Sabine legion marched, and the Gryphon Guard flew, was a war: a defensive line held by snarling, frostbitten raiders, clad in ermine and bearskin and the steel and leathers of war, even as scarlet-cloaked legions marched into their homelands, taking advantage of the onset of summer, and the shrinking frosts along the southern stretches of the Northern Tundra.

A reminder of what was at stake. Enough to force Jai from the warm confines of his chamber, back out into the light. He stopped for but a moment to watch Winter's silhouette bank high above, momentarily blotting the sun.

Then it was on, back up the peak, to meet the Speaker. The man had been in the midst of a lesson, but he was swift to usher Jai to his place once more, tantalisingly close to the faucet of mana, billowing high above.

From his vantage, Jai could see two roqs circling, following the mana where it went. It seemed the Caelite's beasts too benefited from the conflagration of majick, absorbing the ambient mana as all soulbound beasts did, unable to soulbreathe themselves.

'Swifter than expected,' the Speaker muttered, as Jai sat, cross-legged, at his feet.

Jai looked away, knowing his shame was plain on his face.

'The sixth level, then,' the man sighed. 'It is one of the hardest to achieve. And a slow process for many. Only those that have achieved it have the right to join the Caelite.'

He pressed his hand to Jai's chest, and Jai knew he was doing the same as Eko had, examining Jai's core.

'Your core is large,' he muttered. 'Ascended, of course. Thick walls, too. Signs of a soulgem's work?'

Jai nodded slowly.

'Your channels are well formed already,' the Speaker mused. 'Signs of hemlock poisoning, successfully fought – you're all the stronger for it. Hmmm . . . your meld with your beast is better than expected.'

Jai grimaced at that, but the man tutted nonetheless.

'It seems your beast has been sending you mana, reinforcing the meld,' he remonstrated. 'But allowing your totem's core to drift far from your side has stretched and weakened it. You must keep her core close, and reinforce the bond with mana.'

Jai went to ask more, but bit his lip in time. The Speaker shifted nearer.

'Your core is a shapeless mass. The mana it filters is watered down. Golden, rather than pure white.'

Now Jai's face fell in earnest.

'Your spells will be all the weaker, and cost more mana,' the Speaker stated. 'They will be longer in the casting too.'

Jai knew it to be true. He had seen the pale light of Erica's core. Still tinged with yellow, but far purer than the molten gold that Jai filled his own with.

As if he could read his mind, the Speaker leaned close.

'To reach the next level, you must shape your core. Mould and prepare it, such that when the mana reaches its centre, it is as pure as you can make it.'

Jai's mind flashed to the beauty of Erica's core. Could he truly match something so perfect? It had looked so complex and intricate, patterns upon patterns. The most complicated thing he'd ever drawn was a toy soldier, and when presented to Leonid he'd been congratulated on the fine whale he'd drawn.

'How?' Jai whispered.

The Speaker could not possibly have heard, for Jai barely

gave it voice. But it seemed he was adept at reading lips, for he clucked his tongue and waved around them.

'Mana is formed of life,' he said. 'But its quantity, its purity, is derived from order among the chaos. Life, Jai. It is for you to seek out the patterns of the natural world. Form their images in your mind, learn them absolutely. Imprint these upon your core, shape it to your will.'

He clicked his fingers impatiently, and tugged Jai to his feet.

'Come,' he muttered. 'See.'

He did not take Jai far, virtually dragging Jai by the scruff of his neck in his haste. There were other acolytes waiting, heads bowed, crouched in silence nearby. The lessons here were swift, and unforgiving, doled out like bitter medicine. Jai would sup it all.

The Speaker pointed a finger at the rock, and Jai's eyes widened. There upon the sheer rock where the mountain's spike had been sliced away . . . was a spiral.

A concentric circle of expanding size, segmented along its side. A seashell of some kind. Long dead, crystallised into rock and pushed from the sea's depths to the mountain's peak, driven by ancient machinations that had grown this ridge in aeons past.

'Start with that one,' the Speaker said. 'And seek out others, in your mind's eye. Trace the flow of mana, seek out their shape, their form. You may now sample the mana from the font.'

Jai watched him stalk off. No sooner was the man's back turned, he rolled sideways into the spurting mana, his fingers tangling in the perforated ground.

Entering the trance, Jai began to soulbreathe, his lungs taking their first lungful of the billowing fountain of golden light.

It was like breathing effervescence itself. His body heaved, and he let out a cough, but his next breath was just as full. It took a while for him to become used to the tickling, fizzing air, his body shaking as glittering motes roiled through his veins.

Mana flooded his core faster than ever before, and Jai could only sit and gasp, letting it fill and fill. In a world of golden light, Jai could not even see the colour of the sky.

He supped and supped on it, until his hair stood on end, his fingers crackling with power as mana escaped unbidden. Jai laughed aloud.

This was the true power of the Caelite. And he would take all that he could.

Jai only stopped when his core was full to bursting. No longer would he spend his nights struggling for warmth, hunger roiling in his belly.

Indeed, with the sun near set, its honey light staining the rocky vista, he expected most of the acolytes would be in their alcoves, and the devotees in their silent battle with the cold upon the mountainside.

So it was some surprise when Jai stepped from the mana, leaving his half-trance, that he could make out a faint noise, one he had come to know well since he had arrived in the grasslands.

The clack and rattle of practice weapons, and the grunts and cries of men and women locked in battle. He followed the sound, down the winding path, past the ribbon bridge and the spiral chamber at the staircase's top and further down the mountain, following the spiral slope to its conclusion.

And there, Jai found the spire of a smaller peak, a sister to the one he had just descended. There was a doorway in its side, one so tall, a Mahmut mammoth rider might ride through and hardly graze his head.

It was sealed by a great block of granite, but for a gap where it had not been pushed shut, just large enough for two men to walk through shoulder to shoulder.

The sounds came from within, and Jai hurried through the gap, alive with curiosity. What was within took his breath away.

A chamber of immense size lay within, every inch of its interior smooth and shiny where some great power had been wrought upon it. Crystalline structures hung from the ceiling like fine cut diamonds, reflecting the light of the spinning glint-lights within into wild fractal shapes beneath.

And they lit . . . an arena. A circular depression in the pale floors, where figures swirled in the patterned, ethereal light.

Eko overlooked the fighters, a half-dozen Caelite acolytes at his side, his face implacable as he watched the combatants dance, the *tok*, *tok*, *tok* of weapons echoing in Jai's ears.

None seemed surprised at the sight of him, and Jai joined his fellow devotees, observing the two fighters. One was Erica, he saw, her platinum hair tied in a tight bun, her elfin face twisted in concentration.

She lunged, only for a flash to turn Jai's head, but not before he saw Erica fly back, skidding to the arena's edge. She lifted her blade with a grunt of annoyance, wiping blood from her brow with her fingers.

Only for Eko to clap his hands, the noise so sharp and loud Jai thought the lights above might shatter. The result was instantaneous – the two fighters hurried to stand opposite each other, blades outstretched in what he guessed were their starting positions.

Eko strode forward, and Jai watched with curiosity as the big man spoke. It was strange to hear anything other than a whisper in this echoing chamber, and Jai realised that in this place, away from the sacred peak that the Caelite called their home, speaking was allowed. Indeed, every sound here seemed to be amplified by the concave shape of the chamber itself.

It was hard to make out Eko's advice amid the echoes, but the other acolytes watched intently. He was moving Erica's hands, her feet, pointing to the strange patterns cast on the floor, raising her arm, her shoulder, to show where they met the light.

This was different to what he had learned under Kiran. For while she had taught him much of what she had known, here, his footing, his stance, even the angle of his blade could be measured beneath the fractal lights above.

'Jai,' Eko's voice echoed, the chamber whispering back his name.

'Yes,' Jai called back, his voice cracking, the loud speech strange on his lips.

'Your first lesson in Talvir,' he said. 'It's good to take a break from shaping your core. Come, replace Erica.'

Jai bristled at the assumption, his approach buoyed by a flashed smile of encouragement from Erica as she stomped past him. He stood in the classic pose, legs akimbo, sword tilted at his enemy.

Eko tutted, kicking Jai's feet a hair wider, tipping his blade down a few degrees. Jai's opponent was a Phoenixian by his looks, clad in the same homespun loincloth as Eko.

Jai faced him, his nod of greeting ignored as the man squinted beneath the bright lights. Jai startled as Eko crouched, his great legs bowing and then straightening like pillars, sending the man soaring out of the circle.

'Begin!' he snapped.

Jai was caught unawares, but instinct took over as a bamboo blade flickered at his throat, Jai leaning back and countering like a bent bow.

His blade was slapped down in a spinning parry, and the Phoenixian stepped into Jai's guard in the same movement. Jai knelt to counter a high sweep, their blades locking, straining.

The man lifted a hand from his hilt, and Jai yelled in shock as light flared, and he was hurled back in a tangle of limbs. He lay there, only for a blow to fall upon his back, then another and another, Jai rolling and grunting with pain.

He blasted glintlight back, the shock of light buying him time to scramble to his feet before a series of blinding cuts battered him back to his knees.

He fought on, parrying, countering where he could, but the blows rained incessantly until they stopped, a blessed relief from the pain.

It took a while for Jai to realise that Eko had clapped his hands.

'I see some training,' the big man muttered, as Jai staggered back to the start position, his vision blurred. 'Sloppy, though. See here, where you let him hold the high position in Locked Horns pose . . .'

He shifted Jai's feet with taps of his own, showing Jai where he'd gone wrong, taking him through the motion and positioning his sword where the light met it just so.

'And you should always be wary of the other's hands, in case of majicking. A soulbound can wield a falx with one hand. Mind you do not forget it.'

Jai could hardly do more than nod along. Pain, all over, feeling fast catching up to the whirlwind of blows he had suffered. The Phoenixian was a master of his craft, that much was certain.

'You must infuse your movements with mana, Jai,' Eko muttered. 'And be ready to counter any spells with a shield or spell of your own.'

'Right . . .' Jai muttered, feeling his confidence draining. 'I'll try to remember that.'

Eko clicked his fingers, ordering Jai out of the circle. Jai limped out, stunned at the ferocity of the relentless attack that had left him with a loose tooth, and blood pattering in a steady rhythm on the floor from a cut somewhere on his head.

He caught the others staring at him, and he shrugged.

'First time, didn't you hear?' he said.

'Heal yourself, fool,' another acolyte said, rearranging his loincloth. 'You're making a mess.'

'Oh,' Jai said. 'Right.'

Of course, mana was plentiful here. He happily wiped away his wounds, mana burning in his fingers. He was wasteful in the doing of it, for it was one of the spells he had yet to perfect his finger positioning for. It mattered little, with the great foundation of mana just around the corner.

'Erica,' Eko ordered, having finished instructing the Phoenixian. 'Again.'

Erica rushed past Jai in an eager hurry, careless to heal the bruise blossoming on her forehead as she went in for the attack.

Jai watched, trying to memorise their movements. He couldn't focus on his majicking *all* the time. If he could not bring the Caelite to his cause, then he would learn all he could from them. And if that meant getting the leather beaten off him each day, so be it.

Chapter 72

Jai dangled his feet from the high peak of the mountain, watching the currents of mana as they wafted from the grasslands beyond.

More than a week had passed, and he was beginning to worry he had left his tribe too long. By now, the Kidara had left their camp in the lee of the mountain, and had begun, as instructed, to make a slow journey east, along its edge. He could still make out their fires, just a stain on the horizon, and only the knowledge that he could fly there on Winter's back gave him comfort.

Jai knew he might reach them in half a day, attend to his affairs and return. But to come back riteless, after the ceremony of his leaving, would be seen as weakness.

He knew there were risks. Never before had Tainted and untainted tribes been merged together, and these old rivalries could well lead to infighting in his absence. So too did he know that the other Great Tribes might sense weakness and hunt them, if Teji did not raise an army of mercenaries first. And that was forgetting the legion and the Gryphon Guard that marched the Great Steppe.

Jai knew he should be seeking a wild khiro, perhaps an Alkhara, to return to his people. Or an enemy to face, perhaps one of the legion's scouting parties. Yet he knew what he did here served the greater good for his tribe. For without the Caelite to defend the Great Steppe's skies – this war was already lost.

He was sure of it.

Every day he rolled the dice. But there was still so much to learn here.

He had settled into a routine of sorts. Training in Talvir into the early hours, perfecting his form beneath the lights under the watchful eye of Eko.

Jai had learned plenty from Kiran in the past, who in turn had learned from Zayn. But the teachings here were on another level.

He was taught to infuse his very footwork with mana, let alone his blows and parries. To use majicking in his battle, limited though it was to the kinesis spell in practice, lest they kill their opponents.

It was a difficult thing to cast and fence at the same time, no less because the falx was a two-handed weapon. But he was becoming adept at snatching away a free hand, be that in attack or to absorb the spell of another with a shield spell of his own, the kinetic energy blunted in a hollow of his ethereal light.

Sleep was hardly needed, for it could easily be staved off with mana, alongside his hunger. The limitless font at the mountain's zenith cured all ills, all wants. And it bought him the time he needed to take full advantage of this place.

So, when the sun's rays first bathed the mountainside, Jai would soulbreathe through the day, and work on the task as the Speaker had instructed. Now, in his trance, Jai let his mind's eye wander.

To follow the currents of mana where they willed, exploring his line of sight, leaving his core, his soul, behind. Travelling beyond his physical form, tracing the eddies as they billowed into the endless sky.

From his vantage, Jai could see the entire grassland spread out beneath him. And amid the gold falling into the sky, he looked for the paler, whiter motes, using every bit of the gift of his soulbound sight.

So too did Winter search, scouring the cliffs and mountain streams for spirals and natural shapes. In this, the soulwalking was most useful, for she could go where he could not, and he could etch the patterns from memory.

They sought where the life produced a filtered form of mana. Where the motes were thick, and white, and bright. And if he spotted some, somewhere within the swirling sea of rising mana . . .

There. It was so faint, he had to stare for a full minute before he was sure. But there it was. A rising, paler, globular drop of mana, drifting up from the ground amid the golden mist. He had seen it once, too high to figure its location.

Jai called out to Winter within, summoning her with a thought. She came swiftly, for she took any excuse to race to him, cutting and soaring through the ravines below.

'Flying again?' Erica asked.

Jai looked behind him to find Erica grinning at him, arms crossed.

'Jealous?' Jai asked.

She chuckled drily, but he could see he'd touched a nerve.

'Regin will come around. Seems he's a little distracted of late.'

Jai grinned. When Winter was not flying him on their excursions, she was courting Regin. Following him with dogged abandon, getting plenty of exercise as he tacitly avoided her flybys, hiding within the depths of the mountain.

Sometimes, Jai thought he could learn something from his erstwhile dragon, for Erica had thrown herself into her own training with the same abandon he had, exchanging only pleasantries and advice in a businesslike fashion.

Today, it seemed, was different. She hesitated, and Jai was surprised to realise she appeared almost . . . self-conscious.

'Let me come with you,' she blurted.

Jai looked at her, amazed.

'You sure?' Jai asked. 'I don't have a saddle.'

She scoffed.

'The Dansk have been riding bareback for centuries. But don't worry, the Caelite have saddle makers of all kinds in their flock. I've taken the liberty of requesting one made for the both of us.'

'You can do that?' Jai asked.

Erica grinned.

'Just because there's no speaking here doesn't mean you can't ask for things, Jai.'

Jai rolled his eyes. The speaking rule was grating on him, not least because it limited his and Erica's discussions to the training arena, or a more remote part of the mountain where they were now.

It was a strange rule, one that sought to still wagging tongues, and turn the focus of their energies inwards on their progress down the path. He felt good flaunting the Caelite's rules as they were now, though he did not relish the thought of a night spent in the snow or a beating in the arena, the punishments for breaking them.

'Their gallipot prepares pills, powders, tinctures and all kinds of things down there too, you know,' she said. 'Not that they have much need of them, with mana so plentiful. Mind you, it is only for the Caelite but—'

Winter's arrival brooked further discussion, snatching away the last of Erica's words with a last flap of her wings. She knelt a foreleg, waiting for Jai to mount her back.

'Can she handle two?' Jai asked, pressing his heels tight to Winter's sides, his groin sandwiched awkwardly between her spikes.

'Ask her,' Erica chuckled.

Winter's enthusiastic yawp as Erica leaped fluidly behind him was answer enough. He felt her arms wrap around his belly, and the softness of her breasts against his back, separated by but a thin layer of cloth.

Jai didn't have time to get in another word, one minute revelling in Erica's closeness, the next his stomach plummeted as Winter hurled them out into the vast sky.

For a few moments, Jai was focused only upon the grip of his hands on the horns at her neck, the padding he'd stuffed down his shirt resting upon the blunt spine beneath.

Then, as his balance set, and his heels found their grip against Winter's sides, he was awash with the joys of flight, revelling in the wind that blew cold through his hair, the sights of a world rendered simultaneously in miniature and larger than it had ever been before.

Erica whooped behind him, her laughter infectious as Winter set her wings, spurred to greater speeds. They were making a beeline for where Jai had seen the pale mana, and he was amazed at Winter's ability to navigate the enormity of the expanse beneath.

She used senses he could not understand, ones that if she sent them to him, no matter how close he'd drawn their cores together in his mind's eye, all that came through was a gibberish that gave him a headache.

So it was with unnerving accuracy that she alighted in the exact spot he had noticed, letting Jai topple off her back, shaking the memory of the tight rictus that had been his legs for the last few minutes. That saddle could not come soon enough, Dansk tradition be damned.

'You should do this more,' Jai said. 'There are more patterns than just the fossils in the rock.'

Erica scoffed. Long had they debated this point, but in truth Erica had little choice, for Regin had no interest in seeking spirals in the grasslands, rivers, ice and streams. She had taken Jai to find those ancient corals in the rock face of the Caelite's lair. They had even visited the mushroom fields below, borrowing the strange furling spirals of the fungal flowers.

'The ones in the caves are the self-same ones used to create the source,' Erica said. 'If they did for the ancient Caelite, they will do for me.'

Jai shrugged and drew his blade, using it to push aside the grass before delving between its blades, seeking out the source of purified mana.

It did not take him long to find it. A succulent plant, its juicy leaves curling in a fractal spiral, surviving amid the tall grasses like moss in a dark forest.

Jai closed his eyes, burning the shape into his memory. His core, by now, had been slowly reshaped into a pearly sphere, its surface scored with the patterns Jai had found already. With focus, and a hefty plug of mana, the lines formed, glowing and then fading as they raised upon its surface, the last section of the core's shell covered.

It was here, in his homeland, that he sought to find the shapes that would take him to the next level of the soulbound path. Already, he had covered much of it in what the Speaker called the fingerprints of the gods.

There were a wide range of choices. A burst of twirling petals here, the splitting of a leaf's veins there. The spiral in a snail's shell, the seed pattern of a sunflower, growing alone on the fringes of a distant oasis. Whereas Erica sought uniformity in her designs, copying the same coral spirals over and over, Jai sought diversity of every kind. According to the Speaker, both strategies were sound – though he was, as ever, cryptic about what came next.

Certainly, Jai's core's stored mana was becoming purer, with every stroke of his mental chisel. But there was more to it than that, Erica said. Though even she had little idea of what came next either.

When every bit of his core's surface was covered, he would be deemed a sixth-level soulbound. Then, and only then, would he be allowed to attempt the final test before he was welcomed as a true member of the Caelite sect, and all the privileges that wrought.

The pattern now seared into his core, Jai smiled with satisfaction. That was the last he needed. A sixth-level soulbound, finally.

If only the seventh was so easy. Jai knew it was considered by many as a second ascension, for it worked in much the same way. He would fill his core to the brim, and keep going. Pressure his core until it blossomed into a new shape. Erica had been trying for weeks, but she couldn't bear the pain.

Jai straightened, looking back at Erica now. She smiled at him, and he plucked the succulent from its place, holding it out to her like a bouquet with a courtly bow.

'Go on,' Jai said. 'Just one plant etching.'

She smiled at him, shaking her head, and Jai felt his heart twist at the sheer beauty of her, wild hair tossing in the wind, the low sun setting her fair eyelashes aglow.

Erica took the proffered plant with half-rolled eyes, but to Jai's surprise, then gave a coquettish curtsy.

'Why, thank you, my prince,' she said, her voice singsong, an imitation of the bardic romances performed in drinking houses the world over.

'Actually, it's khan.' Jai winked. 'I outrank you.'

She laughed aloud. It was a perfect moment, their gazes holding without the urge to flick away, cheeks rouged by the wind's bite, yet warmed by the sun's last rays in that heady, spring evening.

Then her eyes narrowed, her head turned to the side and Jai followed her gaze, confused. It took a moment for him to catch it, seeking the line of Winter's nose as she stared at the same.

Dark, winged forms in the distant sky, arranged in the shape of a V. Heading west, angling away from the line of the mountain.

'The Caelite are on the move,' she breathed. 'Almost all of the fully fledged members, a dozen at least.'

Jai stared, at first in fascination, then slow realisation.

'What business have they to the west?' Jai asked. 'Surely only the Dansk, and the Sabines lie that way.'

Erica's lips tightened, before leaping back onto Winter, her eyes turned to the skies.

'Come on,' she said. 'Before we lose them.'

Chapter 73

Jai was glad of the dark of night, and the great cloud bank that covered much of the sky. Their quarry, the Caelite, moved with such speed, there was no time for subtlety in their pursuit.

In truth, with her burden, Winter could hardly keep up, and were it not for her strange senses, they might have lost them in the clouds.

As they flew, Jai looked out to his right, where the lights of the Kidara could be seen in the distance, tantalisingly close. He was glad, at least, that there were as many fires there as he had left behind, and that they still followed his instruction.

Still, he had seen those lights many times on his wanderings, and his focus was to the formation of Caelite ahead.

This was further, already, than Jai had ever flown, and he was glad of the time Winter had had to practise in these last weeks. Since she'd stopped sending her mana to Jai, and spent a few hours circling above the mountain's mana plume, she had a full core, but Jai kept an eye. With Erica on her back, this journey would be harder too than any she'd faced.

He wished he could speak to Erica, as they flew silent through the mist, his chest dripping with caught condensation. But he knew, even if she could make out his words amid the rushing air around them, it was best to keep quiet, lest the roqs caught wind.

It amazed Jai just how far they could travel at these great heights, without the cloying tug of the grasslands. Already, they had travelled as far as the Kidara might hope to travel in a day.

With each hour, he grew more nervous. He was sure Winter could find her way back home if they lost them, but this far west, he knew the Sabine legion and the Gryphon Guard that accompanied them would be near.

He felt a squeeze of his shoulder, and Erica's hand extend. Pointing at something, far ahead. At first Jai had thought them more clouds, but they were too dark for that. And there, beneath it. An orange glow, as if the sun had reversed its journey beneath the horizon.

Winter dipped her wings, her keen eyes making out the Caelite's sudden descent. This was the place. They burst beneath the moonlit cloud bank, the world darkening as they emerged.

And Jai saw it. Fires, smouldering in the grasslands. And a smell, like no other. Blood, burned hair and spilled entrails. The stench of battle, of human suffering.

The Caelite were already settling amid the devastation, their great birds hop-skipping into the air no sooner had their riders leaped from their backs.

This was a battlefield. One that had taken place right in the centre of a Sithian camp. The last remains of the tents still smouldered, the flames' spread still battling with the stubborn grassland.

Jai did not bother to hide their pursuit now, instructing Winter to head straight for them – this was no secret meeting with their enemy. This was something far worse.

He saw the bodies before they reached the ground. Many had been lost to the grass, where they had escaped the camp and fallen there. But most were in the plaza at its centre. By its size, Jai guessed this was a tribe almost as large as his own. This was a Great Tribe.

They landed amid a massacre, such that Winter took care to alight where the corpses did not cover the ground. The Caelite stood among the bodies too, their fluting language strange in the still air. Their glintlights rushed back and forth, illuminating the devastation.

The Speaker looked at Jai, gripping Eko's arm as the man began to stride towards them. Eko relented, but his face was dark and troubled. The others, bald and strange though they were, looked much the same, staring with horror.

Jai did not want to look at the dead. But he forced himself to, kneeling and rolling over the body of a young woman. Stab wounds marked her body, blood from the wounds blossoming through the robes of her torso. No slashing wounds. The work of a gladius, chosen weapon of Sabine legionaries. A blade was still clutched in her hand, a small, pathetic thing. She'd never stood a chance.

He could feel the blood pulsing in his ears, the rage building. Winter too was enraged, letting out a low rumble that Jai felt in his chest. Even a sob from Erica, her tears streaming, could not turn his fury to sadness.

'Who were they?' Erica breathed.

Jai could see the markings upon the clothing of the wounded, the pale yellow of their robes stained red. Their symbol, a black rose on a yellow field, was stitched upon a crumpled blanket that swaddled an infant, its head stomped into nothingness by legionary boots. Jai knew not the tribe's name, but he was certain that Feng would. Not that it mattered. These were innocents. His people, even if they weren't necessarily his tribe.

Then a screech from above. A roq swooped low, letting a figure fall from the clutches of its claws into the pile of corpses. A man. A Sithian.

He cringed away at the sight of the bald strangers, his word obscured by snot and tears.

'Please, please, please . . .'

Eko lifted him to his feet.

'What happened here?' he growled.

He wore the same yellow robes as the others, but they were muddied and bloodstained. Clearly, he had been hiding in the grass nearby, his movements picked up by the sharp-eyed roq circling above.

The man was clearly still terrified, repeating his mantra, his dangling feet kicking until Eko slapped him.

'The legion,' the man whispered, gulping in a sob. 'We could not outrun them. We were too many. The warriors rode out to face them, buy us time. They . . . they . . .'

The man trailed off, and Eko let him fall into a heap, still crying. Jai could not imagine the courage of the warriors to face an army of five thousand, when their own army could not number far more than Jai's own. But he could imagine the charge, direct at the legion's lines. The legion's column folding into a square, the pikes of the triarii hurrying to the front lines. Their sudden, devastating drop as the khiroi neared.

Jai did not understand. How had the legion caught up to a tribe, even a slow-moving great one, when they had been unable to in Leonid's time? Such that their warriors had been forced to ride out to face their pursuing enemy.

But then, he remembered how the Kidara too had been slow until the tribe's divide, and how Teji had been forced to abandon many of his belongings, leaving all his citizens vulnerable, to chase Jai down.

It seemed in the new era, many of the tribes had lost their way. For it was clear, what the legion could not easily carry, they burned. And there was a lot to burn. Jai could still see the remains of the dark wood furniture, silken sundry, shards of fine crockery, all smouldering where the fires had burned down to coals.

'How did they travel?' the Speaker asked, his voice kinder.

'Once they caught our trail . . .' the man whispered, 'they could follow in our wake. We'd already beaten down the grass. Their flying beasts, they killed our scouts. We did not know they were so close until it was too late.'

Jai strode closer, picking his way between the bodies, his anger such that he wanted to scream.

'Do you see what the Sabines do?' Jai hissed. 'You heard the man. Their warriors weren't even here.'

The Speaker ignored him, as did Eko. For they were chattering away in their strange, fluting language, ignoring his presence completely.

But he would not be ignored. Jai reached their huddle, laying a hand on the Speaker's shoulder.

'Have you seen enough?' he snarled. 'You cowards.'

The Speaker moved so fast, Jai had no time to react. One moment his hand was on the man's arm, the next he was bent over, his offending arm twisted painfully behind his back, an iron grip upon his neck.

'Go back, Jai,' the Speaker said, his voice soft.

'Cowards,' Jai spat again, his tears running down his nose, dripping into the dirt.

He strained to free himself, but it was like trying to escape the grasp of an iron statue. Only a threatening rumble from Winter earned his release, the Speaker kicking him back towards Erica and Winter.

'You can address the Caelite when you are one of us,' Eko boomed.

He stabbed a finger into the sky, back the way they had come.

'Return to the mountain,' he said. 'On your own or strapped to the claws of my roq.'

Chapter 74

Jai sat within the plumes of mana, sucking it in with great heaves of his chest. He had no time to wait for the Caelite to return. No time for Erica, or lovesick Winter.

Not now. Not when the Great Tribes were already beginning to fall. He heaved in another breath, letting the mana roil within his core, its crystalline shell straining.

He felt pain, like no other, as if his very soul might split in two. It built and built, until he could push no harder.

Still, he maintained the pressure, hoping something would shift. But it seemed no matter how hard he tried, no matter how much pain he endured, nothing happened. The shell remained stubbornly the same, refusing his attempts.

He pushed the stray thoughts from his mind, trying to shake free the distractions. The memory of his flight back, tense with silence. Of Jai leaving Winter and Erica without a word, ignoring their attempts to comfort him.

His rage . . . it was so great, he could hardly contain it. He put every ounce of it into his attempts to advance. But it was not enough. He could not summon the strength to blossom.

Jai cursed, feeling hot tears upon his cheeks, though if they sprung from pain, rage of helplessness he did not know.

He felt a presence beside him. Opened his eyes, allowing

himself momentary pause. Eko. Sitting amid the mana with him, his dark eyes staring into Jai's own.

Eko reached out a slow hand, laying it upon Jai's chest.

'Beautiful,' he said. 'But . . .'

He trailed off, catching Jai's expression.

Jai stabbed his finger west, his brows raised, his face set with a scowl.

Eko sighed, and Jai left the half-trance, the golden mist surrounding them fading away, until they were just two men on the high peak of a windswept mountain, deep in the shadow of an overcast sky.

'We buried the dead,' he said. 'As many as we could. Put out the fires. Sent word to the Great Tribes. No harm in that.'

Jai turned away, his jaw set. He wiped at the tears that sprung, but they soon froze on his cheek.

No harm . . .

'When you ask your favour,' Eko said, 'you ask it of all the Caelite. We vote, you see, if we are not of an accord. All of us.'

Jai looked at him, his brows furrowed. The man knew Jai's mind was made up. Yet he seemed . . . sympathetic, in this moment. Jai listened, closely.

'The others have kept themselves apart for so long,' Eko said. 'So focused on the path, the search for life eternal, they ignore their flock, their acolytes. The Speaker and I . . . we are the oldest. We still remember when the Caelite cared. Buying the fettered of the world, providing them safe haven . . . they were more than just cattle to feed our hunger for mana.'

He sighed, and stared out into the darkness.

'When your father came to us, we numbered almost a hundred. And we had seen the slaughter of your people. Many of us were Sithians too. So when he asked us to join in the war, our sect rose to the occasion. Only the Speaker and I survived. We have rebuilt our numbers, slowly. What you saw today is the sum total of our forces. A dozen, against the Gryphon Guard's fifty knights.'

Jai hissed through gritted teeth, unable to hold back his words.

Rules be damned!

'I am not asking you to fight them all at once,' he replied. 'Hell, the dragons of the Dansk are probably keeping most occupied right now. But they fly the skies with impunity, guiding the legion, massacring traders and small tribes. You know it, and I know it. If this continues, it will not be long before all the Great Tribes are hunted down, one by one. They will burn the grasslands, turn it to wheat and corn. Fetter my people by the thousands to work them. Is that what you want?'

Eko was silent.

'You tell me to ask for something else,' Jai asked. 'I tell you I cannot. If you have anything else to say, then say it.'

The big man shook his head softly.

'Your core is too thick to blossom,' he said. 'You won't have the strength to pressure it enough. Thin it down from the inside, or you will never force the metamorphosis.'

He stood, and walked a step, before hesitating, his back stiff.

'Remember, the others care little, even for their own.'

And then he was gone, striding into the darkness.

Jai cursed bitterly beneath his breath. Too thick? He had spent a great deal of care to thicken its walls, to make it blossom as large as it could. Now he learned he had been overeager.

He held his head in his hands, staring at the perforated floor. The holes yawned black, like the eyes of the dead. Jai brought his mouth closer to the hole, and found he was able to suck in mana a little more effectively, the mana jettisoning into his mouth.

It was strange, for there was barely a draught, so his lungs filled as normal, even if mana flowed like a fountain down his throat.

He tried once more, and found it easier than ever to soul-breathe. It made little difference to the quantity he managed to take in, but the passage of mana was effortless, borne by the pressures that pushed the mana through the fountain.

It allowed him to pressure his core more than before, but despite the pain that almost made him scream aloud, his core was still too thick.

He cursed once more, slamming his fists, only to make out another figure on the approach. Flying in, just visible against the dark sky.

At first, he thought it was Winter, but she was elsewhere, sulking at Jai for cutting off their communication. But no . . . it was Regin. With Erica upon his back.

She laughed aloud as she alighted on the mountaintop, the dragon hop-skipping sideways, unused to her weight upon his back. Then she was there, her smile fading a little at Jai's grim, tear-frozen face.

Still, he pawed his wrist across his eyes, and forced a congratulations.

'Just like that?' he asked.

Her smile widened.

'He's a jealous boy, aren't you, Regin?' She pulled his snout close to her, and gave it a kiss. 'One whiff of how much I liked flying with Winter and he came nosing around.'

The dragon snorted, and turned up his snout. Erica reached down and unknotted something heavy from where it was strapped to the dragon's belly. A saddle fell to the snow.

'A graduation gift,' she said. 'A little early.'

Jai looked at the saddle in awe. He could see a channel down its centre within, where the spines of Winter's back would slot. By now, he was used to pain up here, for they beat the leather off him each day in their training, but it would be sweet relief to be comfortable when he flew.

'I don't know how to thank you,' Jai said.

She glanced at him, a smile playing across her lips.

'Want to go on a gryphon hunt?'

Chapter 75

They flew in darkness, just below the cloud bank, racing the rising sun. Early morning was just beneath the horizon, but Jai cared little. He wanted to be seen.

The leather of his new saddle creaked beneath him. It was a marvel, seated firm where it slotted over the spines of Winter's back, and a steel pommel at its front where Jai could grip, or strap himself to.

Jai was glad of it, a rope pulled through his belt loops and knotted to the saddle giving him comfort for the fight to come.

Aerial battles were something that even the Caelite knew little about, for much of it was done by the totems themselves. But Jai knew that majicking was chief among the way their riders would fight.

Still, Erica was bullish about their chances. The Caelite had learned in their assessment of her accompanied flight back to her homeland that much of the Gryphon Guard were busy with the war far in the west, and that only a few accompanied the lone legion cutting its way through the Great Steppe. Four of them, split in pairs to cover enough ground to find their quarry, travelling at nightfall, but always returning to the legion just before dawn. Easy enough for two dragons to take on, right?

He had a full core, and a suite of spells he'd now had some time to practise within the Caelite arena.

Still, doubts plagued him. Engaging with the Gryphon Guard was surely a breach in the Caelite's rules – would this be enough for him to be expelled?

His rage was abating, and in the growing glow of dawn he was beginning to regret their hasty choice to fly towards the legion. Where the reinforcements would not be far from whatever Gryphon Guard they caught.

Already, they could see the perfect square of the legion in the distance, and he knew the Gryphon Guard would be returning from their night scouting soon. He only hoped they did not return at the same time.

'There!' Erica called.

Winter saw it too, and it took Jai a while to see them. Two specks upon the horizon, growing larger by the second. She signalled with her thumb for them to ascend into the cloud bank, and Jai's world turned wet and dark and cold, his vision becoming a grey blur.

He closed his eyes, letting the shock of cold shake any blood lust free, his mind focusing on their circumstance. An aerial battle.

It was a terrible time to fight. For it was the first night Erica had ridden Regin, and he was hardly an expert rider himself. And neither of them were trained in how to fight from dragon back.

They would throw their beasts into the fray, forcing them into a battle not of their making, against likely veterans of such fights. But he could feel Winter's thoughts pulsing, her twinges of alarm as she tracked the approaching enemy through the clouds.

She was eager. Angry. She knew they hunted those responsible for the massacre. She wanted this.

There was no time to think now. The enemy were close. Any moment, they would be beneath them. Jai drew his blade, feeling the wind try to tug it from his grasp. He gripped with his knees, and lifted the other hand, charging his body with mana in preparation for his spell.

He raised his blade, and Erica the same, her outline murky

in the rushing clouds around them. Jai stabbed down, and Winter plunged like a falling star, their twin pulses quickening with the rapid descent.

Below was a Gryphon Rider, cloaked in a gleaming golden armour. His gryphon saw them the moment they were through the cloud bank, a screech piercing Jai's ears. It angled upward to meet them, the mighty wings of his beast flaring out like a war banner.

Winter's roar reverberated through the sky, an indomitable call that Jai joined with a battle cry of his own. Water blurred his eyes, and the world lurched as Winter collided with a gryphon, her claws taking its side, feathered wings battering Jai's face.

They fell in a spinning clash of claws, beak and talons, the two beasts snapping at each other like snakes, entangled limbs sending them tumbling. The world flipping once, twice. Then again, again, Jai hardly able to keep his grip.

The gryphon's wings battered Jai with such force that for a brief, terrifying moment, he felt himself unseated. His blade became ensnared in the sinewy mass of the gryphon's wing, pinning him in a precarious embrace.

A hailstorm of molten sun burst from the armoured knight's hands, wild and desperate as they plummeted in their death spiral. The heat was scorching, blasting close by, and Jai could only grip his pommel, heave back and stab the wing through, blood spitting before the blade was yanked from his grip. Time felt as if it was stretching, each second a painful eternity. He couldn't see, couldn't think.

Panic, however fleeting, gripped him. The ground was rushing towards them, a vast expanse of unyielding earth. Each second brought them closer to its embrace.

Drawing on his reserves, Jai contorted his bladeless hand. With a cry, he unleashed a surge of kinetic energy, careless of its target, of its waste. It rippled outwards in a wave, blasting the gryphon rider and his steed away.

Winter's wings flared, and they swooped, Jai flipping and

dangling from the pommel, his feet scrabbling at the side of her neck. No time to clamber back, Winter pulling out of the dive, flying higher and higher.

A beam of pale light flashed past him, and Jai smelled the stench of burning hair, and a flare of agony along his shoulder. He spun, blasting his own wave of flame, hearing the gryphon screech as it banked away.

Far above, lights flashed like lightning in a storm, the sound of Erica's own thunderous battle. Winter was in pain, her foreleg hanging limp, her neck bleeding from a dozen claw marks.

Yet, as Winter banked and spun to face their pursuer, he saw the gryphon had turned back, circling down in a limping spiral. One of its wings was flapping awkwardly, and Jai could see his blade hanging from its wing.

'On, girl,' Jai hissed. 'We have him!'

Winter, loyal beyond measure, ignored her pain, dipping her wings with a determined growl. They plummeted in pursuit, wind tearing at them, ground rushing closer and closer. Spells blazed by, and she banked left, then right, a zigzag that nearly threw Jai from his seat, his returning balls of flame sporadic, pathetic.

The gryphon skidded to a halt, Winter hot on her trail. No sooner had the gryphon spun, her armoured rider raising his hand, did they slam together.

Jai fell, his line snapping, rolling and tumbling into the grass. He came to a halt, staggered to his feet. Saw the knight, a long blade in his hand, stabbing at a writhing mass of scale, fur and feather.

Rage. Jai screamed, hurling a burst of lightning from his fingers, sparking the very air itself. The knight spun away, even as Jai pursued him through the grass.

He almost tripped on the armoured figure, the man struggling to stand in the tangle of vegetation. Bladeless, Jai straddled him, placing his hand upon the helmet, summoning the last dregs of mana he had within. He blasted fire through the slit, seeing the eyes widen, then peel away, the mailed hands snatching for his neck falling limp.

Behind him, he heard the gryphon scream, as its master's soul shattered. Enough for Winter to wring its neck with a savage shake of her head.

Above, Jai saw Regin circling down, Erica's blade drawn. There was no sign of her quarry.

He staggered to Winter, kneeling to see where her leg hung limp and broken.

Sobbing, he tried to heal it, but his mana was all gone. She lapped at his face, bloodying his cheeks. Jai hugged her close, relief flooding him. Never again.

Such risk, and for what? Petty vengeance? Now, in the dirt, with his love wounded and broken, their victory felt hollow. He had barely survived, surprise and luck winning the day. The Gryphon Guard were formidable indeed.

'What happened?' Jai called, hearing the thud of Regin's landing.

Erica leaped down, her eyes searching above.

'Injured, but we lost him in the clouds,' she said, pushing her way through the grass. 'Regin wouldn't follow.'

The dragon snorted, licking at a burn seared across his shoulder. Jai could hardly blame him.

He turned and kicked the fallen gryphon, its beak half-open, its strange animal stench heavy in his nostrils.

Jai pulled his blade free and stabbed it deep into its chest, sawing until he could reach in and pull the soulgem from within, his hand struggling to tug forth the clotted rock.

It came away with a sick squelch.

Erica stared in awe, for it was larger than a grapefruit, a lump of golden crystal filled with liquid light.

'We should move,' she warned. 'He'll be back with the others if we're not careful.'

Jai sniffed, and raised the blade one more time.

'Just one more thing,' he said.

Chapter 76

'Come on,' Erica urged.

They were back on the mountain, and Jai was kissing Winter goodbye, stroking her snout the way she liked. It had taken them all day to restore enough mana to heal their injured dragons, both of whom were a mess of fractured limbs, gashes and burns. It was lucky that injuries from duelling were so common there, or the Caelite might have caught wind of their night's activities. It was easy enough to sneak off to where Winter and Regin were resting and heal them of their wounds.

All he wanted to do was sleep.

'Jai,' Erica repeated.

'All right,' he said, giving Winter one final kiss. 'Off you go.'

His dragon turned and flew off in a gust of wind, Regin hot on her heels. The two dragons seemed to have reached a new understanding after their battle. A kinship that Regin could no longer deny. As a result, they'd found the pair curled against each other when they'd returned, though they'd done nothing more than nuzzle and rest.

In truth, Jai could tell Winter was keen for him to leave, so the two could frolic in the air, revelling in their survival.

'Jai!'

'Coming.'

He followed her down the mountain's path, clutching the

soulgem in the cloth sack he had hidden it in. For that was what this visit was about. They were headed to the Caelite's gallipot.

The soulgem was too large for Jai to swallow whole, as he had done with that of Erica's dragon.

The woman who ran it lived close to the Caelite, but it still took a good half hour to get there, clambering down narrow mountain paths, descending deep into a ravine.

So it was with some surprise when Jai found a windowed stone-built cottage backing into the very rock itself, one replete with statues, mosses and trickling waterfalls of water.

'She lives well,' Jai said.

'Just be polite,' Erica said. 'Chen only works for the Caelite. Acolytes and devotees are at her discretion.'

Chen emerged from the cottage, at first cracking the door and peering with a beady eye, scuttling outside, her back hunched, hair pale and lank.

She was a crone if Jai had ever seen one, though not as old as Meera, for she seemed spry in her movements. He bowed low and extended a hand. She slapped it away with a cackle, instead gripping him by the ear and pulling him close.

'Rohan's boy,' she muttered, peering at him. 'Took you long enough.'

Jai tried to resist the urge to pull away, for her breath stank of pickled onions. Finally, she released him with a tut.

'Got something for me?' she asked, snatching the bag from his hand. 'A gift?'

Jai stammered, and she snapped her fingers, shutting him up as she withdrew the bloodstained glassy nugget from the bag.

She sniffed it, then dipped the tip of her leathery tongue.

'Gryphon,' she said, spitting aside. 'Mature too. You two've been up to no good.'

Again, she held up a hand before Jai could speak, then pressed it to Jai's chest.

'Thick walls,' she muttered, shaking her head. 'But well formed, good size. Ready for the seventh level, I'll wager?'

'Yes,' Jai blurted, before she could cut him off again.

'Wait here,' Chen snapped.

She disappeared back into her cottage, the door slamming behind her.

'That's the most I've heard her speak the whole time I've been here,' Erica said. 'Mostly she'd order me about. Fetch this, deliver that. But I got something for my troubles.'

She fished into her own cloth bag, and proferred Jai a small, glowing vial of green liquid.

'When I'm ready for the seventh level . . . this'll make it easier. Need to practise pressuring my core a bit more first.'

'What did you do to get that?' Jai asked, jealous.

'She took a liking to me,' she said. 'Eventually.'

JAI AND ERICA SAT in wait, the sun slowly turning more orange as it approached the horizon. Their conversation had taken a natural lull as they dozed in the rare light, both exhausted from the last day's happenings, and appreciating the rare warmth of the late spring sun.

But as Jai rested, Winter and Regin were alive with emotion and excitement. Chasing each other through the mountains, lost in the attention of the other. This was a dragon's courtship, and Regin had finally allowed Winter into his domain, showing her the places he knew, the lairs he had found in the great expanse of the mountains.

And it was strange, but in the joy of their romance, so too did Erica calm in Jai's presence. The formality had gone, replaced by a head upon his shoulder. And Jai could only sit and smile, unwilling to disturb her sleep.

It was almost disappointing when Chen's door creaked back open and Erica jerked awake, giving Jai an apologetic smile and rubbing her cheek.

'Come here, Rohan's boy,' Chen called out.

Jai approached, wary of the hand she kept behind her back. He bowed again, and she gave a slight nod of appreciation, and extended the hidden item.

'Take this philtre,' she said. 'When you make your final attempt, it'll help smooth the way.'

It was a vial filled with contents not dissimilar from Erica's, though the quantity was considerably greater for this vessel was the same size as his soulgem.

She spun on her heel, and Jai called out.

'How will I know if I'm ready?'

She stopped, and looked over her shoulder, a glint in her eye.

'You're ready now,' she muttered. 'If you can bear the pain, risk its shattering. Just need to know *where* to do it.'

'What does that mean?' Jai called out.

A slammed door was his only answer.

His soulgem had likely been an ingredient, but it was a happy sacrifice. A soulgem would only provide him with an enormous burst of incoming mana, but there was plenty of that at the top of the mountain. But this potion, customised to his exact needs, was likely better.

'Perfect,' Erica said when he walked back to her, shaking his head. 'Back to it, then. It's either sleep, or soulbreathing so I don't have to. Might go for the former today.'

She began the journey back up the mountain, and Jai longed for a few moments longer, here in this quiet, trickling haven amid a barren landscape. Here. Alone. With her.

The sun was nearly set, though, and soon they'd be in darkness once more. And Jai realised how much he longed for sleep, too. To put it all off for another day.

Instead, he looked to the mountaintop, far above them. Chen had given him an idea. And he'd not sleep until he'd tested it.

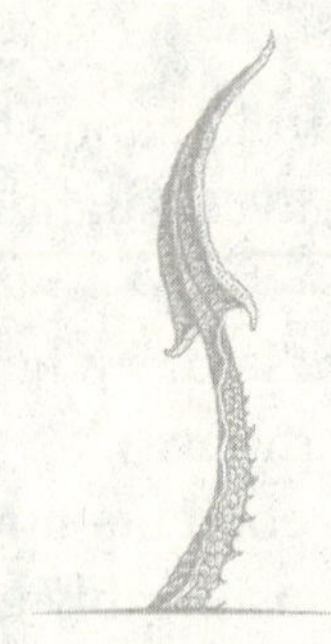

Chapter 77

Jai stared into the roiled mass of mana, watching as it swirled through the strange channels in the stone. He was standing in the hollow beneath the peak, the great spiral filter beneath the perforated platform above.

The Speaker was there, as he so often was, soulbreathing at the cavern's entrance. In his half-trance, Jai could see the mana coiling away from the rushing torrent within, passing through the man's nostrils.

Jai strode to the torrent's edge, the rope and dagger he had used to climb there clutched in his hands.

'What are you doing, Jai?' the Speaker asked.

'What I have to,' Jai replied.

He reached out a hand, feeling the rush of mana, tingling like pins and needles in his hand. As an acolyte, he was allowed here now. To touch, and explore the crucible, through which all the mana above poured.

This place filtered the mana, emerging in a purified form above. Not so pure as if filtered through a blossomed core, or indeed any core at all. But a good start.

Jai's eyes turned skywards to where the spinning mana emerged into the stone above. Only, it was not perforated holes in the ceiling, but a single tunnel, one that divided into a network to send the mana to the great source above.

He took a breath, and reached for the wall, digging the blade into a furrow there. Then he began to climb.

It was strange to climb in this hollow, in one world dark and silent, another glittering, swirling, golden light. He found it easier to progress with the former, able to see his handholds in the gloom.

Every few yards, he yanked the blade free from its purchase, and made another hold for him to move further. Finally, he reached the ceiling, where the runnels that guided the mana to the exit above made for handholds, allowing him to monkey his way across the ceiling, his legs dangling, one slip from a bone-breaking fall below.

So it was some relief when he made it to the tunnel itself, manoeuvring his body to spreadeagle across the entrance, looking down into the warren of channels, holes and strange carvings beneath.

He secured his place with the dagger, digging it deep into a fissure in the rock within. If this was to be the moment of his blossoming, he knew he might fall in the distraction of his pain. This, at least, would keep him from death.

He was almost scared to enter the trance. For he could feel the mana coating his body, his body tingling all over as it was covered in the invisible golden dust. This was different to above. For here, the mana was concentrated into a single pipe, blasting him with fast-moving particles he could not yet see.

Jai pulled the vial free from his pocket, yanking its cork with his teeth. He gulped it down, grimacing at the acrid taste. It was metallic, and earthy. Mushrooms, then.

I should have guessed.

He thought he might have to wait to feel its effects, but it was almost immediate. His body felt . . . liquid. It was hard to keep his limbs stiffened, holding him in place. And his vision . . . it was alive.

The world was a mess of fractal lines, patterns appearing in searing blue in his vision. Within the dark cavern, he was seeing the mathematics of the carvings, the patterns in the stone. A hallucinogen, he was sure. But something else too was happening to his core. Its surface rippled, the raised lines of his core seeming to shift and move. Rearranging themselves into cleaner patterns, merging and melding mathematical perfection.

'Jai!' the Speaker called. 'I know what you're doing. It's too dangerous!'

Jai ignored that, steeling himself. He could die here. He knew that.

But he also knew, if he did not reach the seventh level soon, he could not join the Caelite, and ask his favour of them. And he was beginning to understand what he had to do.

'Come on,' Jai hissed, urging himself on. 'Come on!'

'Jai!' the Speaker yelled.

He gritted his teeth . . . and entered the trance.

Instantly, his world became filled with golden light, so bright he had to close his eyes. He could feel the rushing mana, the gale so strong he felt it might sand the flesh from his bones, so thick and voluminous it was.

He almost choked on his first lungful of mana, for it came the moment he entered the trance. But he centred himself and found it easier to take it in before it could overwhelm him.

His channels were swiftly alive with mana, the pale motes swirling through him, blazing into the chamber that held his core. Already, the mana was piling up against his core, the very surface rippling as more and more mana oozed through its surface, gathering thick and gelatinous within. It was not long before his core was full to the brim, and Jai could feel the pressure building. He could hardly see his core for the mana, the current that blasted it into his lungs like a roaring river.

His crystalline core swelled . . . the pressure continuing to grow. Jai felt the pain, at first dull and specific, then fierce and overwhelming, as he felt the very borders of his core begin to stretch. It was—

Agony.

He did not know where his mind began and his body ended. All was pain. He hung there, his hands and legs shaking as he held himself in place, the mana burning down his throat, bursting out of his eyes in glowing points of light.

His core rippled. Creaked.

His mind stayed firm:

More.

Jai took a huge, gasping breath, filling his body with a great lungful of mana. Felt it flood his core chamber, another layer upon the thick carpet of golden light that surrounded it, drawn there like a moth to a flame.

And with that, his core *stretched* . . . and Jai screamed, his soul splitting.

He did not feel his limbs fall limp. Nor did he hear the snap of the rope that held him. Only felt the lurch of his fall, and his core swelling.

Then nothing. Darkness.

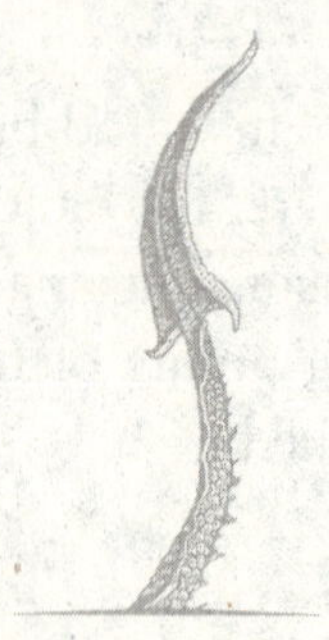

Chapter 78

Snapping fingers. Wet, splashing his face, cold as ice. Pressure upon his chest, *a shove*, *shove*, *shove* that made his ribs creak.

Lips, upon his own. Breath, pushed in, hot and moist. The healing spell, constant, flooding white over his chest.

He jerked, spluttering, and saw the Speaker staring down, his dark eyes wide with concern. Other bald-headed men and women peered from behind.

Jai sat up to find himself in a strange place. A large nest. There was no other way to describe it. He was in a hollow of woven branches, lined with feathering, grasses and fur. They were nestled in the hollow of the mountainside, in a space large enough to fit all the Caelite, though their beasts seemed to be away, perhaps resting in their individual nests, as they were wont to do.

'Fool boy,' the Speaker snapped, even as Jai coughed, more of the world swimming into focus. 'Do you have any idea how close you came to death?'

Jai ignored him, instead looking within. And breathed in glorious relief.

For his core . . . was different. It had blossomed indeed.

Gone was the pearlescent, ornate marble that had been. In its place was an ivory conch-shaped cornucopia, replete with swirling channels, spiralling indents, all leading to a great hollow at its centre. And it was larger. Perhaps three times larger than it had been before.

It lay empty, but was no less beautiful. It might have been a living thing, found amid the corals at the bottom of the ocean. And there was intelligent design behind it. Not random, not symmetric, but somehow perfect in every way.

Still, a swift jerk of his arm brought him up to his feet, before he was pushed into a kneeling position by the Speaker's iron grip.

'You are a seventh-level soulbound,' the man said, somehow angry and impressed all at once. 'You have the right to join the Caelite. Do you choose to?'

'I do,' Jai said with no hesitation.

'Will you return to defend our fortress and our flock, should an enemy choose to invade us?'

'I will,' Jai said.

'Will you follow our rules and customs when you remain in our sacred places?'

'I will,' Jai said.

'Then rise and ask your favour, Jai,' Eko boomed, standing head and shoulder above the rest of the Caelite.

Jai stood on shaking legs, his head swimming. He had just been brought back from the brink of death. Advanced to one of the hardest levels one could achieve, such that no man could join the Caelite without it. And even though he had already accomplished what he needed to here, he also, somehow, wasn't ready for this. But he had to try.

'As a new member of the sect, I bring a warning,' Jai said, addressing the strange, silent bald men and women among them.

'Then give it,' one growled. 'And be on your way. We know your commitment to our cause is weak.'

'His father's son,' another muttered. 'All take. Nothing to give.'

'Do you blame me?' Jai snapped back. 'After what you saw the other night?'

They had no answer for him. Because how could they?

'Your stronghold is not hard to find,' Jai said. 'You know the Gryphon Guard covet it. Only the fragile truce between the Sabines and my peoples kept them from crossing the border, to reach you. Now that truce is over. Even at this moment, they are distracted with the dragons of the Dansk. But when they are done with them, ask yourselves: what is stopping them from descending upon this place?'

'Then we will beat them!' another sect member cried, a Phoenixian woman with a cherubic face. 'On home ground. But we will not strike the first blow, far from where our roqs fly, far from the source.'

Jai let out a deep breath, trying to still the rage within him.

'Why wait until they are done with the Dansk, with us? Why risk this sacred place? Why not fight them by our side?'

Again, a question that evoked silence.

'Years ago, your forebears allied with my people. And while they lost much, in the act of their defiance, in exhausting the might of the Sabine Empire, you preserved this place.'

'Eko has told us of your intentions,' the woman said. 'Our minds are made. Ask your question so that we may end this charade.'

Jai felt the tiredness of these last days. His core was empty of mana, and exhaustion was setting in with nothing to keep it at bay.

He was close to swaying on his feet, but knew he would show these men and women no weakness. Standing tall, he made his request.

'I will not ask you to join me in war.'

The woman – and many of those around her – looked shocked by this. He pressed on.

'No, I ask a different favour: fly far and wide. Gather the

tribes of the steppe, great and small. Summon a High Council for me, to forge an alliance between the tribes. And attend too. If you are to abandon us, then say it to all the Sithians, not just one khan.

'Not just to Rohan's son.'

Eko blinked with surprise at Jai's words. The corners of his mouth tugged, just a little, and Jai knew he'd played this right. The Caelite muttered in their strange fluting language, one Jai imagined he might learn, in time, if he chose to stay.

'This, we can grant you,' the Speaker said finally. 'When? And where?'

Jai hesitated. He knew of only one landmark in the Great Steppe. Where his mother had been buried.

'How far lies the Blue Mesa?' Jai asked.

'Two weeks' ride from here,' Eko said, swiftly. 'Or a day's flight.'

'Most of the tribes have moved east; they will be close,' Jai said. 'Two weeks, then.'

He summoned Winter with a thought, feeling her relief at his return to consciousness. He felt too her reluctance to leave Regin's embrace, even as she had lain in terror, watching Jai's soul waver between the land of the living and the dead. The two dragons were ensconced in his lair, not far beneath them. But loyal beast that she was, she came.

Jai stalked to the great nest's edge, waiting for her return.

'Two weeks,' Jai said, as they stared at him, brows furrowed as they tried to understand what game they played. 'To prepare your explanation for your cowardice to the peoples of the steppe. Your brothers. Your neighbours.'

He caught Winter's outline, gliding up to meet him.

'You have till then to find your mettle,' Jai said.

Then he leaped . . . and was flying.

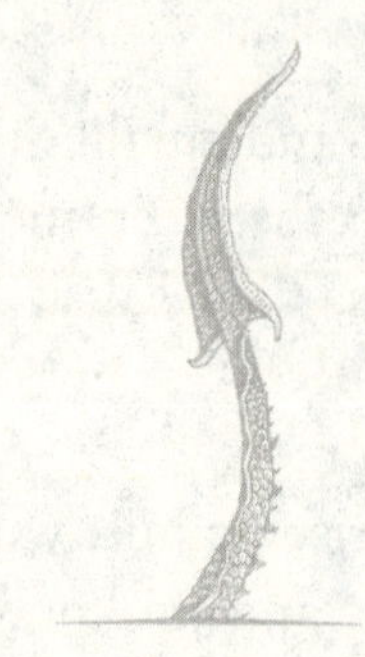

Chapter 79

Jai circled above his tribe, making sure no gryphons lurked on the horizon, before making his descent.

He was a mess, he knew. Ragged, topless, and filthy, for the Caelite did little more than scrub themselves with snow, and his shirt had long been lost in the climb. But he'd had no time to ready himself. Hardly time to collect his things, or give Erica a proper goodbye, her promise to come to the High Council almost snatched away by the wind.

The wheels of the world were turning. And he was coming to realise he could be the axle that drove them. He had done all he needed in the mountains. It was far past the time for his return.

Winter began her descent, eager for the food she had so missed – apparently curried khiroi was preferred to the hoary goats of the mountain.

Jai could see the upturned faces of his people, a thousand smiles, hundreds of hands raised to greet him. The plaza was thronging, and he headed for the empty fighting circle at its centre, guiding Winter with a thought and a stroke of her neck.

They landed gracefully, Winter's wings furling, and Jai stood upon his saddle as the people gathered, their cheers not just for his return but with the assumption their khan had returned rited.

And they were right. For Jai raised the sack strapped to the saddle and delved within to reveal his prize. He pulled forth the helmet of the Gryphon Guard, sooty and gory though it was.

He held it aloft, and the crowd's cheers grew louder. Jai let it tumble from his fingers, though, and the cheers faltered. He smiled mischievously, and reached in again, yanking free the feathered head of the gryphon. This is what he had asked Erica to wait for after he'd taken the soulgem. An offering for the Mother, to his peoples.

'With this blood,' Jai roared, above the shouting throngs, 'I join my people.'

They roared back, a wall of noise and fists punching the air. Jai leaped down, sticking the head upon a bamboo spear from a rack, holding it aloft for all to see. Hands pulled at him, people shoving gifts and foods, their smiling faces all awash with awe. He pushed through the throngs, even as guards cleared a path towards his tent.

He was surprised by the adulation, but only for a moment. Because he understood that he was more than a prince returned in their eyes. He was a *man*, a true member of the tribe reborn. Too, never had his people seen him fly, and he could see that he had grown beyond a mere curiosity in their minds. It was one thing to keep Winter close, like a well-fed leopard on a chain. But to ride her, as they did the khiroi . . . that was true mastery of a wild and fearsome beast.

Jai was back, but so was the Kidaran khan, bloodied and proven and powerful.

It was a heady thought, and when he reached his tent, Jai stabbed the spear into the dirt, letting all the plaza see what happened to his enemies. Once more they cheered, and he looked at the crowd that had followed him, taking it all in. He turned then, moving past the guards and away from the grasping hands of his people, back into the soft, silent world of his royal tent.

It was a wonder to be somewhere that wasn't a cave. Outside, Winter remained, guarding the entrance, distracted though she was by the foods that piled like religious offerings at her feet. Jai salivated at the familiar scents that greeted her.

It had been a long time since Jai had eaten anything, reliant on mana alone. That was the first thing he'd call for. Then a bath, and his Small Council.

Jai stretched, glad of the full core he had harvested from the fountain before his departure. He had let mana leak out to soothe his aches on the flight, for he was not yet used to riding Winter in the saddle.

Every now and again, he still entered the trance to glance at his new core. It was glorious, and contained a deep well of mana, so large he could hardly believe it possible. In time, the Gryphon Guard would come in numbers he could not handle. But with the power he now held . . . and some help from the soulbound among his tribe, they might just hold their own against one of them. Two, with the element of surprise.

At least, for now. And with the Caelite spreading his call for the High Council, so too would they bring the message of the slaughtered Great Tribe. Already, he knew, word of Rohan's son's return would have spread. And now rited, he was as legitimate as any other khan that rode the steppes.

'Jai!'

Feng was first through the door, Sindri and Harleen pushing through a few steps behind. More clamoured at the flapping entrance, but it seemed the guards would not let them through. Still, every now and then, a hand reached through the partition or a guard's leg as he braced against the crowds, only to be snatched back. They all wanted a piece of him, and he didn't blame them. He'd been gone so long. And yet . . .

Jai collapsed onto his throne, wishing for just a moment's peace. He knew, though, time was short. It was the late afternoon, and he had much to set in motion before the day was out.

'I take it I have passed the Rite?' Jai asked, too tired for formal greetings.

'You're a madman for taking on a Gryphon Knight,' Harleen said, shaking her head in awe. 'But it is undeniable, and any who might have doubted have already come to me professing their admiration.'

'And to curry favour,' Feng muttered.

'It's the way of kings,' Harleen responded, turning back to Jai. 'You are khan now in more than name alone.'

She bowed low, and Jai inclined his head, wishing Winter was there beside him. This room held memories of his long hours, ruling in the dim light. He remembered when he had not left for days, so long was the queue of those that needed his judgement. That would only increase now that the people actually respected him as rited. Too, there was surely now a backlog that would need to be addressed. Which he would – just not now.

'I want a full accounting of our soldiers by morning,' Jai instructed Harleen. 'Real numbers, every soldier we can field on the back of a khiro with a few weeks' training. I want lists of armour, weapons, experience – everything you know.'

'It is done, my khan,' she said.

'Sindri,' Jai said. 'I need you to gather the soulbound among us, and have them training under Kiran and Meera. If we are to defeat the Gryphon Guard without the Caelite to aid us, I will have need of their skills. They must work on their ascension. Magnus's men may rule the skies, but we will keep them from the patch above us even if we have to set the sky afire to do it.'

'Of course,' Sindri said.

'Feng, how many traders do we have with us?'

'Only a few, my khan,' Feng replied, awkwardly formal in the presence of the others. 'Lai and her ilk still follow; the rest departed soon after you did.'

Jai steepled his fingers.

'Figure out how much gold we can spare,' Jai said. 'And sell every luxury I have. Then go to Lai and have her send word to her friends among the traders of the steppe. Tell them the Kidara tribe are buying for war.'

'War?' Harleen asked.

'Where should I tell them to find us?' Feng asked. 'Do we ride east, west?'

'We ride for the Blue Mesa on the morrow. I have summoned a High Council.'

AFTER A FEW MORE hours of instructions and petitions that could not wait, Jai had dismissed his advisers. He meant to rest then, but found he was buzzing, unable to simply fall asleep. There was too much still to do, too much in doubt, and he wondered if they'd accomplish it all in time.

For some reason – maybe it was the focus on logistics, of running a war – but his mind turned to the diary. Meena had brought it back to him, and he looked at it now, sitting on the table. Although he rarely found much of use from Leonid's musings, the kernels he did glean were often worth their weight in khiroi.

He picked up the book, finding where he left off, and read.

Forgive my scattered thoughts and crooked pen, oh, Leonid, of years to come. I am weary, for I joined my men in training to lift their spirits, and my body is not what it once was. But I suppose at the time of reading, you will know this well enough, future self.

We survive another day. This Rohan has cobbled together an alliance that will break me if I am not careful. Three legions may not be enough to fight the horde that follows us as we retreat back across the grasslands.

I have seen their great birds in the sky, and

the mammoths on the horizon. The latter set my men's tongues wagging like the tails of scared pups. But I have faced these beasts' bald cousins in the desert plains of Shambalai. They will fall like any other animal. Soon enough, they will be no more than petty marvels for the Colosseum.

We return not in fear, but because my men are near mutiny. Imagine a year without the touch of a woman. A year of boiled grains and heathen savages your neighbour. No. It is time we left this place.

I am beginning to think these lands are not worth the trouble. What need have we of grass? But the people . . . that is another thing. My lands are vast, and someone must work the soil. Constantine says we should fetter them all, still green in his defeat.

Still, to the present. With all of Rufus's gryphons ferrying us food, their raids stalled, there is no point in festering amid this grass, waiting for the enemy to grow some balls and fight us in open battle. A siege is not a siege if the fortress can move. We rebuild our camp each night, and march in battle dress throughout the day, cutting our way through the grasslands. It is gruelling, but the men have no alternative. They are just happy that we march in a homeward direction.

It is clear to me now that I must return to where my supply lines are no longer in danger, and Rufinus's men can return to what they do best. Only when they act in savagery does this Rohan seem to baulk.

He closed the book. He knew he was on the right track. The Gryphon Guard only knew barbarism. Violence on the scale of being atrocity. That was all Leonid had in his favour, and all Magnus had now. Leonid had been so close to giving it all up if it hadn't been for his gryphons.

I'll just have to make it that way for the Sabines again.

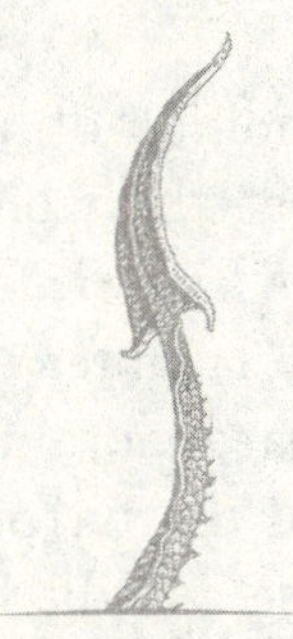

Chapter 80

Jai rode at the head of his tribe, the leather of his saddle creaking, Navi snorting as she set the pace, tirelessly clomping on through the grasslands. Above, Winter's shadow flitted, as she patrolled the tribe's edges, watching the horizon for enemies.

It was near the end of a clear spring day, a week since he'd returned, with nary a cloud in the sky, the sun full and bright on Jai's face. The warmth was strange upon his skin, and it felt almost odd to not let out a constant stream of mana to fight the bitter freeze of the mountains.

In that week back with his people, Jai had come to realise his stay among the Caelite had done more for him than reaching a higher level or allowing him to summon a High Council with the Caelite as his respected messengers. Down here, he was almost lightheaded in the thick air close to the ground, his body abuzz with energy – he felt he could run a mile full tilt without using his mana at all. The little majicking he had done since his blossoming had cost far less mana too, for it was pure as quicksilver, and it was a wonder to watch the mana turn from gold to the purest white as it dripped into his core.

His body, once wiry, was now rippling with muscle, with nary a pinch of fat. Such was the consequence of a diet of pure mana, got in great quantities from the mountaintop.

He was in the best condition of his life, and even if he had not noticed it immediately, the women of the tribe certainly had. Never before had Jai experienced the feminine whispers as he passed, followed by laughter that set his cheeks aflame. His soulbound hearing heard more than they needed about the shape of his buttocks and the furrows above his hips. It was embarrassing and flattering and, he had to admit, alluring.

But as much as he might be tempted, he knew these weren't the women for him. There was only one on his mind, one that fuelled his dreams and his hope and heart.

He let them stare and giggle, and focused on what was crucial. For one thing, he knew he could not sustain this level of mana-fuelled euphoria, for down here on the ground, mana was precious once more. If he emptied his core in place of feed or sleep, it would take him the better part of a month to recover it on the Great Steppe.

No, it had been a return to sleep and solid food, both of which he had made the most of these last days. He'd got to bed each night with a protruding belly of curried khiro and sweet potato, his skin softened with the hot rosewater of his bath, his body clad in muslin and silk.

It was good to be khan. Even if he'd spent every waking hour that he was not on khiro-back, or on his own back in his bed, dealing with the affairs of state.

A literal thousand people sought audiences. Indeed, Feng had received at least a dozen requests from Meera alone, the first in the form of a note alongside the return of Jai's diary, demanding to speak with her khan urgently, and privately. But there was time enough for him to tell her of his adventures for her memory keeping. There was more important work to do now, particularly in balancing the disparate elements of his khanship.

The Tainted and the Kidara were getting on well enough – knowing their rivals' additional soldiers were all that kept them from being put to the fire and sword helped. But there were still disputes to settle, for which Feng had been invaluable, for he knew both cultures intimately.

Jai had been working his way through as much as he could before they reached their destination. Now he could see it in the distance. A block of rock, emergent from the land, as if a sheep's knuckle had been tossed by the Mother on a board of green velvet. Its colour was a strange grey that gave the place its name, a grey that looked almost blue beneath the open sky.

Winter had spotted already a dozen tribes, all gathered at its base, taking advantage of the oases that surrounded it. Seeing through Winter's eyes from the sky, it was like a great grey-dark pupil, surrounded by a turquoise moat of water, ringed by the trees and bamboo groves.

Legends told the Blue Mesa was the Mother's iris, crying her endless tears for the warring of her children. She might have to cry a little longer. But at least her children might unite in common cause.

Already he could see the crisscrossed paths of their rival tribes' passage, and the going was easier as they followed the beaten trails. Jai turned in his saddle as they approached. He had instructed his tribe to ride in full battle dress on this last day, and all bore the Kidaran colours emblazoned alongside flashes of their own.

It was a sight to behold, an army of five hundred warriors, riding at the head of a great moving herd of sleds, carriages and men, women and children.

Lai had been as good as her word, summoning the traders to meet them at the Blue Mesa. He'd emptied her stores of blue cloth, cladding his warriors in the colours of his house. Others had come in dribs and drabs, and Jai's coffers had slowly emptied as he'd purchased weapons and leather armour for his army, such that all had at least a breastplate, helmet and blade.

His Small Council, the nobles and his advisers rode at their head, resplendent in the finery that befitted their houses. Jewels, beads, gold and silver flashed, and Jai knew that there could be no doubt among his rivals that his people was a true Great Tribe of the steppe, no matter what they said about the so-called Tainted among them.

A horn sounded ahead, followed by another, then another. Jai's flag bearer responded, though Jai had little idea of what it meant. But soulwalking from Winter's gaze above, he found a gap amid the dozen camps that crowded about the Blue Mesa. There, he aimed his tribe, such that they too could find their place amid the bounty of the oases, and reap the harvest therein.

'Tighten up!' Jai called out, his flag bearer signalling frantically, a horn in one hand, a flag in the other. 'Backs straight, eyes bright! Remember who we are, the legacy we protect. Remember we are Kidara!'

The folk cheered, and Jai rode on, to where the fates of all the Sithia would be decided. To the High Council.

Chapter 81

The camp is a charnel house, but we dare not leave. We cower behind our walls, while the enemy celebrate a victory. But it was no victory. No battle. Just butchery.

The courage of my enemy cannot be discounted. Their mammoths came in the night, thundering out of the darkness without warning. They broke our walls. Made easy work of our rotted, salvaged wood that we have torn down and built up a hundred times in this cursed expedition, careless of our javelins, our blades, until they fell.

And then they came. Screaming from the grasslands, their beasts abandoned, throwing their bodies into the breach. They fought like the savages they are. It was a bloody business. Twice, I rode into the breach. Twice, I was thrown back by their courage.

They lost as many men as I, perhaps more. But you would not know it, the way they crow from outside our walls, taunting my men. I write to the tune of my men's screams as the healers go about their work. We run low on catgut, on honey for the wounds. The sawbones do their *bloody business with blades dulled from work, but there is no time to sharpen them.*

I see now they will not let us leave freely. They will hunt us to the edge of our homelands, so I head for the prison garrison of Porticus. There is nothing for me here – their only resource is the people themselves. Let them face an arrayed legion, defending a narrow passage. Let them follow beyond their grasslands, into my territory. Then we shall see their mettle.

Jai sat in the still waters, setting the diary aside and listening to the creak of the boughs above, and the chirr of the insects that called the oasis their home. Vines hung from the trees, sheltering him from the sight of the rest of the tribe, who had, as one, shed themselves of clothes and entered the healing waters upon their arrival.

They had no need to fear ambush now. No Great Tribe would sully this sacred place with battle. No khan would war in the sight of the Mother's eye.

Jai understood now why his mother had been buried here. He hoped that he would be able to find the grave in time, but he could not do so this night. Because to go into the High Council in grief would be folly. No, he needed all his resolve. Now was the calm before the storm, and he would rest his mind, gird his loins and cleanse himself of the past. For the future beckoned, the spinning top of the world at a precipice.

If ever there was a place to rest, this was it. The Blue Mesa and its surroundings were a strange, beautiful place. He could hear the laughter of children through the trees, though he'd waded further away, so he could be alone with Winter. She relished the water, for Jai knew her species frequented the geysers of the Northern Tundra, and hunted whales and dolphins in the icy seas.

Even now, she circled him in long, lazy strokes of her tail, as at home in the waters as the sky. Jai felt a pang of regret that he had condemned her to a life upon the ground, for the flats of the Great Steppe were the antithesis of her natural habitat. Through their umbilical, she reproached him, reminding Jai that he was her home, first and foremost.

Then she splashed him with her tail, and he laughed.

She swam away and Jai lay back, letting the eddies of the spring that fed this place float him where they willed, staring up at the stars through the underbrush. The moon was as full and bright as he'd ever seen it, such that its ethereal light allowed some colour to remain amid its silver sheen. He was . . . content?

It was a strange feeling, considering the past few weeks.

Considering my entire life, he thought ruefully.

Winter sensed it before he did. A twinge of recognition from her consciousness, a scent on the wind, a stir in the air. Jai stood, anxious, moving back to the shallows, where the water trickled from above, and a narrow strip of pebbled beach separated the jungle.

There was a crackle from above, lianas raining down, and then Regin was flopping into the water, Erica diving gracefully from his back. Jai stepped back as she emerged in a burst of water, wiping her eyes, and pulling her hair back.

'Phew,' Erica breathed. 'You have no idea how good that feels. Beats snow by a square mile.'

Jai stared, and broke into a grin.

'You sure know how to make an entrance,' he said.

She smiled and shrugged, the swathe of cloth about her clinging provocatively to her body. He was suddenly aware of his own nakedness, glad he was underwater, his clothing draped over a branch a stone's throw away.

'Regin could smell Winter from up there,' she said. 'We're camping on the mesa.'

'The Caelite are here, then?' he asked, both intensely interested in the answer and also not able to care less. She was *so* close. More, he had nowhere to go, his back pressed against the mossed stone of the mesa. He was glad of it. He liked her close.

'A detour on the way home,' she said, oblivious to his thoughts. 'I'm ready. Blossomed core and everything. Here.'

She took his hand and placed it on her chest. Jai thrilled at the intimacy, and yet was equally thrilled as he entered the trance and saw within, the spiralled shape that closely matched the coral she had based her etchings on, but expanded in all directions in perfect symmetry.

She held Jai's hand in place, long after Jai had left the trance. They were so close. He could feel her pulse quickening as he leaned in, daring, hoping. Her head turned just a touch to face him more fully, eyes flashing.

Erica's lips met his, a soft brush, then she pulled into the kiss, pressing her body – somehow firm and strong yet soft and warm – against him. He was lost in it, her embrace, her lips parting as he ran his fingers up the nape of her neck and into her hair.

She broke off, gasping for breath, as if shocked at their daring.

'By the All-Mother, I've been wanting you to do that forever,' she breathed into the shelter of his chest. He held her, questioning if this was even real. He leaned in again to make sure, but her soft palm held him back.

'This is ours and no one else's,' Erica said, looking into his eyes. 'We are leaders, Jai. Our lives are not our own. But here, now . . . I want this. I don't care what it means.'

Jai could tell her mind was spinning. His was as well. In the moonlight, he could see her lip trembling – he wondered if she could feel his own knees doing the same. But even though he was nervous, he knew this was right. He reached out and stilled her lip, pressing his forehead to her own.

'It can mean whatever you want it to,' he whispered. 'In this, we are beholden to ourselves, and no one else.'

She pulled away again, and looked into his eyes once more. There was a fragility there. A fear. Of him.

'First loyalty to our peoples,' Jai said firmly. 'But our hearts also deserve loyalty . . .'

Her hand played with his chest, raking the soft down along its centre. She stood, water splashing, and slowly removed her clothes, revealing her nakedness.

She was . . . perfect. He had dreamed of her since the moment they'd met, but even his vision of her was nothing compared to the woman that stood before him. So strong. So vulnerable. So assured yet nervous.

Just as he was.

Jai stood, meeting her lips, and pulled her further into the shallow water, their hands grasping, teeth clashing as they fell into the soft moss that surrounded the pool.

It was a battle, of the best kind. Talvir of the heart and soul, as each fought to consume the other. Nails raked his back, even as his fingers gripped rough enough to bruise and never let go.

Jai may have been inexperienced, but he knew what he wanted and she responded, helping him, helping herself. She guided his hands, his mouth, his fingers. Showed him what made her gasp, made her twitch, made her back arch. He loved the taste of her mouth. The smell of her skin. The feel of her spreading before his tongue.

They had been breathless on the Caelite mountain, yet nothing suffocated so deliciously as they bucked the air from their lungs, mana fuelling their movements when exhaustion would otherwise stop.

Soon it was too much for each. Jai strained and Erica groaned, their rhythm such that they rolled over in unison. She straddled him, her hands seizing his stiffening self, making quick work as she guided him against her. He hissed in anticipation, so sensitive he had to spend mana to not release too soon.

'Not yet,' she breathed. 'Not yet . . .'

He drew Erica to him, crashing their mouths together in a

kiss of affirmation, a promise that he would wait for her, and she bit his bottom lip, the pain a perfect acknowledgement. Her breasts heaved as she worked in the silver light, nipples pink and pert. Jai sat up, taking her breast in his mouth, before she shoved him down once, mounting him with a single, anguished thrust.

THEY LAY TOGETHER, THEIR dragons gambolling in the shallows, revelling in the afterglow of their twin souls. Erica lay upon Jai's chest, spinning the hair around a finger, her breath tickling his neck.

'Imagine a week here,' Jai whispered. 'Just us, our dragons. We could eat the fruits, the herbs of the land. Winter'd hunt us down a fish.'

Erica chuckled.

'Regin's the better fisherdragon,' she said, teasing. 'He's the scourge of the mountain's streams. Even snuck me a couple, before the Speaker caught wind.'

'I can imagine the bards singing now,' Jai replied. '"Regin, oh, Regin, scourge of the mountain streams, slaughterer of trout."'

She gave him a playful slap to the chest, and sat up, bundling her hair in a knot. Jai traced the lines of her back with his fingers, feeling the muscles bunching and coiling. Her body was so beautiful, he tried to burn the memory of it into his consciousness. To savour every moment, so he could relive it in the days to come.

Because even in the throes of joy, there was sadness there too.

Erica was going home. And even as allies, he knew it would be long before he saw her again. She had her war to fight, and he his. They had done important work, bringing themselves to the same level most Gryphon Guard began at. With any luck, they would be well matched in a duel. As important as all that was, though, it didn't make the knowledge that they'd soon part any easier.

She caught him looking at her and flashed him a smile, before lying back down, her head resting on her hand.

'So you think this will work?' she asked, breaking the spell. 'All this?'

Jai sighed, letting the dread of what was to come spill back into his mind.

'I don't see how the other tribes have a choice,' Jai said. 'The legion just took down a Great Tribe. Slaughtered them, to a man. They're all at risk. No one tribe can face a legion and win. Without some sort of alliance, we're all prey to the Sabines. But then, they were always prey to each other too. Always a bigger fish. They just don't realise a shark just slipped into their pond.'

'And the Gryphon Guard?' Erica asked. 'There's still three of them with the legion. And only one of you.' She took his hand. 'Don't fight them alone,' she said. 'We were lucky last time.'

Jai shook his head, his mood darkening.

'We'll do what we can. I have a half-dozen soulbound training right now to fight them. They may not be able to fly, and none are yet ascended, but with some training, focus, their spells will knock one out of the sky same as any other beast.'

Erica nodded grimly. 'But what about the next battle?' she asked. 'There's fifty Gryphon Guard flying above my homeland right now. Burning villages, raiding our supply lines. The Dansk's dragons hold them at bay, but that could change. And when they're done with us, they'll turn on you. You and I both know this legion is just the beginning. More will come.'

Jai turned his gaze up to the skies, shaking his head.

'I don't know,' he said. 'I'll shame the Caeilite into joining us. That's all I can think of.'

Erica ran her thumb along his cheek, as if trying to smooth out his frown.

'I've ruined it, haven't I?'

He forced a smile and sat up. 'You couldn't ruin this if you tried. It was perfect. You're . . . you're perfect.' She blushed, and he once more wished they weren't who they were, didn't have the responsibilities to anyone but each other.

But they did . . .

'I should go,' he said, even as much as it pained him. 'My people will be worrying where I've gone. We're lucky one hasn't come looking already.'

She nodded, her face a little sad, and it tore at his heart. He had finally found her, and more, they had finally found each other. If he could, he would fly off with her. It wasn't like anyone could stop them . . .

No one but ourselves.

And that was the sobering reality. That as much as his heart belonged to her, his destiny belonged to his people. He was soulbound to a dragon, not to fly off and live in peace and love, but to fight for the Kidara. For the Sithians. Maybe one day . . .

Just not today.

'Don't leave without seeing me,' Jai blurted. 'I mean. If that's okay.'

She smiled at his awkwardness.

'Count on it.'

Chapter 82

Our borders near by the day, but the men grow more hollow. Our food supplies dwindle, for Rufinus's men must scout our vicinity, for fear of the mammoths' return.

These walls are both a prison and a dam, and even my centurions whisper in the dark. They say the expedition is forever cursed, for we did not bury our dead. They forget, it was they that clamoured to leave, when the bodies began to stink, and none dared leave the safety of our walls to put them in the ground.

At least the way we came is an easier path. And for now, my enemy has retreated. Rohan is a wily fox. But the lion rules the savannah.

Jai stomped up the stairway of the mesa, Feng hurrying behind. It was awkward to climb in the regalia of his royal house, and he was trying not to sweat through the makeup that caked his face.

This was more than he'd ever worn before, and he'd been woken in the early hours not long after his parting with Erica to begin the long process of getting ready. His eyes were caked with kohl and his cheeks striped with henna, and the folds of silk swathed about his body made him feel more a cosseted concubine than a king.

He'd rather have been in full battle armour, but this was a holy place. One that it seemed had hosted past meetings of the tribes before, if Feng's words rang true. Indeed, it was here that the peoples of Rohan's alliance had sheltered throughout the war. It heartened him to know he'd chosen here, as if both his Sithian heritage was in his blood *and* his mother was guiding him.

Feng stopped when they reached the top of the plateau, staring out over the horizon, at the lagoon and forest that ringed them, enshrined by the infinite halo of green grassland.

'Never been this high,' Feng said, short of breath. 'Is this what you see when you ride Winter?'

Jai appreciated the break in tension.

'This is nothing. You should see it from the mountains,' he said. 'It is like a glimpse of how the Mother sees our world.'

Feng gave a jealous sigh, and tore his gaze away. The mesa was near flat, a slight slope dragging Jai's feet on as he headed for the glowing torches at the mesa's centre. The Caelite birds circled above, shepherding the High Council. Winter and Regin were among the roqs, flying side by side, giving the strange avians a wide berth.

Jai was glad of them, for if the Gryphon Guard were to strike, they could take out the entire Sithian leadership in a single attack. It was one of the many reasons it was unlikely they could ever have a gathering like this again. At least, not with their entire tribes in tow.

'Remember,' Feng whispered. 'You called this meeting, and they came. That says a lot. Have confidence, you are as much a khan as any of them, maybe even more. Your father was High Khan, for Mother's sake.'

Jai hushed him, a smile tugging his lips.

'Don't worry, Feng,' he said. 'I've got this.'

Ahead, Jai's tent had been set up for their guests, and each khan had brought their throne ahead of them, such that all would sit tall around the table.

As Jai marched to the tent entrance, he saw Kiran and her bodyguard, armed to the teeth, their eyes fixed upon the skies.

'All clear?' Jai asked.

'Nothing yet,' she said.

'Good,' Jai said. 'First sign of trouble, don't worry about interrupting, just let us know. And put out these torches if you please. It'll look like a bullseye from above.'

'Right away, my khan.'

Jai ducked through the tent's flaps. Within, there were no partitions, just the grand table set up in its usual position. But there were new thrones there, alongside his throne.

He recognised the Mahmut tribe's leader instantly, not because he'd met the man, but because he sat on a mammoth tusk throne that nearly dwarfed Jai's own, with a swarthy, barrel-bellied occupant to fill it.

He stood as Jai entered, as did the others, each with their own great chairs of bone, horn, carved wood and plush cushion. Each khan had a man hovering at their shoulders, the viziers of a dozen tribes brought to advise. Already, he could see them leaning in, whispering.

Only the Caelite sat on a bench, one borrowed from the Kidara. Eko and the Speaker shared it, looking small alongside the raised thrones of the others. Jai was glad to see Erica there too, standing behind them, dressed in a simple smock that did nothing to hide her beauty.

Jai took his place in front of his throne, only to see one man had not stood at his arrival: Teji. His uncle sat upon a throne near identical to Jai's, only the horns were still fresh, the blood still drying at their bases.

Nazeem stood smirking at Teji's side, and Feng let out a growl that Jai stilled with a grip of his wrist. Jai nodded respectfully to each khan in turn, four women and ten men in total. All but his uncle.

Then he sat too, tugging at the silks about his neck before speaking with a steady voice.

'I thank you for your council,' Jai said, speaking the words Feng had instructed. 'Be welcome. Please, sit.'

There was a rustle and creak as the others followed suit, the eyes of the most powerful men and women in the land all on him, silent except in whispered replies to their incessant viziers.

'I am Jai, khan of the Kidara,' Jai said, as was proper.

'I am Tenzin, khan of the Mahmut,' the large man said, leaning deep across the table.

'I am Teji, khan of the Tejinder,' Teji said in a bored voice.

'I am the Speaker, and this is Eko, leader of the Caelite.'

More introductions rippled around the table, until the last had spoken. Jai took a deep breath, and stood, motioning at the map laid in front of them. The mesa had been well rendered by Jai's cartographer, and the legion had been represented by scores of eagle-headed figurines. The poor man had worked his hands bloody to prepare the pieces, but it was well worth it, for now the khans stared at it, some pointing to their viziers and whispering.

Good, Jai thought. *You should be concerned*. Because the map laid out their situation in a way that could not be ignored.

'A lifetime ago, my father met with the khans of the Great Tribes to form an alliance,' Jai intoned. 'An alliance that held firm against the Sabine threat, and secured a peace that has lasted a generation.'

'*I* secured it,' Teji said. 'I met with the Sabines. Agreed to terms. Your father *lost* the war. I ended it.'

'Be careful of what you claim credit for,' Tenzin growled. 'That peace was paid for in the fettering of tens of thousands of our peoples.' Others around the table nodded, while some shook their heads, clearly happier with Teji's take on history.

For himself, Teji shrugged, petulant as a child. Jai spoke on, but not before leaving a moment for Teji's behaviour to be felt.

'We have no choice but to fight this war anew. This time, however, it is different.'

'Go on,' Teji chuckled, shaking his head with exaggerated disbelief. 'I can't wait to hear this.'

'Is there something funny about the massacre of the Cimmer?' Jai demanded, speaking the name of the slaughtered tribe.

There were murmurs and nods from around the table, and Nazeem whispered urgently. Teji sat straightened from his relaxed pose, giving a mute shake of his head.

'Do not let the shame of your defeat colour this discussion, Uncle,' Jai snapped. 'You disrespect the time of my esteemed guests. And by coming here without invitation, I will remind all that you are no guest of mine.'

'Speak, runt,' Teji snapped. 'It is you who wastes time.'

Jai gritted his teeth, wondering what would happen if he tried to throw out his uncle. Then he caught their gazes, and realised he'd lost his place in his speech. Tenzin raised a hand, nodding to Jai.

'No need to wax eloquent, Khan Jai,' he said, his voice polite, but firm. 'Many of us here were in the tent for the first alliance, some of us even sitting behind our fathers. What do you propose?'

'Suicide,' Teji spat.

Jai bit back a retort, and spoke on, even amid growing murmurs.

'Leonid is dead,' he declared. 'And not by my hand. Titus killed him. Killed his father too. Seized power for himself. Blamed my brothers, my *amah*. Blamed me. Cut their throats right in front of my eyes.'

The table fell silent, the whispers stopped.

'I know the man. More boy than man, in truth.'

'You're one to talk,' Teji muttered, but Jai ignored it.

'He is not the general that Leonid was. Just a spoiled pup, eager for glory.'

'And what of Magnus?' Teji said, Nazeem whispering frantically in his ear. 'The Gryphon Guard in the last war numbered but a dozen. Now, they are fifty.'

Jai nudged Feng as he spoke, the signal they had agreed to.

His vizier hurried to the nearby entrance, and reached into a sack he had stashed there. Without ceremony, he tossed its contents onto the table.

The gryphon's head rolled alongside the golden helm, the stench of the vinegar they had preserved it in since taking it off its stake messing the air. The khans recoiled, the whispers turned to speech as they voiced their disbelief.

'They are not so tough,' Jai growled. 'Here is the last one that crossed my path.'

'A parlour trick,' Teji said, even as his eyes bulged from his head.

'I am soulbound to a dragon!' Jai replied, his voice rising above the murmurs. 'And I am in alliance with the Dansk, who have a dozen of their own. If the Caelite join with us' – he stabbed a finger at Eko – 'we will have no trouble holding our own against them.'

Yet Eko shook his head, a rueful smile upon his face. 'We are here to provide the meeting protection. Nothing more.'

Jai turned to the remaining khans, slapping the table to get their attention. They were still staring at the gryphon's head, and Feng snatched it back, out of sight.

'Tell that to them,' Jai said, pointing at the others. 'Go on.'

Eko inclined his head, as if this was of no moment.

'The Caelite will have no part in this war.'

Jai waited, but the khans were silent. Indeed, they seemed in awe of the strange, hairless men that sat beside them. Clearly the Caelite were as much a mystery as they had been when Jai made his climb.

'We also will have no part,' another khan said, a buck-toothed man with red silks all about him, the crest of crossed impala horns emblazoned upon his chest.

'We too,' said another, one of the women, emblazoned in orange and the symbol of a setting sun.

Jai stared, shocked at the response. Only now did he see them exchange glances with Teji, and his uncle's open smile. Nazeem's dark eyes bore into Jai's own. There was . . . hatred there.

Of course. The cowards were working against him.

'There must be five thousand warriors gathered here,' Jai said. 'And more, if the smaller tribes join us – I hear some journey here now, even as we speak.'

'They will,' Tenzin muttered. 'Join us, I mean. It is they who will suffer most under the gryphons.'

'Five thousand,' Jai said. 'Against five thousand legionaries.'

'Wrong,' Teji said.

'How so?'

'The Sabine army is vast.'

'It is but one legion!' Jai snarled. 'We could crush them!'

'For *now*,' Teji retorted. 'How many march into the Northern Tundra as we speak? How many more garrison the forts along our border? Ten legions, at least, with more being called up by the day. Fifty thousand warriors of the greatest fighting force in the world. They outnumber us ten to one.'

'The Dansk hold their own,' Jai said. 'They have thousands of warriors fighting right now, and a dozen dragons to keep the Gryphon Guard at bay. Even now, the legion that approaches had but three Gryphon Guard accompanying them, so great is the dragon threat.'

'Who cares about the Dansk?' Teji laughed. 'Drunk savages, all. If Titus wants to swallow that lump of ice, so be it. We'll be next.'

Jai glanced at Erica, but she shook her head. Not yet.

'Titus fights on two fronts,' Jai said, raising his voice to be heard above the murmuring. 'We cannot discount them.'

'The Dansk will not help us against the Gryphon Guard,' Teji asserted. 'When the beasts ravage our lands, do you think they will send their dragons to defend us?'

'I do,' Jai said.

'You are delusional,' Teji roared. 'A pup with no head for politics. No experience. And if you want to follow him into war, then you are just as foolish as my late brother was.'

'The Dansk and I are in alliance,' he said firmly. 'They *will* come to our aid, if we will come to theirs. And right now, that means defeating the legion, and invading the Sabines' eastern territories. Titus will have no choice but to pull legions from the northern front.'

Silence met his words, but he could see the doubt in the eyes of the others, even those who had not yet made their position clear.

'Jai,' Tenzin said quietly. 'Who are you to speak for the Dansk?'

Jai looked to Erica, and caught her smile.

'I don't,' Jai said. '*She* does.'

Eyes swung to Erica as she leaned across the table, resting on her knuckles as she met the eyes of those seated.

'Perhaps I should have spoken earlier,' she said.

'I am Erica, Queen of the Dansk.'

Chapter 83

'Twenty thousand warriors,' Erica said. 'Twelve dragons. That is what holds off ten legions and the Gryphon Guard.'

Jai caught the gazes of the other khans, looking at him with new eyes.

'So they outnumber you,' Teji blurted, but his bulging eyes told Jai he had been caught unawares.

'A Dansk warrior is worth two legionaries,' she asserted, giving him a withering look. 'I dare say a Sithian knight is worth as many too.'

'Hear, hear,' another khan said, a woman with white hair who thumped the table.

'And you hold your own?' Tenzin asked Erica.

'We've been fighting the Sabines since my father's birth,' she said. 'They invade our land, and expect to best us. It is a bitter fight. My people suffer. But we have the measure of them, yes.'

'The numbers do not work,' the buck-toothed khan, a man named Hari, said. 'Let us imagine, for a moment, that the Dansk lose. Call it a tragic defeat.'

He held up his hands as Erica started, asking for the opportunity to finish his thought.

'Fifty thousand legionaries march into our lands. As much as I love my people, I do not think those odds can be beaten.

Leonid marched on us with only fifteen thousand. Think on that.'

Jai clenched his fists beneath the table, trying to slow his racing heart. This wasn't going as he'd hoped. He had not expected Teji to come. Indeed, he had told the Caelite to leave the man off the invitation, but it seemed the wily old politician had caught wind.

You either battle on the terrain you find yourself, or you retreat.

Retreating wasn't an option.

'That will not happen if we fight now,' Jai said. 'Imagine the blow to Sabine morale when we ride on that legion and carve a path into the heart of their eastern territories. Titus has left himself completely exposed.'

'And what if their Gryphon Guard abandon the Dansk front, and come to ravage our peoples in return?' Teji snapped. 'The Cimmer tribe was just a taste of what is to come if we do not make peace.'

Jai turned to Eko, who bowed his head low.

'The Caelite will defend the Great Steppe,' Jai said.

'We will not,' Eko replied in a low voice. 'Not unless all the Sithia join this battle.'

'I concur,' Tenzin said. 'It must be all of us, or none of us.'

'What is our alternative?' Jai said, trying his best not to let his temper colour his words.

'Make peace,' Teji said. 'And give them what they want.'

'What do they want?' Jai asked, genuinely puzzled.

Teji pointed at Jai.

'*You*.' Teji pointed around the table. 'He killed Leonid. He plotted with the Dansk to assassinate Constantine. Isn't it obvious?'

Jai stood, stabbing a finger in his uncle's direction. 'That is a lie!'

Teji threw up his hands, smirking from ear to ear. 'I am only saying what everyone else is thinking.'

And the truth was, there was little Jai could do to refute him. It was word against word, and even though Jai had the respect of some of the khans, he was still an unknown. And the rumor Teji bandied about had been among the Sithia far longer than Jai had been khan.

'It is obvious Teji's mind is made up,' Hari said. 'And if it is, then this has been a waste of time. Either we all do this, or none of us do.'

'What, then, do you suggest?' Tenzin asked.

Hari shrugged. 'Titus has won his victory. We send Teji to seek terms, and the imperial pup can say we are beaten. Let him crow.'

'You don't know him,' Jai said. 'He killed his own *father* for glory. His grandfather too. You think he'll stop now he's won a single victory?'

'So you say,' Hari snapped back.

'We give him to the Sabines,' Teji repeated.

'Just try it,' Jai hissed, his hand straying to the empty scabbard at his side, once again cursing this costume he had been forced to wear, rather than his battle dress. Khans stood, shouting across the tables.

'No tricks this time,' Teji snarled. 'We're ready for you.'

Tenzin called for silence, his deep voice booming, beard bristling as he slammed his meaty fists against the table, knocking the figurines askew.

As quiet returned, Tenzin turned to Hari, speaking with measured voice.

'If Teji's men joined the war, would you follow?'

Hari vacillated, looking to Teji for guidance and finding none.

'We all know the Tainted mercenaries he has hired to bolster his ranks.' Jai's head jerked at this; it was news he hadn't heard. Hari continued, 'We will need his men. So . . . yes.'

'It is clear we have two paths,' Tenzin said. 'One where we sue for peace, another where we go to war.'

Nobody disagreed, and he nodded slowly.

'Good. Then let the Mother decide.'

Jai stared, confused. Tenzin caught his gaze, even as Teji seemed to understand, his face paling.

'A duel,' Tenzin said. 'The old way. We need a strong, united Kidara tribe more than ever. No big battles between each other. The winner takes the other's tribe. The loser banished, if they survive. Then we will know who to follow.'

'No,' Erica said. 'That's madness.'

'I'm sorry, Queen,' Tenzin said. 'We welcome you, but this is the High Council of the Great Steppe. Let us sort our own affairs.'

'Agreed,' Teji snapped. 'But she speaks sense. The boy is soulbound. Even a warrior of my standing could not hope to defeat him.'

Tenzin laughed aloud, and the potbellied khan crossed his arms.

'Yes, Teji, we are all aware,' Tenzin said. 'It will be a fight the old way, in the sight of the Mother. No mana. No totems. And you can choose a champion.'

Teji stared at Jai, and Jai smiled at him. But then Nazeem leaned in close, whispering in Teji's ear. He was shaking his head.

'I'll fight,' Jai said. 'I'll do it.'

Nazeem paused. Smiled. He whispered again.

'I'll agree it,' Teji said suddenly. 'But only if the boy fights it himself.'

'Aye,' Hari growled.

Jai knew he would face Priya. The woman who had bested him once before. But he had been a different man then. The training with the Caelite had taught him much.

'Jai, don't do this,' Erica begged.

'She's right, Jai,' Feng whispered. 'There are better ways.'

Jai tried to think, closing his eyes. He could get everything he ever wanted. The Kidara tribe, reunited. The Sithia all under one banner. And he, to be High Khan, just like his father.

'If I do this,' he said, looking to Eko. 'Will you join us? Or will you give Magnus free rein over the Great Steppe, to slaughter where he wills?'

'As I said, we will not accompany your armies to battle. But, yes, we will defend the innocents you leave behind. Keep your peoples east, and close to our mountains, and we will protect them from the Gryphon Guard.'

Jai's heart soared. One more chance. One last roll of the dice.

'So be it,' Jai said. 'I accept.'

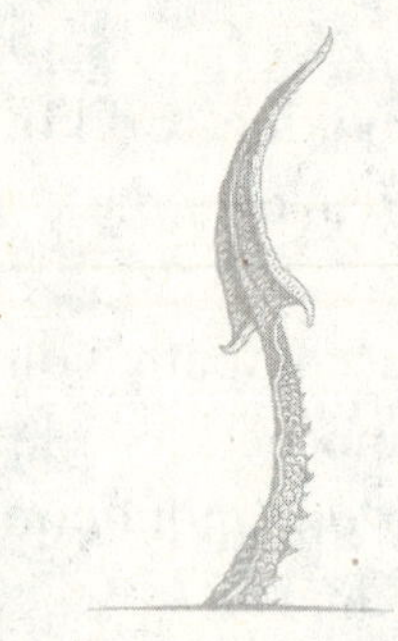

Chapter 84

They gave him the night to prepare, for the tribes could not linger long. Still, a dozen more, smaller tribes had reached their camp during the negotiations, awaiting the decisions of the High Council, and Jai could see the lights of their campfires.

The Caelite had done their job, at least. Now he had to finish his.

One night was hardly enough time to work up a sweat, let alone practise for a duel against Priya. Jai had never fought without mana before, and he knew it would be an entirely different beast. Still, he'd take all the practice he could get.

Kiran and Erica faced him, their blades raised high, eyes fixed upon him.

'Again!' Erica yelled.

Jai swept in close, his bamboo blade flicking high, then low, driving the pair back. He pressed closer, locking blades with Erica, and lashed out with a boot, kicking her back just in time to parry Kiran's swing.

The pair grappled, the test of strength in Jai's favour, until a low-swept boot had him flat on his back. He stared up at the night sky, his fists gripped tight with frustration.

'You're trying too hard not to use mana,' Kiran said. 'But you are anyway – it's too ingrained. You should drink the potion now, get used to it. Meera worked herself to the bone to get it ready in time for you to practise with.'

Jai struggled to his feet and stared at the green glass bottle, sitting on a spot on the top of the mesa. They trained upon it, for this was to be where their duel was to be fought, and Jai wanted to get used to the terrain.

'Fine,' Jai groaned. 'Let's do it.'

Kiran hurried to do his bidding, bringing Jai the bottle. He swigged the acrid liquid in a single gulp.

'How long?' Jai asked, feeling the liquid settle uncomfortably in his stomach.

'A minute,' Kiran said. 'Maybe less. I've only ever seen Zayn take it, and he's much bigger than you. Should last a few hours – you'll have to take it again tomorrow.'

Already, Jai could feel the potion working, a black tar that seemed to coat his very veins, spreading like an infection through his body. He lay there, hating every second, Erica kneeling beside him, gripping his hand.

'The mana lock should be in effect now,' Kiran said. 'Try a spell.'

Jai stood with Erica's help, feeling . . . *different*.

He lifted a hand, and sparked a fireball with a flick of his fingers. Only . . . nothing came. His mana remained within his core, locked away.

'Good,' Kiran said. 'Now . . . ready!'

Her blade lanced forward, and Jai raised his blade in return. His move felt sluggish, tiring, and the blow knocked his blade back, the force near wrenching the blade from his hands.

He danced back a few steps, ducking her blows, until he stood apart, aghast.

'I . . .'

'No mana to strengthen your parry,' Kiran said. 'You'll be slower, weaker now. No spells, no healing. Your body may be ascended, so you'll be stronger than any normal man but . . .'

She sighed and looked out over the crowds.

'Just be glad Priya is not used to it either. I bet right now, she's practising the same.'

Jai looked down at his body, already soaked with sweat from the exertion of their training. Poison aside, he was in the best condition of his life. Ascending had permanently strengthened his body, mana or no, and a diet of mana, relentless exercise and exposure to the elements had left him lean and muscled. Even the air felt heavy somehow, and he'd found it far easier to catch his breath down here.

Erica flashed him a smile of encouragement, and Jai realised he was not doing a good job of masking his fear.

'Come here,' Erica said, pulling Jai aside as Kiran swigged water from a flask.

Jai could hardly look at her, his mind racing. He should have taken this potion ages ago.

'Jai,' Erica whispered, cupping his chin, bringing his attention back to her face. 'You've faced worse than this. Both of us have. Look how far we've come.'

Jai stared, and kissed her, careless of Kiran's surprised expression. Erica cared little either, whispering.

'This is destiny. Right here, right now.'

And Jai wanted to ask her, if they too were destined for more.

'My khan!'

Jai turned, only to see Feng emerging from the stairway at the edge of the mesa, not far from where they trained. His face was pale and drawn, and he fell to his hands and knees after a few staggering steps.

'Not . . . Priya,' he managed, before retching.

Jai knelt at his side, rubbing his vizier's back.

'Take your time,' Jai said.

Feng shook his head, before retching again. He must have taken the stairs two at a time. What could possibly be so urgent?

'I should have known,' Feng moaned, wiping his mouth with the back of his hand. 'The moment Hari mentioned Teji's Tainted mercenaries.'

Jai felt his heart drop.

'Some of the Kidara went to the Tejinder to see their families . . . and they bring news.'

'Out with it,' Jai said.

'It's not Priya,' Feng choked. 'It's someone else. Someone . . . better. A mercenary, that's all we know.'

Jai gritted his teeth, and raised his bamboo sword once more.

'Kiran, Erica . . . again!'

Chapter 85

The fighting ring was so large, the entire Kidaran plaza could fit within and hardly touch the sides. It was a simple thing, a depression at the mesa's centre, encircled with bales of dried grasses.

Already, men and women had staked their claim to this dubious seating, while the khans and their entourages sat one step behind, raised platforms of cut bamboo there for the royals to have full view of the proceedings.

By now, the stairs to the Blue Mesa's top had been blocked, for there were so many people crowding it that it was becoming a hazard.

Jai didn't mind. If he won, the more people to see his victory the better. If he lost . . . well, it wouldn't matter much then, would it?

He sat at the arena's edge, Kiran kneading his shoulders, Erica urging another gulp of water down his throat. The midday sun beat mercilessly on the makeshift arena, scorching rock and skin alike. The air carried the tang of sweat, steel, and anticipation.

'Enough,' Jai groaned, pawing at the water gourd, 'else I'll be caught short mid-battle.'

Erica ignored him and shoved the gourd under his nose.

'Our strategy is to wear them out, take advantage of your

condition,' she snapped. 'Won't be much good if you're gasping for water after an hour.'

Jai gave her a rueful smile and took another sip.

'Make way!' a voice called.

Jai turned to see Teji making his way through the crowds nearby. He could see the Tejinder banner, a copy of Jai's father's but with the Alkhara it depicted in deep black, rather than the silver sigil of Jai's own house, and their colour was blood red. Strange choice, for a man who did not desire war.

And behind Teji, standing head and shoulders above the rest . . . was Zayn.

'No,' Kiran breathed. 'It can't be.'

Jai felt the blood drain from his face. His own stomach seized, and he sat back on his haunches, staring into the dark of the horizon.

'He's the best I've ever faced,' Kiran whispered. 'He's . . . he's a monster. The size of him . . .'

Zayn was indeed a monster. The man stood a foot taller than Jai, and perhaps twice that in width. The former Valor prince was a veritable mountain of muscle. Without mana . . . that muscle and height would count far more.

'He knows how to fight with the mana lock,' Kiran whispered. 'It's how he trained with the men before I bonded with my khiro and became a sparring partner. They didn't stand a chance otherwise.'

Jai felt dizzy. The shock of Zayn, now grinning at him as he stretched in the bright sunlight, had thrown Jai for a loop.

'You have watched him fight,' Sindri said. 'He has never seen you. Use it.'

Jai glanced at her, where she sat cross-legged nearby, her lips chewed to bleeding from nerves.

'He favours the crane stance, with the high blade.'

'What else?' Kiran muttered, kneeling to tighten the laces of his boots.

'He has an old wound in his left knee,' Jai said. 'Right, Sindri?'

'I used to massage it every night,' she whispered. 'A donkey kicked it, when he was a boy. Our master almost sold him on, thought he'd make a poor groom. Hard days.'

Jai shook his head.

'I'm sorry,' he said. 'I wish it wasn't this way.'

Sindri shrugged, though he could see the pain in her eyes.

'The boy I knew is gone,' she said. 'The man you face . . .'

She trailed off and lowered her head.

'Anything else?' Kiran asked.

Jai closed his eyes. He was tired, for he'd only allowed himself a few hours' sleep, wrapped in Winter's embrace. It was hard to learn the new rhythms of his body without mana. To understand his speed, his strength. But in the last hour of his training, he felt something click into place.

'He's arrogant,' Jai said. 'Quick to anger, fast to react.'

'Good,' Kiran said. 'Use that.'

Zayn wore no armour, as was customary for these duels. Only simple silken trousers, and a silver belt to keep them in place.

Indeed, Jai himself was bare-legged and chested, his skin oiled such that he would be hard to grip and grapple, his hands dusted in flour and salt, so he could manage the same. He wore a silken pair of shorts, voluminous in case they might tangle or slow a blade, and wide bottomed so as not to restrict his movements.

His hair was braided in a tight knot upon his head, and his beard braided into a dozen points, such that neither could be grabbed in battle. A trick from the Dansk, and done by Erica's own hand.

He was as ready as he'd ever be. Now he took his blade, fresh sharpened by his blacksmith, its razor edge gleaming in the high midday sun.

Tenzin stomped out to the arena's centre, his hands upon his hips, a lackey at his side. The lackey raised a mammoth tusk horn to his lip, and let out a short, loud blast that silenced the mesa within seconds of its sounding.

Jai watched as Zayn strode out of the crowd, his head high, blade slung flat over his shoulder like a club. Nazeem followed him.

'Good luck,' Erica whispered.

Jai felt the brush of her lips across his cheek, and her hand squeezing his so hard it hurt. Then his feet were moving of their own accord, sending him into the depths of the arena.

The walk felt like it took an age, and he found Feng hovering at his side. Finally, the whispers of a thousand onlookers stirring the air, he took his place opposite Zayn, Feng hurrying to Tenzin's side.

Tenzin held out a silver coin, one Jai did not recognise – though the phoenix embossed on its side left him in no doubt of its origins.

'The younger gets the toss. Choose.'

'Heads,' Feng said.

Tenzin flipped the coin, and showed it to Feng. The vizier pumped his fist, and flashed Jai a smile.

'Go on,' Tenzin said, proffering two vials of black liquid, each as large as a mug of ale.

Feng's hand hovered for a moment, and picked one, while the other was offered to a glowering Nazeem.

The man's face was inscrutable as he handed Zayn the bottle, but the big man's own was full of rage. He downed the vial and cast it aside, in a tinkle of breaking glass.

'Pick your position,' Tenzin said.

Jai gulped down the bitter liquid, casting the vial aside too, and circled until his back was to the sun, where its continued trajectory would only serve to blind Zayn more.

Seeing what he'd done, Zayn let out a chuckle.

'It will not matter, runt,' he said. 'That toss is all you'll win today.'

Jai met his gaze, his opponent's eyes bulging from their sockets. He was angry, and Jai knew that was a double-edged sword.

Already, Jai could feel the blackness spreading within him,

his connection to Winter fading to but a whisper. It was just as well, for his dragon's fears were compounding his own. He glanced above, and offered Winter a silent kiss. The dragon dipped her wings in response, two Caelite flying on their birds behind her, shadowing her in the sky. Should she try to intervene, they would fall upon her, and stop her from interrupting the sacred duel.

'To the death, or surrender!' Tenzin bellowed.

Feng hurried away, giving Jai a last quick hug before he departed.

'You can do this,' Feng said. 'I believe it. Now you do the same.'

Then he was gone.

Seconds ticked by, Tenzin jogging back, his lackey at his side. Only when all but Jai and Zayn had cleared the arena did Tenzin turn, and nudge his companion.

The horn sounded once. Twice.

Silence.

Then a roar from Zayn, his blade raised high, feet thundering across the mesa. Jai stepped back, and braced for the blow.

It was on.

Chapter 86

The blades clanged, sending reverberations through Jai's wrists that near turned them numb, such was the force of the blow.

Jai had hardly time to dance back before another deep swing almost gutted him, the air thrumming as Zayn threw great haymaker blows, his vast reach such that Jai could not hope for a swift counter.

Instead, he kept his distance, side stepping with careful feet, gauging his closeness to the arena's edge by the roar of the crowd. He could hear Zayn's huffing breaths, feel the sweat sting his eyes, the sword hilt gritty and heavy in his hands.

Zayn lanced forward, his blade stretched far, enough to slice past Jai's deflection. The blow glanced from his shoulder. Jai felt no pain, only the blood spring hot and wet on his arm, and the grunt of success from his opponent.

Jai leaped back, pumping his legs. Zayn was happy to let Jai scurry out of reach, for his chest was heaving, his skin already soaked with sweat. The big man was in fighting shape, but was clearly unused to battle without mana.

Jai took the time to rip a swathe of cloth from his silken shorts, binding the cut to his shoulder in an ugly, rushed knot. By now, the wound was beginning to sting, and Jai winced as he rolled his shoulder, lifting his blade once more.

Already, Zayn had caught his breath and was lumbering towards him, pressing him back against the watching crowd. Now they had fallen quiet, anticipating the next clash.

Another great swing deflected, the blade clanging against the ground, throwing up a spurt of dust. Jai was careful to never meet the blows, only knocking them askew, keeping his movements small, his energy conserved.

Zayn seemed of opposite mind, pressing forward in keen anticipation of easy victory, one Jai refused to grant him. Already, he could hear the booing from the crowd, eager for blood.

Still, he circled, the blade held outstretched in front of him. Now Zayn panted, his eyes narrowed, tongue poking between his teeth.

Jai knew he could not let the man catch his breath again. He probed, a quick step in and out of reach, his blade flicking close to the man's face. Zayn did not even flinch, his focus razor-sharp despite it all.

'So much for becoming a khan,' Jai hissed, goading him. 'A mercenary is but a step above a cutpurse.'

Zayn's eyes widened at the challenge. But he smiled darkly in return.

'When your lifeblood drains, Teji takes your throne,' Zayn chuckled, his voice low so that no other could hear. 'He will pay me well. Your treasury will buy me enough khiroi for a Great Tribe of my own.'

Jai let out a laugh, probing with his blade, Zayn batting each slash aside with grunts of exertion. With each blow, Jai let vile venom drip from his lips, prodding the enraged bull with any insult he could think of, though they felt strange in his mouth.

'You whore yourself to a disgraced khan, nothing more. Just an attack dog for oath breakers and murderers, fighting in their pits for scraps.'

Zayn let out a roar and rushed Jai, his blade flicking left and right, Jai forced back on the defensive as the big man's blade sliced ribbons of the air. Jai met the blade, only for

Zayn to barrel forwards, letting the blades slide and lock in at the hilt.

The big man grinned, his face a rictus of effort, veins bulging, breath seething between gritted teeth. Jai screamed in return, straining against the unrelenting force that toppled him back.

Jai spat plum in Zayn's face, the man's shock giving Jai a chance to twist away, the blade clanging to the ground. Jai stumbled back, for his trousers had been caught in the blow, a flap of garment draped at his shins. Only luck had saved his leg, and Jai knew he could never let himself be trapped like that again.

Zayn pawed at his face, and Jai forced a grin, despite how close he had come to death.

'Come on, big man,' Jai said, beckoning him with his chin. 'Come get paid.'

Zayn bellowed his frustration, but approached slowly, his legs in wide stance, sword steady.

Jai took in a deep breath, his chest heaving as he assessed the dire situation he was in. He was outclassed in strength, outreached by arm and blade, but not outwitted. The sun had moved overhead and shone directly behind Jai. Even now, Zayn squinted through sweat and sunlight.

Zayn would not chase him all over the arena. If Jai was to exhaust him, he would have to force the issue.

'You and Teji are birds of a feather,' Jai growled, closing in. 'Traitors to your own blood, blinded by your ambition. Scrabbling in the dirt for a coin.'

Zayn shook his head, as if to shake the words from his skull. He stood firm, letting his blade do the talking.

'What if I go left,' Jai said, feinting left, before cutting low and right.

Zayn stutter-stepped, awkward in his parry, his weak knee slowing his turn, but the blow had never meant to land. Only to unbalance, frustrate.

'Let's try again,' Jai said. 'Left!'

He cut left, and this time, followed through, even as Zayn countered slow and late, backing away, confused at Jai's wordplay. He was used to being in command, to fighting those weaker than he. Not used to being teased, to being treated as inferior.

'You yip like a pup,' Zayn snarled. 'Come, let me snap your neck.'

Jai charged, his blade high, meeting Zayn's counter before dancing to the side, his blade whipping left, right, low, high, the tempo fast, random.

Zayn's swordsmanship was flawless, but he parried hard, and countered harder. As a man of great strength would, if he had reserves of energy to power him. But he did not.

Jai was panting too, now, for the exertions on him were almost as great, the jarring clash of blades leaving the sword heavy in his hands, his arms screaming for relief.

Still, he forced himself to slash and cut, trading his speed against Zayn's strength. Already, the big man's blows were slowing. Twice, Jai's blows slipped close, and the big man stumbled back, giving up the field, stopping only when hands reached out to press him away from the arena's edge.

'Enough!' Zayn roared.

He lowered his head, and charged, his sword swooping low. Jai leaped away, even as the man barrelled into him, Jai's hilt slamming ineffectually against the great back, before a shoulder took him in the chest and they tumbled to the ground.

Jai felt the man's meaty hands seize his throat, the blade clanging away as they rolled over and over on the ground. His fingers scraped at the man's hands, the world's edges darkening.

It was like plucking at a steel vice. Jai scrabbled for the blade, his hands slapping at the sun-hot rock, finding nothing.

His vision darkened, and above, Jai saw Winter plummeting towards him, the Caelite in pursuit. Then his vision was filled with Zayn's spitting, bulging face.

'Die,' he hissed, leaning close. 'I'm going to enjoy watching you piss, shit and twitch your way to hellfire.'

Jai heard a screech from above, felt Winter siezed in the air, far above. No help coming.

His world shrank, and darkened. Pain, but it was fading. The *world* was fading.

I . . .

I lost.

Chapter 87

Jai's hand flared with pain, as his palm dragged through shards of glass, the remains of a broken vial skittering away.

He choked, and Zayn spat in his face, leaning close and redoubling his grip.

'Easy now,' Zayn whispered, malicious and gleeful. 'Let go, it's okay.'

Jai felt veins pop in his eyes. Gripped a handful of glass, barely feeling the shards embed in his palm. With the last of his strength, he raked Zayn across the face, and was rewarded by a shrill scream.

The vice-like grip around his throat loosened – not fully, but enough – and Jai sucked in a sharp, ragged breath. The world snapped back into a painful clarity, Zayn, face contorted in pain, but still straddling Jai, blood streaming from an eye.

Jai gasped another breath, before a punch knocked his head down into rock. His head lolled, the world spinning once more, pain blossoming across his face, radiating from the back of his skull.

The only respite was that Zayn must have thought the punch enough to allow him to paw at his own face, blood streaming down, dripping upon Jai, clotting hot on his chest. Glass peppered the man's cheeks, and his eye was a mess of blood.

So Jai took advantage and hit back, his blow weak and

ineffectual, but his thumb fishhooked the man's mouth, yanking Zayn's head to the side. Jai used the momentum to wriggle free, taking another punch to the back of his head as he rolled away.

He was in agony, his head on fire, yet he somehow staggered to his feet, turning just in time to grapple with Zayn as the man staggered close, their blades forgotten on the ground as their heads pressed together, their arms hugging tight.

This wasn't even a fight anymore. It was pure survival – animalistic and raw. With that realisation, Jai turned his head to the side, seized a hunk of flesh with his teeth, ripped with savage abandon. Zayn shoved him away, and Jai reeled back, gasping through his bruised throat, trying to catch his balance as he stumbled for the nearest blade.

He snatched it up and kept moving, his steps – like his breathing and vision – unsure, even as Zayn reached the other. Jai cursed momentarily as his hand adjusted to the hilt: for this was Zayn's blade, longer and heavier than his own. Zayn's eye was closed tight, blood running down his face in a rivulet, dripping from the braids of his beard. Jai could feel the glass in his own hand, but he dared not lift it from the hilt to see the damage.

Jai held his two-handed, the weight dragging the tip low. Zayn twirled Jai's, laughing at the lightness of the smaller blade. The crowd, once baying for blood, now watched in rapt attention as the two circled each other, the combatants' blood freely flowing, not in the way of ballads, but in the way of nature – brutal and unpoetic. Jai pushed them out of his mind, watching Zayn. He held the blade like a spear, glad of the extra reach it gave him despite it all.

Zayn was quiet now, blood bubbling from one nostril as he breathed out.

'Yield,' Jai whispered. 'You can still walk away. Nobody will fault you. You lose nothing.'

'Shut your cunt mouth,' Zayn spat.

Jai shook his head, knowing the man would never accept

– knowing, perhaps, that there was no reason *to* accept – and snatching a few more breaths, letting the world settle. Then he stepped forward, raising his blade.

The two staggered close, their swords clashing. The tempo of their duel had evolved. Gone was the frantic pace of the beginning, replaced by a calculating dance where every step and strike mattered. Zayn began to rely on sheer brute force. Each of his blows, though, while formidable, lacked the surgical precision Jai had faced earlier. He swung wide, leaving gaps in his defence that Jai could exploit if he dared.

Jai, however, didn't quite dare. He was sure he'd have but one chance, and so he waited for an opening, taking no risks, giving the blade the respect of distance, never ranging far enough that Zayn could let the blade fall.

Seconds ticked by, feeling more like aeons, but eventually Jai saw something. Moving with the grace of long practice, Jai parried a reckless blow from Zayn and quickly sidestepped, positioning himself for a counter. The moment felt as if it stretched, elongating like the shadow their moving forms cast. And then, with a calculated lunge, Jai struck, his blade gliding past Zayn's defences to score a deep cut across his opponent's chest.

Zayn staggered back, surprised, and Jai pressed forward. He darted forward again, feinting a high strike only to dip low and deliver a swift cut to Zayn's thigh. Then another flick, swifter than the last, sliced across the wrist, starting blood and drawing a guttural roar from the giant.

'Enough,' Jai snapped. 'It's over!'

But Zayn, his pride overwhelming reason, bellowed in rage and dashed forward, his sword swinging from on high. Jai expected this, knowing Zayn could never surrender, and lunged into a sidestep, his blade blazing in the daylight, cutting through air . . . then flesh. A gash appeared in Zayn's side as he stumbled past, just under his ribs.

It was deep. Deep enough, Jai knew, that it hadn't just cut through skin and muscle.

Zayn's blade fell from his fingers, ringing against the rock. The bigger man followed, collapsing to his knees. Jai, forcing a strength that belied his pain and exhaustion, approached his fallen opponent, his blade held steady at Zayn's exposed throat.

The arena was a cacophony, yet through the noise, a clear voice cut through. Sindri's call, tinged with desperation.

'Mercy, Jai! Show mercy!'

'Surrender!' Jai roared into Zayn's face.

The man said nothing, refusing to look at him. He knelt, staring at the ground, blood dripping and sizzling on the hot rock.

'Mercy!'

Yet Jai lifted his sword and swung . . . only for the flat of his blade to knock into the side of Zayn's head with an anti-climactic thud. The man fell, face down. His breath came in snorting snores. Out cold.

'Is this enough for you?' Jai bellowed, turning to the crowd, letting his own blade fall from his glass-studded hand.

If they responded, he didn't hear. The world was swaying, and only now did Jai see the blood flowing freely from his shoulder, the bandage long since fallen away. He staggered, crimson dripping a trail in his wake.

Teji lurked, half-hidden by the crowds that rushed across the arena's edge, men and women eager to congratulate Jai. The man's face was scrunched up like a babe's, even as Nazeem dragged him away, his dark eyes panicked.

Run, you cowards. If I see you again . . .

What he would do, Jai couldn't say; he fell to his knees, the focus that had held him upright receding into blurred vision, the dusted rock of the arena rushing close. He saw faces, felt hands plucking at him, tugging tourniquets tight, plucking glass from his fingers, but recognised no one.

Healing light flashed, both above and nearby. Cool, spreading like ice water, replacing the pain. He could feel a rushing.

'. . . Too much blood,' Feng's voice came, echoing from afar. 'He's going into shock.'

No, Feng. I'm in *shock*.

And then. Finally, blessed silence.

Chapter 88

Jai's consciousness swam back to the surface, the flurry of movement around him slowly coming into focus. He was sitting in his throne, Winter's head in his lap, lapping the dried blood from his fingers.

He felt no pain, only a lingering . . . what would he call it? Weakness? It seemed little time had passed, for the black cloud that infected his body, and stilled the mana in his core, remained.

Indeed, Jai was in his own tent, the room arrayed as it had been the night before, Kidara rushing to carry thrones, furs and the banners of each house into the chamber. It seemed the khans of the Sithia waited for no man, even the one that had just fought to unite them.

Absent was the Tejinder throne, and Jai could see Feng instructing servants to leave a space.

'—Remind them of his failure,' Feng said. 'Wider. Wider I said!'

He looked up, as if feeling Jai's gaze upon him, and hurried to Jai's side.

'You're awake,' he said. 'Kiran said you would return to us soon. Forgive me – there was not time.'

Jai nodded slowly, feeling his senses find their way back to the fore. He gestured to the thrones quizzically, his throat too parched to speak.

'The smaller tribes say they will leave before sunset,' he said. 'There is word that the legion marches this way, and many lose their nerve. We dared not wait.'

Jai nodded slowly, taking a gourd of rosewater offered him by a nearby Kidaran servant, dashing it over his sweaty body. Now that he was awake, others rushed forward, only for a warning growl from Winter to send them scampering back.

The dragon looked up at him, and gave a snort that told Jai he was not to be forgiven in a hurry. It appeared her clash with the roqs had left her none the worse, though there was a scratch along her snout that had not been there before.

He stroked it, wishing he had use of his mana to heal her. Her eyes gazed up at him, a dull sense of concern drifting down their muted connection. Jai kissed her snout, sending her all the love he could muster.

But there was work to be done, and he could still see the blood that caked his fingernails. Jai coughed, and took a proffered wet cloth, using it to wipe the worst of the grime and blood from his face and arms. His hand was dotted with fresh scars, where the glass had dug into his palm. He felt like some small fragments remained within, sharp and painful, healed over by the spell.

He would dig them out later. Later . . . what came later? His mind was dull.

'My khan,' Feng said, motioning behind the throne. 'We have your vestments here for you. There is time yet to dress.'

Jai waved away the suggestion.

'Let them witness the warrior, not the royal,' he muttered, his voice hoarse. 'They have more need of the former.'

He closed his eyes, tried to think.

'Where is Teji?' Jai asked.

'Gone, my khan,' Feng said. 'Nazeem and some small number of his nobles and liegemen with him. They and some Tainted mercenaries, members of Nazeem's former tribe. Teji took all he could carry, but the treasury remains intact. And he has Zayn too.'

Jai sucked in a breath.

'How many fresh khiroi do I now command?'

'A moment, my khan.'

Feng's feet thudded away, a whispered conversation that Jai would have usually heard, were the mana not sealed within his core. But it was slow fading, and already a trickle of mana was bringing him back to his senses. He straightened his back, and took another swig of water.

The thrones were crowding close now, far more than the last meeting.

'From the Tejinder we have gained two hundred mercenaries,' Feng said, hurrying back. 'And another hundred former Kidara. Their mounts are either the poor stock we gave them or fresh caught from the wild, no breeding at all. But in all, more than a thousand riders under your rule alone. No other tribe commands such a force.'

'Make sure these so-called Tejinder are treated well,' Jai said, leaning close. 'Harleen will see that there's no bad blood, now our brothers have returned. Have Sindri invite the Tainted mercenaries to join the tribe, and pay them whatever Teji owes.'

Feng bowed. No argument now, it seemed. Jai had proved himself to more than just the khans of the steppe.

'Your will, khan,' Feng said.

After all he'd done, it was a simple duel that confirmed his place.

This is a world of violence, he thought, and hated the truth of it.

Jai longed for a kind word from his vizier. But that was not the life of royalty, of khans immemorial. Friends would never be equals. Only family . . . and he had none.

'Where are the Caelite?' Jai asked. 'Where is Erica?'

Feng shook his head.

'The Caelite claim they have said their piece. They will protect the innocent, nothing more.'

Jai cursed, but knew he should not push his luck. In the end, they had given them what he needed. He could wage war against the legion without his soldiers worrying about the Gryphon Guard running rampant across the steppe, slaughtering at will. No more would innocents suffer.

'And Erica?' Jai asked.

'She did not wish to intrude, she said—'

'That's all of them!' one of the servants called.

'Sire,' Feng said. 'We should not tarry.'

Jai sighed, but lifted Winter's head from his lap. She sat straight, and readied herself, unfurling her wings in a grand display.

'Send them in,' Jai said.

Feng gave the command, the partition of the tent thrown back, men and women pouring through. Many took halting steps as they entered, transfixed by the sight of the bloodied Jai, his dragon casting shadows from the fire in the hearth behind.

Now as many as thirty khans took their places, their viziers perched in awkward stances, crowded by the many thrones. These new ones, further away from the main table, were less grand in design, many made of simple bamboo, some no more than a saddle mounted upon a wooden block.

These were the smaller tribes, those who had no sooner arrived than wished to leave, thanks to the legion in supposed pursuit. But they were here now, because of him, and that was all he could ask for at the moment.

Looking at the table, Jai saw Feng had laid out in clear detail their position. The legion was no longer moving east. Indeed, the meeting of the many tribes had changed their direction, if they had caught wind of the council. Not west . . . but south.

Jai pondered this, as the khans took their places, some jostling for position, scraping their thrones closer, others complaining their positioning was not proportionate to their importance.

A fist slammed upon the table silenced them – Tenzin's. Jai nodded to the man, then stood . . . and spoke.

'There will be no ceremony today,' Jai said. 'You only need hear one name spoken – mine. I am Jai, son of Rohan. I have done what has been asked of me, and you know what I am here to ask of you.'

He let the words settle, sweeping his gaze, meeting their stares with one of his own.

'I was raised a captive in the court of our enemies, learning at their greatest general's feet. I have proven the rumours false through my duel – I did *not* kill Leonid. Rather, I was there when Titus spilled my brothers' blood, and in turn, that of his own lineage. All for a war of vanity.'

Now Jai heard the anger among the khans, whispered curses, dark glances. They believed him. He could feel it.

'I stole a dragon in my escape, and was hunted the breadth of the empire until I was fettered in the great prison of Porticus. Even then, my resolve would not be broken.'

He leaned over the table, knuckling it with his fists.

'I broke out with new allies, the Dansk's queen and Huddite warriors, men who will rally their brethren to our cause. Even now, the Dansk pledge their dragons to come to our aid, should the Gryphon Guard return to our skies. These dragons are more than up to the challenge. I myself have killed a gryphon and its knight.'

Fresh whispers now, from those who hadn't been in the tent during the first council, but Jai ignored them, raising his voice above.

'I climbed the Yaltai's highest peak, and joined the sect of the Caelite, as my father once did. They will protect our tribes when our armies ride to war. Now I return to you, my people, to continue my father's legacy. We will drive these legions from our borders, and ride on, into the heart of their rotten empire!'

Voices, raised in agreement, fists thudding upon armrests, feet stamping on fur-clad rock.

'Fifty. Thousand!' a voice bellowed.

Jai saw Hari, standing upon his throne, his hand raised for silence. It came, and Jai allowed him to speak, for to try to hide this truth would be seen as weakness.

'That is how many legionaries march in the Northern Tundra, right now,' Hari said, stabbing a finger to the west. 'And when they're done with the Dansk, they'll march on us. This warmonger seeks only revenge, for his brothers, for his father, for himself. Do not be dragged into his vendetta. We must sue for peace!'

Applause, at first hesitant, then louder, as Hari nodded, smiling, before gesturing at Jai.

'He is young,' Hari said. 'No man here doubts he is a warrior born. But he will not be the one riding his khiro into a line of glittering steel. He'll be flying above on his pretty dragon.'

'Enough!' Jai said. 'All may speak at this council, but I will not be insulted in my own tent.'

Hari bowed. 'My apologies, khan,' he said, his voice slick with sarcasm. 'I seek only to speak the truth. Tell me, have I lied?'

'Tell *me*, do you not distort the truth? Do you really dare to suggest in the presence of your equals that I am afraid to get my hands bloody?'

He spread his hands flat across the table, where blood remained beneath the nails, and caked the soft hair of his arms. Hari looked away, cowed.

'I thought not,' Jai said, disgusted. 'How many men can the gathered tribes muster?' he asked, leaning close to Feng.

Feng chewed his lip, calculating, before saying, 'Ten thousand. Perhaps five thousand more eventually, but it would take time to break the khiroi, forge the weapons.'

He took in that information, and then addressed those gathered once more. 'Hari indeed speaks the truth about one thing,' Jai said. 'Though the legion that marches our lands is only five thousand, ten times more may follow. But it is for this very reason that we must fight!'

His words were met with worried glances, viziers once again leaning in, their whispers stirring the air.

'We are fifteen thousand riders,' Jai called out, his voice settling the room to a low buzz.

'Fifteen thousand cannot defeat fifty,' Hari said, nodding sagely. 'That is more than three times as many. So it is decided. Let us send an envoy to the legion that marches on us.'

'It is enlightening to see you know your numbers,' Jai said, and Hari flushed. 'Do your calculations take into account that they are on foot in the Great Steppe, then, while we ride the mighty khiroi and are born of this very land? Of course they don't,' he said, dismissing the man. 'Even as you again obfuscate the truth.'

'How so?' Hari dared ask.

'In that they do not march on us,' Jai snapped. 'They run for the Kashmere Road to the south. They will seek reinforcements, or retreat back home.'

'Then our job is already done!' Hari called as if in victory. 'Let us wait, and see how the Dansk war fares.'

It was disheartening, the murmurs of agreement, scared men and women already shifting in their seats, looking to the door.

'Wait for them to bolster their ranks? Let them escape when we can finish this before it starts?' Jai looked around the table, pinning to their chairs those that were growing restless. 'Most of these legions are untested, green boys from the fields. Would you place such a child above a Kidaran knight?'

'You should know more than anyone that the Sabine war machine is the single greatest force in the world today,' Hari said, seeming to gain confidence once more and preaching to the crowd around him. 'Or are you so foolish as to forget the lesson your father never learned.'

Jai had to resist the urge to strike the smug man, whose eyes gleamed with a light that told Jai he was goading him. Whatever the outcome of the duel, Hari was still Teji's man. And still a khan in his own right – the fact that he hadn't been challenged by the members of his tribe spoke of something that kept them loyal and in line.

He spoke like a fool, but he still had power. Just as Teji did. So just like with Teji, Jai needed to take down this man.

'How quickly your word changes, Hari,' Jai said. 'Last night, you agreed we would war against the Sabines if I won my duel. Now you go back to begging surrender.'

'I said no such thing!' Hari cried, turning to the khans around him. 'Did you agree to such a thing? Why, the boy thinks himself High Khan!'

'We were not there,' a lesser khan called. 'The Great Tribes do not speak for us. We have chosen no High Khan.'

'And why not?' Jai demanded. 'Am I not my father's son?'

Shouts of agreement, angry khans standing, stabbing fingers in Jai's direction.

'We can beat them,' Jai said, his voice near lost in the din. 'Titus is no Leonid.'

'Prove it, then!'

Jai turned, for it was the booming voice of Tenzin that had spoken. The big man got up, towering tall even beside those standing upon their thrones. The leader of the mammoth-riding tribe commanded respect, and even Hari fell silent under his dark gaze.

'To become High Khan of all the Sithia is no small thing,' Tenzin said, his voice low and serious. 'You have achieved much, Jai, but you are a young man still. One with blood hot for battle.'

'You were the one that—'

Tenzin held up his palms in peace, and Jai bit his tongue.

'You command an army of one thousand, against the legion's five,' Tenzin said. 'With a few hundred more men, you'll match the odds we might face in this war.'

Jai did not like where this was going, but he had no way of changing things.

'What of it?' Jai asked.

'If such odds can be beaten, then prove it. Prove yourself worthy to be our High Khan. Lead your army against this legion. Give us such a victory that will strike fear into the hearts of our enemies, and make them dread the day they set foot on our lands again.'

Jai stuttered, even as the khans began to bang their fists and stomp once more, calling out support for the plan.

'You want me to fight your battle for you alone?' Jai asked, sweeping a stabbed finger across the arrayed khans. 'While you hide like cowards far from harm, under the protection of the Caelite that I myself secured for you?'

The khans avoided his gaze, their shame evident. That was exactly what they wanted.

'Oh, I wouldn't say alone,' Tenzin chuckled. 'You'll still need another . . . what, five hundred warriors?'

He thumped his chest.

'The Mahmut tribe rides with the Kidara, now and hereafter. Any who wishes to join us can.'

Jai stared, his grip on the meeting fast unravelling.

'Know this,' Tenzin growled to the others. 'You are to prepare for war. Sharpen your blades, wean the calves and tighten your lassos. When you hear of our victory, you will answer the call, to your new High Khan. Or we'll come back and take your tribe for ourselves, mark me!'

He glowered at the khans around him, then turned, and winked at Jai, as if he'd somehow won Jai some great victory. Jai was speechless.

'Swear it now,' Tenzin growled. 'You first, Hari.'

Hari paled, clambering down from his perch. Jai could see the fear in the man's eyes. He was scared of the Sabines, of their legions. But it seemed the idea of the combined might of the Kidara and Mahmut tribes riding him down seemed all the more real, here and now.

'Hari!' Tenzin roared.

'All right,' he snapped. 'I swear it. High Khan, if such a victory is possible.'

More murmurs came, half-hearted, none spoken in loud voice. But Tenzin was undaunted, staring down each khan until he had verbal confirmation from everyone.

'It is agreed,' Tenzin said, finally nodding.

'Anything else, Khan Jai?' Tenzin asked, turning back to him.

Jai gulped. He had not had time to think, to plan. He had expected to lead a great army to crush the invading legion. Instead, he would be fighting a battle with a force smaller than he anticipated . . . and he did not yet know how to win.

Still, with his mind racing, he beckoned Feng closer, keenly aware of the gazes of the rest of the khans, boring into him.

'Pretend I'm talking to you,' Jai whispered. 'I need time to think.'

Feng murmured, 'Aye, my khan. Then . . . I will think also.'

They stood this way for a few heartbeats, enough for Jai to contemplate his next move. Finally, something clicked, and he turned to the khans.

'If I am to fight for you, I will need your blacksmiths, and steel.'

'They will give it,' Tenzin assured, brooking no refusals. 'I'll make sure of it.'

'They will not give khiroi or their weapons,' Feng hissed. 'What else?'

'I want all the spare bamboo, and any pelts for leathers, too,' Jai called.

'That too,' Tenzin said, daring the khans to dissent. None did. Indeed, many of their faces were a picture of relief.

'Swear it,' Jai said.

'Go on,' Tenzin barked. 'Swear now, in the sight of the Mother's eye.'

'I swear.' The response was weak, but Tenzin once again glared until all had spoken.

Jai nodded, slowly. There was no changing this. Their path was set.

'So be it,' he said. 'Join us, if your conscience allows. Tenzin and I march at first light.'

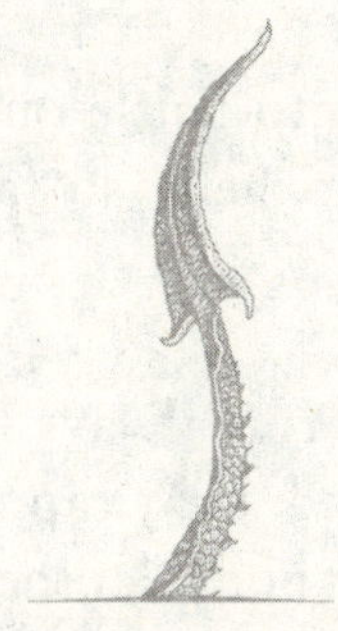

Chapter 89

Jai sat upon the mesa's edge, staring out at the many tribes, moving away into the depths of the grasslands once more. He could make out the humped backs of the mammoths far beneath him, the strange, trumpeting calls of his new allies' mounts small relief to the growing worries that pervaded his thoughts.

Just once, he wished time would stop, and he might catch his breath. But the world slowed for no man, and he knew that no sooner did his head hit his pillow then the morning sun would come, and with it the troubles of the morrow.

So he sat, letting mana stave off his exhaustion, watching the sun set. His freshly healed hands were still pink with scars. In time, they too would fade.

'You should be celebrating,' Erica said.

Jai turned to see her dismounting from Regin. He'd been so deep in thought, he'd not heard her arrive. No sooner did she leap down, Regin was off once more, making a beeline to where Winter glided on the wind above, still sulking after Jai's near brush with death.

'Celebrate what?' Jai said, forcing a smile.

'You got your tribe back,' she said, sitting close, and laying her head on his shoulder. 'All of them.'

Jai sighed, turning and kissing her forehead.

'Only to throw them into battle once more,' Jai said. 'With only the Mahmut tribe to help, so far. We'll know who else tomorrow.'

She shrugged.

'You'll win,' she said. 'You always find a way.'

Erica shifted closer, and Jai wrapped his arm around her, letting the softness of her body soothe his weary soul.

'I'm worried,' Jai said. 'My new bodyguard of soulbound won't be much use against the Gryphon Guard if the bastards keep to the skies . . . and I cannot cede them that space, lest they rain fire upon my soldiers. But Winter cannot take on three alone.'

She looked at him, understanding, but also with refusal. 'I can't stay,' she said. 'My people need me. I've already tarried far too long. If the Caelite would accompany me sooner . . . I'd already be gone.'

'I would not ask you,' he said. 'I could keep my distance,' he then mused. 'Stick to the clouds. But then I won't be able to command the battle.'

She chewed her soft lip before her eyes widened.

'What?' he asked.

'Better they were not there at all,' she breathed. Erica turned to him, seizing his shoulders. 'How long until you battle with them?'

Jai furrowed his brow. 'Ten days, maybe more,' he said, confused. 'Why?'

'Then nine days from now, I will send a raiding party to lay siege to Porticus,' Erica said. 'Free whatever fettered remain there. With any luck, the men there will send word for the Gryphon Guard to help – they're closest after all. My dragons will hide in the mountains, ambush them when they arrive.'

Jai stared before breaking into a grin.

'You would do that?'

She grinned back. 'It's a sound strategy – don't think yourself special.'

He leaned forward and kissed her. She kissed him back, softer than before, then pulled away.

'We . . . this is why we can't do this again,' she breathed, pressing her hand against his chest. 'For all that I want to.'

Jai let out a breath he had not realised he'd been holding and pulled her close into a hug.

'Okay,' Jai said. 'We will stop . . . just not tonight.'

She grasped his face, and kissed him, her tongue flicking between his lips. Jai stood and pulled her to her feet, back to where his tent lay, at the centre of the mesa.

'Come on,' Jai said. 'It's early yet. Let's make the most of the time we have left.'

ERICA WAS GONE WHEN Jai awoke. All that remained was the indent of her head upon a pillow, and at its centre, a lock of hair, bound like a bundle of thread. He gathered it close and breathed in her scent, wishing he could turn back time, and relive the night all over again.

Instead, he rose, glad the black that had enveloped his core was gone. He used some mana to shake off the aches of the morning, and walked through the partition to the outer chamber. There, tired servants waited for him, apparently having stood all morning to attend to him.

He apologised and let them ready him for the day, wishing for a long, hot bath but making do with the warm, damp flannels they rubbed him up and down with.

Winter was flying alongside Regin, accompanying Erica and the Caelite as they flew north-west, where they would hug the edge of the Yaltai Mountains until it met the Petrus. Jai did not deny her this simple pleasure. For Winter too was bidding farewell to a lover.

Soon enough, he was ready enough to leave the tent, and it was just as well – the servants were dismantling it even as his hair was being oiled, perfumed and combed.

His Small Council were waiting for him, hovering like cats

at a fisherman's doorstep. He called for silence and walked on, down the steps. It was time to be away from this place.

As he stomped down the steps, his nobles hot on his heels, Feng hovered at his elbow, muttering what he thought Jai needed to know.

'—stripped the Mesa of all the bamboo it has, and more besides. Our army won't want for—'

Harleen's voice cut him off.

'—blacksmiths have been set to work, we'll have a falx apiece by the week's end. What—'

'Who commands the Tainted? We need—' Sindri said.

Jai stopped, and turned.

'Can I have one minute of quiet, please!' he demanded.

They fell silent.

He took a deep breath. 'I'm sorry – it's just . . . I trust you to do your jobs. Now let me do mine.'

They nodded and they walked the rest of the way in relative silence. At the bottom, in the dappled shadows of the trees, Jai turned back to them, regretting his outburst.

'I know there are a hundred decisions to make, and not much time to make them in,' Jai said. 'As I said, I trust your judgement. You know that we march for war. Know this too – we leave our people here, where the Caelite can watch over them when they return from escorting Erica. But I want every man and woman who wishes to fight and is worthy of holding a blade to come with us, whether they have khiroi to ride or not. We are not fighting another tribe now, we are fighting infantry. That means we may need foot soldiers of our own. We can ride two men to a knight, or sledges if we have to. If it takes us a few more days to catch up to the legion, no matter.'

'It will be done, my khan,' Feng said.

'I want you to write me a report, Feng, of all I need to know,' Jai said. 'Right now, I need to see what our new allies bring to the table. Make your preparations, and be ready to ride before the sun begins its descent.'

There was a chorus of assent, and then they were hurrying away, leaving Jai alone in the jungle, the air stirring with the birdsong that accompanied the morning.

He oriented himself to where he had seen the mammoths the night before. Tenzin had played him like a fiddle that night. Beneath the gruff, bluff exterior, the man was a shrewd tactician. Yet he'd still thrown in his lot with Jai, even sworn everlasting alliance.

The man was an enigma, and Jai intended to solve it.

'OUR WARRIOR RETURNS,' TENZIN bellowed, as Jai trudged into their camp.

The Mahmut cheered at the big man's words as the Mahmut khan stomped past the enormous tents scattered at the edge of the oasis, seizing Jai's hand in his enormous mitt and shaking it.

'Is that not how they do it in Latium?' he chuckled.

Jai withdrew his hand, and shook his head.

'I am no Sabine,' he said.

Tenzin's grin softened a little, and he pulled Jai aside.

'Come,' he said. 'There is much to discuss.'

It had taken a while for Jai to make his way around the enormous mesa, and already the Mahmut were preparing for their march. Tenzin guided Jai into the tall grass, pushing ahead to where the Mahmut's mammoths were gathered.

Jai had only seen a mammoth once in his life, and it had been a thin, sickly thing, goaded to death with spears by Constantine's prized gladiators in the capital city's Colosseum. More often, their elephantine cousins were seen in Latium, from the Shambalai region in the empire's southern reaches.

These were different beasts entirely. They towered at ten feet at least, with long yellow tusks stretching out ahead of them, like the great ribs of a whale. Instead of saddles upon their backs, there were baskets, upon which several men and women sat.

Stranger still were their weapons. For enormous pikes were strapped to their sides, so long as to be impractical in any other circumstance. But Jai could imagine the men and women leaning out and stabbing them down like bargepoles.

Others had bows in their hands, the first Jai had seen in the Great Steppe. It seemed that it was more the mammoths themselves that did the fighting, and as they approached the largest of them, one that stood twelve feet in height, its great trunk reached out, running its soft grasping tip over his face like a blind man might.

'My girl,' Tenzin said. 'Munnar. She begot half the mammoths we have here.'

He smiled and rubbed her trunk, stroking the orange-red fur that coated it.

'She's a good judge of character,' Tenzin said. 'The best. Except for me of course.'

He brought his face closer to Jai's, and smiled at him through his beard.

'I rode with your father,' he said. 'I broke the walls of Leonid's camp, and helped drive him back to his homeland. I was there in the final battle, when Rohan fell from his Alkhara. And I was there when Teji negotiated our surrender, and condemned my brothers, my cousins, to a life in fetters.' He sighed, and laid a hand on Jai's shoulder. 'What I did last night, I did in your father's memory.'

Jai shook his head. 'You have a strange way of showing it.'

'Don't you see, Jai? The ones who want to fight have stayed. Smaller tribes, true, but this is all you were ever going to get. More, even.'

Tenzin pulled Jai aside.

'See, they wait there.' He pointed at a group of men and women, many of them far older than he'd expected. But none looked like a khan, for most were dressed no better than the Valor once had.

'Old allies of your father,' Tenzin said, beckoning them closer. 'Some of them once led Great Tribes of their own. Now . . .'

He trailed off as the khans approached.

'Jasdeep, my khan,' one of them said, bowing arm in arm with a man who looked his twin. 'I rule with my brother, Rajdeep. Our sister was queen of the Cimmer tribe.'

'Welcome,' Jai whispered, returning their bow.

'Simran,' said another, a woman with grey streaks in her beard, and old armour covered in a patchwork of where it had been repaired. 'I served with your father.'

Jai greeted each in turn, as more still introduced themselves, each more ragged than the next. Some even were Tainted tribes, eager to join the Kidara under his banner. None had more than a score of khiroi under their command, but together they bolstered his cavalry by almost two hundred. He tried to remember each name.

'You will be well rewarded for your show of loyalty,' Jai said, grasping their hands, and meeting their eyes. 'But please, do not wait here on my account. There is much to do, and little time to do it in. In time, we will talk – you ride with me at the head of our army.'

They thanked him and dispersed, their haste telling Jai he had been right to dismiss them. Soon, Jai and Tenzin were alone once more.

'How did you know?' Jai demanded. 'That these were the only ones that would have joined me.'

Tenzin looked him in the eyes, his jaw set.

'I know,' he said. 'Those khans are cowards all. This was going one way – a vote. One you were going to lose. But now, they've sworn an oath to raise you to High Khan. Then they'll have no choice but to follow.'

'Just need to defeat a legion to do it,' Jai said. 'Outnumbered three to one.'

'Depends how you look at it,' Tenzin said. 'I've got thirty battle mammoths that'll make those Sabine farmers' sons shit their skirts.'

He grinned, and Jai could not help but meet it with a weak smile.

'How many legionaries did you say a Kidaran knight was worth again?' Tenzin winked.

He clapped Jai's shoulder, and stepped up into a trail of rope loops that encircled the mammoth's body.

'Come, ride with me,' he said. 'You'll find it more comfortable than that dragon's back, I'll wager.'

Jai followed, clambering up the hairy side, the ribs expanding and contracting with each breath of the strange beast.

'Are you soulbound?' Jai asked, as he half-fell into the basket, finding the inside lined with a pelt of the same orange fur, a surprisingly comfortable seat.

'Me and all the rest, one for every mammoth,' Tenzin replied, clucking his tongue to set Munnar on her way. 'Mammoths are not like your khiroi. They are wild beasts, impossible to tame without the meld to keep them on side.'

Jai shook his head, incredulous. That was thirty soulbound warriors.

'Don't get too excited,' Tenzin chuckled. 'Most of them can hardly spark enough of a flame to set a fire. Only I and my two sons are ascended.'

Jai tried not to let his disappointment show, instead letting his eyes stray across the grasslands, to where his own tribe prepared for the fight ahead.

'I've said my goodbyes,' Tenzin said. 'My men are ready. Look, your warriors gather for the march as well. Let us join them.'

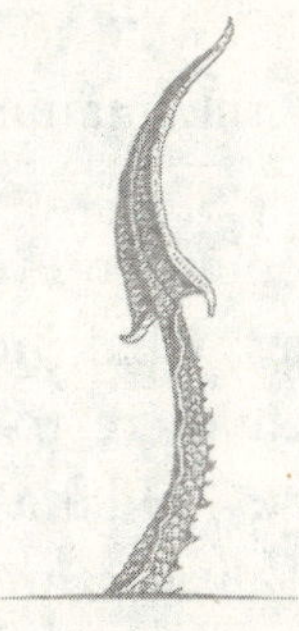

Chapter 90

Sweet hope. I taste it.

The Petrus Mountains are in sight, and the enemy fall away. But the rumours of sedition spread. An empire is a fragile thing. This force is not the total of my armies, for they are spread in garrisons across my lands. But three legions, battered though they are, could march on Latium itself, and seize power for themselves.

The return of our baggage trains has been sweet relief, and we eat like kings. Rohan dares not raid them so close to the fringes of my empire. But the damage is done. The men still remember the hunger. The long, hard marches. The slaughter, and retreat.

Gold no longer moves the centurions. Each man, legionaries included, will leave this place a rich man, yet so too does gold breed delusions of grandeur. I know the ones who plot, yet I dare not move on them yet.

They made camp before the sun set, for they had made good progress. A tribe had followed this path to reach the High Council in the days past, so the grass was still low and manageable for the mammoths and khiroi as they stomped across the Great Steppe.

Above, Winter flew, keeping an eye out for Gryphon Guard. And beneath Jai's haunches, Chak lumbered.

For Zayn had not been there to claim the great Alkhara, when the Tejinder and the Keldar's herds had been reunited, and Teji and Nazeem had disappeared into the night.

Jai only wished Navi was there to accompany her old friend. But Feng was elsewhere, busy overseeing their supplies.

'I've never seen a force like it,' Harleen said, breaking into Jai's thoughts.

He rode with his nobles, and along with Tenzin, they surveyed their troops.

Thirty battle mammoths led the way, their tusks now capped with barbed steel spikes, and squares of beaten metal in makeshift chain mail draped down their sides.

But the true bulk of the army lay behind.

A thousand and two hundred mounted khiroi warriors. Most were armed with a blade, and Feng had seen to it that the blacksmiths' forges would blow all through the night as more were made for the battle to come.

Some were Tainted, some were not, but Jai could hardly distinguish between the two, for the traders had walked away rich in coin from Jai's new treasury. The blue fabric of Jai's house was emblazoned throughout, even if some wore a simple swathe of it across their chests.

Only the smaller tribes stood apart, some two hundred in array of their own colours, even a handful of riteless who wished to fight the Sabines alongside them.

Behind these khiroi, five hundred men and women rested, volunteers from the Kidara and the other, smaller tribes' citizenry. The infantry, if Jai could call them that. These there had been little time to arm and clothe, and they were a motley crew with an assortment of weapons ranging from wooden clubs to falx blades of their own.

Among them were the Huddites, brought by the terror birds some nights before, along with a few countrymen they had found among the flock. Only fifty soldiers, but Jai was grateful to them. For while the citizenry could hardly wield a blade, the Huddites had fought much as the Sabines did, and even now they trained the remaining infantry to hold a shield wall. Even if the shields themselves were hastily made of flattened bamboo and a single layer of leather.

They would not last long against a trained legion, inexperienced though their enemy may be. But Jai was not sure he needed them for that.

'Your bows,' Jai said, leaning forward in his saddle and patting Chak's neck. 'Are they easy to make?'

Tenzin grunted.

'Not easy to make what we use, but my men can make a poor imitation fairly quickly. Why?'

Jai chewed his lip, staring at the five hundred.

'You know of the testudo formation,' Jai asked. 'Leonid's invention that brought victory over the bow-folk of Shambalai?'

'We faced it, in the old days,' Tenzin said. 'A roof of shields. Clever of your mentor.'

Jai nodded.

'Few used bows against the legions after that. But Leonid hated them. He thrived in a fluid battle, moving his formations when needed. The testudo takes its name from the turtle, not just because of the steel shell it mimics, but the slow pace of its namesake. It fixed his men in position, kept them in tight formation. He had to rely on his cavalry. This legion has none.'

'Sure enough,' Tenzin said. 'But we face not a turtle, but a porcupine too. There will be an array of pikes to breach, whether they can manoeuvre or not.'

'Let me worry about that. Have your men train the infantry to pull a bow. There's bamboo and steel enough for that.'

'I'll make it happen,' Tenzin said.

Now Jai called over Sindri and Harleen, the pair of whom Jai had made generals of their respective peoples. Though he loathed to keep the Tainted and untainted separate, each had their own way of doing things, their own brothers and sisters in arms, and he would not have time yet to teach them to fight as one people.

'If the legion is marching south, they know of our High Council,' Jai said. 'They fear us, seek the safety of the road. But they cannot know the army that now pursues them is but a fraction of those that gathered at the Mother's eye.'

'We are the lone hound hunting a fox,' Sindri said, sagely. 'It runs, hearing only the barking.'

'And I would bark all the louder,' Jai said. 'Tonight, I need every man and woman to set five campfires. And set up our spare pelts with bamboo, as if they were tents, beside them.'

'To what end, my khan?' Harleen asked. 'Our people are weary enough.'

Jai pointed to the empty skies.

'The Gryphon Guard know we're coming. But they dare not come near in daylight – not after Erica and I ambushed them, with Winter flying above. But they will haunt our camp at night, to glean all they can. So we set the fires. Let them think we have five times our number. Let the boys shake in their beds, and fear what lurks in the shadows.'

Harleen bowed her head.

'I shall pass the word. If it pleases you, the blacksmiths say they will have blades enough for our riders. But the infantry . . . they'll have to make do.'

She fell silent, and Jai caught a look upon her face.

'Speak your mind,' Jai said. 'Your opinions mean much to me.'

She gestured at the people.

'We could catch the legion in just a few days, if we cut these so-called infantry loose. Let them return the way they have come. What use have they against ten times their number? They muddy the battle.'

Jai shook his head.

'The Cimmer charged the legion with their khiroi alone, and

not a single warrior returned to tell the tale. Would we have won the battle against the Tejinder were it not for our infantry, without a drop of blood spilled?'

Harleen looked away.

'Sometimes, the old ways are better,' she said.

Jai pointed at his blade in response, though. 'The art of Talvir is not for petty duels between rivals alone, or when a knight falls from their khiro. It was meant to be used in battle, on foot. It is an ancient art, passed on from a time before our peoples tamed the first khiroi, and drank of their blood and milk. A warrior is more than the khiro they ride.'

'They are not warriors,' Harleen insisted. 'They are citizens.'

'And that is why I will not ask them to fight,' Jai said. 'Only use their bows.'

Harleen spat off to the side, warding off evil.

'These are not little toys to push about a map,' she said. 'No good will come of it.'

'I assure—

'I will make the fires – the hour grows late.'

She kicked her heels, lost in the sea of waiting riders, still on parade for the nobles.

'Forgive her, khan,' Sindri said. 'It has been no small thing, bringing the Tejinder back into the fold. Her authority is questioned and you . . . you have left it all to her.'

Jai cursed, and signalled the order for the cavalry to dismount and return to their campfires. Already, he could see Harleen spreading the word, men and women carrying glowing embers to start small fires elsewhere.

'Her heart is in the right place,' Jai said. 'Before you rest, find Feng, have him send the Tejinder nobles to my tent. I will have them swear the blood oath, and make clear Harleen's word is law. Make sure Priya is among them – I heard she's abandoned Teji. Have you any troubles with the Tainted?'

Sindri shook her head, and gave him a forced smile.

'Nothing I can't handle. Devin and Anita have lent me their

support, and the rest fell in line. They are glad to call themselves Kidaran – you have made quite a name for yourself among our people. Beating Zayn didn't hurt.'

Jai grinned, even as Winter caught his intention and swooped low, soldiers cheering as she swept overhead.

Enough. Time to fly the skies with Winter. See what lay ahead.

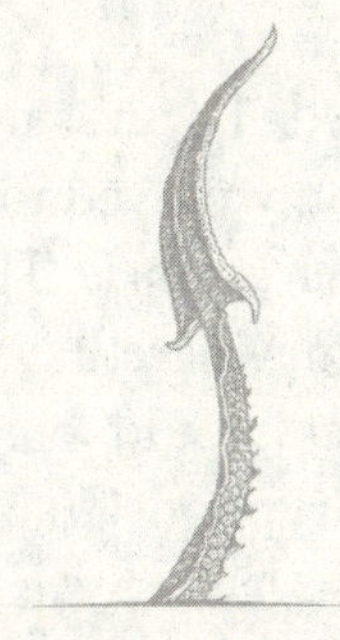

Chapter 91

This is a battle for the hearts and minds of the rank and file. And if gold will not settle them, then perhaps a taste of home will. It is an old trick of the corsairs of Damantine, to pull into port and seek out the cathouses there when whispers of mutiny are heard.

So I will bring the cathouse here. Let them get a taste of my so-called fabled whorehouse. I have called for the courtesans of the eastern territories. And I confess, I too miss the comforts of home.

I miss my loved ones. So I send for Miranda, my port in the storm. Her mother will come too – they will feel at home among the courtesans, and when they arrive, they can move into my tent. I will triple the guard on that baggage train, so her delivery will be assured. I miss her kind caresses, for she cares for these aging bones.

Now, I count the days. They cannot come soon enough.

In the days that followed, Jai saw no Gryphon Guard as he patrolled the skies. He only prayed they had seen the fires, and that Erica would keep her promise. The nights came, and went.

And Jai prayed that somewhere, far to the west, a dove with a note attached to its feet would be winging its way to the legion, there to call the Gryphon Guard for aid.

Even so, the path of the legion was clear, and each day, the grass grew shorter, the scent of it stronger until it pervaded Jai's very dreams. For the legion did not trample it underfoot, but clear cut it with their blades, leaving a wide swathe of devastation.

Jai found it hard to read beyond the pages where his mother's name was mentioned. It was why he had avoided visiting her grave, back at the Blue Mesa. He hadn't earned it yet.

To learn she had been Leonid's favoured courtesan was painful. That the old man had known his mother in that way . . . it made him wonder if she had been to the palace. If she had once frequented the very bedchamber he had grown up in.

Leonid had lied to him. Never mentioned Jai's mother, not once. Perhaps he did not know. Even Jai had not known, after all.

The writings were becoming more infrequent, scattered with the detritus of administrative notes, battle plans, sketches and philosophical ramblings. They were coming to a close, and Jai had realised the diary was incomplete. It seemed Leonid had ended the diary on the return from his expedition, and there was no accounting of his great loss against Jai's father, and the final battle that came some months after.

Jai wished it did. For he could use every clue he could glean from the battles past. For his own was soon to come.

Winter saw the dustcloud first, yawping with excitement, her body shuddering beneath Jai's thighs. A yellow haze on the horizon, growing larger by the hour, until at last they saw the shimmering silver stain beneath.

Yet the sun was fast setting, and Jai knew that soon, they would make camp. And he had no desire to siege one. He knew from Leonid's diary where that ended.

'We ride!' Jai cried out, as Winter swooped down to within earshot of his generals. 'Before their walls are raised!'

Jai kept Winter low, grass whipping beneath her belly as they glided at their head, the khiroi rampaging behind, their low moans and grunts accompanied by the yips and cries of his riders.

With the setting sun casting long, dark shadows over the plain, the gleam of the legion's armour was the only beacon that guided them. He could see the enemy now, individual figures, hastening to form ranks against the coming onslaught, moved by the dull booms of Sabine war drums and the brassy notes of the cornu.

The once-disciplined march was fast becoming a hasty scramble. Banners flapped wildly, the lion and eagle emblems barely distinguishable in the dim light.

'Ride on!' Jai roared, drawing his blade. 'Form up! Form up!'

Winter echoed his cries, her roars reverberating across the open plains, echoed by the war cries of those that followed.

Could it be? Had they caught the legion unawares?

Riders behind Jai echoed his call, signalling the horde to tighten their ranks, preparing for impact. Winter's wings beat hard, the gusts flattening the grass below. The distance closed rapidly.

The legion's centurions shouted orders, attempting to form a wall of pikes and shields. The front line was an amalgam of young faces, barely old enough to hold the weight of their shields. Among them, Jai could see those that could easily be the kitchen boys of the palace.

As they braced themselves, Jai could see the fear in their eyes, see their chests heaving. These weren't battle-hardened soldiers, they were the youth of Latium, thrust into a war they didn't understand. But they had slaughtered an entire tribe. They were complicit.

A horn sounded, shrill and alarming. The front line of the

legion lowered their pikes, aiming the sharp points at the charging khiroi. Jai cursed.

'Pull away!' he cried, veering Winter sharply to the left. The khiroi, sensing the change, skidded and swerved, some tumbling but most managing to redirect their momentum. His riders followed him, shouting and signalling to others. The charge dispersed, pulling back just a stone's throw from the legion's desperate pike formation.

The expected clash, the clang of metal on metal, and the screams of the dying didn't come. Already, Jai's flag bearer was signalling the retreat. Jai circled back, Winter's wings creaking against the tight turn. Jai guided Winter to land between the two groups, his silhouette cutting a lone figure against the dying light.

Behind him his riders massed for the charge, even as the centurions shuffled their lines straighter, careless of the enemy that stood close enough to shout at.

Finally, the drums halted, the cornu trumpets sputtering to a halt. There was an uneasy silence, save for the panting of the beasts and the soft murmurs of the legion's ranks.

'I do not wish to shed the blood of Latium's sons tonight,' Jai cried out, addressing the silent legion. 'Behind you lies the Kashmere Road, just out of sight. Surrender now, swear to never return and you leave safely.'

Silence. Then a javelin, soaring high above the massed shields, landed woefully short of where Jai sat. Another smattering followed, and Winter reared back, as one spattered mud close by.

Jai had his answer. He signalled the return to his flag bearer, and Winter leaped into the air once more. He flew higher, Winter's wings pumping, until he could see all the legion arrayed, a warped line of silver drawn across the sea of green.

And yet Jai saw as many as five hundred men, separate from the rest behind that line. Most wore little clothing at all, and many held scythes in their hands. These were fettered, brought by the legion to cut their way across the Great Steppe, just as Leonid had used the Huddites, all those years ago. Indeed, Jai would not be surprised if these were Huddites themselves, captives from the battle he had witnessed, all those months ago.

It was shocking to see them here, in this place. They complicated things.

Winter banked her wings, and Jai was glad that the skies were clear, for there was nowhere that the Gryphon Knights might ambush him from above. Indeed, there seemed to be no sign of them, though there were tents and cut poles enough there that they might be hidden.

Jai looked west, and gave a silent thanks to Erica. With any luck, they would not return before the battle was long won.

Now Winter approached his warriors, and Jai could sense her fear, her desire to be upon the ground among friends once more. She too was wary of lurking gryphons, and Jai knew that he had no time to waste. By the morrow, this had to be finished, one way or another.

His own men massed beyond, somehow seeming many more than the legion, spread out and with the bulky forms of the khiroi. Far behind, Jai saw the mammoths, finally catching up to the khiroi, and further still, his infantry, trudging a mile beyond.

Jai hugged Winter's neck close, as they angled down to return, the wind tearing his hair as they swooped towards the ground.

There was much to do. And only one night to do it in.

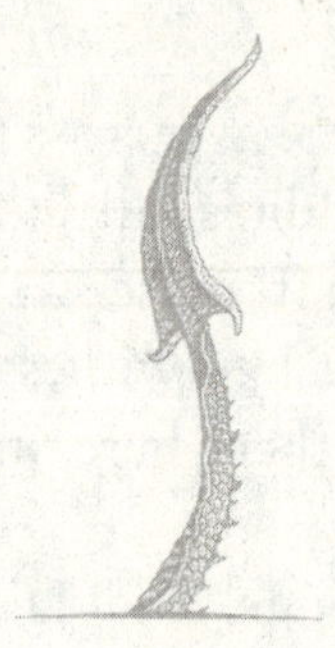

Chapter 92

'We should have met them,' Harleen growled. 'Right there and then, infantry and mammoths be damned.'

'The pikes were lowered,' Jai said. 'It was too late, and I'll hear no more about it.'

Jai and his Small Council were gathered in Jai's small travel tent, looking at the map arrayed in front of them.

'Their pikes will be lowered tomorrow too,' Harleen said. 'And they'll be even further dug in by then.'

Jai sighed, and let his silence draw out, to let them know that was the end of it.

'We know the legion races for the Kashmere Road,' Jai said. 'Now, it is just over the horizon.'

'And we'd have caught them earlier if . . .'

Jai closed his eyes, his exasperation evident, and she trailed off.

'Why do you think I made that speech to them?' Jai asked. 'Do you think I thought for a moment they would surrender?'

Harleen shrugged.

'I wanted them to know where safety lies. It gives them somewhere to run to.'

She looked back, her brows furrowed.

'Imagine, if you will, you are a legionary in the middle of

the Great Steppe. Surrounded by so-called savages that'll skin you alive, drink your blood, take your head.'

His words drew chuckles from the rest.

'Now, imagine you are in battle, and all seems lost. What do you do?'

He was met with blank stares.

'You fight on. There is nowhere left to go, no other choice. But what if your salvation lies in the distance? What, then?'

He stabbed his finger southwards.

'We do not want to surround them, to force a battle of the death. We want them to turn tail.'

'They'll never make it,' Sindri said, shaking her head.

'An army's rout is never logical,' Jai said. 'If you think each of our knights will kill four legionaries apiece and live to tell the tale, you are mistaken. Our best chance of victory is to break them. Then cut them down while they run.'

'But we have to make them run first,' Tenzin said, leaning over the map and peering at the neat lines that Jai had drawn up. 'My mammoths can lead the charge, but pikes'll work against mammoth flesh same as khiroi.'

Jai nodded slowly. He had been working on this plan all week, but he had not yet shared it with his generals. His father's supposed betrayal was still remembered, especially by him. Still, now that it was time to voice it, it seemed the work of an infant, of a child general.

Unfortunately, he had none other to suggest.

'They'll draw up battle lines, in the half-moon formation. That is what any general with sense would do.'

He pointed at the legion, a series of toothpicks and wooden squares, where he had arranged the line in a shallow curve, bending in to prevent a flanking manoeuvre.

'So we bring our archers forward, pepper them with arrows. With our cavalry so close, they'll not dare break ranks and charge. We'll have them at our mercy.'

Feng leaned forward, shifting a large block, marked with a simple bow and arrow, towards the legion.

'They'll draw together into testudo – a tight formation of men, shields above and to the front, pikes extended.'

'So we go around,' Sindri said.

Jai nodded.

'Exactly. But not behind them – we do not want to block their way to the road. To the sides, like so.'

He took the slider from Feng, shifting half of his khiroi to the left of the legion, the other to the right.

'With their flanks threatened, they will close the half-moon – that is their doctrine. We will have them in a tight ring of men – a circle. And all the while, as they manoeuvre, gaps appearing, our arrows will fall.'

Jai turned to Tenzin.

'Have we bows enough?'

'They're simple things, bamboo and rawhide, but they'll pull an arrow.'

'Good,' Jai said. 'And have we arrows?'

'Enough for a few volleys, no more,' he said.

Jai shook his head.

'I want the men fletching arrows all night. Knights included. If we can't forge arrowheads fast enough, sharpen the wooden tip and harden them on the fire.'

'Why, my khan?' Sindri asked. 'Surely they will be useless against the testudo?'

Jai shook his head.

'Not so. Some will slip through; it is not impregnable. Enough to injure some, kill fewer.'

'Then why—'

'Because their shields will be weighed down by the arrows by the time we're through. And they'll be worried there will be more. Shocked by the onslaught. It will soften them up before we strike.'

'You want our knights spending their night fletching arrows instead of resting?' Harleen said. 'Sire, you go too far.'

'I don't go far enough,' Jai said. 'Now, watch.'

He pointed at the legion, pushing them into place until a rough circle had formed.

'Tenzin's mammoths will charge their front,' Jai said. 'The khiroi will sweep back his way, and follow behind him.'

Tenzin huffed, as the mammoths were shoved home, their rough-carved pieces clacking against the spines of the legion.

'So your khiroi ride over the bodies of my mammoths, is that it, Jai?' he said.

'No,' Jai said. 'Because now they are so tight-packed we need only break a hundred feet of their lines, to make a breach our men can ride through and put to slaughter.'

He pointed at each mammoth.

'Our best soulbound will ride with you,' he said. 'Before you meet, they will blast a hole in their front lines. It is for you to hold it, and my khiroi to exploit it.'

Tenzin hesitated, staring at the map, before nodding grimly.

'I did not doubt your father when he had my father breach Leonid's camp. Many mammoths were lost, but we won the day. Sometimes, victory requires a little butchery.'

'One last thing,' Jai said. 'At the moment our lines meet, your soulbound will not be alone.'

He plucked a wooden figure from his pocket, one he had commissioned some days before.

'I will fly the line,' he said, tossing the sun-bleached miniature dragon into the midst of the legion, sending them scattering. 'I will burn a hole so deep and wide, they'll see the flames from the Blue Mesa itself.'

The room was thick with tension, the atmosphere heavy with anticipation and doubt in equal measure. Every pair of eyes turned to the miniature dragon in the centre of the map, a mark of Jai's commitment.

Harleen's hardened expression softened just a bit.

'If they target you, if you fall, it is all for nought. You carry more than just flames, Jai. You carry our hope.'

Sindri nodded in agreement. But Tenzin, resting a hand on Jai's shoulder, said, 'It is as sound a plan as any. He is his father's son, a general born.'

Harleen relented, a hint of a smile playing on her lips. 'Perhaps.'

Jai returned her smile. 'Let's hope I make a better High Khan.'

'Let's hope you survive,' Feng muttered, then looked up, aghast that he'd said it aloud.

But Jai just stared at him . . . then laughed.

Chapter 93

The steppe lay silent and expectant, as if the very winds held their breath, waiting for the impending clash. The setting sun gilded the grasslands, turning the pikes of the legion into a forest of gleaming silver, catching the light as they swayed in nervous hands.

Their half-moon formation spread across the horizon, a steel barrier that promised slaughter to any who dared approach.

Jai's forces were arrayed opposite, the calls of his generals stirring the air as they cajoled their knights into position. The khiroi, their hides gleaming with anticipatory sweat, snorted and stamped impatiently, while the mammoths grumbled, shaking their heavy heads. Ahead of this front line, Jai's archers notched their arrows, their gazes fixed on the target ahead.

Jai, elevated upon Winter's back, addressed his troops, his voice carrying over the steppe, filled with all the authority and conviction he could muster.

'Sithians! Warriors born! This day, we stand for the hope and future of our people. The legion before us trample our land, breathe our air!'

He paused, letting his words sink in, eyes scanning his audience.

'We are not here just to win a battle. We are here to show

their pissant emperor his armies will never darken the Great Steppe again.'

The warriors cheered, but still more stared at him, grim in their silence. Nearby, a boy barely older than Sum threw up over the side of his beast.

Taking a deep breath, Jai continued.

'When I fly, know that I am with you, not above you. And together, we will see the dawn of a new day for our homeland. Archers, let the skies darken with our promise! To war, my friends. For the Mother!'

Now more warriors cheered, their blades held high, khiroi rearing, generals shouting to loose their deadly hail.

With his words still hanging in the air, the archers released their first volley. The sky was blotted dark, hundreds of whispers cutting the wind.

Then the staccato sound of arrows thudding into the ground, shields and flesh, punctuated by screams from beyond.

'Now, Winter,' Jai breathed. 'We fly!'

The world lurched as Winter hurled herself into the sky, even as the khiroi split beneath them, thundering the ground. Harleen leading half, Sindri the rest, curving east and west. No sooner had he climbed, a second volley followed the first, whistling under Winter's dangling feet as she beat higher and higher.

The legion, as Jai predicted, formed the testudo, their shields lifting into an interlocking shell, but even now the formation was warping, struggling to form up even as centurions cried for them to fold their wings as their enemy encircled them on either side.

Jai soared, watching the mess of reforming men, teetering on calling the charge now, while the legion struggled. But doubt snatched at him like the wind, and the moment was lost.

He circled above, watching the warped circle of the legion below, the fettered Huddites running free, leaping and shouting through the tall grass, heading for the Kashmere Road.

Another volley, buzzing like angry hornets. He could hear

the screams in earnest now, see the shields darkening, thickening with arrow shafts. His five hundred archers looked so small, so motley compared with the scarlet block of fighting men beyond.

He could hear Gurveer's cries.

'Loose!'

The clunk of strings, the hum and patter as they made their marks.

'Nock!'

Silence.

'Loose!'

Jai banked Winter in a tight curve, feeling the tension ratchet higher. The misshapen testudo ring shuddered with every volley, and he could see Harleen and Sindri's khiroi formed in twin masses, readying for the call to charge.

'Not yet,' Jai breathed. 'Not yet.'

The hail of arrows was faltering, as one by one, the archers ceased, their ammunition spent. Still, Jai waited. Let them cower, a moment longer. Let them hear the silence, before the ground shakes.

'Now!' Jai bellowed.

His voice was lost to the high winds, but the glintlights that burst from his fingers were not. His flag bearer raised Jai's banner, and Jai kissed Winter's neck, his hand extended, mana roiling within.

Jai could see Tenzin rallying his forces. The mammoths began their charge, their massive feet thudding on the steppe, echoing the heartbeat of the land itself. Their trumpets were as shrill screams, drowning the ululations of Jai's riders, curving back to merge behind Tenzin in a single mass of shrieking knights.

Jai angled Winter down in a steep dive. He felt the wind whistle past, every detail of the battlefield sharpening. Mana roiled in his veins as he drew upon the deep well within, twin spots of light appearing on Winter's plunging neck as his eyes were set aglow.

The legion's lines rushed closer, and Jai leaned out, seeing eyes turning up to meet him, their shadow blotting the sun.

Fire burst from his fingers, a cascading inferno channelling a path straight through the heart of the mass of scarlet-clad men. The silver shields blazed, fire branching and flattening, the front ranks became a writhing mass of flame. The very air crackled with heat, buffeting Winter high, the green steppe scorched brown in an instant.

A shock wave rocked Jai's senses, Winter knocked back, her wings spasming. Jai's nerveless hand twisted the fire's path, spiralling upwards, an ascending vortex that painted the sky orange.

Winter had but a moment to right herself before a gryphon erupted from the centre of the burning legion. Its armoured rider, falchion raised high, drove the beast straight at Jai.

The impact was violent, the two beasts roaring as their talons met, the world spinning out of control. Jai saw but flashes – feathered wings, the blast of spells rippling through the legion, mammoth heads sweeping tusks low through screaming men and metal. The expanse of the sky, the chaos of the battle below, the green of grass, rushing to meet them.

Tangled with Winter, they hit the ground in a tumble of scales and limbs. The gryphon landed nearby, its armoured rider vaulting from its saddle before impact, his blade in one hand, the other raised, twisting.

Through a blur of confusion, instinct took over. Jai rolled aside, narrowly avoiding a ball of golden light, the explosion behind raining soil.

Jai drew his blade just in time to parry a second strike, before a kick bowled him over Winter's tail.

The gryphon knight's face was hidden behind a cold steel helm, eyes narrow slits of merciless intent as he raised his hand, the fingers glowing. Winter's teeth clamped about the man's wrist, pulling the spell into the ground. The explosion hurled Jai back, and he could smell his hair, burning as he rolled over and over.

Jai staggered to his feet, blade raised, eyes searching.

'Winter,' he croaked.

He was in the crush of battle, mammoths swinging their great barbed tusks, reaping a heavy toll. Beyond, the khiroi crushed forward, their riders' blades rising and falling, even as those at the bogged-down edges were pulled from their mounts, the legionaries chopping at them where they fell.

A legionary ran towards Jai, screaming, and Jai lunged, punching through the armour and skewering the boy's chest. Jai sidestepped, letting the weight slide from his blade as he searched for Winter in the morass.

A mammoth reared, a pike shaft trailing from its belly, trunk misting the air red as the beast let out a shrill screech. It fell, clearing Jai's view. Winter lay just beyond, her long tail lashing, teeth clamped about a legionary's neck. And nearby, the gryphon knight, kneeling at his totem's side, the white of the healing spell flashing bright.

Jai locked eyes with the golden knight, who stared back. Frozen, as if in shock. The knight tugged their helm, letting it fall from their fingers before stepping over the rising gryphon, gripping the falchion in two hands.

And Jai saw a face he had seen so long ago in the savannah, hunting alongside his brothers. The face that had sold him to a life of fettering, abandoning him to the bowels of Porticus.

It was Silas.

Chapter 94

Jai's heart raced, time moving slowly beneath Silas's gaze.

He stepped forward, pooling mana in his palm, shaping a shimmering shield. With a contemptuous sneer, Silas hefted his falchion in one hand, a pulsing ball of yellow light forming in the other.

They charged, the gap between them closing, the world blurring, the cacophony of battle becoming a distant murmur.

Silas sent the yellow energy hurtling towards him, striking Jai's shield, sending spiderweb cracks across its surface. The explosion rocked Jai back, his feet scoring channels in the scorched earth, yet he did not fall.

Mana surged from Jai's core, repairing the shield in great dollops of mana. It used precious reserves, for he had blown much of what he'd saved into the sky, and he could feel the drain, a creeping weakness that made his knees buckle. But there was yet enough.

Silas pressed forward, his hand contorting. A stream of fire burst forth, licking around the shield, the heat intensifying, sizzling Jai's boots and scorching the flesh of his arms. His beard crackled, the stench terrible as he squinted through the heat, falling to his knees as his skin began to peel.

Jai dove to the side, rolling along the trampled grass, mana surging in a twisted hand. He pulsed a kinetic energy in a raw, unfocused blast. The ground trembled in a shock wave that shook the earth, radiating dust as it plucked Silas from his feet, sending him and those behind skidding and tumbling.

Jai felt the void where his mana had once been, the exhaustion dragging at his limbs. He stumbled, his thoughts turning to Winter. Blinking through the afterglow haze, he saw Winter on her back, her scaled belly ravaged as the gryphon scrabbled on top of her.

Jai ran, falling and rising as he tripped over the detritus of battle. Staggering close, he stabbed his blade deep into the maelstrom of ripping teeth and talons. It bit into the gryphon's flailing wing, and the creature screeched in pain. But Jai barely registered the sound, for Winter's own agony tore at his mind, louder and more piercing than any cry.

A flash of gold made him turn, and then Silas was upon him again, falchion swinging high. Jai met his charge, the two blades singing as they locked. The world seemed to pause as the two men stared each other down, mana pulsing through their limbs, eyes straining, teeth gritted.

The blade edged closer, closer, until Jai twisted a hand, electric energy crackling up the blade, sending Silas whirling away, twitching and shuddering as he staggered. Jai pressed home, slashing once, twice, his blade riving the golden breastplate, the cuts too shallow to kill.

Yet his third blow was countered, knocked back by sheer force, then another that shattered Jai's blade in a spray of screaming metal. The blow carried on, clanging against Jai's gorget, hard enough to knock Jai to his knees.

Jai stared at the stump of his weapon, even as Silas raised his blade high.

'Second time's the charm,' he hissed, raising his own, very intact, blade.

Jai saw Winter struggling to escape her fight, her claws scrabbling in the soil, her jaws snapping, just out of reach.

The blade swung, even as the world blazed blue. A wall of searing fire engulfed the space between them, twisting back to send Silas staggering, a shield spurting into life as the man careened through the air, smoke rising from his armoured form.

Jai turned to see Winter, her throat expanding and contracting, eyes glowing a lightning shade of cerulean. She had breathed *fire*, flames dripping from her mouth as the gryphon twisted away in shared pain from her master.

Yet, before Jai could muster an attack, legionaries approached the smoke, closing in on him like wolves on injured prey.

Jai scrambled for a fallen blade, but found instead that Winter's massive head had swooped down, her jaws seizing him by the scruff of his shirt. He could smell the acrid scent of her flames, and feel the burning heat of her teeth – and he thanked the Mother for it. With powerful beats of her wings, they erupted into the sky, sending legionaries staggering and leaving the battle below.

From his elevated vantage, the scene was dire. The battle had turned into a charnel house. The charge had broken through the legion's centre, but the enemy's left and right flanks had held their ground. The once-proud knights, despite their strength and courage, were being hemmed in as centurions reformed their soldiers into two islands of determined legionaries.

That was not to say they were completely unbroken. Legionaries peeled away from the battle in dribs and drabs, but Jai could see their hesitation. For beyond, the fettered Huddites had run. Half a thousand men, who would take easy vengeance on a lone legionary running from battle.

'Easy, girl,' Jai whispered, for he could not tell where his pain began and hers ended. His arms and shins were badly burned, and his mana was all but spent. Winter's pain was diffuse, spread across extremities and wings that made their flight an agony. Her mana too was almost spent, and it was a miracle they were still aloft.

Now was not the time for half measures.

Jai signalled to his infantry with a second burst of glintlights, calling them to charge, throwing his reserves in to break the nearest island of embattled legionaries. The infantry roared in response, their myriad weapons raised high as they tore across the trampled grass, heading for the exposed flanks of the embattled legionaries.

Jai turned his gaze to the retreating backs of the fettered Huddites, and a mad idea sparked in his mind.

'Come, Winter,' Jai breathed, reaching up and stroking her leg. 'We've one more card left to play.'

Chapter 95

Winter carved a path through the smoke-filled skies as she swooped towards the fleeing fettered Huddites. Jai clung on, his gaze unwavering on the retreating backs that held a promise of redemption, for his knights, his country and himself.

The Huddites continued their desperate flight towards the Kashmere Road. Freedom beckoned them east, promising sanctuary, away from blood-soaked fields and the steel of the legion. Behind, Jai could hear the trumpeting of the legion's cornu, and the rise and fall of screams, clangs and shouted orders.

Jai dropped in front of the vanguard of the escapees, Winter's teeth bared and wings spread, a monster blocking their path. The Huddites came to a halt, some trying to edge around, exhaustion evident in their eyes, weapons gripped weakly in malnourished hands. They had not made it far, for the grass was virgin here, and they had chosen to push through rather than cut a path.

'I am Jai, son of Rohan, leader of the army that has bought your freedom. Who speaks for you?' Jai called, suddenly aware of his empty core, and the scabbard that matched it. The men slowed, seeing he had no intent to harm them.

'I,' a man called. 'Mago.'

A tall Huddite, his body a mass of welts and dirt, hands

manacled together by a short chain, pushed his way past the others.

He faced Jai, his chin high and defiant, eyes blazing as he weighed the scythe in his hands. It was a rusted, ancient thing, but its blade's edge had been sanded sharp and gleaming. Jai eyed it and held up his hands.

'Do you think the Phoenix Empire will strike your chains, when you reach its borders?' Jai called. 'They will be thankful you have come, ready shackled for work.'

Mago spat, in answer. Already, the stragglers were catching up, crowding behind Mago, urging the man to move in their language.

'Your countrymen fight with me,' Jai said. 'Hanebal, freed from Porticus, and scores of others.'

'No country,' Mago said. 'Nothing left to fight for.'

Jai stabbed a finger west, marching closer, careless of the blades that threatened him.

'The Sabines, in their arrogance, leave their eastern flank defenceless, pulling all legions west for the fight against the Dansk.'

He turned to all the others, beseeching them with as much conviction as he could stir, even as he swayed on his feet, his fire-dried eyes blurry in the light.

'Join me, and I will guarantee your freedom. And you can march at my side as we ride into the Sabine heartland, freeing your people where they work the fields stolen from them.'

Mago stared, the men clamouring behind, careless that Jai could not understand.

'With these?' Mago asked, brandishing a scythe.

Jai nodded, and took the implement from Mago's hands. The man released it, as if glad to be free of its weight. Then Jai pushed through the Huddites, marching towards the enemy, picking up speed over the half-trampled grass.

'Run and live as the fettered they made you,' Jai called, lifting the scythe high. 'Or fight like the warriors you once were!'

Jai kept walking, the weight of his words left behind him.

He dared not look back, not wanting to seem desperate, refusing to betray the hope that they might listen. Yet, through the bond he shared with Winter, he could see everything, hard though it was to walk in the half-trance.

Through Winter's keen eyes, Jai saw the turmoil among them. Men shoved each other, heads turning between Jai's departing figure and the uncertain horizon to the east. Some continued walking, but still more stood as if rooted, caught between distant sanctuary and duty that tugged at their souls.

Then movement. Mago, whose defiance and pride had first met Jai, swung around, striking a wailing Huddite across the face, snatching his weapon from him. The other man stumbled, then recoiled, eyes wild with confusion and anger. But Mago, unmoved by the confrontation, merely turned his back and began walking in the direction Jai had taken.

Like a wildfire, the spirit of vengeance spread. One by one, men began to break from the throng. Some shouted out to their retreating brothers in chains, imploring them to remember who they once were. There were curses, pleas and even maddened laughter – a raucous mess of raw emotion.

Others simply fell into step with Mago. The sight of each seemed to pull more with them, and soon a procession of men, once broken, now followed in Jai's footsteps.

The grass whispered as he waded through, as if the Mother herself was trying to hold him back, but Jai kept moving, trusting in the pull of destiny.

Winter caught up to him in leaping bounds, nudging her head under Jai's arm until he allowed himself to be shunted into her saddle. She limped on, scrabbling through the grass, picking up speed as the cries of battle neared.

'On me,' Jai roared, raising his scythe high. 'We break their flank!'

As Winter surged forward, the eastern flank of the Sabine legion was close enough to smell, a charnel house of blood, of burning hair and cooking flesh.

It was a scene of utter chaos; the Sabines engaged with a mass of bellowing khiroi and hulking mammoths, Jai's infantry pressing from the sides, making little progress. Their attention was such that they cared nothing of their rear. The legionaries' shields were raised against the arrows and spears coming from the mammoth riders, their formations broken beyond the front line.

Winter ran through the pain, charging with energy borne of desperation, leaping high, her wings flaring, swooping.

Few legionaries noticed, all too late. Hoarse cries, desperately calling 'Behind, behind!' But their warnings were lost amid the roars of the mammoths and the cacophony of battle.

Winter smashed into the back rank, claws raking wide as she burst through, jaws clamping about necks, then shaking them like a dog with a rat before seizing another.

Jai, wielding his scythe with a deadly grace, one hand gripped about the saddle's pommel as he rode the bucking Winter, the other yielding a deadly harvest until the head splintered away.

Huddites followed in his wake, swooping with their scythes low, cutting through the vulnerable backs of the legionaries' legs, felling them like timber. A swathe of bloody destruction was carved deep into the Sabine ranks, even as they turned to face the new threat.

Men pressed against each other, crushed between the sweeping Huddite blades and the heaving khiroi, their half-formed ranks crumbling like a clay house in a monsoon. It was every man for himself, a free-for-all for survival.

Winter scrambled for a reprieve atop a fallen mammoth, even as pikes stabbed at her, cutting her flanks, the blades sliding across her ribs. Atop the furred hump, she was just out of reach, hissing and slashing at any who dared attempt to mount it.

Jai, from his vantage point atop Winter, scanned the battlefield. There were pockets of resistance where the Sabines had managed to regroup, forming small fortresses with their shields. They held out hopelessly, the enemy too close to wield their pikes, Jai's infantry making short work of men whose weapons were not designed for the heavy crush of fighting.

Jai turned to look back at Winter, and followed her gaze. Far in the distance, limping in lopsided flight in the skies, was the outline of a gryphon.

Fleeing.

Winter, in her rage, raised her head, letting out a guttural roar of challenge. For a moment, the sounds of battle lulled, the terrible noise a fleeting shock. The change was slow, halting, yet it came. Legionaries began to peel away, at first in ones and twos, then entire lines of men, leaving their comrades to the slaughter for the false hope beyond the horizon.

Jai could see Harleen so close he could touch her, leading her khiro in pursuit, an arm hanging limp, the other stabbing and hacking at the enemy they drove like cattle before them.

The Sabine resistance was fleeting. With their formation broken and threatened on all sides, discipline evaporated, the enemy becoming a panicked mob. The pressing wall of pikes and shields fell away, turned to a mass of running, frantic men, their weapons abandoned as the pressure broke, the khiroi trampling over the fallen, their pursuit relentless, their blades rising and falling in tandem with screams of pain and terror.

A young Sabine soldier, not much older than a boy, lay on the ground, his entrails spilling out, his eyes wide with shock, slowly losing their light. The weight of the moment pressed on Jai as he looked into the boy's fading eyes, bringing Jai to his knees.

He heard his infantry cheering, even as more among them continued a grim slaughter, their blades rearing and lancing down to finish the Sabine wounded.

The battle was won, the field theirs. But the lingering stench of flame and butchery was the cost. He scrambled up the slope of the mammoth's belly, where Winter lay, the adrenaline that drove her fast fading in the face of her wounds, her flanks heaving, eyes unfocused with pain. Blood ran freely from the cuts on her side, her pearlescent scales stained crimson.

Jai's fingers traced the weeping cuts, feeling the warmth of her lifeblood wet his fingers. He cursed, realising that he had no mana to heal her, his fingers sputtering, half-sealing what he could before he ran dry.

He cradled her head in his lap, calling for help that did not come. Closed his eyes, whispered a prayer to the Mother.

Winter gazed up at him, lapping his face with a rough tongue. They hurt, but they would survive. They would fight again. Soon enough, the pain and scars would fade, but their victory burned bright on this day and hereafter.

Epilogue

'It lies that way,' Meera's apprentice murmured.

Jai gently extricated himself from the young woman, who had helped him hobble much of the journey there. He let his crutch fall away as he approached the overgrown hollow in the Blue Mesa's lee. He would walk the last steps to his mother's grave unaided, no matter the pain. He owed her that at least.

He wished Winter could be with him, but he could not wait any longer. She had remained in the great litter that had carried her on the long journey home, and though she was fast recovering, she had slept for much of the journey and he had chosen not to wake her.

She needed that rest, for while Jai had healed her with what mana he could spare – even as he'd soulbreathed, nestled in the hollow of her belly – there were hundreds of men and women waiting for the ministrations of the few soulbound that had survived the battle.

Even now, he allowed his body to heal on its own, saving whatever mana he could for the mortally wounded that still clung to life.

The victory had been bittersweet, for many had fallen in battle. A full third of his army had been wiped out, spread across khiroi, mammoths and men, and another third were injured and might never fight again. But the way his men told it, he had won a great triumph.

Jai had avoided the celebrations, calling for Meera and finding her apprentice instead, the old woman's whereabouts unknown. He was sure she was angry at how he'd ignored her entreaties to meet urgently in the days since his return from the mountains. He did not begrudge her for it.

But it was his mother he first had a duty to and he would not tarry longer. Even now, he could hear the laughter, the khymis running freely as soldiers drowned their sorrows, and citizens celebrated their victories.

Not for him. Not tonight. He'd earned this moment. His head was clear, and the weight of destiny, for now, had lifted. There was time for grief, now. Time to think.

'Thank you,' Jai said. 'I can make it from here.'

Jai left the young woman waiting in the shadows, and ducked beneath the hanging lianas, wishing he had mana to see clearer in the darkness. But his destination was unmistakable.

It was a beautiful place. An oxbow lagoon, with a small mound at its middle, alongside a simple gravestone. Willows trailed their long leaves into the water, and the jungle was alive with the chirr of insects, the night calls of birds and the croaking of frogs.

Jai could see why his father had chosen this site. He wondered if he had brought Jai here, as an infant, before leaving for his final battle with Leonid. Meera would know.

He approached the grave, collapsing in front of it. Flowers, fresh cut, had been laid before the gravestone, and he saw a name scratched in the rock, barely legible for the moss and wearing of time.

'Miranda.'

It might have been the first time her name had passed his lips, and Jai felt tears spring unbidden to his eyes. He pressed a hand against the cold, uneven stone, as if he could somehow bring himself closer to her.

'It took you long enough,' Meera's voice said.

Jai turned to find the old lady hobbling out of the darkness. It seemed she had been lying in wait.

'Meera,' Jai said, a little angry at her interruption, but the feeling faded fast as he caught her expression. She was sorrowful, her face a picture of pity.

'This is a private moment,' Jai said. 'You may have your audience in the morning.'

Meera nodded, inclining her head and backing away.

'Your will, my khan,' she said. 'I only offer myself to answer you. It was I that laid the stone some years later, when your father did not return. We used to play here, with your brothers. Before your uncle came, and took you.'

Jai held up a hand as she turned to leave.

'Wait,' Jai said. 'Did my mother have time to name me, before she died? Or was it my father?'

Meera turned back, her face twisted in a strange expression.

'Your father named you,' she said. 'He met you but once. Flew back here with the Caelite, buried her with his own hands, plague be damned. But you had another name, one he refused you. She named you for her father.'

Jai furrowed his brow, confused.

'What do you mean?'

She sighed, and looked at Jai.

'Only now I have read the diary, as you have, do I know why she chose it. I had thought it was to spite Rohan, for abandoning her to war . . . How wrong I was.'

Jai stared at her.

'Make yourself plain, now.'

Now it was Meera's turn to stare, her hands raised to her face.

'You did not . . . you have not . . .'

Jai reached into his pocket, pulling the diary free.

'I never finished it, Meera. Who was she?'

She pointed a finger at the diary, her finger shaking.

'I did not know, truly. I thought you had always known. That you gave me the diary because you were too . . . because you could not tell me in your own words. I am so sorry, my khan. Read it. Read the last page.'

Jai did, flipping through, his hands shaking. There, scrawled in a small note, amid a mess of wage bills, maps and camp plans. It was Leonid's very last entry.

I will not rest. I will show no mercy. I will bring his people to their knees.

He has stolen my heart. Begotten her with child, and now she lies dead.

He took her from me.

Now I will take everything from him.

I mourn her, and yet I cannot share the pain. For how can I tell my men he has taken my heart, my only daughter? My Miranda.

The End

Dramatis Personae

JAI – The protagonist and heir to the Kidara tribe, raised as a hostage in the Sabine court.

WINTER – Jai's soulbound dragon, who shares an emotional and mental bond with him.

THE SITHIA – Also known as the Steppefolk, they are a diverse people of the Great Steppe, with some marginalised as 'Tainted'.

THE VALOR TRIBE (TAINTED) – Marginalised within the Sithia due to their cursed status.

SINDRI – Khan of the Valor tribe, a powerful and complex Steppewoman who is both Jai's captor and protector.

ZAYN – Sindri's brother, a cruel soulbound warrior and prince of the Valor tribe.

KIRAN – A soulbound warrior of the Valor who guides Jai in the Sithian martial art, Talvir.

THE KIDARA TRIBE – Jai's ancestral tribe, known for their khiroi.

ROHAN – Jai's father, the former Khan of the Kidara tribe and High Khan of the Sithia, who united various tribes through his legendary status and strength.

TEJI – Jai's uncle and current ruler of the Kidara, becomes Kahn of the Tejinder.

NAZEEM – Teji's corrupt vizier.

HARLEEN – Leader of Rohan's old nobles and loyalists.

GURVEER & SIMRAN – Nobles still loyal to Rohan.

NAVI – A khiro who accompanied Jai in his escape from the Sabine Empire.

MEERA – Kidaran keeper of memories.

MANU – Jai's flag bearer.

SONY – Jai's cartographer.

BALBIR – Jai's former nursemaid, murdered by Magnus and Titus.

ARJUN & SAMAR – Jai's brothers, murdered by Magnus and Titus.

TRADERS – Known to frequent the Steppe in great caravans.

FENG – Jai's translator and minder of mixed Phoenexian heritage. He and his sister, Sum, are captives of the Valor due to his valuable skills in diplomacy.

SUM – Feng's sister, kept apart from her brother by the Valor tribe's decree

LAI – A Phoenexian silk trader.

SITHIAN RULERS – Khans of the many tribes of the Great Steppe.

HARPAL – Former Khan of the Valor.

RAJDEEP & JASDEEP – Twin Khans of the Cimmer.

AMAN – Khan of the Gujara.

TENZIN – Khan of the Mahmut.

DEVIN – Khan of the Keldar.

ANITA – Khan of the Maues.

HARI – Khan of the Ordun.

THE SABINES – An empire at war with the Dansk and the Sithia.

LEONID – The former emperor, Jai's former master, and Titus's grandfather.

TITUS – The Sabine emperor and usurper, who killed Jai's brothers.

MAGNUS – Leader of the Gryphon Guard.

RUFUS/RUFINUS – Former leader of the Gryphon Guard, Magnus's uncle and Jai's mentor.

SILAS – Gryphon knight who once sold Jai as fettered when working for the Guild.

MIRANDA – Jai's mother.

THE DANSK – A kingdom in the Northern Tundra that was betrayed and invaded by the Empire.

ERICA – Queen of the Dansk, Jai's close friend and romantic interest who escaped with him from Porticus.

REGIN – Erica's soulbound dragon.

THE CAELITE – A soulbound sect that ride upon Roqs and live in the Yaltai mountains.

EKO – 200-year-old leader of the Caelites.

THE SPEAKER – Eko's second in command.

CYRUS – Leader of the Caelites' flock.

THE HUDDITE KINGDOM – Defeated by the Sabines, with most of their civilisation fettered.

HANEBAL – Former fettered soldier and leader of the escaped Huddites from Porticus.

MAGO – Former fettered soldier and leader of the escaped Huddites from the Legion.

Acknowledgments

First and foremost, my heartfelt gratitude goes to my editors, Rachel Winterbottom and David Pomerico, for their support, patience, and commitment to this novel. The guidance you provided has been indispensable, and I feel fortunate to have had you both by my side throughout this journey.

I also wish to express my thanks to Juliet Mushens, my agent. Juliet, your wisdom and belief in my work have made all the difference. I am deeply thankful for your guidance and persistence.

To the broader team at Harper Voyager in both the UK and the USA, that worked tirelessly behind the scenes, I am deeply grateful.

Frankie Gray, Natasha Bardon, Catherine Perks, Chloe Gough, Hannah Stamp, Emily Chan, Terence Caven, Toby James, Sian Richefond, Libby Haddock, Holly Martin, Rosie Hawkins, Harriet Williams, Ruth Burrow, Mireya Chiriboga, Gregory Plonowski, Michelle Meredith, Jennifer Eck, Jennifer Chung, Richard Aquan, Lara Baez, Catriona Fida, Isabella Ogbolumani, Hope Ellis and Dionna Bellinger.

Every book takes a village, and I am profoundly grateful to have had such an incredible team behind me. Your collective talent, dedication, and passion have left an indelible mark on this novel. Thank you all for being a part of this journey, and helping bring this story to life.

About the Author

Taran Matharu is a *New York Times* and *Sunday Times* bestselling author. He was born in London, where he found a passion for books, writing his first novel at nine years old. Taran started writing *Summoner* at the age of twenty-two on Wattpad.com, with the story reaching over three million reads in less than six months. After being featured by NBC News, Taran decided to launch his professional writing career, with ten books written to date. His Summoner series has become a worldwide phenomenon, selling millions of copies in more than seventeen languages. Book one in The Soulbound Saga, the *Sunday Times* bestseller *Dragon Rider*, was Taran's adult fantasy debut.